W9-DBW-321

2-16

TOO DANGEROUS FOR A LADY

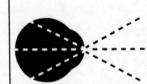

This Large Print Book carries the
Seal of Approval of N.A.V.H.

Too Dangerous for a Lady

Jo Beverley

THORNDIKE PRESS

A part of Gale, Cengage Learning

GALE
CENGAGE Learning·

Farmington Hills, Mich • San Francisco • New York • Waterville, Maine
Meriden, Conn • Mason, Ohio • Chicago

GALE
CENGAGE Learning·

LIBRARY OF CONGRESS CATALOGING-IN-PUBLICATION DATA

Beverley, Jo.
  Too dangerous for a lady / by Jo Beverley. — Large print edition.
    pages cm. — (Thorndike Press large print romance)
    ISBN 978-1-4104-8178-8 (hardcover) — ISBN 1-4104-8178-6 (hardcover)
    1. Aristocracy (Social class)—Fiction. 2. Revolutionaries—Fiction. 3. Large type books. I. Title.
  PR9199.3.B424T66 2015
  813'.54—dc23   2015013829

Published in 2015 by arrangement with New American Library, an imprint of Penguin Publishing Group, a division of Penguin Random House LLC

Printed in Mexico
2 3 4 5 6 7 19 18 17 16 15

For Persephone,
who will be one year old
when this book is published

ACKNOWLEDGMENTS

I had help from various people in researching this book, including a doctor who declined to be named.

I'm a "Lancashire lass," so it was a pleasure to set a book partly in the northwest. My friends Anne and John Ward have shown me around the Wirral on many occasions, inspiring me to set part of this book there. Anne also did a bit of local research for me.

Fellow author Lynne Connolly advised me on Warrington.

The Birkenhead Historical Society supplied the date of the introduction of the steam ferry from Tranmere, which, as it was in 1817, mattered to me. Yes, Hermione can see it chugging across the Mersey.

My friend John Park, a science fiction author and chemist, was very helpful about the chemical side of antimonial medicine and about explosive potential.

In searching the Web for information

about Northumberland coal mining in the Regency period, I came across Alan Fryer's fascinating blog, Northumberland Past. Alan cheerfully put up with my questions and supplied maps and technical explanations so that I could tie up a thread. You'll see what I mean as you read.

CHAPTER 1

September 1817
Ardwick, Lancashire
The King's Head Inn

The church clock began to strike. Lady Hermione Merryhew prayed throughout the nine slow tolls that they wouldn't wake the two boys in the big bed. She'd only just settled them.

At ages five and nearly three, Billy and Roger should have been asleep hours ago, but the family had been late to arrive here, and an inn was a novelty for them. It was a particularly noisy place, for the walls were thin, and even now she could hear indistinct conversation from one side and someone yelling out in the innyard. It was cheap, however, which had been the main consideration.

Even after their supper the boys had been bouncing with excited energy, but it was important they get a good night's sleep. If all went well, tomorrow they'd arrive at Great-uncle Peake's house, and rambunctious children could be disastrous. In the end she'd extinguished the candles and pretended she, too, was ready for bed.

That wasn't far from the truth, but now that they were asleep, she needed a little time to herself. She'd lived with her sister and brother-in-law for the past year and enjoyed her niece and nephews, but she wasn't accustomed to having sole charge of them. At least baby Henrietta was with her parents next door.

She would have liked to relight at least one candle and read a little, but it wasn't worth the risk, especially with the bed-curtains still undrawn. She'd begun to draw them, but the rattle of the rings on the pole had caused Billy to stir. *Let sleeping dogs lie, or rather, sleeping puppies.* They looked such darlings now, their lashes resting on round cheeks, blond hair curling against the pillow, but there'd been moments when they'd seemed monsters.

Such folly to drag them on this journey, but her sister, Polly, had been willing to do anything to secure Great-uncle Peake's money, and she'd been sure her darlings would turn the trick. After today, Hermione feared the children would have the opposite effect, and then she'd have to marry Cousin Porteous.

She began to take pins out of her hair, gloomily considering her fate. Porteous Merryhew was a distant relative who'd inherited her father's marquessate. Hermione and Polly had wished him well of it, for her father, her grandfather, and his father before him had each been known as "the Moneyless Marquess." Then, intolerably, Porteous had discovered coal on the Northumberland estate, and now he was on his way to being rich.

A month ago he'd written to Hermione to offer her the honor of becoming his bride, mentioning what a pleasure it would be to be in a position to be generous to her struggling sister's family. "In a position." He could be as generous as he wished right now, but no, he was using his money like bait in a trap.

She shivered, wishing she could indulge in putting more coal on the fire. There wasn't much left in the scuttle, however, and it would be extravagant to order more. In any case, part of the shiver had been at the thought of marrying Porteous.

He wasn't revolting — which was unfortunate. If he were, no one would expect her to marry him. As it was, he was

11

a man in his forties of acceptable appearance, high rank, and growing fortune. Many would expect her to weep with gratitude, but she couldn't imagine spending the rest of her life with such self-righteous pomposity. She especially could not imagine sharing the intimacies of a marriage bed with him.

He was a thin, abstemious man, who looked at rich food as if it were poisonous. If she became his wife, she'd never see a cake or a sauce again. His mother was just as thin as he and ruled the roost. She'd make any wife's life intolerable. Above all, Hermione didn't *like* Porteous. She wouldn't harm her family by insisting on love in a beneficial marriage, but surely she shouldn't have to marry someone she didn't like.

She'd responded to his proposal with a request for time to think, claiming discomfort with his replacing her dead brothers. He'd not pressed his suit, but she imagined him now like a cat watching a mousehole, confident that she'd have to emerge into his claws in the end.

Please let Great-uncle Peake be as rich as we think, and please let our interpretation of his invitation be correct — that he's dying and intends to leave his all to us, his only close

12

living relatives. Please!

She was urging her wish upward to whatever powers attended to a selfish maiden's prayers when the door to the corridor opened. She turned quickly to whisper to the servant to be quiet. But the man coming in was no servant. He closed the door, flipped the rotating bar into place, and then leaned his ear against the wood, listening.

Even from where she sat, Hermione heard rapid footsteps in the corridor and urgent voices. She stayed fixed in place, hoping the intruder would leave before noticing that she was there. Then she thought better of that and eased to one side, toward the poker.

He turned sharply, and across the room his eyes caught and reflected the light of the flame. Heart thumping, she grasped the poker and stood on guard. But rather than attacking or fleeing, he raised a finger to his lips in a clear *shush* gesture. Stunned, she couldn't think what to do. She should shriek for help, but that would wake the boys. Even worse, anyone who ran to her aid might leap to scandalous conclusions.

And he wasn't attacking her yet.

The room was lit only by firelight, which hardly reached his shadowy corner, but she could make out a tall man wearing an ordinary outfit of jacket, breeches, and boots, though he lacked a hat and his hair hung down to his collar. Who was he? What was he?

Tinker, tailor,
Soldier, sailor,
Rich man, poor man,
Beggar man . . .

Thief.

As if he'd heard the thought, he turned toward her again.

She made herself meet his eyes, trying not to show the fear that had dried her mouth. She could hear no disturbance in the corridor now, so she jabbed a finger outward, mouthing, *Leave! Or I'll scream.*

His response was to lean back against the door, arms folded.

She glanced at the door to Polly and William's room, but it was in the wall closest to the invader. He could block her way in a couple of strides. She was going to have to scream. Then two-year-old Roger stirred and whined, "Minnie . . ."

The man looked sharply at the big bed. Hermione dashed to put herself between him and the boys, poker in hand.

"He's not really awake," she whispered, "but you must go — now."

He relaxed again. "I'm afraid that's not quite convenient." At least he, too, spoke softly, and with a surprisingly well-bred accent. That didn't mean he was safe or honest. Times were hard for everyone.

"It's not at all convenient for you to be here," she said. "I will scream if you don't leave."

"You'd wake the children."

"And the whole inn, including whoever is after you. Begone." If he'd made a move toward her, she would have screamed, but it seemed an odd thing to do when he remained leaning against the door. "If you fear people inside the inn, leave by the window."

He pushed off the door and walked with easy grace to look outside. "You think I have wings?"

She could escape through the door now, but she couldn't abandon the boys. "I thought thieves were adept at such things."

"That's doubtless why I'm not a very good thief." He turned to her and a touch of moonlight illuminated one side of a sculpted, handsome face, tweaking her memory.

Did she know the rascal? How could that be?

"The window looks onto the innyard," he

said, "and there are people down there. Someone would be bound to notice me scrambling down the wall, and then . . ." He drew a finger across his throat.

She sent him a look of powerful disbelief.

He nodded.

It must be playacting, but she didn't want to be responsible for a death. "The corridor seems quiet now. Leave that way."

"They'll be watching. I'll have to spend the night here."

"You most certainly will not!" She was hard put not to shriek it.

"Minnie . . . I'm thirsty."

Perhaps she'd raised her voice. Five-year-old Billy was sitting up. What would this desperate man do if the child saw him and cried out?

"I'm coming, dear." Hermione sidestepped to the bedside, keeping an eye on the intruder, though she had no faith in her ability to hold him off, poker or not. In any case she had to put it down to get the water, but she kept half an eye on the intruder as she poured some into a glass and gave it to the lad.

Billy hadn't noticed the man and was still mostly asleep. He drank, murmured thanks, and settled again. But he mumbled, "Want to go home."

"Soon, dear," she said, smoothing blond curls from his brow.

Six days would not be soon to a five-year-old, but it was the best she could offer. She took the risk of drawing the bed-curtains in the hope the boys wouldn't be disturbed again.

"So you're Minnie," the man said, speaking as quietly as before.

She saw no reason to reveal her real name, so she agreed. "And yours, sir?"

"Ned."

It was more convincing than John or Henry, but it wouldn't be real.

"Am I allowed to stay?" he asked.

"No."

"I won't harm any of you."

"Why should I believe that?"

"For no reason at all."

Even so, her instincts said he was safe, which was ridiculous, except . . . *Dear Lord, could it be . . . ?*

"You could tie me up," he said.

She started. "What?"

"If you tied me to that wooden chair, you'd all be safe and you could sleep."

Still distracted, Hermione could hardly make sense of his words. "You imagine I travel with rope in my valise?"

"Stockings would do."

17

"You're deranged."

"Not at all. Think about it."

But instead she was thinking that he just might be, could possibly be, the dashing dance partner, the man who'd almost given her her first kiss, the soldier she'd never been able to forget. Thayne. Lieutenant Thayne. She'd never known his first name. It could be Ned, but if so, how had he sunk to such a state?

One thing was clear. If there was any possibility, she couldn't eject him to possible death.

She forced her mind to clarity. "It won't work. In the morning servants will come to build up the fire or bring hot water."

"Servants won't come until you summon them, and no one can enter if the doors are barred."

He flipped the latch on the adjoining door, then walked to the chair. He moved it to face the fire and then sat down, presenting his back to her. She could pick up the poker and hit him over the head with it, except she would never do such a thing and apparently he knew it.

Did he know why?

That would mean that he'd recognized her just as she'd recognized him.

18

CHAPTER 2

She'd attended her first true ball in May 1811, aged seventeen and giddy with excitement. She and her friends had spun to even greater heights when some young officers had arrived, having ridden five miles from their billets. Their gold-braided uniforms had sparkled beneath the hundreds of candles, but they'd stirred every lady's heart because they were soon to sail to Lisbon to join Wellington's army in the Peninsula. She'd felt their heroism strongly because one of her brothers, Roger, had been a soldier and had died at Corunna two years earlier.

The six young subalterns had not all been handsome or charming, but their regimentals had made them the stars of the night. One had been splendid, with a dramatic dark-haired, dark-eyed appearance uncommon in England, but so very common in the novels she'd loved back then.

Someone had said he had French blood, but that hadn't shocked her. There were a number of émigré families whose sons fought Napoleon.

She'd been thrilled when he asked for a dance, and felt queen of the ball when he'd later asked for a second. The waltz had not yet become acceptable, so they'd enjoyed only country dances, but the holding of hands and the occasional turn close together had been enough to sizzle her. After all, it had been her first true ball, and the first time she'd danced with a stranger.

No wonder she'd allowed him to coax her onto the moonlit terrace. When she'd realized they were the only ones out there, she'd trembled in the expectation of her first kiss and been a little disappointed when they'd only talked. Soon that had become magical. She didn't know why it had been so easy, but she'd talked with him as she had never talked with anyone before or since, as if they were the oldest, closest friends.

She'd told him about Roger and his death, and about the trials of being poor.

He'd spoken of his need to defend Britain from Napoleon and of how his mother's family had been slaughtered in the Revolution.

She'd complained of her parents' fractiousness, her older sister's temperament, and her brother Jermyn's dull wits.

He'd said his mother was an invalid, but that his parents' marriage was a great love match. That had led to a discussion of the nature of love and whether it was a rational or an irrational force. Dizzyingly deep waters for a seventeen-year-old. No wonder she'd never forgotten.

He'd been two years older and had lived the typical life of schools and sports, while she'd been educated by a governess and raised to be a perfect lady, yet there had been no barriers between them. She'd willingly let him cut a silk rose off the bodice of her gown to be his talisman, and she'd always treasured the brass button he'd given her in exchange.

They had been about to take the final step, to kiss, when her mother had rushed out to herd her back into the safety of the flock.

Despite her mother's whispered scold, she'd known he was no wolf and when he and his fellows had left at midnight, she'd had to conquer tears. She'd heard no more from him, but then, he could hardly write to her and had probably not felt the encounter as much as she. But she'd dreamed, when she'd allowed the folly, of encountering him at another ball, both of them older, when there'd be more possibilities.

Never like this!

She walked round to study him. Everything was blurred by his unkempt hair and a dark beard shadow. His loosely knotted neckerchief didn't help, especially in garish stripes of red, green, and black. The clean-cut features were older and harsher, but surely it was him.

He must have thought she was considering her actions, for he said, "My life truly is in danger if I'm caught, and I give you my word I'm not a villain. If you please, fair lady, tie me up and allow me to stay."

"What's your surname?" she demanded.

"Granger."

If he'd sunk to a life of crime, he'd use a false name. Thayne or Granger, she couldn't send him out to his death, but if he stayed, she'd have to tie him up or she'd never sleep a wink. "Very well." As she went to her valise, she probed for more information. "You don't speak like a thief."

"You don't speak like a nursemaid."

"I'm a governess," she said, pulling out a pair of stockings. They were her best pair, however, and this business could snag them.

She put them back and chose the most darned ones and approached the chair. "Put your hands behind you."

"A good move," he said approvingly, doing as told.

She knew nothing of tying secure knots, but surely multiple knots would do the job. She knelt to use one stocking to tie his wrists together against the central bar at the back of the chair.

"What's your surname, Miss Minnie?"

"None of your business," she said, disturbed by touching his hands. A lady didn't handle any part of a man like this, and his hands were very fine — long fingered but strong. Nothing to help her recognition there. He'd worn gloves at the ball. A scar ran across the backs of the fingers of his left hand. Some mishap when picking pockets? Or in battle.

"What did you steal?" she asked.

"Only papers."

"That could mean bonds, money drafts, or banknotes."

"It could," he agreed.

She yanked another knot tight. She'd almost used up the stocking. "Once you're tied, I could search you."

His fingers tensed. "I wouldn't if I were you."

Dangerous papers, then. With dangerous people after them, who might not hesitate to harm innocent children. She walked round to the front of the chair, the remaining stocking in hand, and studied him again. He met her eyes guardedly. Her heart pounded. Oh, yes, this was the man. Years older and eons more experienced, but this was the onetime Lieutenant Thayne.

He met her eyes braced for trouble.

Clearly he didn't remember her. That hurt, but why should he? After the ball she'd had nothing of importance to distract her from memory and infatuation, but he'd gone to war. When not fighting, he'd doubtless dazzled and sweet-talked a score of girls in Portugal, Spain, and France, and forgotten every one. He'd probably thrown away the silk rose, having already forgotten what bodice he'd cut it from. Even if he remembered, why should he connect a dancing partner with a "governess" in a plain brown gown, whose hair was half in, half out of its pins? She was twenty-three years old. Well enough for her age, but there was a special glow to a pretty girl in her teens. Better he not remember. She knelt to tie his ankles together.

"I'd take the boots off first," he said. "They might be loose enough for me to take my feet out of them."

She was annoyed not to have thought of that. She needed to be clear witted, not enmeshed in girlish memories. "Thank you. Raise one."

She grasped the boot and it came off easily. It was the sort a man could get into and out of without a servant, and there were other signs of poverty. The boot was well-worn, down-at-heel and scuffed, and when she had it off, his worsted stockings were darned in the heel. Lieutenant Thayne had been from a noble family headed by a Viscount Faringay. How sad to see him in poverty, but he wouldn't be the only one.

The pay of army officers was barely enough to keep up the style of living thought suitable to their rank, and the half pay they got when they weren't fighting only just kept body and soul together. Many had extra income from their families, but some, like Roger, hadn't. His letters had often mentioned privations, though he'd made them part of the adventure.

His rare letters had presented army life as an enjoyable adventure, and she hoped that had been true. Though he'd been a man in her young eyes, he'd been only twenty when he died. She pushed such thoughts aside for fear of crying, but realized that the dashing officer of her dreams had been even younger six years ago. What had happened to bring him to this state?

"The other." It came out more brusquely than she'd intended. "I'm tired and I want to get this done," she added, dragging off the second boot.

"Now tie my ankles to the chair legs," he said.

She dropped the boot to thump on the floor. "I don't know why you don't do it for yourself."

"Untie my hands and I will."

She glowered and returned to her task, but saw a problem. She needed to tie each ankle to a front leg of the chair and had only one stocking. She grasped the woolen stocking on his right leg and pulled it down.

A naked lower leg.

She'd seen such a thing before. Some workingmen did without stockings in the summer. Some poor ones did without shoes. All the same, in the intimacy of a firelit bedroom his bare calf made her quiver with embarrassment, and perhaps with something else.

"No need to risk more of my stockings," she said, pulling it all the way off.

"None at all," he agreed.

Did she hear humor? She wasn't about to

look up and reveal her blushes. She took off his other stocking, and then paused. The long, jagged scar down his calf swept away irritation. Whatever Thayne was now, he'd fought for their country and been wounded, perhaps even at Waterloo.

She tied his right ankle to one chair leg, finding his bulky woolen stockings more awkward, but unable to ignore his feet. She'd never thought about men's feet, but his were excellent specimens with straight toes and no bumps or bunions. She felt sure Cousin Porteous had bumps and bunions.

The thought of tying Porteous to a chair pushed her perilously close to giggles and she bit her lip as she tied the other ankle. Thayne would think her ready for Bedlam. Eventually she stood and backed away to assess her work, nodding with satisfaction. He wouldn't get out of that — which made her softhearted. "I hope you won't be too uncomfortable."

"I'm sure I will be, but needs must."

"Yes, they must," she said firmly, which was difficult with the atmosphere in the room — the atmosphere created by naked limbs, proximity, and memories. She couldn't help it. She had to know more. She sat on the upholstered chair facing his. "Have you always been a thief?"

He gave an irritating impression of ease. "I assume not in the cradle."

"Have you had any other means of survival?"

"Yes. What of you? The infants seem young for a governess."

"Billy is learning his letters and numbers."

"But you were born for better things."

"Why think that?"

He cocked his head, considering. "I don't know, but I'm sure of it."

Was he remembering? "You, too, were born for better things," she said.

"Was I?"

"You weren't born to be a thief. No one is."

"I'm sure there are larcenous lineages. Our birth can direct and constrain our path. As yours did?"

Being born the child of an impoverished marquess had created many problems beyond the need for economy. People had always expected a grandeur and generosity they couldn't afford, and some took exception to the lack of it. Some had sneered at the Miserly Merryhews. Others had thought them eccentric and perhaps even insane for their simple way of life. She'd spoken of these things that night.

"My story isn't uncommon," she said.

"I'm wellborn but poorly funded, and I've chosen honest labor."

"How wellborn?"

"You or me?"

"Either."

Perhaps he was chasing memories as she had — but then she remembered that she shouldn't want him to remember. Despite that ball and their instant closeness. Despite that almost-kiss, dreams and longings, and a treasured button, she couldn't afford entanglement with an impoverished criminal pursued by dangerous victims.

"Enough of this," she said, standing. "Now you're safe, I can go to bed."

The word "bed" hung dangerously in the firelit room, especially with her nightgown draped over a nearby rack to warm. It was a perfectly decent voluminous garment of white linen, but its presence made everything wicked. She'd never had a man in her bedroom in her life except for the doctor twice when she'd had a fever. How was she to prepare for bed? The washstand was behind him, and there was a screen around it, but even so . . .

"I don't have eyes in the back of my head," he said, and yes, there was definitely a tease in it.

"I wish you'd invaded some other room,

you wretch."

"I, on the other hand, am happy with my choice." Looking directly at her, he added, "Will you honor me with a kiss, sweet lady?"

The exact words he'd used six years ago.

They'd talked and they'd talked, and he'd claimed that rose, and then he'd tried to claim a kiss. She'd been so torn, yearning for her first kiss and feeling it her duty to grant the warrior his due, yet terrified that it would be the first step to ruin. His lips had barely brushed hers when her mother had "rescued" her. It would only have been a kiss, but back then she'd felt as if she'd escaped the fires of hell. And regretted it a little.

"A kiss won't ruin you," he said. That was the next thing he'd said that night, too. Before he spoke, she knew what would come next. "It might be the request of a man soon to die — Lady Hermione."

Despite a racing heart, she managed to speak calmly. "We've been here before — Lieutenant Thayne."

"Not quite, but we do have unfinished business." Oh, that lopsided smile! She'd never forgotten that.

"It was a long time ago," she said.

"Even so."

Unfinished business. That elusive kiss had

haunted her dreams. She'd progressed as far as real kisses with other men, but pleasant or unpleasant, those kisses had never been the one.

"You're bound," she pointed out.

"Are you going to take advantage of it?"

The idea had never occurred until he mentioned it, but now it was irresistible.

"Probably," she said, smiling as she stepped closer, heat spreading through her at the answering gleam in his eyes. Oh, this was wicked, but again there seemed no barriers of convention or propriety to save her from herself.

On the terrace he'd been taller, but now she looked down at him. He'd been the stronger one, but now he was her captive. He'd been in control, but now she had command. When she'd allowed kisses over the past six years, the men had played the masterful part once she'd permitted their attentions. This man couldn't hold her, direct her, or keep her close if she wanted to retreat. He couldn't escape her, either, and there was no mother to rush in and save her.

She rested a hand on his broad shoulder, vibrating at his strength and warmth, and lowered her head to press her lips against his.

So sweet.

So wicked.

So thrilling.

Still kissing, but in the slightest way, she put a hand on his other shoulder, and then slid both to cradle his face. Warm skin and the roughness of whiskers, and his lips teasing at hers for more. She drew back to look at him, seeing clearly his long lashes around widening dark eyes.

He felt it, too, this wicked reversal. He, too, wanted more.

It will be my pleasure, sir.

She returned to her kiss, tantalizing him with butterfly touches until she could bear it no more and pressed hard against him. He opened to her, hot and moist, and she sank into that, exploring a new pleasure, for she'd never gone so far with any other man, and never in a situation like this. His tongue taught her new excitements and she almost drew back, but she couldn't, wouldn't.

She was in command.

He was safely bound.

She relaxed into magic, letting him explore as she explored, settling against him, trusting his strength. And she was lost — not in memory, but in something entirely new, something meltingly sweet and so deeply stirring that her heart beat like a drum and a demanding ache stirred deep inside. She tingled — no, burned! — all over and her breasts felt confined by her light corset.

Simply from a *kiss*.

She pushed away, then had to brace herself against his chest. She recovered, retreated, standing to smooth down her skirts. "I apologize. I shouldn't have. . . ."

"Never has a lady transgressed so delightfully. Please, don't stop for my sake."

"There are children nearby!" She'd spoken too sharply and she froze, listening for a response from behind the bed-curtains, or even from the next room. How could people have slept though the earthquake that had rocked her?

She and her aching body wanted to return to destruction, but she grabbed her nightgown and fled behind the washstand screen, where she stood, breathing deeply, trying to regain sanity.

Merely from a kiss!

No wonder her mother had rushed her back into company. But then, it wouldn't have been like that six years ago. They'd been different people and it had been a very different situation.

But now it was over. There must never, ever be anything like that again.

Even though he couldn't see her, she

couldn't bear to take off any item of clothing. She'd undress in the concealment of the curtained bed even though that meant she couldn't have a proper wash. In any case, she hadn't rung for hot water and certainly couldn't now, so she'd have to make do with the bit of cool water left in the jug from when she'd been putting the boys to bed. As she washed her face and hands, she tried to clean her mind as well.

She would not, *could* not, allow herself to be swept into disaster by lust, even if with a magical man from the past. She paused, towel in hand, dreaming, but then dried her face. Polly's marriage showed that marrying an inadequate income was unwise, even for love, and Polly had married a baronet with an estate, not a threadbare thief!

Marriage. The tickle of temptation was warning enough. *It's been six years. You know nothing of him now, and all you do know is bad.* Rolling her eyes at her own idiocy, she peered around the screen, just in case he'd managed to get loose, then hurried to bar the doors. But of course he'd done that earlier. If Polly tried to get in, she'd think it odd, but better that than Polly coming in before Thayne left. Despite him being tied up, despite Hermione having once known him, Polly would see only that her beloved

34

children had been in danger, and she was inclined to overreact.

Perhaps it wouldn't be an overreaction.

If her actions tonight were ever discovered, people would think her mad, even without the kiss.

But she couldn't regret giving the onetime Lieutenant Thayne refuge from his enemies. Despite all logic, six years ago they had become friends, and even more than friends. If he hadn't had to leave for the Peninsula, she knew they would have grown even closer. Despite his misfortunes he was still the same man at heart.

She didn't regret that shocking kiss, for it had completed a circle, but in the morning she'd untie him and force him to leave, no matter what danger lurked for him.

She wanted no part of a criminal's life.

CHAPTER 3

Mark Louis Thayne, Viscount Faringay, smiled wryly at the low-burning fire. He'd survived his dangerous life by planning carefully and keeping a cool head, so how had he ended up tied to a chair in a lady's bedroom? Being tortured in a lady's bedroom by the rustling sounds from behind the curtains that clearly meant that Lady Hermione Merryhew was undressing.

She must be wearing the lightest of corsets to be able to undress without help and that explained the softness when she'd pressed against him in that kiss. A man became so used to the ridges and bones of a corset that the lack of them could make him lose his wits. As he had.

By Jupiter, that kiss. Nothing like the one they'd failed to achieve on that terrace six years ago. Once he'd recognized her, the years had evaporated and he'd seen in the plainly dressed woman the girl who'd

36

enchanted him at his last English ball. Lady Hermione, glowing in pink and white and sparkling with anticipation and zest for life. After she'd granted him a second dance, he'd coaxed her out onto the terrace. He should be ashamed of his younger self except that he'd had no vile intent. The evening had been cool and everything still damp from a rain shower, so he'd known they might be alone out there, and he'd wanted her to himself.

She'd been as innocent as a lamb and expected to walk and talk. He hadn't minded and he'd soon become lost in it. He'd never before or since felt such open ease with another person, and as they'd strolled back and forth, he'd found himself telling her about his parents, even about his mother's peculiarities, something he'd rarely spoken of with anyone.

Perhaps it had been the thought of death that had lowered his restraint, for with youthful drama he'd anticipated a glorious one. Certainly that had been behind his request for a token to take into battle. The white silk rosebud, much battered by time, was in his breeches' right-hand pocket, where it always lived. The thought of her finding it there if she'd searched his pockets had alarmed him, but it had done its job.

He'd survived.

She'd demanded something in return and he'd cut off one of his buttons. Did she still have it? She seemed too sensible for that. Only then had he tried for a kiss, simply to seal the moment — the knight leaving his lady to go into battle.

It would have been the sweetest, most reverent kiss.

Their kiss tonight had been of another order, just as she was a different person and even more remarkable. But he could no more pursue her now than he had been able to back in 1811. Duty called then and it did now. What was more, he needed his wits and a cool head. He hadn't lied about his peril.

He was in this room because of instinct and impulse. Both had won the day at times during the war. This time, he didn't know. He could feel the stolen papers in his breeches pocket, but he hadn't had the chance to read them, so he had no idea whether he'd risked everything for a good reason or not.

The day had gone as expected, with him playing a minor supporting role as Julius Waite had given speeches and accepted the adulation of the Ardwick crowd of weavers and other working people. They'd cheered

Waite for his condemnation of corruption in high places and his demands for honesty and justice. They had no idea of his true plans — that he was paving the way for bloody revolution. Nor did Waite have any idea that Mark was not who he seemed, and had infiltrated his organization only to destroy it.

Waite's organization was called the Three-Banded Brotherhood, after the flag of three colors adopted around Europe by revolutionaries. The prime example was the French *Tricolore,* but Waite's flag was black, red, and green. Black for the pernicious current state, red for the blood that would destroy it, and green for the glory to come.

There were members of the Three-Banded Brotherhood throughout the country, numbering thousands. They wore the three colors in whatever way they could so as to recognize kindred spirits. This had been one of Mark's first suggestions when he'd gained a place on the central committee, the Crimson Band. The committee had seized on the suggestion, not realizing how it could mark the members to the authorities. Mark had found that even the cleverest of them were blinded by their fanatical dreams. They'd stop at nothing, but Mark would stop at nothing to destroy them and their cause. From his mother's experience, he knew what evil revolution had created in France. He had pledged his life that such horrors would never happen in England.

Now he had a new embodiment of his purpose. Hermione Merryhew, "aristo," as the French revolutionaries would have called her, would never see her family murdered, or need to flee in terror, or face the guillotine's bloody blade.

The papers in his pocket might at last be the key that would lead to the Crimson Band's arrests, convictions, and deaths.

There were members of the Brotherhood all around Britain, but the Crimson Band was based in London, where they hoped revolution would erupt as the French one had in Paris. They'd traveled north to attend the ceremonies to commemorate the third anniversary of the death of Thomas Spence, hoping to inspire the crowd to march on London.

Spence had been a revolutionary, but of a more Utopian type. He'd never advocated slaughter or violence, but had wanted to completely reorganize England on egalitarian principles. He'd wanted land divided equally among all, and government by parish councils supervised by a national senate. Some of his plans might have worked in the Middle Ages, but not in the modern world of industry and cities.

Spence had worked for change with his pen and he must be weeping from on high to see his work exploited by men like Julius Waite and Arthur Thistlewood, who wanted total destruction of law and order. Waite was more subtle than Thistlewood, who'd been on trial for high treason earlier in the year. A shame he'd been acquitted, for he was half-mad and capable of extremes Waite and the Crimson Band would blanch at.

At the memorial service today Thistlewood had ranted, but Waite had spoken in his usual calm and noble manner, urging the return of habeas corpus, drawing on the fact that Spence had been unfairly imprisoned a number of times. It was a safe subject, for many of the most righteous in Britain felt the same way, but he'd managed to turn it toward a general criticism of the government without saying anything to rouse the crowd. Yet.

Tomorrow would be different.

Tomorrow, thousands, perhaps tens of thousands, of people from all over this part of Lancashire would hear more Spencean speeches. Waite would again be moderate, but Thistlewood could be depended upon to let rip. With the crowd well seeded with

Brotherhood members, the inflamed mob would set out for London on what would be called, apparently spontaneously, the Spencean Crusade. The name had been another of Mark's suggestions, and applauded by the rest of the Crimson Band. Crusade or not, the marchers wouldn't make it five miles, if they left Ardwick at all. The magistrates were ready and the military stood by.

There could be trouble in the town, however, for many of the Brotherhood would be armed, and he realized Lady Hermione and her family could be in danger. He was tempted to wake her and warn her, but she'd think him mad, and she and her party could hardly leave in the middle of the night. He'd stir alarm early in the morning — once he got out of here. He tested his bonds. He'd suggested stockings because they had stretch, but she'd tied them thoroughly. Getting free could take a while.

By the time the Crimson Band had sat to dine in a private parlor, they'd all been satisfied with the day. Waite, a gray-haired patrician man, had sat at the head of the table opposite his French wife, Solange. Despite her nationality, Solange Waite enhanced his apparent respectability.

Her public story was that she had fled France in the Revolution as upper servant to aristocratic émigrés. She claimed to have seen vile Jacobins at their murdering, pillaging worst. In fact she'd been a Jacobin herself and in private boasted of bloody deeds. She played her part well, however, emphasizing her solid, middle-aged respectability with sober clothing and decent white linen.

Pete Tregoven had been given the place of honor on Waite's right, and Mark the seat on Waite's left. The other two present had been Benjamin Durrant, scribe and speechwriter, and Isaac Inkman, the very odd young chemist.

Waite had begun the toasts with a reference to his choice of inn. "To the King's Head. Soon we'll have the king's head off on our guillotine!"

Indeed, they had a beheading machine built and stored in a warehouse in East London, so everyone had drunk to that.

Solange had added, "And the head of the monkey-faced queen and her far too many whelps."

The woman disgusted Mark, but he'd drunk and added, "Especially the fat Regent's."

"And his p-pampered daughter," said

43

Benjamin Durrant. "B-before her whelp is b-born." Durrant was a bitterly frustrated man. He had the words to be a great orator, but his stutter betrayed him. He could only compose speeches to be delivered by men like Waite, who had the voice and manner, but no true oratory of their own.

Durrant might have had trouble commanding a crowd even without the stammer, as he was thin and bespectacled, with a high-pitched voice, but he blamed the injustice of fate. Perhaps that had turned him to the extreme of revolution, for in other respects he'd been given a comfortable life.

None of the men in the Crimson Band had suffered poverty or hardship, and they were all involved in revolution for their own gain. Waite intended to be a British Napoleon, rising from the ashes to rule. Durrant needed to hear his words move crowds to action. Tregoven was a wastrel in it for the spoils, and Inkman enjoyed blowing things up.

Only Solange was honest, and that made her the most dangerous of all. She proved it by saying, "If the revolution is delayed, we can make a grand display of dashing out Charlotte's baby's brains as we guillotine the mother."

The other men smiled, though perhaps uneasily. For sanity's sake Mark had established a distaste for crude violence, so he was able to say, "The child is an innocent. It can be reared by a simple family to be of use."

"Its public death will be of more use," Solange said. "You are weak, Granger."

"I look to our main purpose. Many will be disturbed by the death of a child."

"They will feel as we wish them to feel. Durrant will ensure that, won't you, my friend?"

Durrant actually flushed with pleasure as he agreed.

Mark disliked them all, but he detested Solange Waite. He detested her vile plans, but he was revolted by her past for personal reasons. She'd been an ardent supporter of the revolution in France twenty-five years ago, and active in the worst times, commonly called the Terror. She claimed to have killed a number of "aristos" with her own hands, including women and children, and to have been present to see both the king and the queen lose their heads on the guillotine. She had dipped her fingers in their blood and smeared it on herself, and danced the day and night away in celebration. A celebration she hoped to repeat here.

45

Had she been present to see his uncles, aunts, and other relatives perish that way? Had she dipped her fingers in their blood? Such murder was why he'd fought Napoleon, and why he'd sunk himself into this work — to keep Britain safe from the bloody French.

How she'd come to marry Waite, Mark didn't know, but she'd turned a muddled Spencean organization into a dangerous revolutionary one. Despite her sober appearance, she was the vicious goddess of the Three-Banded Brotherhood and Mark knew he should kill her. It might come to that, but he'd never killed anyone in cold blood and hadn't yet been able to bring himself to do so. He planned to bring them before the law and see them all hang.

Dinner over, they set to a review of the day. It was tedious, for Waite was like an accountant about such things, going over and over details as if in search of a missed penny. He fretted about whether enough people would turn up tomorrow.

"They will flock to hear you speak, sir," Pete Tregoven said, "and the Brotherhood members will bring their women and children as instructed, to deter any soldiers who are ordered to attack."

Tregoven was a toadeater, who could be

depended upon to stroke Waite's pride. He dressed his wiry frame like a dandy and was overly fond of gaming and drink. His only useful service was as an artist. He created scurrilous cartoons showing royalty and government in the worst light, and noble illustrations of Waite addressing the multitudes. These were printed off and sent to Three-Banded Brotherhood groups around the country.

After a bit more fretting, Waite closed his record book and Mark hoped they were done, but Solange spoke again. "Isaac has something to say."

Solange had found Isaac Inkman early in the year and brought him into the Crimson Band despite objections. She appeared to dote on him, and perhaps she did, for he knew a lot about the destructive capabilities of chemistry. He was a pale, pudgy young man who hardly ever spoke for himself and now his eyes shifted. Mark thought he wouldn't say anything, but then his eyes flickered with excitement.

"Exploding letters," he said.

"A, B, C?" queried Tregoven with a sneer.

"Correspondence," said Solange coldly.

"A damp letter," Isaac said. "When it dries . . . bang!"

Even Waite seemed unimpressed. "How is

it damp, Isaac?"

"Sent damp. In an oiled pouch."

It sounded idiotic, but Mark didn't under-estimate Isaac's notions. None had proved effective yet, but all were alarming.

Solange took up the explanation. "When the recipient opens the pouch and finds the letter damp, he will set it to dry so as to be able to read it. Perhaps even by the fire."

More interested, Waite asked Isaac, "How big a bang?"

"Shattered a pot nearby. Set things alight."

"Imagine if the recipient was actually holding it," Solange said. "The prime minister, for example."

Good God. "It won't explode in the prime minister's hands," Mark said.

"It will if we plan it correctly," Solange said.

"Why not?" Waite asked, but attentively.

When Mark had infiltrated the Three-Banded Brotherhood three years ago, he'd known he wasn't actor enough to pretend to be lowborn, even with a scruffy appear-ance, so he'd constructed a story of being a lord's by-blow. He claimed to have been raised by the family but then unfairly ejected, which had given him a hatred of the nobility and a thirst for their blood. Waite had liked the idea of a scion of the nobility in their midst, and Mark's knowledge of that world was part of the reason he'd been brought into the inner circle. His other skill was organization. Good thing none of them knew that had been honed in the army.

"Such a man doesn't open his own correspondence," Mark said. "The damp letter will either be discarded or left to dry by a secretary or clerk."

That had them all frowning. Thank God.

Waite said, "It is an intriguing idea, Isaac. We'll think more about it. . . ."

"Love letters," Solange interrupted. "A perfumed billet-doux. Might not that be opened by even a prime minister, and be set to dry by him?"

"Not all men have secret lovers," Mark said.

Solange smirked. "If they don't, they wish they did. They will wish to see."

Mark had to admit that to be possible, silently damning the woman.

"Isaac must work on this immediately," Solange said. "Only think of such devices exploding all over London on the day the Spencean Crusade arrives there and the mob pours out to join them. Rioters smashing windows, armed mobs breaking open the prisons as we did the Bastille, and at the same time key men alarmed, perhaps even crippled by Isaac's letters. It will be glorious!"

"It will achieve our end," Waite said, trying for a more sober note, but with the same glitter in his eyes. "My dear, you and Isaac must travel to London with all speed to prepare the letters. Granger, you know the world of the powerful. You will go with them to choose the targets and decide how best to ensure the men open the letters themselves."

Returning to London quickly fit in with Mark's plans, but he had no intention of traveling with Solange. "We could set out on the night mail coach," he said, knowing what the reaction would be.

"Me, I do not travel on an overnight coach." Solange had a terror of being outside four strong walls at night, probably because of a guilty conscience. "Tomorrow will be soon enough."

"You follow on, then," Mark said. "I'll go ahead and get things under way."

"An excellent plan," Waite said.

Tregoven was eyeing Mark. "Not sure why you came north, Granger. We've needed no fancy organization here." Tregoven had been tossing darts like that recently. The Crimson Band was aware that the government had spies within subversive organizations, and they were alert for a traitor in their midst.

"Plans can go awry," Mark said.

"With you around?" Tregoven asked.

"You imply?"

"Information seems to be leaking fast these days."

"If any of us is suspect, it should be the one who can't resist cards and dice."

Tregoven half rose, but Waite waved him back into his seat. "We will not bicker on the brink of victory. There need not be a traitor around this table. In fact, I can't imagine how that might be. There will be agents in this inn simply because I am here, but they will discover nothing unless we allow cracks in our unity."

"Or speak t-too loud," said Durrant.

He'd pointed out the thin walls and suggested dining elsewhere, but Waite hadn't liked the implication that he'd chosen their meeting place poorly. He'd instructed his bodyguards, the Boothroyd brothers, to stroll up and down the corridor in case anyone paused to listen at the door. This parlor was bracketed by the two bedchambers used by Waite and his wife. Mark did wonder whether the marriage was consummated. It was a strange mating.

The security arrangements were

51

inconvenient, as Mark had a few new details about tomorrow he must pass on. He would dearly like to know more about the exploding letters, in particular the chemicals Isaac planned to use, but saw no way to ask and the meeting was over.

He rose. "I must pack and buy a ticket."

Waite blessed him with a smile. "We all know your fine mind will ensure success in London, Granger."

"If the Spencean Crusade arrives, sir, London will be primed and ready to explode." Mark picked up his wineglass, which still contained an inch. "To the revolution!"

They all repeated the toast and drank, but Solange made her own toast. *"À la lanterne!"* The old cry of the vicious Jacobins. Hang the enemies from the lampposts — men, women, children, they hadn't cared.

Everyone else rose, rolling shoulders, gathering papers, but Waite asked Durrant to remain to discuss messages to be sent along the route.

Mark turned to the door, but heard Solange say quietly, *"Il y a une autre question à discuter."*

CHAPTER 4

Waite and his wife often spoke in French between themselves and none of the others thought anything of it. None of them spoke much French, but Mark had had a French mother and spoke it well. He'd kept that secret, which had enabled him to pick up a number of details not revealed to the others. Such as the fact that Solange now had something else she wanted to discuss with her husband.

Waite turned to Durrant. "Isaac deserves a drink, my friend. Take him below for some gin. I'll send for you soon."

Durrant pulled a face, but he steered Isaac out of the room.

Tregoven approached Waite, doubtless with some oily words of praise. If there was a traitor here other than himself, he'd pick Tregoven, who'd sell his mother for money, but at the moment he was being useful. He was delaying the private words between

Waite and his wife.

If Mark didn't immediately prepare for his departure, someone might notice, so he left the room. Nathan Boothroyd was patrolling the corridor. His brother, Seth, was nowhere in sight.

The Boothroyd brothers were close to identical — stocky, muscular young men with limited brains, but well able to follow commands. Mark thought of them as dogs — short-legged, muscular hunting beasts, but for some reason they always dressed well. Nathan was in brown jacket and breeches, striped waistcoat, white cravat, polished boots, and tall beaver hat.

"You can go now," Mark said. "The meeting's over."

The square face showed no expression and Nathan went into the room to confirm the order. Very well-trained beasts. Mark hurried on his way, hoping Waite dismissed the guards.

He entered the room he was sharing with Durrant, shoved belongings into his valise, and then ran down and across the road to the George and Dragon, a much grander place where the London coach would halt. He bought a ticket, left his bag there, and hurried back to the King's Head.

When he entered, he saw both Boothroyds

coming downstairs. They went into the taproom, and a glance showed Durrant and Isaac already in there. Surely Waite would have dismissed Tregoven quickly when his wife clearly wished to speak to him.

No time to waste.

He went upstairs and turned into the corridor toward Waite's parlor, but then ducked back out of sight. Tregoven had just left the room. Fortunately the man needed to go in the opposite direction to reach his own room, but Mark resented every second it took for him to do so.

Once the corridor was empty, he hurried to the parlor door, hoping the flimsy structure of the King's Head would allow him to hear. He wasn't optimistic. Conspirators spoke softly.

However, the words were clear. Waite and Solange must feel safe when speaking French. He felt lethally exposed standing there with his ear to the door, but if anyone came, he would knock and say he had a final question.

"Revolution is not for the softhearted," Solange was saying, with a sneer in the tone.

They were arguing?

"May I remind you that your revolution failed, perhaps because the bloodbath became too deep for most."

"It failed because it was betrayed! By those who saw only a vehicle for their own aggrandizement."

Tregoven had recently portrayed Waite in a toga and crowned with a laurel wreath, but he didn't react to the words. Instead he said, "We are pure of purpose."

A pause made Mark take a step back in case one or the other came to the door.

But then Waite said, "Need you have put Isaac's plans in writing? Such a document could hang us all."

"Plans seem to fly out of his head as quickly as they fly in, and this must not be lost. The details are beyond my memory."

"Even so . . ."

"The notes will be safe with me. You foolish men respect women too much."

"Not generally," Waite said drily.

"Most respect the sober, middle-aged lady, and all of you underestimate women's brains. Even if they imprison us all, they'll never imagine I know anything of importance. I'm a mere wife. An appendage, and too decent to search."

"If they suspect you, they'll find a woman to search you."

"I won't hide them in a pocket, silly man." Mark was astonished by the scathing dismissal in Solange's voice.

"Where, then?" Waite asked. "Come, Solange, if anything happens to you, I need to know."

"Very well. I have a secret section in the lining of my spare corset. A very stiff, whale-boned corset. Nothing will be found there unless it's ripped apart. I must go now to prepare."

Mark hastily retreated, but he did it backward in case the door opened before he could reach the bend in the corridor. Just as well.

Solange came out and stared at him. "Not on your way yet?"

"A final question. Waite is still in there?"

"Yes. *Bonne nuit.*"

Mark only just stopped himself from responding in French. He hoped his hesitation would fit with confusion over the switch in language. He simply bowed to her, but as she went into the room next door, he wondered whether that had been a test. Solange was a very clever woman, and she wouldn't hesitate to order the Boothroyds to dispose of anyone she believed a traitor. His predecessor in the Crimson Band had been found beaten to death in an alley. If she suspected him, stealing her notes might be even more dangerous than he'd thought, but he had to do it. Now he had to speak to

Waite first.

He knocked and entered to find Waite looking worried. Perhaps he was having doubts about his wife. The more distrust among the Crimson Band, the better. "What do you want?" he asked curtly.

Mark asked a few pointless questions.

"You're becoming fretful, Granger. Losing your nerve?"

"Only concerned that everything goes perfectly this time. We've had bad luck recently. The attempt to assassinate the Regent. The Blanketeers. The plan to explode the armory."

"Bad luck or betrayal, and the suffering in the country won't last forever."

"I can't help hoping it won't."

Waite sadly shook his noble head. "You have too tender a heart, Granger. Remember that everyone will benefit when the rot is dug out and the state is whole again. Even amputation is to be blessed if it heals the patient."

"Thank you for reminding me, sir. We will meet again in glory in London."

Waite straightened, a new light in his eyes. "Yes, this time we will succeed. You will see wonders."

Mark lingered, hoping Waite would let something slip about the wonders, but that was all, so he had to leave. He hesitated outside Solange's room, but there were things he must do before attempting to get the details of Isaac's new idea. He had new nuggets of information about tomorrow's gathering to pass on, so he found a quiet corner and wrote them down.

He advised the magistrates to move in early but handle the true Spenceans as gently as possible. Oppressive force would be oil on the fire and Waite was ready to exploit that. He considered adding a warning about exploding letters, but that danger was directed at London and he'd carry the news himself — if all went well. He rolled the paper thinly and tucked it beneath the cuff of his shirt. He went downstairs, hoping it would take Solange a long time to unpick and then repair her spare corset.

He strolled into the taproom and ordered a glass of punch. As he sipped, he looked around idly and soon spotted his contact. Tom Holloway was sitting at a table close to the fire, and not by chance. There'd be nothing suspicious in another man going to warm himself nearby.

By the stocky, middle-aged man sat a book, half-hanging off the table, again not by chance. Mark walked toward the fire and knocked the book to the floor. Apologizing, he picked it up, replaced it, and moved on to enjoy his drink in the fire's warmth, his note passed on.

He must linger for a few precious minutes, just in case he was watched, though the only Crimson Band member here now was Isaac, abandoned by Durrant. Isaac was sipping gin and staring blankly at the wall. At moments like this the young man looked such a dull pudding. Would that he were.

Mark checked his pocket watch. Twenty minutes till the mail coach passed through, and it wouldn't linger for a missing passenger. He should go upstairs, but could he get more information out of Isaac? He had to try, and with luck Holloway would catch a bit of the conversation.

Mark went over. "That ABC stuff. I don't think it'll work."

"What do you know?" Isaac muttered.

"No one of importance will open them," Mark said. "So they won't have any impact."

Isaac smirked. "Wait till you hear about the gas."

"The gas?" Mark asked loudly.

Isaac scowled and sipped his gin. "None of your business."

Mark leaned in to speak quietly. "It is if you'll need new supplies in London. I'm off soon and I'll be there a full day ahead."

Tell me what you need and it might tell other chemists what you're up to.

"Oh, I'll have what I need," Isaac said, with a hint of sly humor.

Mark would dearly love to question him more, but neither Solange nor the mail could wait. He drained his glass, took leave of the young man, and went upstairs, trying to come up with a devious plan. He failed. Brute force be it, then. He opened the first door he came to. A half-dressed man turned, startled.

"My apologies!" Mark said, and moved on.

The next one rattled against a latch and someone called, "What do you want?"

Mark moved on, hoping that person wouldn't bother to open the door to look out. The guest didn't, but luck could last only so far.

He heard voices in the next room but silence in the one after. He again went in, ready to apologize, and at last found a deserted room. He took a pillowcase off one pillow, rearranged everything, and went on to Solange's bedchamber. The first danger was that Waite had joined Solange there, but that seemed remote. The next was that he'd lingered in the parlor, with only a thin wall between.

That was in the lap of the gods.

Mark approached Solange's door, unable to slow his heart rate.

This could go wrong in so many ways.

He could easily lose his hard-won position in the Crimson Band and could even lose his life. The risk was worth it, however, and it felt good to be taking direct action instead of conniving. Spying from within the Three-Banded Brotherhood was surprisingly tedious work.

A couple came out of a room and he had to stroll in an opposite direction until they turned to go downstairs. Once they had, he returned to the parlor door, steadying himself as he approached. He knocked, then flattened himself against the wall.

Solange opened it. "What?"

As she stepped out to look, he pulled the pillowcase down over her head and bundled her back into the bedroom, kicking the door shut. As he'd hoped, she was fighting rather than screaming and he saw why. She wouldn't want people to see the folded papers on the table along with a partially unpicked corset and sewing things.

He picked her up and flung her on the bed, then rolled her up in the woolen coverlet. It wasn't easy. She might look like a soft matron, but she was sturdy and strong. Breathing hard with the effort, he tucked her up tight, grabbed the papers, and left. He was halfway toward the stairs and escape when he heard another door open behind him.

Waite's?

He tried the door by his left hand and thank God, it opened. He went inside and closed it, heart thundering. When he looked around, he saw yet more good fortune. The room was in use but lit only by a low fire, and if the occupants were there, they were in the half-curtained bed asleep.

He pressed his ear to the door and heard Solange say sharply in French, "The papers. They're gone!"

"Who?"

Jupiter, it *had* been Waite, and Solange had freed herself far faster than he'd hoped.

Then, distantly, he heard the clarion call of the London mail. He could just make it if he ran, but he was trapped here. The Waites could still be in the corridor, and even if not, he could bump into any of the Crimson Band on his way through the inn and the game would be up.

His only option was to stay concealed. They'd assume he'd left on the coach and thus could not be the thief. He'd stay in this room until the inn was sleeping and then slip away.

That was when he'd heard something behind him and turned to find a lady arming herself with a poker.

CHAPTER 5

Hermione had been desperate for sleep, but she lay awake, aware of the man so near. She felt turned inside out and not herself at all.

She sat up, being careful not to disturb the boys, and fumbled among the clothes she'd laid over the bottom of the bed. She found the belt of her pair of pockets and drew them toward her. She reached inside the right-hand one and brought out the cool, hard disk. She didn't need light to know it was a military button.

After the ball she'd never mentioned Lieutenant Thayne to anyone, because everyone would think the intensity of her feelings idiotic. But in private she'd relived their time together and often taken out the button to polish and cherish, hoping her silk rosebud would be the talisman he'd hoped.

She'd imagined him traveling to

Portsmouth to take ship. She'd known nothing of the way soldiers were transported to war and had never traveled by ship, so from then on, she'd had only vague notions and prayers. She'd heard of major battles, of victory and loss, but her family took only the local newspaper, so she'd known he could be in the casualty lists and she'd never find out. Surely, though, she'd know in her heart if he was dead.

She'd tried to draw his image, but her efforts were too inadequate to keep. Over time her memories had weakened so she hadn't been sure what was true or false, and inevitably her emotions had become less raw. But she'd never forgotten. From that day she'd always carried the button, and at times she'd taken it out and prayed that he be alive and happy, somewhere in the world. She'd never prayed that they meet again, for through family strife and death she'd lost all faith in fairy stories.

Yet here he was, on the other side of the heavy, musty curtains.

There was still no fairy story, however. She was an impoverished spinster, dependent on her sister's husband for a roof over her head. He was a down-at-heels thief. Such logic didn't help. All the magic had returned — the connection that made it effortless to share her thoughts, and gave such pleasure simply from his company.

And then there'd been that kiss. Far more of a kiss than she'd dreamed of six years ago, but proof that the situation wasn't a fairy tale at all. He was real. Their connection was real. Their earthy passion was desperately real.

She couldn't, wouldn't, do anything about that, but the thought of him tied uncomfortably to a chair wouldn't let her sleep. When the clock tolled eleven, she gave up. She put the button back in the pocket and slid out of the far side of the bed to put on her slippers and brown woolen robe. She hesitated then, but she was more covered, neck to toe, than in most of her daytime clothes, and it was dark. The fire must have gone out and only moonlight lit the room.

As she fumbled her way toward the back of the chair, he said, "What?" perhaps alarmed.

"I'm going to untie you," she murmured, kneeling behind him to undo his hands.

"Is that wise?"

She unpicked the first knot. "You won't hurt us."

"You can't be sure of that."

"Are you going to scold me? If so, I'll leave you as you are."

"Then I should."

"Oh, be quiet. A pest on these knots. Why did I tie so many?"

He didn't respond and she lost patience. She found her sewing kit and used the small scissors to hack at the stocking until it fell free.

She went round to the front, but rubbing his wrists, he said, "I'll do the legs. I have no other pair."

"Are you truly penniless?"

"Not quite, but I'm not sure where my luggage is."

As he bent to work at the knots on his left ankle, she perched on the nearby chair, despite the cold, tucking her hands up the sleeves of her robe. The boys were sound asleep and the bed-curtains drawn. A little more quiet conversation should be safe, and she needed to know how he'd come to such a state.

"Can't you tell me what's going on?" she asked.

"No."

"You did fight in the war?"

"Of course."

"At Waterloo?"

"No."

"Your regiment was sent to North America?"

"I sold out in 1814." One stocking was done. He started on the other. "Why aren't you married?"

"Is it an offense?"

"I'm merely surprised. The pretty daughter of a marquess."

"Flattery, but thank you. I've had offers, but none that suited me."

He glanced up. "You prefer being a governess?"

"They're my nephews. My sister and brother-in-law are next door with the baby."

"No nursemaid?"

"No room for one in the coach."

"Only one coach?"

There was nothing for it. "Didn't you know we're the Poor Merryhews?"

He unfastened the last knot and stood to stretch his legs and arms, tall and so handsomely built. His shoulders were broader now. "How can a marquess be poor?" he asked.

"The same way as with any other impoverished peer. Unproductive land, bad management, indulgence, a gamester or two along the way."

"Marquesses should have been able to marry a fortune every generation."

"You'd think so, wouldn't you? It's not as if they romantically married for love. They simply drifted into the easiest option."

He sat down again opposite her, nothing but shadows with the window behind him. "I'm surprised some ambitious heiresses didn't present the easy option."

"Northumberland."

"Why is that important?"

"Carsheld Castle is in Northumberland and rich heiresses seem to favor the south. That was part of the reason for our move to Hampshire." Here they were again, in easy conversation, even about personal matters, perhaps more intimate because of darkness and the late hour.

He began to pull on his stockings. "I was wondering about that."

"Mother lost patience with the crumbling discomfort of Carsheld and insisted on the move, but she also hoped that in the south my brother Jermyn would tempt a fortune. It almost worked. He was betrothed to twenty thousand pounds when he died from eating bad shellfish."

"Careless of him. No other brothers?"

"Roger, but he was already dead." She hadn't grieved deeply over Jermyn, who'd been selfish and stupid, but her heart still ached for Roger, who'd burned brightly and deserved the name Merryhew.

He looked at her. "Ah yes, you mentioned him."

"You remember?"

"Deceased heroes were significant to me then. Still are," he added.

"You must have lost many friends."

He didn't respond to that. Of course not. "Is there a new marquess, or has the title died?"

"There's a new one, though they had to hunt up and down the family tree for him. Porteous Merryhew, who before his elevation was some sort of official in the Public Accounts Office. I know it's horrid to sneer at that."

"He must rejoice to be a marquess, even a poor one."

"I'm sure he did, but he's become a rich one, damn him."

"Lady Hermione!" he protested, laughter in his voice.

She had to smile. "I've frightened off some suitors with my bold tongue." Then she heard what she'd said. "I didn't mean . . ."

"Of course not."

"Absolutely not." But that was too definite. "I mean that Cousin Porteous has found coal on the Northumberland estate. If only Father had thought to look."

"Ah, no wonder you cursed him. If your

father had grown rich that way, the money wouldn't have been entailed and you and your sister would have inherited his wealth."

"It's maddening to think about. I try not to, but Polly can't help it."

He stretched out his long legs. "Polly?"

"My sister, Apollonia."

"No one ever shortened your name?"

"To what? Hermy?"

"Minnie," he teased. "The new marquess doesn't share his good fortune with his family?"

"Why should he? We're strangers. So you see, I have only a tiny portion to tempt the gentlemen."

"Thus you live with your sister and she uses you as a servant."

"Heavens, no. I live with her, but we do have the normal complement of servants."

"But travel in one carriage and stay at a cheap inn?"

She shook her head. "My turn for questions. Where is your home?"

"London as much as anywhere at the moment."

His family came from Berkshire, she remembered. Perhaps he'd been disowned. "You'll return there tomorrow?" she asked.

"Yes."

"With your ill-gotten gains."

"Yes."

"Aren't you at all contrite?"

"Not a bit of it."

"You should be."

"I'm sure you're right."

She desperately wanted him not to be a thief, not to be poor, not to be any of the things he so clearly was. "An impoverished gentleman has many ways to make his fortune, so why turn to crime?"

"What profession would you prescribe for me?"

She couldn't resist the whimsy and cocked her head in thought. "Not the church, I think, and you're too old to join the navy."

"Not a promising path anyway in peacetime."

"The law?" she suggested.

"Too much book work."

"Diplomacy?"

"Too much wandering."

"Not trade, then. I have it. You must become a Bow Street Runner and put your wicked ways to good account."

He chuckled. "Perhaps I should. It's a shame ladies have so few ways of earning their keep. I'm sure you could turn your hand to any profession."

She shook her head. "Too much book work or wandering."

"Trade?"

"I'm not at all enterprising or adventurous."

"Perhaps you don't know yourself. Remember how you ventured onto that terrace with me, ripe for adventure."

"That was different." Thank heaven dim light would hide any blush.

"I wonder. Was your mother very cross?"

"No. She understood. I miss her."

"When did she die?"

"Four years ago."

"My condolences."

"Thank you. Are your parents still alive?"

"No," he said, but his tone was odd and she remembered some things he'd said six years ago. His mother had been French and had been caught up in the violence of the revolution there. She'd been of a nervous disposition, but she'd been deeply loved.

"What is it?" she asked, and, without thinking, leaned to touch his hand.

He turned his hand to take hers, rubbing her fingers with his thumb. The warm connection rippled up her arm. "My father died in 1814 and my mother a year later. But she'd not been fully alive for a long time. Perhaps as long as I've known her."

"Because of her experiences in France?"

"You remember. She saw a brother

murdered by a mob, and she and her mother only just escaped with their lives. Her father sent them to safety in England, but later he, another brother, and many relatives perished on the guillotine."

She tightened her hold. "How horrible. It's scarcely believable that such things happened just across the Channel and not that long ago. How could people become so cruel?"

"Cruelty seems to lurk like a plague. It takes only a fissure in the social order to release the poison."

"It could never happen here."

"I pray not." He looked down at their joined hands. "She could seem fairly normal when I was young, though we all knew she could be upset by crowds or any hint of violence. She stayed close to home and everyone shielded her from disturbance. That sufficed until my father died. I was away in the army, but when I came home, I heard the story. Despite seeing his body, she insisted he'd been guillotined and hid away for fear of the same fate. She became terrified of strangers, especially men. Then, perhaps a blessing, she slid back into her youth, when her world was tranquil and her family and friends were still alive. Early in the marriage my father had some rooms done over in the French style and after his death she lived entirely in them, with two French servants, and responded only to her maiden name. In that world I didn't exist. I became a stranger to her."

All she could do was squeeze his hand.

"It's cold. You should go to bed."

She rose but lingered. "You'll feel the cold, too."

"I've known worse." Then he drew her into his arms. "That interrupted kiss," he said, and put his lips gently to hers.

It was, she supposed, exactly the sort of kiss he'd have claimed from a seventeen-year-old at her first ball — slight, but sweet beyond bearing. When it ended, she rested her head on his shoulder, wishing hopelessly for everything to be different. How cruel it was that she'd found him again only to have him snatched away by poverty.

Great-uncle Peake.

If he was rich and dying, and if he truly intended to leave his money to her and Polly, perhaps the fairy tale might become real after all. She didn't dare to believe that, but she'd keep the possibility in her heart.

She wanted to stay in his arms all night, but she moved away. She was tempted to share her hope, but she was still sane enough to realize that he might not feel as she did about their connection and their future.

She returned to bed and took off her robe just before climbing in. Then, impulsively, she returned and gave it to him.

"Something to keep you warm," she said, and fled in her nightgown into the conceal-ment of the curtained bed.

CHAPTER 6

Hermione was woken by Roger pulling at her sleeve, "Miony? Miony?" That was his version of her name. "I'm hungry."

It was morning, for some light was coming through a chink in the bed-curtains. Perhaps it was late, for there seemed to be a bustle from the innyard. Time to get up and on their way.

Then she remembered Thayne. Billy was waking up, yawning and rubbing his eyes. The children mustn't see him!

"Yes, it's morning, loves, and we'll have breakfast soon. Stay under the covers, though, both of you, while I make up the fire so you don't get a chill."

She tucked them up again and slipped out through the curtains on the side away from the fireplace. The chair was empty except for her robe draped over it. She hurried to put it on, looking around the room. He wasn't there. He'd left, and without a proper farewell.

He'd left before they'd had chance for more speech, and she'd failed to get any means of contacting him. How stupid. She could be a rich heiress soon and not be able to let him know. What if he was caught and put on trial? Or caught and murdered? Or escaped, only to steal again?

"Miony?"

She pulled her wits together and realized that the room wasn't as cold as it should be. A small fire burned in the hearth. There'd been little coal, so he must have left recently, but she couldn't pursue him, especially in her nightgown. The scanty fire wouldn't last long, so they should dress quickly.

"Come on out, loves. I'll ring for washing water and then we'll have breakfast."

The adjoining door rattled and Polly shouted, "Hermione? Why is this locked? *Open it!*" The shriek seemed an overreaction even for Polly, but Hermione rushed to lift the bar, preparing an explanation.

She didn't need it. Polly dashed in, clearly scrambled into her clothing. "You're up. Thank heavens! We must leave immediately!"

"What? Why?"

The boys ran to hug their mother's legs,

but Polly only patted their heads. "Why are you just standing there? Our lives are in danger. A mob is gathering. They're being inflamed by speeches. We have to leave, *immediately*!"

Hermione scooped up little Roger. "Polly, love, you're frightening the children. A protest gathering won't affect us."

"It's a mob. You know what mobs are like. They break windows. They set fire to buildings. They steal weapons with intent to kill! William's gone to prepare the coach. Get dressed. Get the boys dressed. Be quick, *be quick*!"

She dashed back into her own room. Hermione wanted to protest, but once Polly ran on her wilder emotions, there was no reasoning with her.

"Who's going to kill us?" Billy asked, eyes huge. Roger had his thumb in his mouth, which he did only when anxious.

Hermione knelt to gather them both into a hug. "No one's going to hurt you, loves. But sometimes people become a little wild when they gather in a big group, so we're going to leave and be out of their way. Let's get dressed. You start for yourself, Billy, while I help Roger."

Hermione was still gathering the boys' clothing when Polly dashed back in, hair somewhat tidy and bonnet in place. "Why aren't you ready? Really, Hermione! I'll dress Roger." She picked up the lad and his clothes and carried them into the other room, where baby Henrietta was beginning to wail.

Hermione smiled for Billy and turned his stocking so it would go on properly.

"If we're not in danger," Billy asked, "why are we in a rush?" He was a clever and observant little boy.

"We could become in danger if we stay, but we're leaving, so we're in no danger at all."

He let her do his other stocking. "What's a mob?"

"A lot of people gathered together."

"Like at church?"

"No. In the open air, and getting overexcited."

"Like at the fair and the greasy pig contest?"

He was clever, observant, and persistent. "A bit like that. You know how sometimes people start to argue and fight?"

He nodded, apparently satisfied. "I want my breakfast."

So did Hermione, but she said, "We'll halt as soon as we can. Let's get your shoes on." She brushed his hair, put his jacket in his hand, and shooed him next door to his mother.

She closed the door with a sigh of relief and took off her robe, but then she wondered whether Thayne could be hiding somewhere. "Thayne?" she asked softly, but of course there was no response. She had to hope he was far away and safe.

From the next room her sister cried, "Where are you, Hermione? *Hurry!*"

"Coming!"

Her traveling corset was light and front-fastening, and her gown crossed over at the front with side ties, so she could manage quickly and without help. Once she was ready, she stuffed items of clothing into the valise, then hunted around for anything she might have missed. Satisfied, she joined her sister.

She, Polly, and the children made their way along the corridor and downstairs to a crowded entrance hall. They struggled in the crush even though the flow was all in one direction. It seemed everyone was fleeing, so perhaps Polly's reaction hadn't been overblown.

"The mob is planning to march to London," a man said as he pushed by them in the hall. "Carrying petitions."

"Carrying *petitions*!" Polly gasped, as if

he'd said, "Carrying guns."

"Then it's good we're going west, not south," Hermione soothed. "Once on our way, we'll be out of all danger."

"Pray God you're right. Come, come." Polly rushed toward the innyard, carrying the baby.

"Polly!" Hermione protested to her back. She was left with two children and a valise.

She looked around for a servant, but it was hopeless. She saw a flash of black, red, and green stripes and thought it was Thayne, but it wasn't a neckcloth — it was a bunch of ribbons on a lady's black hat. The colors must be a fashion, like tartan. The middle-aged woman caught her staring and stared back in an almost threatening way. This panic was affecting everyone.

Quickly Hermione arranged the boys on her left side, saying, "Roger in front, Billy behind. Both of you hold tight to my skirt and don't let go. Billy, keep an eye on your brother."

With the valise in her right hand and her left ready to grab a wandering child, she steered a course through the melee of passengers. The people were close enough to a mob of their own, buffeting her and the children, intent only on their own direction.

When they achieved a bit of space in the

innyard, Polly was waiting. "What happened to you? Really, Hermione." She grasped Roger's hand and towed him onward. Hermione took Billy's hand and smiled at him.

"There's nothing to fear, love. I see your father and the coach. We'll be on our way soon."

Then they were almost knocked to the ground by a big-bellied man bullying his way through to where a public coach was ready to go, full inside and crowded on top. There must be at least one space left, for the coachman was calling, "All aboard for Stockport! All aboard. I dare not dally!"

"Hold, coachman," the man bellowed. "Double fare for a ticket!"

Hoping the bribing oaf didn't get a seat on the coach, Hermione wove over to their sturdy old coach, where Polly's husband, Sir William Selby, took the valise to stow in the boot. He was a slimly built, sensible man, but even he looked worried.

"There, see," Hermione said to Billy as she guided him up the steps into the coach. "We're safe now."

Soon they were packed into the carriage and their coachman could steer out into the street, but there was almost as much chaos and crowding there. It looked as if all the coaches and travelers in the area had the same idea.

"We're on our way," Hermione said cheerfully, "and many of these people are traveling north or south. We're going west, so we'll soon have the road to ourselves."

Perhaps the lads relaxed a bit, but baby Henrietta was grizzling. That could be because she was held tight in Polly's arms and Polly was intent on the street, seeking any threat. So was William, who didn't frighten easily, his long face anxious. Hermione couldn't stop herself doing the same, though there'd be nothing any of them could do if they were surrounded by an inflamed mob. William didn't even travel with a pistol.

She remembered how earlier in the year the London mob had turned on the Prince Regent's carriage as he returned from opening Parliament. Stones had been thrown and even a shot fired. In March there'd been an enormous gathering in nearby Manchester, which had become known as the Blanketeers' March because the protesting weavers had all carried blankets. The march had been stopped before it left Lancashire, but for a while it had seemed to herald disaster. Hundreds had been arrested.

The government had suspended habeas

corpus and enacted new laws to control seditious meetings, but it seemed to be like putting a lid on a boiling pot — seething unrest kept bursting free. Hermione couldn't believe that violent revolution could happen here as it had in France, but perhaps most French people had thought the same.

The situation in France had begun with moderate demands for reform, but ended up in rivers of blood — blood that had included that of Thayne's family, breaking his mother's mind. In the worst time, the period called the Terror, the *sansculottes* had stopped coaches to haul out families they thought privileged and hack them to death, or hang them from a lamppost. *"À la lanterne!"* had been the cry. And *"À bas les aristos."* Bring down the aristocrats.

Some of the French nobility had fled early, but most had been sure the insurrection would fizzle out. The royal family had waited too long to race toward Austria, the queen's homeland. As a result many, including the royal family, had ended their lives on the guillotine, men and women both, their only crime their high birth.

If this local mob attacked their carriage, would it help to protest that they were impoverished nobility? Not when they had wealth beyond the dreams of many. Her stockings were darned, but she had stockings. They were traveling in an old-fashioned and quite uncomfortable coach, but many people must walk if they wanted to get anywhere. Most of the time they ate simple, frugal food, but they never went hungry or cold, and they always had good shelter.

Yes, they were privileged, and if some of those suffering the harsh effects of the postwar privations resented them, it wouldn't be surprising. At home everyone would know that William was a good landowner who found work for as many as he could and paid fair wages. They'd know how the family provided charity for those in need. Here, no one knew any of that. The streets were crowded with people watching the coaches go by. Was she imagining sullen glares? At least there were no curses or shaken fists.

But then some soldiers came into view — foot soldiers under the command of a mounted officer. People fell back to make way for them. Hermione had enjoyed soldiers on display, looking fine in their uniforms, and had once been as entranced by a uniformed officer as any young lady. Now she saw them from a different angle. The men seemed hard-faced and grim, and many would have seen bloody action in the Peninsula and Waterloo. If the Riot Act was read, they would follow orders. Their bayonets would be lowered and their rifles fired.

"It seems wrong that they might soon be fighting fellow Englishmen," she said.

"Don't be ridiculous!" Polly protested. "They are all that stands between us and the guillotine!"

William took the fretful baby from her. "Try to be calm, dearest. It's not so dire yet."

"Yet!" she echoed, but she did calm a little. William was good for her. "You can't deny that there are people who want to bring about a revolution. Lord Sidmouth, the Home Secretary, said as much. People have been arrested for it."

"Most reformers want change by legal means, love, and heaven knows reform is needed. But let's not speak of it here." He glanced at the boys. Billy in particular was following intently. "See, we're away from the crowded area and can make better speed."

He was right. They'd turned off the north–south road and were heading west.

Billy asked, "Can we have breakfast now?"

Roger removed his thumb to echo,

"Breakfast."

Henrietta began to whine.

The poor children were used to a comfortable routine and their nursemaid, Minnie Lowick. They were so attached to her, little Roger had even called her name instead of Hermione's last night. Polly and William were loving parents, but much of the children's care fell to Minnie, and nine-month-old Henrietta probably thought she'd been torn from her arms forever. Indeed, waving good-bye at the doors of Selby Hall, Minnie had looked as if she'd like to snatch back her charges from the unreliable arms of their parents. With hindsight it might have been worth squeezing her into the coach, but four adults plus three children really wouldn't have been possible, and they couldn't have asked Minnie to travel with the coachman, exposed to all weather.

"Not quite yet, boys," William said. "We'll stop when we're well out of the city."

Billy slumped and Roger stuck his thumb back in his mouth, but Henrietta gave up protest and fell back asleep. Hermione could relax a little, but this allowed her mind to return to the adventure in the night. In hindsight she couldn't believe she'd let a man stay in her room — but it had been Thayne. She'd finally met Lieutenant Thayne again. It was delicious to accept that fact by daylight, but she must also accept that he was now a criminal. If she had any sense at all, she'd wish they would never meet again, even if this venture left her rich. She'd fallen into this entanglement as quickly as she had in the past. And that passionate kiss. She'd nearly lost all control!

But please let him not be dead.

She must hope they never met again, but she couldn't bear the thought of him dead.

As the coach rumbled on, she couldn't resist memories. When he'd told her about his mother, she'd wanted to take him into her arms. How horrible that must be, to not exist for a parent. Worse than a death. She'd nursed her dying mother. Her death had come quickly after a carriage accident. She'd nursed her father, and that had been much harder. He'd been old, for he'd married late, and he'd declined over months, frequently in pain, frightened and angry. He'd been himself, however. Neither had slipped away in life.

She wished she knew his real name. She couldn't keep thinking of him as Lieutenant Thayne when he was no longer in the military, and she was sure his name wasn't Ned.

He'd be Thayne, then. Simply Thayne, and by that name surely she could find him. Against her will her mind slid toward dreams. If Great-uncle Peake was all she hoped he would be, there might be a future for them.

CHAPTER 7

At last, they stopped for breakfast. Polly didn't think three miles far enough, but William overruled her. In the common dining room of the Three Bells they were the first ones bringing news of mayhem. Some people were alarmed, but it was clear others felt some sympathy for the Spenceans.

"Time Lunnon paid 'tention t'plight of t'north," one burly man said in an accent so thick Hermione found it hard to understand.

"But not by public disorder," said a pinch-faced clerical type.

"Orderly march, that's all."

"It'll turn into disorder. You mark my words."

"And why not?" asked a gray-haired man who'd been observing from the fireside, puffing on a pipe. "Think back to the Magna Carta. Where'd we all be if Bad King John hadn't been stopped? Then there's the

92

Glorious Revolution that put Queen Mary and King William on the throne. Without that, we'd all be Papists. Or burning at the stake."

"Lord have mercy!" exclaimed the clerical man's wife. "When was that?"

"Not a hundred and fifty years ago, ma'am, after Charles the Second died and his brother James became king. Rabid Papist he was, and tried to foist a false son on us all. The warming-pan baby," he reminded everyone.

"Oh, that," said a big-breasted matron in a fur-trimmed cloak and a grand bonnet. She'd made no secret of being a wealthy widow who ran her dead husband's saddlery business. "A substitute baby smuggled in by means of a warming pan when the queen's child was stillborn? I've never seen a warming pan big enough."

The man's face twitched with annoyance. "We'll be thinking you a supporter of the Stuarts, ma'am."

"Only if you're a fool," she dismissed. Hermione delighted in her effortless authority. How splendid to be a wealthy widow running her own business.

"A *royal* bedpan," the man persisted. "Everything they have is bigger than normal."

Some of the people in the room were nodding, but the widow hadn't finished. "You'll be saying next that they have extra-large royal chamber pots. Those changes you talked of, sir, were brought about by the nobility squabbling among themselves and had nothing to do with folk like you and me. Look at how the first King George came upon us. He didn't even speak English, but we had no say."

"There you are, then," said the man with the pipe. "That isn't right."

"But it preserved law and order from Papists and Scots. That's all that matters to law-abiding folk."

There was a murmur of agreement and the man fell silent, but Hermione noticed that his waistcoat was made of a fabric striped thinly in black, red, and green. Like Thayne's neckcloth. And the bonnet of the woman in the innyard. Three very different people to be following a fad, but her main concern was stumbling across arguments in favor of unrest in such an unlikely place.

Once in the coach, Hermione wanted to discuss it with William, but it would upset Polly and disturb the boys. The boys were content now their stomachs were satisfied, but her own breakfast sat heavily inside her. Perhaps Polly was right to be fearful. It was as if there were a contagion in the air. She watched men digging out a drainage ditch, while others mended a nearby fence, and wondered whether their glances at their coach showed resentment or worse. Could they turn their tools as weapons against her family?

Oh, nonsense. This was England, and those were honest workingmen, just like the ones she'd known all her life. In Yorkshire she often passed time with their wives and daughters, talking about the weather and sharing wisdom about how to get the hens to lay, and how to preserve meat longer into the winter.

This journey could benefit everyone on William's estate. With Great-uncle Peake's money William would be able to hire men to do necessary repairs to Selby Hall and other buildings. There'd be improvements to the land and the laborers' cottages. Polly would hire more servants in the house and dairy, and be able to be less frugal all around. What a merry Christmas the next one might be.

And Cousin Porteous would lose any ability to force her into marriage. She might even have a dowry large enough . . .

No. Despite magical memories and astonishing kisses, Thayne was a thief. There had to be many decent ways for a man like him to make his living, but he'd chosen to steal, which meant other people lost their hard-earned property to him. Even if he did reform when he could marry a rich woman, did she want a man like that?

Yes, said her weak and wanting part.

"Oh, you idiot." She'd actually mumbled it and the others looked at her. "Sorry, nothing. Where do we stop next?"

"In Warrington," William said, consulting a map and a guidebook. "We'll dine there and give the horses a long rest. Our route crosses the main Carlisle-to-London road, so there are any number of inns. We have no need of the hustle and bustle of the center, so we'll stop earlier." He ran his finger down a page. "The Lamb sounds tranquil."

In time, the coachman steered under an arch into a small innyard, but an ostler urged them through another arch into a more spacious area. "For there's plenty of space back there, sir, and a lane back to the street."

"And the small yard will then look more inviting to another coach," Polly murmured.

"Nothing wrong with that," William said as the coach just made it through the second arch. "And look, there's a grassy area and a pond with ducks. After we've eaten, the boys will enjoy playing here."

Not just ducks but ducklings, so the boys had to be compelled to eat first. As soon as they'd finished, they were fidgeting to be off. William said to Polly, "I'll take them out there. The horses need more rest, so why don't you and Hermione stroll around the town a little?"

Henrietta was asleep, so they soon set off, sharing the task of carrying her.

Hermione knew this jaunt was to help settle Polly's nerves, for she loved to shop. Selby village offered no opportunity for this pleasure, and if they went to nearby Wakefield, Polly was more likely to be upset about all the items she couldn't afford. This was shopping for amusement only, but it was spiced by possibility. Beneath every discussion of a bonnet, a china dish, or a bar of French soap ran, *If we get Great-uncle Peake's money . . .*

The amusement was ended by an ominous rumbling sound from the infant, accompanied by a smell. Thank heavens Polly had charge of Henrietta at the moment. "Time to go back," she said, in the manner of one forced back to grim reality.

"But toward our future," Hermione said. "What do you say to my stopping at the shop to buy a bar of that soap? It's not a great deal of money and it will remind us of all the other pleasures."

"Oh, do! But I must hurry back."

"I'll be perfectly safe on this busy street for five minutes, and indeed if I were set upon by brigands, I don't see what you could do."

Polly laughed. "You're always so practical, dearest. Very well, but don't dally. I'm sure we must be off soon."

She hurried back toward their inn, but Hermione dawdled, enjoying being on her own for a while. She wasn't solitary by nature, for in Hampshire she'd enjoyed many social occasions, but she'd always been able to spend time alone, sketching, reading, playing music, or simply whiling away time. That seemed sinfully indolent now, for at Selby Hall the family worked as hard as the servants. It was probably a sin to want to be able to afford indolence, but she did.

She entered the aromatic shop and lingered over the pleasure of choosing between a plain soap, a rose-scented one, and a lavender. In the end she chose the rose because Polly would prefer it, and the shop assistant wrapped it neatly in silver paper and tied it with a pink ribbon.

Delighted by the prettiness of it, and completely satisfied with her purchase, Hermione left the shop — to almost bump into Thayne.

His apology was distracted, but then he truly saw her. And smiled in a most satisfying way. "Lady Hermione."

"Sir." She dipped a curtsy, unable to suppress a smile of her own, even though daylight didn't amend his shabbiness. His hair was still too long beneath his unfashionably low-crowned hat, and his jacket had seen many better days, and he was still a thief. But his dark-lashed eyes were as fine as she remembered from the ball and her heart was dancing.

"How do you come to be here, wandering the streets without escort?" he asked.

"How do you come to be here without pursuers? Aren't you supposed to be en route for London?" Suddenly she wondered whether he'd followed her there.

A number of romantic fancies were exploded when he said, "The road to London threatened to seize up because of the Spencean Crusade, so I traveled west to avoid delay. You've done the same?"

"Our route continues west. To Tranmere, in the Wirral."

"Thus we cross by happy chance. May I

escort you to your inn?"

Good sense commanded that she say no, but she was incapable of it. "So you've escaped pursuit," she said as they strolled along.

"With your help."

"Which I'm sure I should repent. Any theft has a victim."

"I assure you, the victim in this case doesn't deserve your sympathy. No, I'll say no more, but I hope you believe me, for I'd not want you to suffer any qualms."

"Then I will believe you. I prefer to think myself in the right at all times."

She meant it as a joke and he chuckled. "Delightful as ever. Or is that too bold?"

Inside she purred, but she kept the tone light. "Any lady is pleased to be told she delights, sir. You should scatter your praise with abandon."

"A very risky course."

She raised a brow at him. "Are you claiming to be hunted by ladies with marriage in mind?"

"Some disregard my rags in favor of my charms. Not you, I assume."

"If only I were a grand heiress, sir, I might be able to afford you." She said it lightly, but watched his reaction. It was unreadable and they'd arrived at the innyard of the

Lamb. There was nothing for it. She offered her gloved hand. "Good-bye, sir."

He took it, saying, "Good-bye," but raising it to his lips.

Despite sturdy cotton gloves, she felt a frisson, and his eyes held hers. Surely it spoke of emotions similar to her own.

Thief! she reminded herself. *At the very least you must go carefully.*

She pulled her hand free and hurried into the innyard, not allowing herself a backward glance, but she paused as soon as she was out of sight to gather her composure. Her heart was racing and she was almost in tears. Over a rascally thief.

A completely unrepentant thief. Good riddance — and yet she had to dab her eyes and blow her nose. It would never do for Polly to see signs of distress. She was just putting the handkerchief away when Thayne ran into the innyard.

Coming after her? No, he was surprised to see her still there. He hesitated, then took a letter from a pocket and thrust it into her hand. "Put it out of sight and into the post as soon as possible. It's of crucial importance. Good-bye indeed!" With that, he ran toward the arch into the back area and out of sight.

Hermione gaped after him, then looked at

the letter. It was addressed to Sir George Hawkinville, Peel Street, London. That seemed respectable, but the wretch had foisted his stolen goods on her. She was tempted to toss the thick letter on the muddy ground or to find the nearest fire, but he'd seemed so serious. "Crucial importance." "Out of sight," she remembered, shoving the letter in a pocket while she tried to make sense of it all.

Another man ran in from the street and paused, looking around. If Thayne seemed poorly dressed for his state, this man was too well dressed for his nature. His fashionable jacket and breeches stretched over bulging muscles and there was something about him that made Hermione think of a hunting dog sniffing for prey.

The turning head stilled to look at her. "Seen a man here?" he growled. "Brown coat. Low hat?"

"No!" She gasped it, for his brutish face terrified her. Her hand was to her throat, the packet of soap still clutched in it, the sweet rose perfume at odds with everything else.

He stepped closer, nose twitching as if he truly could smell his prey. His head was unnaturally square and that nose was fat, but it was the small, cold eyes that had her backing away, heart pounding.

"Begone, you wretch, or I'll scream for help." *And this time, I'll do it.*

He smiled as if he found her threat amusing, but then turned his head sharply toward the back of the innyard. She looked that way and saw Thayne clearly visible in the archway. Why on earth wasn't he far away by now? This peril was clearly what he'd fled.

He disappeared again, and his pursuer leapt into a run exactly like a hunting dog — all muscle and trained to kill. He raced through the arch and Hermione moved forward as if to run after, to protect and defend . . .

"Are you all right, ma'am?"

She turned to find an aproned servingman had come out of the inn carrying a broom. "Yes. No! A man ran through here and another pursued. I'm afraid there will be violence done."

The servant shrugged. "Some private brawl, ma'am. Don't you distress yourself. Is there anything I can do for you?"

Sweep away the past twenty-four hours and restore my orderly life.

"Hermione!" Now Polly was waving to her from the very arch where Mark Thayne had shown himself — in order to draw the cur away, she now realized. Polly and the others could have been put in danger by that.

"Come along!" Polly cried. "You've been an age and we're ready to leave."

Hermione was about to join her, but then remembered the wretched letter. She didn't want to take the dangerous thing into the coach with her family.

"I just need to go into the inn for a moment!" she called, and went inside. Polly would assume she needed a chamber pot and couldn't object to that. She entered the inn and went down a cramped corridor into the crudely paneled entrance hall, which also served as the taproom and had the beer smell to suit. A coal fire gave off an acrid stench. It would serve Thayne right if she threw the letter there to burn. But that man, that predatory brute, had been vile. If he was a minion of the victim of the crime, she could believe no pity was needed.

People were staring at her.

An elderly couple sat at a small table, his clothing announcing him to be a clergyman. Two young women sat on a bench, shawls around their shoulders and bundles at their feet. Three sturdy workingmen stood between the kegs of ale and the fire with flagons in their hands.

The hard-faced woman stationed by the

kegs asked, "Can I 'elp you, mam?"

"Can you tell me where I may post a letter?"

Before the woman could answer, the gray-haired innkeeper entered, all apologies. "I gather you have been discomforted, ma'am."

"I was merely startled."

"T'lady wants to know where to post a letter," said the barmaid, as if that was deeply suspicious.

"The post office is but a short walk, ma'am," the innkeeper said, "but I believe your party is ready to leave. May I have a letter taken there for you?"

Hermione stood pinned in indecision. She couldn't bring herself to burn the letter in her pocket, but handing it over to the innkeeper felt like a betrayal of trust.

"Ma'am?" the innkeeper prompted.

"I thought to write one," she said, "but I see I don't have time." No wonder the man looked as if he thought her deranged, and the barmaid as if she was sure of it.

Hermione hurried away to the carriage and endured Polly's scold. They were soon on their way, but she felt as if she carried danger in her right-hand pocket and dearly wished to have that decision back to do again. Stolen papers. What if she was caught with them? Could she go to jail? Or worse?

If the papers were banknotes, theft of money was a hanging crime.

If that horrid brute had caught Thayne, it would serve him right. At the next stop she'd get the letter into the post if she could or burn it if she couldn't, and she'd allow no more foolish yearnings over a long-ago dream.

CHAPTER 8

Mark ran for his life, aware that he was insane because he was enjoying it. He had no doubt that Nathan Boothroyd would kill him if he caught him, for he'd have no chance against the man's brute strength short of a pistol, which he didn't have. In any case, he wasn't sure one pistol ball would stop a Boothroyd quickly enough.

All the same, he was grinning as he ran, because he was damned tired of skulking and conniving. He dodged through the laundry pegged to lines across the back lane, trying not to soil any of it, and down a narrow passage between high walls. He was probably faster than Nathan, but he didn't know this town or any hiding places. He might be safer in the high street, but he wasn't sure a Boothroyd would let a crowd stop him and innocent people could get hurt.

He twisted into a slightly wider lane that

ran between the backyards of two rows of houses, but it was too long and without concealment. At any moment Nathan would turn into it and see him. Nothing for it. He scrambled over a head-high gate, hoping he managed it before Nathan glimpsed his disappearing boots.

He was in a small backyard that held no greenery except weeds and stank of slops thrown out of the back door. He stood still, listening for Nathan's footsteps on the other side of the brick wall.

A dog snarled.

Mark stifled a laugh.

He was facing a real beast this time — a bull terrier guarding its territory with bared fangs. It wasn't barking, but such a dog could attack without warning. He stayed still, silently urging the dog not to make a noise beyond the rumbling growl. He could hear Nathan crunching along the rough surface of the lane now, going slowly, trying to sniff out his prey. The footsteps passed the gate and moved on. Mark let out his breath.

Then the dog barked, once, twice, three times.

The back door opened and a woman said, "What's the matter with you now, Rowley? Here." She threw out a knucklebone.

The dog whined its dilemma, but then clearly decided if the mistress was here, his job was done, and settled to gnawing the bone with excellent sharp teeth.

But out in the lane, Nathan's footsteps had stopped, and now the woman had seen the intruder. She was probably in her thirties, with loose, slovenly red hair but a decent enough green gown. She wasn't afraid. He tried last night's trick and put his finger to his lips. *Shush.*

She looked at him as if he was crazy.

Aware of Nathan listening, Mark chose another route and dug out a coin — fortunately he found a five-shilling piece first — and showed it to her. She tilted her head to indicate he could enter the house. As he passed the dog, it gave a growl for honor's sake, but hardly stopped its work on the bone.

Mark paid his dues and entered a small kitchen where a crone stirred a cauldron over a fire. Had he stumbled upon a witches' coven? He went through a curtain into a front room and realized that, no, he'd found a bawdy house, and not one of the most salubrious in town.

Two thickly painted women lolled on a sagging sofa with their heavy tits hanging out of gaudy gowns. A third was plying her trade, straddling an elderly customer on a wooden chair. Perhaps there were beds upstairs. Perhaps not. The two available whores smiled invitingly, one showing missing teeth.

The woman who'd let him in said, "Suit yourself, sir. You've paid for them twice over."

Fighting a wild bubble of laughter, Mark bowed to all of them. "My apologies, ladies, but I have pressing business elsewhere."

"I can work quick, me 'andsome," one of the whores called.

Mark sent her a regretful smile, opened the front door, and stepped out. He found himself on an alley so narrow two fat people couldn't walk abreast, with the high street visible nearby on his right and a green area to his left with houses beyond.

He had two pressing but conflicting imperatives: one, get out of Warrington in one piece and on his way to London with all that he knew; two, make sure Lady Hermione came to no harm through his impulsive recruitment. A third was to find out what had happened to the damn letter, but somehow he felt sure she'd have done as he asked and put it into the post.

When he'd escaped out the back of the Lamb, he'd seen an additional area there containing two private coaches. One had been ready to depart. A woman had been leaning out of the window looking for someone — a brunette who bore a marked resemblance to Lady Hermione. She must have been the married sister. Hermione would have posted the letter and entered the coach, and they'd already be on their way and safe.

Alas, his conscience wouldn't let him accept that without proof. When Nathan gave up the pursuit, he could well return to the Lamb to look for another trail. So Mark turned left and plotted a course that would bring him to the rear of the Lamb. He found the coach gone. Thank the gods for that. Now he needed a safe haven for himself. He continued along the lane, alert for a Boothroyd on the prowl.

He'd run because he'd seen Solange arriving in Warrington in one of the outside seats of an overloaded coach. That meant she'd done the same as he and escaped the disruption to the Manchester-to-London road. A piece of bad luck, but he should have anticipated it. Isaac Inkman and Nathan Boothroyd had been with her, and at her word, Nathan had scrambled down off the coach while it was still in motion.

So he'd run.

He'd evaded Nathan for now, but Solange wouldn't give up the hunt. She knew now that Mark hadn't taken last night's London coach, so he'd be her prime suspect for the theft. He'd read through her papers. He didn't understand it all, but she'd be desperate to get such dangerous documents back. He'd booked a seat on the next London coach, which would stop for passengers at the Nag's Head, but it was the principal inn for London coaches. Solange would already be booking seats there, but also asking about him.

So there was another coach seat he couldn't claim. At this rate he'd run out of money.

Would she stay in Warrington to search for him, or would she take the first coach south? Her priority should be to reach London and plan destruction for when the Crusade arrived. If she believed that wouldn't happen, Isaac's destructive ideas wouldn't seem so important.

Mark weighed the situation and decided to gamble that she'd pursue her main plan and take the afternoon coach. He'd wait for the London mail, which arrived in Warrington at midnight, but in the meantime he needed to be out of sight.

As he passed the rear of a string of inns,

he looked for a quiet, out-of-the-way place and settled on the Roebuck. It was too small to cater to public coaches or to tempt many who traveled in private ones. The only vehicle in sight was a light sporting curricle, which no one would use for a long journey, so the owner must be local. As he walked by it, Mark admired the expensive toy with its gleaming paint and shining brass. He wasn't surprised to be glared at by a groom dressed in matching livery who was eating his meal while on guard. Clearly the local was a wealthy man, which promised a decent inn and a fine kitchen.

He went in at the back and followed a corridor to a flagstoned hall with a taproom off to the left and two doors on his right. A plain staircase led to an upper floor. The taproom was deserted and the whole place very quiet.

Perfect.

He went into the taproom and asked a massively bosomed woman for a tankard of ale. She might be a barmaid, but the high-necked dark gown, the voluminous cap, and an air of command suggested she was also the innkeeper. She drew the ale from a cask, but grudgingly. Would she allow him to linger here till midnight for the purchase of occasional tankards of ale? To take a room for the night would deplete his money to no purpose.

He sipped and tried to sweeten her. "An excellent brew, ma'am."

Her only response was a cold stare.

He tried a smile. "The town seems busy."

" 'Appen it is," she said, discouragingly.

He turned away and caught sight of himself in a dingy mirror. Gads! He was dressed shabbily, but he'd lost his hat and his unkempt hair was in disarray. He'd a dirt smudge on one cheek, and when he looked down, he saw evidence of his scramble over the gate, including a rip in his breeches. He couldn't go out to search for his hat and he'd never pass for respectable without one. He was tempted to laugh out loud, but in truth his appearance could make things difficult here, there, and everywhere.

"Faringay?"

Mark turned, shocked and on guard to hear his title. He saw a man who could be his opposite in all respects. Beau Braydon was blond, fine-featured, and turned out to perfection from complex cravat to gleaming Hessian boots. He was hatless, but surely only for the moment, and his hair was perfectly arranged in what was doubtless the latest style.

No point in denying who he was. "Braydon. What are you doing here?"

"It's forbidden?" Braydon said, strolling forward. "I'm on my way south from a family place near Lancaster. I do trust you're not in as dire straits as your appearance suggests."

"Yes and no," Mark said, glancing to see what effect this conversation had on the innkeeper. She resembled the bull terrier — confused, but still inclined to growl.

"You know this man, sir?"

Braydon's lips twitched. "Well enough, Mrs. Upshaw. Clearly I should feed him. Lay another place in my parlor, if you please."

"Thank you, sir," Mark said humbly, and followed through one of the doors off the hall into a private parlor. It was a simple room with whitewashed walls, but a fire burned in the grate and the table was set for a meal.

He and Beau Braydon had known each other in the army. They'd never been close friends, but they'd worked together a couple of times, and passing a few hours in his company would be useful — as long as he could come up with a tale to cover the situation.

A young serving maid hurried in with

plate, cutlery, and glassware. Despite looking only fifteen or so, she dallied at Braydon's side in hopes of flirtation. Braydon gave her smiling thanks and she had to leave.

He poured wine for them both. "Don't strain for a lie, Faringay. I can be remarkably incurious when necessary."

Mark toasted him with a smile. "Noble of you. Believe it or not, mayhem isn't my daily style, but today I had to run from a hunting dog."

"And lived to tell the tale?"

"By scaling a gate and escaping through a whorehouse."

"Unscathed again?"

"Untempted."

"Ah, one of those."

Yes, spending a few hours with Braydon would be no sacrifice, and with such sponsorship, perhaps the gorgon of the taproom wouldn't quibble at him lurking here until midnight. The afternoon coach would soon leave the Nag's Head and chances were good that Solange would be on it. She needed to get Isaac to London to do his evil work, and she'd take Nathan Boothroyd, because she liked to have a bodyguard. What a quivering conscience she must have.

The maid returned with an aromatic tureen of soup and Mark, safe for the moment, settled to enjoy it.

CHAPTER 9

When Nathan Boothroyd came into Solange's parlor in the Nag's Head, she glared at him. "You failed."

"It weren't him, ma'am! Bloody Granger left on the London coach afore you were attacked, so he can't have been here."

"I *saw* him. If you'd not delayed to argue with me before pursuing, you would have caught him."

The loss of the papers infuriated her. Waite had gone so far as to scold her for putting the details in writing, as if she were in truth a meek wife. To him, she'd scoffed at the danger, but her notes about Isaac's explosive intentions could provide an excuse for arrests, which would threaten her grand design. She would plunge Britain into chaos, take over through Waite, and then turn the new republic's might to conquer France.

She could easily murder Boothroyd in her

fury, but he might still be of use. "Tell me exactly what happened."

Despite her calm voice he was wary, which showed his animal instincts were intact. "I went into that innyard where you said he'd gone, but it was deserted except for a woman who said she'd seen no one pass."

"What sort of woman?"

"Ordinary."

"A servant?"

He scowled in thought. "No, but not fancy-dressed. Brown gown, straw bonnet. Ordinary. She had a package in her hand."

"A package?" she echoed.

The Boothroyds weren't entirely stupid. "Not your letter, ma'am. Silvery thing tied with pink ribbon."

All very well, but how could this woman not have seen Granger only moments before? Therefore she'd lied. Why?

Would Granger have disguised the papers in silver and pink in order to pass them to a woman? It implied a devious plan, but she'd been involved in devious plans.

Anxious to please, the Boothroyd said, "I scared her well, ma'am."

"Did she scream?"

"Would have, but I saw Granger out the back of the inn and took off after him."

"So it was Granger."

"I saw the man you'd seen, I meant. Dressed a bit like him. Low hat."

"And he ran."

"People run from me whether they've reason or not, ma'am. I chased him through a bunch of plaguey laundry and down a lane, but he must have gone into one of the houses. So it can't have been him, see? Granger'd have no hidey-hole here any more than I would."

Nevertheless, it had been Granger. Her eyesight wasn't as good as it had been, but it was good enough for that. She had tickets on a coach as far as Worcester, where they'd stop for the night before proceeding on to London. She needed to be in London in case the Spencean Crusade made it there, but she also needed to retrieve those papers. Had he passed them on to that woman, wrapped in silver paper tied with pink ribbon?

She must investigate this woman and the Lamb. She didn't like to leave Isaac alone with a Boothroyd, but needs must. First, in case anything went amiss, she must write a coded letter to Waite to inform him that Granger was the traitor.

She composed it, sealed it, and said, "I go to put this in the post."

The Boothroyd sat down. "Very well,

ma'am."

How peculiar it was that both Boothroyds could sit without occupation for so long. Isaac did the same, but he was thinking and produced brilliant results. The Boothroyds seemed to go into a waking sleep, but they would spring to action if needed, and were generally useful if given clear commands.

She put on her black bonnet and gloves and went downstairs to give the letter into the care of the innkeeper. She left the Nag's Head the perfect image, she knew, of decent, middle-aged womanhood. The only flaw was her accent. After a long war, many in England distrusted a French accent, but not enough to turn away a customer.

She could soon observe the Lamb. It was a simple place, so people here would remember guests and incidents. She entered by the front door and found herself directly in the beer-stinking taproom. It seemed to also serve as a waiting room for various forms of transport. An elderly churchman and his wife sat at a table with a valise and a small trunk, and two rather mousy young women sat together on a bench in cheap clothing and insecure demeanor, with bundles by their feet. A brawny working-man was finishing a pot of ale.

A rough-faced fat woman asked if she

could help her.

Solange put on a meek smile. "I have just arrived in Warrington, ma'am, and as we passed this inn, I thought I saw an acquaintance of mine enter here. A younger lady in brown with a straw bonnet."

At the accent, the woman's lip curled. "You'll 'ave to ask the innkeeper. Mr. Johnson!"

An elderly, gray-haired man came in and Solange repeated her request.

"The lady's name?" he asked, but behind the bland face and smile he, too, distrusted anyone French. She cared nothing for that. He'd revealed that he knew whom she meant.

"Miss Wellingborough," Solange said, for she had to produce a name.

She saw her prompt answer reassure him, but he said, "We've no guest here of that name, ma'am."

"Perhaps she is only pausing for refreshment. I would very much like to speak to her if she's still here."

He shrugged, pleased to disoblige.

But one of the mousy young women spoke up. "I know who you mean, ma'am! Her party ate in the common room at the same time as we did. Looked like a poor relation to a couple with two little boys."

That didn't sound like a conspirator.

Solange was about to leave, but the other mouse, competing for importance, said to the innkeeper, "You must remember her, sir. She was here not long ago, talking about posting a letter."

Solange turned to him, smiling. "That is so like my dear Miss Wellingborough. She is always writing letters. In fact, it is chiefly how we keep in contact, for our paths rarely cross."

The innkeeper wasn't pleased with the chatter. "I doubt that lady was your friend, ma'am, for her party's name was Selby."

"Then it is she! She is unmarried, you see, and the Selbys are her in-laws."

The innkeeper practically growled. "She's left now, ma'am, so you won't be talking to her."

But did she post a letter, or entrust it to you?

Solange spoke at random, fishing for more information. "I believe the Selbys have family near Liverpool. That will be where they are going."

"Not Liverpool," said the clergyman with pinched precision. "I spoke briefly with Sir William Selby and he imparted that their destination was Tranmere in the Wirral to visit a relative there."

"But," said the workingman, perhaps feeling left out, "they could be goin' to Liverpool, then crossin' by ferry, seein' as Tranmere's a ferry 'ouse."

Solange cursed his thick accent. The woman with her papers was going to a place called Tranmere and could be pursued. But which route had she taken?

The innkeeper took command. "Sir William has taken the Chester road," he stated, "though against my advice he intends to turn off early toward Picton. I told him that shorter doesn't always mean faster, but he paid no heed."

How delightful that people loved to be "in the know," as the English put it.

"And they are definitely gone?" she asked. "There is no hope?"

"That is so, ma'am," said the innkeeper with finality.

As if to conclude the discussion, a groom entered to say he'd come to collect Reverend Portercombe and his lady. Attention turned to getting the elderly couple and their luggage on their way.

Was there any more to be learned? Solange sighed, and said to the young women, "So sad to have missed my friend by so little."

" 'Appen you could follow her, mum," one said.

"Alas, my coach to London leaves soon.

Did Miss Wellingborough have a letter to post? I suspect it will have been to me. Such a shame."

"Only a package, mum, and not to post. Ever so pretty. Pink wi' silver ribbons. I caught a whiff. Fancy soap, I reckon. Rose."

"She said as she'd been *thinkin'* of writin' a letter," the other said.

"And wouldn't 'ave time. That's right, Hattie!"

"Ah well," Solange said. "What's done is done."

She left before she roused too much suspicion and hurried back to the Nag's Head, putting the scraps together. It was possible that the young woman was a co-incidence, she and her package of soap. It seemed unlikely that Granger would have gone to the trouble of including a scent in his disguise. He couldn't have had much time.

On the other hand, the woman had enquired about the post office and then claimed not to have a letter ready to post. Odd, very odd, when her party was waiting to depart.

A letter could easily be concealed in a pocket.

If the straw-bonneted woman was an agent working with Granger, she was an

125

inept one. Or did she act that way to throw off suspicion, as Solange herself acted the dowdy matron? Most people would assume a muddle-minded woman traveling with a family could not possibly be dangerous, yet this muddle-minded, ordinary woman had been in the yard of the Lamb a minute or so after Granger had entered it, and had claimed not to have seen anyone of his description.

What was more, Nathan Boothroyd had focused on her. The Boothroyds had limited brains but were doglike even to their instincts. The woman wasn't his quarry, so he should have ignored her, but he hadn't. He'd been going after her until Granger had shown himself.

As Solange approached the Nag's Head, she spotted the key point: Granger shouldn't have shown himself. He knew the sort of danger a Boothroyd presented, and he'd had time to put distance between himself and death. But he hadn't. He'd hovered out of concern for the woman, and when she'd been threatened, he'd shown himself to draw Nathan off.

Solange nodded.

Granger had stolen her papers and missed the London coach from Ardwick. He had come to Warrington to take a coach south, thinking himself out of danger, but had seen her arriving. Whether by prior plan or on impulse, he'd passed the papers to the woman in the straw bonnet, probably already packaged as a letter. She hadn't posted the letter at the Lamb, so she had taken it with her.

Solange returned to her parlor smiling. She would soon have her papers back.

She found Isaac and the Boothroyd exactly as she'd left them, like a tableau.

"Never moves," Boothroyd said. "Hardly ever blinks."

"Never mind that. You are to hire a horse and follow a coach going toward Chester, which will turn off toward a place called Picton to go on side roads to a place called Tranmere. The name of the party is Selby."

"Why?"

"Because the man you chased was Granger and he passed the papers to the lady you encountered in the innyard. She is part of the Selby party. You will follow and retrieve them."

He didn't like being so thoroughly in the wrong. "I should stay with you and him, ma'am. I'm to guard you both."

"The letter presents more danger than anything else. Follow the Selby party and get it back."

"How? I'm no high toby."

It was a fair point, and attempting to hold up a coach full of people in broad daylight would be a challenge to even a clever highwayman. "I gather the side road will be slow and little used. Keep them in sight until they turn off, then watch for them to stop for rest or new horses. The woman in the straw bonnet will leave the coach. You seize her."

"With her family looking on?"

"If you do it quickly, they won't have time to react. You need only carry her far enough to search her. Search her thoroughly. Cut off her clothes if necessary." His small eyes sparked at that. "When you've retrieved the letter, break her neck or she'll describe you to the magistrates."

He chewed it over. She watched for any recognition that the family might provide a description of him. It would be inconvenient to lose him, but that was a risk she was willing to take. As it was, he should have time to get clear away.

He came up with a different, and surprisingly pertinent, objection. "She's seen me. I won't get close to her without a screech."

Solange found a brown muffler she'd knitted for Isaac. "The day is chilly — you have a toothache. Wrap that around the lower part of your face."

He took the scarf. "What do I do with the letter?"

"Burn it. Down to ash. Then you return the horse here and take the next coach to London to join us."

She gave him some money. He put it in a pocket, directed a scowl at Isaac, and left. She could only pray that he be up to the task.

Too late she realized that if he was arrested for murder, he might talk. Did the British government use torture? If not, they were weak fools. If he talked, he'd name her and tell what he knew of the Crimson Band. He knew little of importance, but the possible risk made the next step clear. Enough of Waite's caution. The time to act was now.

She packed and then gently stirred Isaac out of his trance. Soon they were downstairs waiting for the coach that would take them to Worcester. The next day they'd go on to London, where the angry poor and the tumultuous mob needed only a spark to explode into revolution. With or without the Spencean Crusade, she'd give them a spark.

More than a spark.

A conflagration.

CHAPTER 10

"Thank you for this," Mark said, spooning up the last of the mock turtle soup. "It's surprisingly good food."

"For a small and simple place? Mrs. Upshaw worked for my family before she married."

"You come from this area?"

"Not exactly. I've been visiting my grandmother and aunt near Lancaster. Delightfully eccentric, both of them."

Mark just managed not to express surprise. Braydon was one of those self-contained men whom it was hard to imagine in the bosom of any family.

"Where do your mother's family live?" Braydon asked.

"They don't," Mark said.

"Ah, my dear fellow, my apologies. It slipped my mind. They went to the guillotine."

"Not quite. My grandfather did, and others of the family, but my grandmother escaped to England with my mother after they were embroiled in violence. Even so, the shock of their experiences killed my grandmother within two years, and my mother eventually."

"Odd business, France," Braydon said, ringing the bell for the next course. "First they fall into revolution and Terror, horrifying us and sending émigrés fleeing into Britain, and then they embrace Napoleon, terrifying us and sending our armies out to defeat him in all parts. Now they have a king again and the beau monde flocks to Paris to see the latest fashions."

"Not me," Mark said as sliced roast beef and vegetables were laid out, steaming hot and aromatic.

"No tug to your mother's land?" Braydon asked as they served themselves.

"None."

"Weren't you in Paris in 'fourteen?"

"Ordered there because I speak French so well. I'd look at older people in the streets and wonder if any of them had cheered my family's deaths." *Or dipped their fingers in their blood,* but he'd not had that image in his mind then.

Braydon nodded. "As I said, odd. We've been at war with France more often than not since the Conquest and yet we can't help but admire their style. Though I prefer plain cooking such as this."

"And prefer both to the Spanish," Mark said.

Braydon laughed. "Be fair. We rarely experienced the heights of Spanish cuisine."

That led safely into army nostalgia, but when the table had been cleared and they sipped the last of the wine, Braydon said, "I believe you said you joined the army in order to restore the monarchy to France. Any second thoughts?"

"Because Fat Louis lacks noble qualities? No. Any ship of state needs a stable anchor."

"At least he's a substantial one," Braydon murmured, refilling their glasses. "So what noble cause absorbs you now?"

"I thought you disclaimed curiosity."

"Only that I could do so. In truth, I'm hoping you're entangled in something where I could play a part."

"Bored?"

"You always were astute. A few years ago I'd have paid a fortune for a meal like this and a peaceful bed at night. Now . . . A man needs a purpose, don't you think?"

"No estate coming to you? Ah, no. Your father was in government, yes? Son of a younger son of an earl?"

"A mere viscount, but yes, I have no estate. You, however, do. Berkshire, isn't it?"

"Do you remember the details of everyone you've met?"

"Many of them," Braydon said with a shrug. "It was useful at times."

"True enough," Mark said, toasting him, for Beau Braydon's retentive memory had turned a trick or two on the Peninsula. "The place is Faringay Hall, near Abingdon. I thought you'd joined the army with a career in mind."

"I did, but I found I didn't fancy any of the likely peacetime duties and sold out. Then a childless uncle left his all to me. No estate, but a decent amount of money well invested. So here I am, comfortably situated for life."

"Too comfortably?"

Braydon smiled. "Quite. Do say you've some discomfort for me."

Mark smiled back but shook his head. "It's mostly very dull work and you'd never fit in."

"If your appearance is de rigueur, then you're certainly correct. Excuse my curiosity, but can you say how you come to be in Warrington, of all places?"

"That I can do. I was traveling from Manchester to London, but the road threatened to be in chaos because of a thousand or so Spenceans planning to march south to present petitions to the Regent. I took a coach here in order to connect with the Carlisle-to-London road."

"So that explains the crush in town." Braydon took his coffee cup and rose to lean against the window frame looking out at the crowded street. "It's normally brisk in Warrington, but not such bedlam. Look at that coach coming in, packed tight inside and on top, and with baggage hanging off the edges."

Mark joined him. The coach was very like the one Solange had been traveling on, giving her a damnably good view of the street.

"Good thing I'm driving myself," Braydon said.

"Coach?" Mark asked with surprise.

"Curricle."

"That was your rig I saw behind the inn? You drove from London in such a vehicle?"

"I've discovered I enjoy it now the toll roads are good. Didn't have much cause for fancy carriage driving during the war, did we, but I've rather taken to it. Not racing, but simply traveling. Use my own horses all the way and stop if the weather turns foul."

"But it's losing its appeal?"

"Not so much that as what to do in

between journeys, or when the weather turns foul."

Mark considered and then said, "You could contact Hawkinville. There's interesting work to be done out of uniform."

Major George Hawkinville had been a key member of Wellington's tactical and security section in the Quartermaster's Division, and both Mark and Braydon had worked under him at times.

Braydon studied him from heavy-lidded eyes. "There's little cause for spying nowadays."

"There's always cause for spying. The enemies are just different."

"Ah. I think not."

"No?" Mark asked, surprised by the chill in the other man's voice.

"The universal enemy at the moment seems to be the distressed poor. One reason I left the army was that I had no intention of having to order men to saber charge English people who ignored the Riot Act."

"Rebellion can't be allowed."

"Nor should starvation, or men, women, and even children working every possible hour for a pittance."

"Zeus! Are you a radical?"

"No, but I would favor more kindness and less greed."

"You should go into Parliament."

Braydon returned his gaze to the street. "I've thought of it, but reform will be a long struggle and I doubt I have the patience. And yes," he added drily, "if I were a true believer, I'd give my all to the poor and toil alongside them."

"An empty gesture, but you could provide employment."

"I do, but even a luxurious set of rooms in London doesn't need many servants and the truly poor don't seem to be employed providing fine clothes and horses."

"You need an estate. You could purchase one."

"I wasn't trained to it. At school I had a touch for oratory. Perhaps I should inspire the enmassed poor to more effective action."

"No."

Braydon studied him. "Still the fear of revolution?"

"Yes, but I'm thinking of the poor as well, and the saber-wielding military. At Spa Fields last year the enmassed poor almost got massacred."

"There should be means of effective protest that don't break any laws."

"Then someone would make a law against it." But Mark was staring out at the street.

"Damnation."

"What?"

"That man, riding past on the bobtailed black."

"What's up with him other than his seat?"

"He's riding west when he should be on a coach south. Apologies for a hasty exit, but I need to hire a horse."

Braydon caught his arm. "I have horses. Whom do we pursue, and why?"

"The hunting dog, now after another target."

Heaven alone knew how Nathan Boothroyd had learned about Lady Hermione Merryhew and her direction of travel, but pursuit of her was the only explanation Mark could imagine for the man being separated from Solange and riding west. She was in danger and it was his fault.

Braydon called for his bill and paid it, ordering his carriage to be made ready.

By the time they arrived at Braydon's curricle, an ostler was leading out a pair of magnificent matched chestnuts, accompanied by the liveried groom, whose coat was brown trimmed with red and shiny brass buttons. His tall beaver hat was detailed in the same way.

"I need your man's coat and hat," Mark said.

Braydon didn't question it. "Baker, your jacket and hat for my friend, if you please. As he'll be traveling in your stead, he might as well look the part."

The groom scowled, but he surrendered his garments. Mark passed over his coat in return. "A poor exchange, I know, but if you could keep it for me, I'd be grateful. We should be back soon."

Fortunately the groom was tall, but he was lanky and the jacket barely fit. All the same, it and the hat would be some sort of disguise.

Braydon took the reins and skillfully steered the lightweight, two-wheeled vehicle along the back lane and out into the busy high street. The groom might be taking some solace from Mark's having to squeeze into his small seat at the back rather than alongside Braydon. It wasn't comfortable, but Mark would ride on nails if they could travel faster.

He'd put a lady in peril. A special lady.

Braydon tossed back a slim book. "Maps."

Mark found the right page as Braydon steered through traffic out of town. The horses were high-spirited, but Braydon kept them in hand and they were soon in the quieter outskirts. All the same, Boothroyd would have made more speed and might be able to gallop once free of the town.

"I have the page for the Chester road," Mark said. "Damnation. For Tranmere the main route is to go into Chester and turn back north, but there are arrows indicating other options. We don't know which way. We need to keep Boothroyd in sight."

Once they'd passed the toll, Braydon gave his horses their head. Mark clutched onto the sides of his flimsy seat. Once he got the balance of the ride, he was able to let go and ask, "Pistols?"

"Box in a section in front of you. Catch!"

Braydon tossed back a key and Mark caught it. "What if I'd missed it?"

"We'd have had to stop."

The key unlocked a panel and behind sat a fine wooden box with brass mountings. Mark opened it to find one pistol nestled in its spot and all the necessaries.

"Slow down a bit," he called, and set to loading it. "You have the other?"

"Of course. What's the mission?"

"Keeping it short, I had some papers that needed to go to London. I'd packaged them as a letter. Being pressed, I gave it to a lady of my acquaintance and asked her to put it in the post. A snap judgment that I very much regret."

"The hound is after the lady?"

"I fear so. There's no other reason for him to travel west. We're clear for speed."

"He's your villain?" Braydon asked as he steered around a large wagon and then set his horses to the gallop again.

"A minion."

"If I'm to kill someone, I need to know why. And a rabid hunting beast needs to be shot."

"He's not rabid, only under orders, but you're right. A Boothroyd on the hunt won't be stopped short of violence."

CHAPTER 11

Hermione and her party had turned off the busy Chester toll road onto a road that led more directly to Tranmere. She soon had doubts about the wisdom, for it was much less well maintained and the coach rocked and bumped, even at a slow pace.

William had probably chosen this route because there'd be no tolls to pay. Penny-pinching again, and perhaps with poor results. The Chester road might have been faster, even though it was ten miles longer. They'd hoped to reach Tranmere today but could end up spending another night at an inn.

She didn't say anything. The atmosphere in the coach was tense because of Polly's tight anxiety and William's stretched patience with her. At least Henrietta was asleep for now and the boys slumped in passive boredom.

Then the coach swayed to a halt.

William let down the window to call a question.

"Breeching's coming loose, sir," the coachman called back. "We'll need to stop and fix it."

"No," Polly moaned, quite pointlessly. Hermione wanted to shake her, but that only showed that her own nerves were frayed to shreds. William climbed out to consult with the coachman.

Hermione said, "I want to stretch my legs. Do you want to get down?" she asked the boys.

They came to life like switched-on automatons and she had to hurry to help Roger or he'd have tumbled down the steps. As the road was quiet, she didn't try to control their wild running around.

Polly joined her. "Henrietta's sleeping, so I've left her. It does feel better to move around in fresh air. Warrington was so crowded. But the delay!"

"It's only some leather. It shouldn't take long. Fretting won't speed anything. Do try not to."

"All very well for you. You don't have children to provide for. Yes, yes, I know you hope for a handsome dowry, but it's not the same. Disaster doesn't loom over you!"

It was so tempting to tell Polly about Porteous, but it wouldn't smooth this moment, and if there was no money from Great-uncle Peake, the issue would then be in the open. Hermione knew Polly would never try to force her into an unwelcome marriage, but whenever the lack of money pinched, especially with regard to the children's futures, the knowledge would be there, like grit. In fact, if this journey was for nothing, she'd have to marry Porteous. She couldn't live with herself if she didn't.

"Many families do well on an income like William's," Hermione argued. "It's not much less than Father's was."

"My children deserve better. *We* deserved better."

"Because of high rank. Why?"

Polly stared at her. "*Why?* Oh, I don't understand you. Billy, keep an eye on Roger. He's heading for the ditch!"

She ran off after her children and Hermione grimaced. Would family harmony survive this journey?

Billy ran back to the coach to join his father and see what was going on. Polly was trailing Roger, who was engaged in a thorough exploration of the verge. As it provided a variety of plants and insects, he was entranced. Hermione walked up and down near the coach, keeping away from both groups.

A farmer in a cart carrying piglets stopped to offer help, but William assured him the job was in hand, so he went on his way. A while later a larger cart rolled by with what looked like a plow on the back, perhaps being taken for mending. Again the driver offered help and was thanked, but sent on his way.

A solitary rider was coming. He, too, would offer help. People were generally kind and she found it impossible to imagine that the farmer, the carter, or the rider might join a ravening mob. It wasn't in the English nature.

Mark and Braydon had caught sight of the Boothroyd and dropped speed to stay far behind him on the busy road, but about four miles out of Warrington, some piglets had escaped onto the Chester road, causing chaos for carriages, including the curricle. Braydon's high-spirited horses objected violently to the squealing little beasts beneath their hooves.

Mark leapt down to go to their heads and Braydon settled them without damage. But Mark had to lead the horses out of the tangle of vehicles before he could retake his seat and they could race on. Horse riders had been able to navigate better and the Boothroyd was again out of sight.

They'd have hurtled on toward Chester, but Mark shouted, "Stop!" A road was going off to the right, sign-posted PICTON, HOOTON, AND BIRKENHEAD. "Which way?" he asked the universe. "Dammit, which way?"

"It looks a chancy route."

"But more direct. And cheaper. Turn."

"A certainty or a gamble?" Braydon asked as he skillfully turned his team.

"Life's a gamble. The Merryhews are poor, so they might avoid the tolls. In addition, the main route's too busy. The best Boothroyd can do is follow, so they're not in great danger there."

They were on the side road and even at cautious speed the light carriage felt like matchwood.

"Thank you for risking your rig."

"I hope not to injure the horses," Braydon said, "but the carriage is easily replaced. At least the road's wide enough not to threaten the paintwork."

"But not straight enough to spot him at a distance."

"We could come up with him without warning. He doesn't know me from Hades, but you keep your collar up and your hat down."

"Yes, sir."

Hermione spotted some blackberries in the hedgerow and was considering whether she could cross the ditch to get to them, when she heard rapid hoofbeats. The solitary rider had suddenly sped up. Perhaps he'd realized he was late.

She turned back to blackberries, but Polly cried something. Hermione turned back to see the rider galloping directly at her. He wore a scarf of some sort around his mouth and a tall hat. . . .

She saw his eyes.

She turned to run, but it was too late. A hand grabbed the back of her gown and hauled her in front of the saddle with appalling strength. And then they raced on with the saddle bruising her ribs and knocking the breath out of her.

She struggled, kicking to be free, but then she gripped instead — at a coat, at a stirrup leather, at anything — for she was in danger of falling off onto her head!

The curricle was traveling faster than was safe, and Mark was jarred around in the small seat, but he wanted to shout, "Faster!

Faster!"

Had he made the wrong choice? Were they on the wrong road? Was Hermione even now in Nathan Boothroyd's claws?

Then they came around a bend and saw a carriage ahead. That old carriage he'd seen at the Lamb, with the lady who resembled Hermione.

"That's them!" he called to Braydon. But something was amiss. Only the coachman and a gentleman were outside the coach. A woman and children looked out from inside.

"Sirs!" the man shouted. "Your assistance, for God's mercy!"

"What's happened?" Braydon asked.

"A madman. A lady . . ." The long-faced man was incoherent, but he collected himself. "A madman snatched a lady of my party, not moments ago! I couldn't pursue. My family . . . The horses are in harness. . . ."

"We'll take care of it," Braydon said, and cracked his whip, sending his horses hurtling forward without consideration of road or comfort. Mark held on for dear life, but he kept a grip on his loaded pistol as well. Hermione in a Boothroyd's clutches. If she fought him, Nathan would cut her throat for convenience.

The damn road twisted and turned, but

then . . .

A riderless horse stood ahead with two people beside it.

Two live people.

They'd pounded along until Hermione was reduced to wailing hopelessly for help.

Then the horse jerked to a halt and she was tossed off to jar on her back onto the hard ground. Before she could recover, the man was off the horse and pulling her to her feet by the front of her bodice.

"The letter. Where is it?" The muffler had slipped down and he was snarling. His dog-teeth were pointed!

She would have told him anything, but pure animal terror held her mute like a rabbit facing a fox. Her mouth opened and shut, but no sound came out.

He shook her, rattling her teeth. *"Where's the bloody letter?"* When she couldn't reply, he laughed. "Here?" He probed her breasts.

She flailed at him, but had no strength in her hands. He laughed again and patted down her sides, stopping at the shape in her right pocket.

"Take the papers, break your neck," he said, showing those pointed teeth. He repeated it as he slid his hand into the pocket. "Take the papers, break your neck.

But not until I've had some fun with you, my pretty."

"Release her!" someone bellowed.

Her captor whirled her so she was in front of him, shielding him. "Bugger off. None of your business."

They were facing an absurdly elegant curricle. What was *that* doing in the middle of nowhere? Perhaps she'd lost consciousness and was dreaming. The driver was a pink of the ton and he had a liveried groom up behind him. The driver had his whip in hand, but the groom was pointing a pistol.

"Very much our business," said the driver. "Release her now."

She felt the brute chuckle. "Going to shoot me through her? Bugger off or I'll break her pretty neck." He put his big hand half around her neck.

Everything seemed to freeze, even her breathing, because he meant it, and could do it. She managed to swallow and suck in a breath, but her heart was racing too fast for life, which was probably why her head was buzzing and darkness gathering. The brute was saying something about his letter, only wanting his letter. She'd stolen it. A low thief.

Take the letter.

Let him take the letter and leave.

Please!

She tried to speak, but only throaty sounds came out.

Something whistled through the air, over her head like a low-flying bird. She flinched away, but the brute yelled. With anger, she thought. Then the loud crack of a pistol. The brute fell, taking her with him onto the hard ground.

The last thing she saw was the smoke still drifting from the groom's pistol.

CHAPTER 12

Mark dropped the pistol and leapt out of the carriage, leaving Braydon to deal with his panicked horses. The job horse was calmer, but it was snorting and stamping too close to Hermione. He scooped her up and carried her to safety. A quick check assured him she'd merely fainted. As well if she didn't see any of this.

"I need to get her away."

"Yes. I'll drive her. . . ." Perhaps Mark's total rejection showed. "Can you drive this?"

"Just about."

Braydon winced, but he turned the curricle and then surrendered his place and helped Mark get into the seat and settle Hermione at his side, in his arm.

"Apologies," Mark said. "Can't let her out of my sight yet." He couldn't even make complete sentences. He'd almost lost her. Almost seen her killed before his eyes. Until that moment he'd not realized . . .

"Quite all right," Braydon said. "I'll take care of things here."

She was beginning to stir. "You're safe," Mark said to her. "I'll get you back to your family."

He gave the horses the command to go. Still fidgety, and unhappy with a tyro on the ribbons, they were slow to settle to their pace, but then they were on their way. He kept them to a walk.

Hermione was coming alert. "Where . . . ? Who are you?"

"Mark Thayne. I have you safe."

His words seemed to act as well as smelling salts.

"You! *You!*" she spluttered. *"Get away, you!"* She pushed at him and almost toppled herself out of the seat. He dragged her back one-handed, trying to settle the horses again.

"Let go of me!"

"You want to kill yourself?" He had to release her to control the beasts.

"I want to kill you! Let me down immediately!"

"I'm taking you back to your family. They're frantic. Calm down, you idiots!"

"What? *What?* You call me an *idiot?*"

"Not you. The horses. You calm down, too, or we'll overturn."

She went silent, which would do for now, but he could feel her seething animosity and wanted to laugh like a maniac. He'd just realized he was in love with this woman, that the seeds of insanity had been there for six years, and she wanted to kill him.

He managed to relax his hands and the horses settled back into their steady pace, but the occasional tossed head told him they weren't pleased.

"I'm sorry," he said to them.

"*Sorry!*" At least she managed not to screech it. "I wish I could make you sorry, you . . . you wretch, you idiot, you *cur.*"

"Guilty on all counts."

"Is an admission supposed to make it right?" She dragged the letter out of a pocket and tossed it in his lap. "Take it. Take it and begone. I hope never to set eyes on you again." She folded her arms and stared ahead.

He gave her a few moments to settle and then asked, "What will you tell your family?"

"The truth."

"That you allowed me to spend the night in your room, where your sister's children were sleeping? Then accepted a dangerous package, which brought a villain down upon them?"

153

If a gaze could sear, hers would have.

"I'm not blaming you, but your family will. I have a suggestion."

"I'm done with you and all your machinations, sir. I could have been killed. He wanted to . . ." She began to shiver, so he put his arm around her again. She tensed, but didn't fight free.

"You're safe now. I promise. I have the letter, so no one has reason to attack you. We'll soon be back at your coach and I'm sure you don't want to upset your family more than necessary, especially the children."

"Wretch," she muttered, but accepted it. "What can I say? That a complete stranger suddenly ran mad?"

"Yes."

She pulled free to stare at him. "*That* is your brilliant suggestion?"

"We don't have time to bicker. You are mystified. I tell your family there've been previous incidents of a madman attacking women on this road. My friend will corroborate if necessary."

"You had it all worked out? You *expected* this?"

"I've come up with the story on the instant, but it'll work if you do your part."

"What of the brute? Didn't you shoot him?"

"Winged him," he lied. He reached to touch her and she flinched away.

"Don't!"

"Your bonnet is awry and somewhat damaged."

"If so, it's all your fault." She untied the ribbons and took it off. At the sight of the crumpled brim, tears started. She sniffed and wiped them with the ribbons. "Take me back to my family. I'll not contest your clever lies."

Another bend brought the coach into sight.

"Thank God!" William exclaimed, running toward them and helping Hermione down. He pulled her into his arms. "There was nothing I could do! No horse free to pursue!"

Polly and the children were staring out at her through a window in the coach.

"Of course not," Hermione said. "Of course not."

"Then the curricle came by and set off in pursuit. My thanks to you," he said to Thayne, "and to your master." He looked around for Braydon.

" 'E 'as charge of the madman, zur,"

Thayne said in what Hermione thought an overdone and peculiar accent.

"Madman?" Polly asked, rushing out of the carriage. "Are you all right, dearest? Oh, your poor bonnet!"

And my poor back and chest and nerves. But Hermione tried to make light of it. "Nothing but a few bruises."

"Madman?" William demanded.

"Aye, zur. 'E's been reported 'ereabouts in the past weeks, zur, attacking women. Never caught afore."

"Then it's a blessing that he has been now!" Polly exclaimed.

"Indeed," William said, "but I fear this will delay us, my dear."

"Delay us?"

"We'll be required to give evidence to the magistrates, and possibly to speak at the trial."

"No!" Polly looked at Thayne as if he might be able to help. "We are on an urgent journey. To a deathbed!"

Thayne scratched his nose. "Well, then, ma'am, 'appen you could leave it with us. I reckon if we could give the magistrates a means of contacting you, zur, that'd likely be enough, there 'aving been other cases, see?"

It seemed odd to Hermione, but William

grasped at it.

"Good man. Good man. We're traveling to Tranmere." He produced a card, and wrote their destination on the back. "Thank your master for me."

"I will, zur." Thayne touched his hat and turned the carriage. Not without difficulty, Hermione was pleased to see. Then she realized that meant he was no true groom. What was he other than a bundle of lies and danger?

"Why are you glaring after him?" Polly asked. "Did he do something wrong?"

I could give a sermon on the subject. But she said, "Of course not. I'm still all ajangle. It was frightening for a while."

"For a *while*? Oh, you! Terrifying, more like. We didn't know what to do. Oh, William, we don't have the gentleman's name!"

"So we don't. I would have wanted to write our thanks. A true Good Samaritan."

Hermione's teeth clenched, but perhaps Thayne's "master" was an innocent party. Her memory was fuzzy, but full of horrors.

The ride. The violence. That man.

Take the papers, break your neck.

The hand around her neck.

The thing flying at her.

The shot.

The fall.

157

"Come back in the coach, where it's safe," Polly urged, arm around her. "We'll try to mend your hat."

She had the whole world to mend, but Hermione was happy to climb inside the coach and sit down. In fact her legs only just held up.

Take the papers. Break your neck.
Take the papers. Break your neck.

She realized the boys were staring at her, wide-eyed and anxious, so she tried a smile. "Quite an adventure."

They didn't seem convinced.

For once, Polly was the sensible one. "A bad man tried to steal Aunt Hermione, dear ones, but a good man brought her back and all's well now. Papa will soon have the coach mended and we can be on our way to Great-uncle Peake's."

"I want to go home," Billy said, lips wobbling.

Roger nodded, thumb in mouth.

Hermione was in complete agreement.

The brute was wounded, but how badly? What if he escaped and came after her again? *Take the papers. Break your neck.*

Hurry, she thought at William and the coachman. If they were moving, she'd feel less like a tethered goat, and if they could reach Great-uncle Peake's house tonight, she'd bless having four strong walls around her.

Mark headed back to Braydon, driving by a white-wigged clergyman on a sturdy gray horse. The clergyman shot him a look stern enough to make any conscience twitch, but the condemnation was probably only for the fancy curricle and livery.

He found Braydon standing by the stolid job horse, which was cropping the grass.

"Where's Nathan?" Mark asked.

"In the ditch for now. I heard someone coming, so rolled him in there, then pretended to be getting a stone out of Zeno's hoof."

"A suitable name. The beast does seem to be blessed with a stoical disposition."

"What are we going to do with the body?"

"Lady Hermione's party will be passing this way soon, and someone else could come upon us. Let's get him into the curricle."

"Over the horse might be better."

"Too visible. Whatever we do with him, we don't want to be connected."

Hooves and the jingle of a harness gave warning, and when a private coach passed by Mark was mounted on the horse and Braydon was back in the curricle seat, apparently paused to point out some aspect of the scenery.

A curious man looked out, but the coach carried on without interruption.

"Damn your memorable rig," Mark said. "We'll have to take the corpse a long way from here."

Nathan Boothroyd's muscular build made hoisting his deadweight out of the ditch and into the well of the curricle seat a struggle for two strong men, but eventually he was in place with the travel rug over him. Braydon took his seat, Mark mounted the horse, and they set off farther into the Wirral Peninsula. Mark looked for a side lane that would conceal them until Hermione's carriage had passed.

How was she? It had been painful to leave her in such distress, even in the loving care of her family, but she'd reviled him, and with cause.

She never wanted to see him again. With cause.

Despite the pain, it would be better so. He'd lived apart from his old life for three years, and only see what happened when he weakened. Hermione had almost been killed and Braydon was implicated in a suspicious death.

A gig overtook them, driven too fast by a young man who was so enraptured by the splendid curricle and horses that he almost ended up in the ditch. Someone else who'd remember them.

They passed some farm tracks that were too rutted and straight to serve, but then came to a side road that soon curved. The fingerpost was weathered into illegibility, but it didn't matter where it led as long as it took them out of sight. They turned into it and around the bend, where they pulled up. A sparse hedge and a couple of trees provided enough of a screen for them, but would allow a glimpse of the coach as it went by.

"What now?" Braydon asked, at ease with a corpse beneath his feet. "Dump him here?"

"Too close. When he's found, there'll be an inquest and the clergyman and the young whipster will remember your rig."

"Water?" Braydon suggested. "We can't be far from the Mersey."

"Difficult to lose a body without a boat, and we might be seen."

"We don't have the means to bury him effectively."

"No. He's going to have to be found by the road, victim of violent robbery, but not here. Close to the Chester road, where the culprit could have been anyone."

"What about the lady and her party? Will they keep mum?"

"No one mentioned a pistol shot, but they must have heard it. But they were anxious to not be delayed. They're on their way to a deathbed, and with urgency."

"So it will suit them to keep quiet."

Mark took out the card. "Sir William Selby — probably a justice of the peace — Selby Hall, Yorkshire." That must be where Hermione now lived, in penny-pinching dependency when she was made for so much more. He flipped it over. "En route to Riverview House, Tranmere."

Braydon found a map book. "About eight miles from here. They may not learn of the crime at all."

"Especially if it's connected to the Chester road, even further away."

"Do we want him identified?" Braydon asked.

Mark considered it. "I'd rather his disappearance be a mystery to his employers for as long as possible."

"An unidentified victim of violence could become an item in the newspapers," Braydon warned.

"But only after a delay."

Braydon climbed down, flipped back the rug, and searched Nathan Boothroyd's pockets. "Some money, a garrote, no card case."

Mark inspected the garrote with its fine cord and leather handles. "Unexpected sophistication. As for a card case, he wasn't the sort for social niceties."

"Nothing to make identification easy." Braydon checked further, finding a knife in a boot. He kept that, too. "Don't want him to look unusual. He might have been useful in the army."

"He could follow orders."

"Perhaps the blame lies with those who gave the orders."

"It counts against them, but the orders didn't shape the Boothroyds' natures."

"There are more of them?" Braydon asked, climbing back into his seat.

"He has a brother. Two peas in a pod."

"Struth. Odd to think someone might mourn him."

"Seth Boothroyd will certainly want revenge."

"If he undertakes investigations," Braydon said, "the surviving Boothroyd might find a connection to my very distinctive rig."

"You did ask me to make your life more interesting."

"I should have remembered what that might mean around you. No sign of your

163

lady's coach yet?"

"They needed to fix some part of the harness."

"Then as we wait, why not tell me more of what you're involved in?" When Mark hesitated, he added, "I believe I've earned the right."

"You have," Mark agreed. "I'm working with Hawkinville, who's working for the government, but I'm a free agent. I've infiltrated a secret organization in order to prevent bloody revolution and terror."

CHAPTER 13

The ancient Selby coach trundled along beyond the trees. Mark managed not to watch it until it was out of sight. After five minutes Braydon turned the curricle, not without difficulty, and they traveled back toward the Chester toll road with Mark riding Nathan Boothroyd's hired horse. They tried to attract as little attention as possible, but probably failed when many people would never have seen such a fine curricle and team before. Fortunately fellow travelers were rare on the quiet road, and there were no nearby cottages.

Even so, when they passed a field where two men paused in their digging to stare, Mark said, "You see why I choose shabby."

"I don't normally object to appreciation. If luck favors us, these people will remember us passing by without any sign of foul behavior."

"We have to do something about Zeno."

"It's an undistinguished beast," Braydon said. "Someone might steal it if given the opportunity."

"Set it loose without tack?"

"In a field. It could be undetected there for days."

"And when noticed, disappear into someone's shed or stable."

Fortune provided better. They passed a Gypsy encampment, so that when they found the access to a field grazed by cows, and with no one in sight, they quickly unsaddled and unbridled the horse and sent it in there. The amiable beast relieved itself and settled to enjoying the grass.

"You must think you've literally ended up in clover," Mark said to it. "I wish you well."

They hid the tack on the far side of the hedge, hoping the Gypsies would find it, too. If so, Boothroyd's horse would be a mystery forever.

They went a little farther with Mark now in the groom's seat, encountering a few more travelers, including some geese walking to market, until the busier Chester road came into view. It was still far enough away that even someone traveling on the roof of a stagecoach wouldn't see details of what they did next.

Braydon drew up the curricle on the edge

of the road. Mark got down and dragged out the corpse, then booted it to roll it into the ditch. "No one's going to spot him there."

"Until flies, crows, and other carrion eaters signal it."

"By which time we'll be far away and long forgotten."

But then a one-horse cart trundled around the bend, heading toward the Chester road.

Mark considered ignoring the body, which was out of sight. He'd already dismissed the idea when Braydon called, "Ho! Where's the nearest magistrate, my good fellow?"

The cart came alongside and drew to a halt. The leathery driver said, "That'd likely be Sir Hugo Porter, sir. Birkenhead way. Is somethin' amiss?"

"Very much so. There's a body in the ditch."

The driver climbed down and walked to stand beside Mark. "Gentleman, by the looks of it. Shot, I'd say."

Braydon agreed with these insights. "Someone needs to take the body to the magistrates, but I'm in some haste for Warrington. Could you possibly oblige me, sir?"

The man scratched his bristles. "Not to Birkenhead, sir. But I'm travelin' to Chester. Likely there's a magistrate there."

"And you'll take the poor man there? Good man, good man. Much obliged. Baker, help get the body into the cart."

Mark, indulging in the heavy sigh of a burdened servant, climbed into the ditch to haul up Nathan Boothroyd's corpse. For a blessing, the ditch was muddy only at the bottom and Nathan's clothing wasn't sodden. The carter climbed down to help hoist the corpse into the back. Braydon pulled the travel rug from the floor of the curricle. "Baker, cover the poor man with this."

Mark did, smiling at Braydon's quick thinking. Any blood on it would be explained.

"Poor fellow," Braydon said, observing from on high. "I hope the footpads responsible for this are hanged." He gave the carter one of his cards. "My name is Braydon. Be so kind as to give this to whatever official takes the body. I will be willing to give any information I can, though I know no more than you do. Convey my regrets that my obligations mean I cannot linger hereabouts." He offered some coins. "I know you'd do this duty out of Christian charity, sir, but I fear it will take you out of your way and you're sparing me the same plight. Do please take these."

The carter did. "Very considerate of you, sir. I'll take care of 'im right enough."

Mark joined Braydon on the front seat, and they set off at a brisk trot. They didn't speak until they were on the Chester road, traveling fast toward Warrington, the carter far behind.

"Quick thinking," Mark said. "But a damned nuisance."

"You're not the one whose name will be known to the coroner."

"A situation when your fine style will play to your advantage. A less likely footpad is hard to imagine."

"As long as the Selby party don't take a hand."

"If the body goes to Chester, they might never know about it."

There was nothing to be done and they both put the matter aside. "That was a neat shot," Braydon said.

"Heart in my mouth. This damned coat's so tight I couldn't raise my arm fully."

"All the more credit to you, then."

"It was only a matter of yards."

"But with a lady close."

Mark would remember that moment all his life. A frozen moment of fear, but Nathan Boothroyd's gloved hand around Hermione's throat had given him no choice.

"What now?" Braydon asked.

"Back to Warrington as we said. I have a seat on the midnight mail to London and you can continue your journey."

"You won't get rid of me so easily now. What do we do about the Frenchwoman? Won't she wait for her bullyboy to return with her papers?"

Mark was so used to working alone he wanted to protest, but only a fool rejects good help, and he knew he'd made misjudgments today. He could use someone to analyze his ideas.

"She'd want to have them back," he said, "but she needs to get Isaac to London in case the Spenceans arrive and his devious explosions are of use. We can check in Warrington whether she left or not. She's not remarkable, but Isaac is."

They went through the first toll gate and passed some slower travelers. "Why travel to London?" Braydon asked. "You'll be in danger now you're exposed as a traitor in their midst."

"Not for long. These papers will bring them down. I want to be there."

Braydon nodded, and they traveled on in comfortable silence with him clearly enjoying weaving around other vehicles and sometimes squeezing through an alarmingly narrow space. For pride's sake Mark kept silent, but his grip was tight on the side rail.

Five miles out of Warrington they met a delay even Braydon couldn't overcome. Ten brown cows were being moved from field to field, heavy udders swaying, and in no hurry at all.

Braydon relaxed back. "I've been thinking."

"You can think when driving like that?"

Braydon's lips twitched. "Stimulates my brain. How did the rabid beast know to pursue Lady Hermione and what direction to take?"

"I've been wondering about that, too," Mark said, "during our relaxing cruise along the road. If Nathan returned to Solange and gave a clear report, he'd have mentioned seeing a woman in the innyard. Something about that must have caught her attention, sending her to the Lamb to investigate. She would have been desperate to get those incriminating documents back."

"She picked up gossip about who the lady might be?"

"It's the only explanation."

"Including the direction of travel of her party?" Braydon asked skeptically.

Traffic was backing up behind them and one of the riders they'd passed, a young man with pretensions, came alongside with intent to get ahead. Braydon gave him a cold look and he turned to go back in the line.

Once the young man was out of earshot, Mark said again, "It's the only explanation. The Lamb's a small place, so there wouldn't have been many parties. I saw only two coaches. I assume Sir William and Lady Selby talked to other guests and Solange found ways to get people to pass on what they knew."

"To a stranger asking impertinent questions? A French stranger?"

"She's clever and can appear so very decent and unassuming. If opportunity arises, she tells a sorry tale of escaping from the Terror and blesses Britain for giving her refuge."

A cow veered toward the horses, which objected. Braydon had to work to steady them. "Damned beasts," he said, not specifying. When all was calm again and the last cow was beginning to clear the road, he asked, "Could she have learned their precise destination?"

"How?" Mark asked. "But devil take it, you're right. It's possible. I should pursue the Selbys to warn them. Warn Hermione, at least . . ."

"But you need to get to London," Braydon pointed out. "We'll make enquiries at the Lamb. When that final bedeviled cow moves."

At last they could move forward, and Braydon put his team to alarming speed.

"She can't know," Mark said, clinging on, wishing he believed his own words. When Braydon slowed the team, however, he said, "Carry on. I'll gamble London is still her priority, but I'll confirm at the Nag's Head that she left when she should. And I'll put these papers in the post. They'll be safer there and reach London at the same time that I do."

When they arrived in Warrington, they paused outside the post office while Mark went in. The letter would leave Warrington on the same midnight mail coach he planned to take, but lost amid the rest of the mail, it would be as safe as if in a vault.

That taken care of, they went on to the Nag's Head, from which most of the London coaches departed. Mark was still in livery, so Braydon asked the questions. Solange and Isaac were a distinctive couple and had definitely left on a coach heading south.

"Only as far as Worcester, sir," the ticket clerk said, and thanked Braydon for the shilling received.

"Any news of the disturbance in Ard-wick?" Braydon asked the man.

"All came to nothing, sir, God be praised. Riot Act read and most dispersed. Those who resisted are in irons awaiting trial."

"All's well so far," Braydon said as he took the reins again.

A stagecoach rolled in and the clerk announced it to be from Manchester to Liverpool. It was not overloaded. The coachman, in his many-caped greatcoat and woolen muffler, climbed down and received a steaming tankard from a cheerful maid. After the brief flirtation, the man merely observed as some of his passengers climbed out and claimed luggage, and others saw their bags and boxes stored and climbed aboard.

Braydon steered the curricle nearby and asked again for news.

"All over when I passed through, sir, but I hear it looked touchy for a while. The magistrates had the roads into town blocked, but people joined the gathering anyway and plenty were in a mood for trouble. The Riot Act was read and the soldiers moved in."

"Many hurt?" Braydon asked.

"Shots were fired, that's for sure, sir. And

from what I heard tell, from both directions. Wicked, that, and sent honest folk scurrying for safety, which put an end to the whole. Some of those with weapons were caught and taken to Manchester in chains."

As they left the innyard, Braydon said, "Looks as if your Solange will be disappointed."

"Thank God for that. On to the Lamb."

Again Braydon did the questioning, arrogantly summoning the innkeeper out to talk to him.

"I come from visiting Lady Sophinisbe Ecclestall, my good man, and she requested me to leave a small gift here for Lady Selby."

Lady Sophonisbe's name seemed to be magical. In association with the curricle, the innkeeper seemed in danger of prostrating himself.

"Alas, sir, alas. The Selby party left many hours ago!"

Fortunately he was too dazzled to wonder how the lady had known where the Selbys would stop.

"No matter," Braydon said with a lazy waft of his hand. "I hope Sir William and his family are well and traveling smoothly?"

"I'd say so, sir." Then the innkeeper added, "There was another enquiry about them, sir, and one that's left me uneasy. A

Frenchwoman, you see."

"A *Frenchwoman?*" Braydon echoed with suitable astonishment.

"Aye, sir, who said as she'd recognized one of the ladies in the Selby party as an old friend, a Miss Wellingborough. The thing that's been bothering me, sir, is that the lady in question was about half the age of the Frenchwoman. I'm not saying such a friendship is impossible, sir, but she was nosy about it. Very nosy."

"Very astute of you, sir. There is no Wellingborough connected to the Selby family."

"I thought so, sir! But she did seem to know things. She said they had family in Liverpool, which was almost correct."

Clever Solange. This inn sat on the Manchester side of Warrington. Unlikely that anyone traveling to Manchester would halt here. Much more likely that they were traveling west and Liverpool would be the major destination.

"I assume you set her right," Braydon said.

"I wasn't of a mind to tell her anything, sir, but a clergyman who'd conversed with Sir William said as how they were going to Tranmere. I hope they make their destination before dark today, sir, but Sir William was set upon the shorter route even though

I told him it would be faster in the end to go by Chester."

"An odd incident," Braydon said. "Did the Frenchwoman give a name?"

"I don't believe as she did, sir. I hope she's not up to anything." He lowered his voice. "I've been thinking about invasion, sir. I know the French have signed for peace and we trounced them soundly, but with the Froggies you never know. If they tried again, happen it'd be through Ireland, and the coast near here is a likely place."

Braydon nodded. "Be alert, sir, be alert. I feel sure our old enemy is cowed for now, but we must all be vigilant."

The innkeeper almost saluted.

When they were in the street, Braydon said, "That's how your Frenchwoman knew where to send her dog, and all from gossip."

"Skillfully teased-out gossip. She's a dangerous woman."

"But safely on her way south. I'm sure you're itching to pursue and overtake, but that won't make the night mail arrive any sooner. Back to the Roebuck for a good meal. We've earned it."

Mark was itching to turn back to the Wirral and make sure Hermione was safe, but he quashed that. Solange had left. All would be well.

As they settled to soup, Mark asked, "Who's Lady Sophinisbe?"

"My grandmother. Daughter of a duke, but I suspect she'd be as awe-inspiring if born in a cottage. Eccentric as all get-out, but a name to be reckoned with. I hope that if any enquiries are made about me here that connection will be remembered."

Mark smiled. "It's a pleasure to work with you again." The soup was again excellent, but after a few sips Mark put down his spoon. "It won't do."

"What?" Braydon asked with a hint of resignation.

"I can't travel south and leave Lady Hermione unprotected."

"Any danger is traveling south."

"Solange is capable of hiring some local thugs and sending them off as a second wave of attack."

"Local thugs to rescue sensitive papers?"

"Kill the woman. Kill the whole family. Burn down the house. Yes, I know it's far-fetched, but Solange wouldn't hesitate for fear of harming innocents. There's another, more likely danger. If she discovered the Riverview House address, she's fully capable of sending Lady Hermione an explosive letter there."

"Why the devil haven't you killed her?"

The blunt practicality made Mark laugh, though without humor. "That would make me as vile as she."

"You shot Boothroyd."

"With urgent reason. We've both killed in war and lost count, but cold-blooded murder's a different matter, even when I can see the purpose." Mark remembered the cooling soup and ate some more. "I'm going to follow Hermione's route and ensure she's safe."

"What of your pressing need to be in London?"

"If the Spencean Crusade has crumbled, I can afford a few days' delay. Solange will have no incident to exploit. I recruited Hermione, thus carelessly putting her in danger. I can't do that again."

"Again?"

It was something Mark tried hard to forget, but it had risen to the front of his mind. He sipped his wine.

"In Spain. A young widow. I was reconnoitering out of uniform. Spying, by definition. She sheltered me for one night, but then she sent me information. I shouldn't have allowed it, but a body of French were in her area and her information was good."

He put the wineglass down and pushed it away. "They hanged her in front of her farm, doubtless after other atrocities."

Braydon nodded. "Bad luck."

"Luck? I shouldn't have allowed it. I shouldn't have stayed there."

"Not everywhere you lodged led to disaster. War creates these monstrosities, but Lady Hermione is not in the middle of a war."

"She shouldn't be, but I dragged her there. This is a war, Braydon, between good and evil, law and chaos, and like any war, it doesn't care about the innocents."

"So you go to guard her? Indefinitely? Didn't you say she detests you now?"

"With reason. I can guard her from a distance, but I must make sure she's safe. No, I'm not insane enough to sit by her gate forever, but I need to hear from London that both Solange and Seth Boothroyd are there. Once that's confirmed, if no other danger has appeared, I'll leave her to her safe life and take up my work."

Pigeon pie and potatoes were brought in and Braydon served them. Remembering Maria Rodrigo had soured Mark's stomach, but he drank his wine and made himself eat. He'd be no use to anyone otherwise.

"I hesitate to mention this," Braydon said,

"but even without imminent revolution your knowledge of the Crimson Band is needed in London."

"The letter will soon arrive, and I know nothing more than that about whatever Isaac plans for the gas. I included a note about the exploding letters."

"What about the little things? Their individual natures and peculiarities. Their weaknesses and vulnerabilities. All the knowledge gained from a year in their company."

Braydon was coolly pointing out where duty lay, but Mark couldn't abandon Hermione in danger.

"I'll guard your lady," Braydon said.

"Without creating a stir?"

"I can attempt to blend in."

Mark gave him a look. "Have you ever attempted a disguise?"

"I know my limitations."

"And your strengths," Mark said, serving himself more of the rich gravy. "Your remarkable memory. Knowledge can be in any container."

Braydon's knife and fork paused. "You want to turn me into your encyclopedia?"

"If you have some spare room in that head of yours, I can tell you everything I know in the next few hours. But there's more. When

I return to London, I'll have to lie low. Ned Granger's been exposed as the traitor in the Crimson Band, so any of them will shoot me on sight. But you can work openly with Hawkinville and his team, knowing all I know. You did say you wanted some action."

"True, but given the need for speed, I suppose you expect me to take your seat on the night mail."

"Is that so terrible?"

"Yes, but one must be prepared to suffer for one's country. Baker will enjoy driving my rig south, and he deserves some reward for the sacrifice of his livery."

"I didn't cause much damage."

"I'll buy him new." Braydon refilled their wineglasses. "If the Frenchwoman and the chemist can't be brought to trial quickly, I'll kill them for you."

Mark was surprised to be shocked. Such things had happened in the war. "In cold blood?"

"Makes for a steadier hand."

"You won't get near them. You won't be in the Crimson Band."

"I assume they walk the streets and someone can point them out to me. Pistols can work at a distance, and rifles at a greater one. I, too, am an excellent shot. You go to Tranmere," Braydon continued, as if they'd

182

been discussing the weather, "and I to London. I'll send word when I'm sure the vile Solange and her mad chemist are safely engaged there, at which point you will be free to join me. May both our enterprises prosper."

They clinked glasses and resumed their meal.

Mark couldn't truly match Braydon's cool manner, for he burned to leave for Tranmere. He didn't see how danger could already be stalking Hermione, but couldn't shed the fear that it could be on her heels now. That it could even have pounced. He couldn't leave until he'd poured his knowledge into Braydon. Even for Hermione Merryhew, he couldn't neglect his duty so completely.

CHAPTER 14

Hermione had been grateful for the way her sister and brother-in-law continued to make light of the incident for the boys' sake, but she'd struggled to play her part, especially when the sun began to set. She'd never been truly terrified before, and the memory of the threat of casual death threatened to choke her.

Take the papers.

Break your neck.

It was Thayne's fault, but she must take some of the blame. She'd been stupid over him from the beginning, even when he'd confessed to being a criminal, and all because of an encounter six years ago, which she'd doubtless built in her mind. Even if the magic had been real, he was a different person now — a thief who'd made dangerous enemies. She should have forced him to leave her bedroom immediately, and if he'd refused, she should have screamed.

Now all she could do was force him out of her mind and lock the door after him.

A few miles beyond the incident, they'd taken a break for the sake of the horses, but they hadn't left the carriage and they'd pressed on as fast as possible. They must reach Great-uncle Peake before he died, but she knew they all wanted to avoid traveling in the perilous dark.

The sun was down now, though they still had evening light, but they'd not reached Tranmere. They might have considered stopping, but the Wirral was a sparsely populated place and they passed no suitable inn. When darkness settled, the map said they were within a mile, so they lit the carriage lamps and carried on, the children dozing, but the adults awake and tense.

Soon they saw lit windows ahead, but they couldn't make out any details of the buildings. There were other lights scattered across rising ground on their left, and on their right, glimmering at a distance, Hermione saw what must be the great port of Liverpool across the river. Was she the only one wishing they were entering a busy city instead of this quiet place that seemed hardly more than a large village?

The coachman had to halt and ask for directions. They were pointed up the slope and so the weary horses had a climb. In daylight and different circumstances they might have all left the coach and walked to ease the weight, but not tonight. They passed entrances to driveways, reading the letters engraved on pillars, until at last they arrived at their destination. The house was only a pale cube, and the only sign of life a faint glow from the fanlight over the door. Hermione had the irrational fear that they'd be turned away, back into the night. When William knocked at the door, however, it opened and they were soon made welcome.

"When darkness settled, we were sure you'd stopped on the road, sir, but all's ready. I'm Mrs. Digby, Mr. Peake's housekeeper. Oh dear, we weren't told there would be children." Billy and Roger must have looked distressed, for she said, "Never look like that, young sirs! You're very welcome, and we'll set you up in a fine room of your own."

"Not tonight," William said firmly. "They're asleep on their feet, and in a strange place they'll be best sleeping with an adult. Myself, in fact. My wife and her sister can share the other room and have the baby with them. If we could have a quick supper for the boys, Mrs. Digby. Bread and milk, perhaps?"

"In an instant, sir. Nolly, off you go and get it. Mary and Deb, fires, then warming pans!" The maids hurried to their duty and a footman went to bring in the luggage. "A groom's been hired, and the stables made ready, sir, for Mr. Peake doesn't keep horses or carriages at the moment. Come with me, if you please."

"Plenty of servants," Polly said quietly as they went upstairs. In other words, plenty of money.

Hermione and Polly were taken to a pleasant enough bedroom except that it was chilly. The fire had been allowed to burn down, but a maid hurried in with a sling of wood to build it up again.

As soon as the maid left, Hermione asked, "Do you mind William sleeping with the boys?"

"Of course not. He knows I'd want to be with you tonight, and you with me, after such an ordeal. Henrietta will have to sleep between us," she said, placing the sleeping infant there. "I hope you don't mind."

"Of course not. He's very kind. You're both very kind." All the tears she'd been holding back burst free.

Polly drew her to the sofa and rocked her. "There, there. We're safe now and that madman is dealt with. There's nothing to fear.

Nothing at all. Please do stop crying, dearest."

Hermione managed to stop the tears, but she lingered in the hug, wishing she could tell Polly everything. The journey had given her too much time to think, and her thoughts had been terror-fueled. That brute had seemed dull-witted, so he'd acted on orders. There were others involved. She'd given Thayne back his wretched letter, but would his enemies — his throat-cutting enemies — know that? Or would they send another brute after her?

Take the papers.

Break your neck.

Perhaps she should run away from here so as to protect Polly and the children. But how would the villains know she'd gone?

She drew apart and blew her nose. "I'm better now, and I'll be better tomorrow. It's been a long, hard day."

"A dreadful one," Polly said, rising to take off her bonnet. "It seems an eon since we fled the King's Head this morning,"

Hermione realized she wasn't wearing a bonnet and didn't know where her crushed and broken one was. The housekeeper must have thought her very odd to arrive bareheaded.

"I wonder what happened to the Spenceans," Polly said. She didn't wonder long, for she added, "I wonder if Great-uncle Peake will want to see us tonight."

"Oh, I do hope not."

William knocked, then entered. "A couple of maids are helping the boys eat their supper and get ready for bed. I'm told Great-uncle Peake has already retired for the night. According to Mrs. Digby, he is worse by the day. She said we might only just be in time."

"Good that we pushed on, then," Hermione said.

"And that we weren't delayed by magistrates and courts!" Polly exclaimed.

"A supper is being laid out for us below," William said. "A maid will stay with the boys. Another could come here to watch over Henrietta."

Hermione knew she couldn't eat. "I'll look after Henrietta," she said. "I'm not hungry. I just want to join her in the bed."

But in the unpredictable way of infants, Henrietta decided to come fully awake and demand attention. Hermione fought tears again.

"We'll take her down with us," Polly said, scooping up her daughter. "You go to bed, Hermione. Everything will be better in the morning."

Polly and William took Henrietta away and a maid arrived with hot water and a warming pan. Hermione was soon in a cozy bed, but she lay sleepless, in a room lit only by firelight.

It was less than twenty-four hours since Mark Thayne had invaded her firelit bedroom and turned her life upside down. He'd rekindled magic and stirred foolish hope, but then he'd plunged her into danger and fear. She prayed never to see him again, but the tears that came showed folly was hard to destroy.

As they ate, Mark had told Braydon everything he knew about the Three-Banded Brotherhood and the Crimson Band. He included names, the locations of meetings and of stores of arms and supplies, including that guillotine. It would mostly be new to Hawkinville and some tiny detail could be crucial. As Ned Granger, he'd been sparing with communication, because every message had carried risk. Since assuming the alter ego, he'd not met with Hawkinville or any government official. If he'd been detected as a spy, his usefulness would be over, and in the Crimson Band under Solange's guiding hand, suspicion could easily mean death, so he'd passed on information in indirect ways, and only when he had something of imminent importance.

He was hoarse by the time he finished, and he drank some more of the ale that Braydon had sent for an hour or so ago. He glanced at the clock. Half past eleven. Too late to set out to Tranmere tonight. He was tempted to ride through the dark, but it would be demented, and all being well, Hermione was safe in her bed. He could only hope her misadventure wasn't giving her nightmares.

"Mrs. Upshaw won't mind my using your bed?" he asked.

"Of course not." Braydon was packing his valise. "You'll take a coach to Tranmere tomorrow?"

"I believe there are boats. Smoother and probably quicker."

"You'll merely lurk there? Perhaps you should put Lady Hermione on her guard."

"She's been abducted. I think she'll be on her guard already."

"Against explosive letters?"

"Hades, you're right. I'll make sure she understands." *Which will involve another meeting, which I can't regret.*

"Dying relative, wasn't it?" Braydon said. "We'll hope he or she doesn't linger. Once Lady Hermione is back in Yorkshire, on her home territory where strangers would be noticed, she'll be safer."

"She'll be safest when Solange and the rest are either dead or in jail. Those papers should do it."

"What then? You'll become Faringay again?"

"The threat doesn't end with them. Arthur Thistlewood is a greater danger than Waite. He's more like Solange in his demented purpose and without a scrap of Waite's caution."

"Maybe so, but how are you going to achieve anything?" Braydon asked. "You can't be Ned Granger anymore. How long will it take to insinuate yourself into a new group, and aren't there already people there?"

Strangely, Mark had never thought to this point, but the danger remained. He must fight on.

"You work is done," Braydon said with some force. "It's time to return to reality. You are Viscount Faringay, with responsibilities."

Mark contemplated his half-empty ale glass. "Who is Faringay? What is he? I've never used the title. My father died when I was in the army and I didn't fancy suddenly assuming grandeur there. When I sold out,

I slid into being Ned Granger. Can I settle to being a rural landowner, a patron of worthy causes who gives occasional speeches in the House of Lords? Look at you. A brief period of calm comfort and you're leaping back into the fire."

Braydon locked his valise and glanced at his pocket watch. "How have you explained the absent Lord Faringay? I've never heard it mentioned."

"He's on a somewhat vague mission to Mauritius to report on operations against the East African slave trade."

"Which is operated by French slavers, so your excellent command of the language recommends you."

"And Mauritius being so far away, no one is likely to notice whether I'm there or not. The governor stands ready to affirm my presence if asked."

"How pleasant for you now to return to your native land."

Mark played along. "I'll miss the warmth and sunshine of the south Indian Ocean."

"What stories you'll have to tell."

"I have them prepared."

"Of course you do. If you need lodgings in London, I have rooms, and you'll have a transformation to achieve. A new wardrobe isn't acquired in a moment."

"I've become rather fond of the casual way of dress."

"You'll be a shabby viscount? You're too shabby now for even Ned Granger. You at least need a hat and that rip in your breeches mended. I'll consult Mrs. Upshaw."

He soon returned with a beaver hat about half as tall as his own and considerably more hard-worn. Mark tried it on and it was a tolerable fit.

"People apparently leave things behind," Braydon said, "and she holds them awhile in case they send for them. She's assembling a few items and I paid for a cheap valise she has by. If you change your breeches, she'll mend those."

"Thank you."

"You're normally on top of such details yourself."

"It's been a brain-addling day."

Braydon picked up the valise. "Time for me to go. Perhaps you'll have a few peaceful days to recover."

"I hope I've not entangled you in more adventure than you'd like."

Braydon smiled. "I don't think that's possible."

CHAPTER 15

Exhaustion could be a blessing, for despite the horrors of the day, Hermione did sleep. She woke to early morning sunshine and an absence of sickening fear. She lay next to her sister probing for it, as a person probes for a painful tooth, hoping not to find it.

It had gone. She was still concerned, but in a rational way. Her attacker was in custody. Thayne was a wretched man in so many ways, but he wouldn't let the brute slip free to hurt her again. She no longer had those perilous papers and no one of vile intent knew where she was.

She must concentrate on the reason for being here. Today, she and Polly must prove to Great-uncle Peake that they were worthy of the inheritance. The number of servants indicated at least a comfortable prosperity. She slid out of bed, being careful not to wake Polly or Henrietta, and put on her robe, for the fire had gone out and the room was chilly.

Yesterday she'd woken to a warm room because Thayne had built the fire before he'd left. She tried to push all thought of him out of her mind, but he seemed to be hooked in there like a teasel. She couldn't fend off curiosity.

What kind of thievery had caused that horrible man to pursue him and then her, without care or caution?

How had Thayne transformed so quickly from scruffy thief to liveried groom?

Oh, nothing made sense! How had Thayne even known where she was going? Had she told him? If so, it was a lesson not to chatter with strangers, or people she ought to treat as strangers. But if he'd not pursued, who would have rescued her?

Take the papers.

Break your neck.

She shoved that away and drew back a corner of the curtain to look out at the weather, and she discovered a glorious view. No wonder people built houses on this hill. The window overlooked the river and a forest of masts of mighty ocean-sailing ships. Smaller ships and boats plied who-knew-what trades between them. Great-uncle Peake must have chosen to live here in order to watch the living pageant of one of the country's busiest ports.

She saw a boat set out from the nearby shore to cross the river. That must be the Tranmere ferry, and it had a tall chimney puffing smoke. A steamship. She'd never seen one before, but what a clever development, immune to wind and tide. Perhaps it carried milk, eggs, and butter to feed the city, or took people across the river to work. Another boat, this one with sails, came down the river and docked below. Were there ferries up and down the river as well? It was a fascinating scene to watch, so she moved a wooden chair behind the curtain and sat there, happy to be distracted by the busy scene.

The clock struck nine and Henrietta woke, making only little noises for now, but Hermione came out from behind the curtain. Polly was sitting up, rubbing her eyes. "What are you doing?"

"Watching the wider world go by. There's a marvelous view."

Polly stayed in bed. "It will still be there later. Do ring for someone to make up the fire."

Hermione did that, and a maid came in with kindling and wood. When the fire was going, she asked, "Shall I bring up your water, my ladies?" That agreed to, she hurried off.

Polly hugged her knees. "How are you?"

"Better. Did you learn anything new last night?"

"This house is only three years old. Can you imagine? And Great-uncle Peake only has a lease on it."

Hermione understood the concern in that. His owning the house would be more promising.

Polly lowered her voice. "Hermione, there are no oriental artifacts. Suppose he didn't go to India at all?"

"Of course he did. Remember the items we saw when we visited Grandfather and Grandmother Havers? So many intriguing gifts her brother had sent."

"All behind glass so we couldn't touch them. But that doesn't mean the sender has to be rich. I woke in the night fretting that it's all a hum. That he has only a few thousand."

"You can't call it a hum, because he's never claimed to have a fortune. He merely implied that he'd leave what he had to us."

"But . . . Oh, you're right, but after such a journey, and you being attacked, it will be outrageous if it's for nothing."

"Anything is something, dearest, and my being attacked wasn't his fault."

"You're being sensible again." Polly climbed out of bed, put on her robe, and drew back the curtain. "There are certainly a great many ships."

"All implying adventures."

"You've always been the one for romance. To me they imply rough voyages and even rougher sailors."

"Romance?" Hermione protested. "I'm the sensible one."

Polly considered it. "No, you're the level one, whereas I fly high and low. But you enjoy stories of adventure and mystery like *Guy Mannering* and *The Corsair,* whereas I find them unbelievable."

"You're not supposed to believe them."

"Then what's the point to them?"

Hermione laughed. "And there you have it." Had her odd reaction to Thayne's invasion of her room come from a taste for incredible adventures? If so, she'd been cured.

"Take that man you met at your first ball," Polly said.

"What?" Hermione stared at her.

"Perhaps you've forgotten now, but you built dreams around him for months, and after only one dance."

"Two."

"So you do remember."

"Of course I remember," Hermione said, trying for a light tone. "My first gallant at my first ball. He was tall, dark, and handsome and we almost kissed."

"No! I never heard that. Tell."

"Mother caught us too early. Our lips never touched." *Then.*

"Even so, that was bold for seventeen."

"He was the one being bold. I was merely willing to be bolded. When was your first kiss?"

"About the same age," Polly said, going to scoop up Henrietta, who was crawling toward the edge of the bed. "But it was Charles Woolsey, so I'd known him forever. As I said, you're the one for romantic adventures. Do you remember his name?"

"No," Hermione lied.

"Only imagine, you might meet again, especially if you go to Town for a season."

Meet not only him, but the throat-cutting people he knew. At times she'd dreamed of a London season, but they'd never been able to afford it. Now it held no appeal. "I'm too old."

"You're only twenty-three."

"Ancient, and we don't know anyone to present me at court."

"We'll find someone. A marquess's daughter with a handsome dowry."

"If Great-uncle Peake is a nabob."

Please let him not be! A marquess's daughter with a large dowry would stand out from the rest in so many ways, and now, reasonably or not, she felt that to stand out would be dangerous. A comfortable inheritance would do. Enough for an easier life for Polly and a moderate dowry for herself. Yes, that would be perfect. She could husband-hunt just as well in York or Harrogate.

The maid returned with a big jug of hot water and Hermione and Polly prepared for the day — for the momentous meeting with their newfound, soon-to-be-lost relative.

They took breakfast in their room at a small table by the window, and William came to join them.

"There's a competent enough maid called Nolly that the boys seem to like, but they'll have to come here later for the view of the river. The other room doesn't have it."

"They'll love it," Polly agreed as she poured coffee for him. "Any news of Great-uncle Peake?"

"He's no better, but he'll see us at ten. Only us, not the children."

Polly bridled. "Why not?"

"He's a dying man, my dear. It's perfectly reasonable."

"But he invited us."

"Perhaps he didn't expect us to bring the children."

"Leave them at home? Even the baby?"

William shared a look with Hermione, who said, "Polly, stop being silly. People do leave their children to servants, and probably you'd do so more often if you had money for enough of them."

"Oh, very well. I'm all on edge. I want so much for this to go as it should. What should we wear?"

"Exactly what you are wearing," William said. "I refuse to approach this like desperate supplicants."

That ended the conversation. William didn't like feeling that his modest wealth was insufficient. They were all on edge. Polly was desperate, and Hermione was finding that she hadn't shed the horrors of the previous day. She stirred extra lumps of sugar into her coffee, hoping not to quiver when the crucial moment came.

CHAPTER 16

At ten, they went downstairs and were admitted to their relative's room. It was clean and tidy, and well lit by a large window that gave a view of the river. But it had a stale smell of sickness along with a pungency that might come from unguents rubbed into aching joints. On entering, they faced the back of the bed, because it was set in the middle of the room facing the window. It had a high back, but no poles or curtains.

When they walked around, Hermione only just stifled a gasp. It was as well the children weren't with them, for Great-uncle Edgar Peake was enough to give them nightmares. He was heavy-framed but gaunt, and only wisps of white hair showed from under a red velvet cap. The ghastly aspect was his gray skin. He looked as if he'd been dusted with ashes. She was sure the others must feel the same horror, but they all managed to bow or curtsy and say their good-mornings.

He lowered straggly brows. "Here for my money, but took your time about it. I could be dead already."

Polly protested, "We came with all possible speed, Great-uncle."

William put a calming hand on her arm and spoke in his measured way. "As I explained in a letter, sir, your summons was delayed. It went first to Northumberland, then to London, where it lingered unattended for some days before being sent to my wife in Yorkshire."

"Kept me in the dark, all of you. Didn't even know the old marquess was dead. Forgotten about, I was, but now you want my money."

He was as petulant as a two-year-old, but sickness could do that. Hermione had handled her father in the same mood, but she made herself stay silent. Steady William was the one to deal with this.

He said, "Perhaps you were forgotten, sir, when the usual announcements went out. Our apologies for that. But then, we didn't have a direction for you."

"Couldn't be staying in one place to suit people back here," the old man grumbled. "Stuck here now, though. Stuck like a beetle in a box."

"Your situation is most unfortunate, sir. You fell ill in India?"

"India? What's this about India? Last place was Batavia. Moved around, moved around." He plucked at the bedcoverings with darkened nails.

"What ails you, sir?" William asked.

"Kala-azar. The black sickness. Saw it in India, but I didn't get it there or I'd be dead already. Must have been in Morocco."

"Get it?" William asked sharply. "Is it infectious?"

Polly let out a gasp and Hermione only just managed not to. How could they not have thought of that?

The old man cackled. "That's set you spinning, hasn't it? Would I have sent for you if it was? Peter!"

A middle-aged manservant was stationed quietly to one side. "Yes, sir?"

"Getting sick yet?"

"No, sir."

"Anyone else caught it?"

"Not that I know, sir."

"Won't. They say it's caused by tropical air. True or not, it doesn't spread like the plague. It just kills people. Some a bit quicker, some a bit slower. Wish to hell it'd kill me. Doctor was dosing me, but I stopped that."

William seemed to have run out of things to say, so Hermione took up the task. "I'm sorry you're in such a poor state, Great-uncle. We were hoping to hear stories of your adventures."

"No need to butter me up, girl."

"And you've no need to accuse me of it! Oh, dear, I apologize."

But he laughed. "So you've the spirit, eh? Like me sister Anne. She'd have come adventuring with me if she'd not been a female. She'll have run her husband ragged."

Hermione thought of their quiet grandmother. "I don't think so, Great-uncle."

"Oh, have done with the 'great.' Wear out words before we're done here. Call me Uncle Edgar. No, call me Edgar. No one calls me Edgar anymore."

"I'm sure the servants would if you asked them to."

"No, they wouldn't. They'd make a sour face and say it wasn't proper. Wouldn't you, Peter?"

"Yes, sir," the manservant said, but with a slight smile that suggested fondness. Edgar Peake couldn't be as grim as he seemed.

"So Anne didn't fight," Edgar Peake said

with a grimace. "She'd have liked some of the Orient. What of you? Would you like adventures?"

A day ago, Hermione might have said yes, but her frightening experience had taught her better. "No."

The eyebrows came down again. "Why not?"

"Adventures are uncomfortable."

She should have lied. With a look of disgust, he turned to ask Polly. "What about you?"

Hermione saw temptation, but Polly, too, said, "No, sir. I'm sorry, but I can't imagine why anyone seeks adventure."

Edgar Peake's grunt was eloquent. "And the same'll go for you, Sir William. I can tell at a glance. Go away, the lot of you. I need to think."

They had no choice but to obey.

They waited until they were back in the bedroom, but then Polly said, "Oh, William!" and went into his arms.

"I'm sorry," Hermione said. "I spoke too boldly."

"That wasn't the problem," William said. "It was denying a taste for adventure that cooked our goose."

Hermione turned toward the window to hide her expression. Would telling Edgar

Peake about her recent ordeals win them his fortune?

They waited anxiously for the next developments, passing the time in amusing the boys. They wanted to go out to explore, but none of the adults wanted to risk leaving the house and missing a summons. By lunchtime, however, William at least was losing patience.

"I doubt he has a fortune at all," he said as they ate in the dining room. Everything had been laid out and the servants had left. The children were upstairs with two maids. "A lifetime wandering around the Orient need not be profitable."

"I'm quite inclined to leave immediately," Polly said, stirring leek soup without enthusiasm.

"Eat," Hermione said. "It's good. I think he was enjoying pulling our strings, as if we were marionettes."

"Exactly," Polly said, "and I won't stand for it."

"Only because you now doubt there's a fortune to be gained."

"Don't be like that. You want money, too. For a fine wardrobe and a season."

"I told you. I'm not sure I do."

"You must want a husband."

"Must I?"

"Stop squabbling," William said. "This is the consequence of money. It sours people."

"Or the lack of it," Polly snapped, but then she closed her eyes. "William, I'm sorry. Truly I don't mind, but when there might be money for the children, I can't not want it for them."

He took her hand across the corner of the table. "I understand, but we mustn't let it corrode our happiness."

She smiled at him. "You're right. We mustn't. I'll try not to think of a fortune at all, so that if the inheritance is just a little, it will still be a pleasant addition."

He kissed her hand before letting it go. "That's the way, my dear."

Hermione gave silent thanks for harmony.

As they served themselves from dishes of chicken ragout and vegetables, Polly said, "If you don't wish to marry, Hermione, I won't complain. It will be perfectly delightful to have you live with us forever."

Hermione smiled and thanked her, but put like that, the prospect could turn her off her food. Be forever the dependent sister and aunt? Of course, it wouldn't happen. Without a rich inheritance how could she refuse Porteous? If she tried, he'd ask Polly and William to persuade her, mentioning potential generosity to his wife's family.

Polly and William would never urge her to marry for that reason, but the knowledge of what might have been would lurk, like an infection, forever. William was right. Money could sour everything.

After lunch Polly and William rebelled by taking the boys out for a walk. Hermione stayed behind to take care of Henrietta. The willing maids made that unnecessary, but she was staying inside for another reason. She was fearful about going outdoors. The brute was in jail, but what if he escaped and came after her like a bloodhound on the scent? She peered around the window frame, seeking him. Of course she saw nothing, but it couldn't stop her nervousness.

She wasn't going to watch out of a window all day, so she asked the footman whether there was a library and was taken there. It was a small room with well-filled shelves but a very unused atmosphere.

"Did Mr. Peake rent this house furnished?" she asked.

"Aye, milady. On account of his family house not being here anymore."

"His family house?"

The footman was square-faced and solidly built, but clearly willing to gossip.

"Aye, milady. Came here expecting to find some family left, you see. There were Peakes a couple of miles off, near Brimstage. According to Jim Suggs, who's eighty if he's a day, the family fortune dwindled to nothing thirty years or so past, and the house were sold, and then back nigh on twenty years ago, it burned down. Were proper old, it were, built mostly of wood, see?"

"How sad."

"Aye, milady. Mr. Peake rented this place while he decided what to do, but then took a turn for the worse. Wasn't well when he got here, but thought it were something called malery."

"Malaria?"

"Aye, that's it. And according to the vicar, that means bad air. Happen he thought he'd soon be fit, the air here being grand."

The footman left and Hermione looked around the soulless room. Poor Great-uncle Peake. Late in life he'd decided to return home and reunite with his family, and he'd arrived here to find them all dead, with even the house where he grew up gone. It showed the folly of being such a poor correspondent and of assuming life continues as it was, but it was sad.

He'd hoped to recover his health, but when he'd realized that he had a fatal ailment, he'd tried to make contact with his sister's daughter, the Marchioness of

Carsheld, not knowing she, too, was dead. His wandering letter had finally reached his niece's daughters, herself and Polly, the only family he had left, and now they were a disappointment to him.

Why he should think they'd be adventurous she couldn't imagine, for no one in the Peake family except him ever had been. Roger perhaps, but adventure had taken him to war and death. A little of that spirit might run in her blood, leading her to take risks, but only see the consequence — a narrow escape.

She wandered the shelves in search of distracting reading, but the books were all the dullest sorts of treatises and sermons, perhaps purchased merely to fill the shelves. She wished there were a newspaper, for she'd like to know what had happened in Ardwick. It seemed likely she and the family would be traveling home soon and she hoped the way would be clear of all alarms.

Might a newspaper carry news of her abduction? Surely Thayne would spare her that — but if the culprit had come before the magistrates, the story would have been told, with names. A newspaper should refer to her as only "a lady." Or even "a lady of high family." But they might feel no qualms about mentioning "Sir W— S—y." The more scandalous sort could tell the world that "Lady H—e M—hew" had been carried off by a villain. Porteous might decide she wasn't worthy to be his wife. She shouldn't want that, but she did.

She gave up hope of the library, went to get her copy of *Guy Mannering,* and took it to the drawing room. It was a corner room with a window in each outer wall giving excellent views of the gardens, the town, and the river. Again she checked for danger.

And her heart stopped when she saw a man on the road, looking up at the house!

CHAPTER 17

She stepped back, but even as she did so, she realized that of course it wasn't the brute. He was in jail, and the man below was of a different build entirely — taller and slimmer, and quite roughly dressed. She sat on a sofa and opened the book — but then wondered, had he resembled Mark Thayne?

She hurried back to the window, but the man had gone. Idiot to think it could be Thayne, and softheaded idiot to want it so. Did she imagine him like a troubadour trailing after his lady? He would be on his way to London with his ill-gotten gains, and good riddance.

Guy Mannering provided excellent distraction until she heard the party return. The lads sounded pleased with their expedition, so perhaps everyone would be in a better mood. Soon Polly came to join her, bringing Henrietta. She set the child down on the carpet to play with a leather ball, saying, "It was good to have some exercise in the fresh air. I've asked for tea to be served here."

"Lovely. I found the library, which was uninspiring, but I learned a little from conversation." She shared what she knew.

"Poor man. That must have been a bitter brew. I never liked Carsheld Castle, but I'd be upset to find it razed from the earth."

"And your family mostly forgotten."

William came in with the boys, washed and tidied. Billy was keen to describe their discoveries and showed pieces of blue stone. Hermione admired them, and some shells Roger had gathered on the riverside. The tea came and the boys were taken back to their room for their refreshments.

"Now," William said as Polly poured tea, "we must decide what to do if Mr. Peake doesn't grant us another audience. I'm not prepared to kick my heels here like a petitioner at the gate, especially at a time of year when I'm needed at home."

Polly bit her lip, but didn't argue, and indeed September was a busy time of year on an estate. Hermione didn't want to argue, either, but she saw no point in ultimatums when one party didn't know of them.

"I think we should tell Great-uncle Peake

that we must leave tomorrow."

"Force his hand?" William asked.

"Simply because he should know."

"I'm not doing it," William said, making Hermione want to knock him on the head.

"Then I will."

"Are you sure that's wise?" Polly said.

"No, but one of us should." She stood, smoothed down her skirts, then went downstairs to knock on Edgar Peake's door.

It was opened by the manservant. "Yes, milady?"

"I'd like to speak to my great-uncle."

"Let her in."

The man opened the door wider and Hermione walked around the bed to face the old man. Her heart was speeding with nerves, but William wouldn't wait on his whims, and they mustn't throw away all hope.

"I thought you should know that we're going to have to leave tomorrow, sir. William is not a gentleman of leisure and must attend to his estate."

"Humph. Pushing for an answer?"

"To what question, sir?"

"My money. That's why you're all here."

It was like dealing with Billy in a sulk. "You asked us to come to your deathbed, sir. Could we refuse? Yes, if you wish to leave your all to us, it will be welcome, for despite our titles, we're not wealthy, but we're here because we're your family."

"Spirit after all. Sit down and tell me about my sister."

The manservant brought a chair and Hermione sat, still not sure whether she was helping or harming. "Grandmother Havers? We didn't see a great deal of her. She lived in Derbyshire, and we lived first in Northumberland and then in Hampshire, but we did visit them occasionally. The exotic gifts you'd sent her always intrigued us, but they were kept in glass cases."

"There's folly. None were precious."

"It was a very orderly house."

He grimaced. "I feared as much. I had a few letters from her years ago. Never a tidy moment with Anne, so it'd be her husband's doing. She married wrong."

"Grandfather Havers was a highly respected gentleman, a member of Parliament for most of his life. He even held a place in the government at one point."

"Did you like him?" the old man demanded. His sagging gray skin still dismayed her, but now she noticed that his eyes were bright with life.

Hermione sighed. "No."

"See. Married wrong. Make sure you

don't do the same."

"Perhaps she didn't have much choice. Would she have had a large portion?"

"Ha! Our parents frittered away everything. Couldn't even waste the stuff grandly — that'd be something. No, they just let money run through their hands like water. Do you have much to take into marriage?"

"Father was known as the Moneyless Marquess, and his father before him."

"All the same, don't marry wrong." He sat there, his mouth working, perhaps at a loose tooth. Then he grunted. "Tell 'em they'll get my all, and I expect them to use it well. And you, of course. It's to be divided evenly between you and your sister."

"That's not necessary."

"It's as I say it'll be. You spend your part on you. Don't give it to your sister."

"You can't compel that," Hermione protested.

"I can ask for a promise."

"Is that a condition?"

She saw it tempt him, but he stuck out a sulky lip. "No."

It seemed unlikely that there was a fortune, and she did want to make a reasonable marriage. She'd become sour as a lemon if stuck as a dependent sister forever and even worse if she married Porteous.

"Then I promise."

"Off you go, then. No point the others coming here. Tell 'em what I said."

Hermione rose. Because she could feel his loneliness, she wished she could kiss him, but his gray skin put her off. Instead she curtsied and used his name as he'd asked. "Good-bye, Edgar." He nodded, but perhaps, she thought as she left the room, his eyes had been a little moist. His story was so sad.

She went to report to the others.

"He'll leave us his money?" Polly asked, to be sure.

"That's what he said."

"Oh, thank heavens!"

"There's no promise that it's much," Hermione warned.

"Even a little will be welcome. Isn't that so, William?"

"I can't help but wonder how he made it."

Hermione held her temper. "I don't care if he was a pirate. I'll still put an inheritance to good use."

"And we can set off home tomorrow," Polly said.

William rose. "Then I need to know if the roads are safe. I'll walk down to the ferry-house and see what news there is."

When he'd left, Polly sighed. "It's not like him to be so sharp."

"So much about this has him on edge, Polly. The need for more money than he has, and then the misadventure on the way here."

"He felt dreadfully about not being able to race after you."

"Even if he could have, I'd not have wanted him to abandon you and the children. But I quite see how it upset him, and Edgar Peake is like a sulky child."

"Exactly. I'll be glad to leave."

Hermione looked out at the busy river. "I'm not sure it's good for him to be facing this view all day long. So much life, travel, and adventure, and him as he said, stuck like a beetle in a display box."

"It's his choice."

"He didn't choose to be so ill, or so alone in the world."

"He's well taken care of."

"By servants. I think of Father in his last months. He was difficult, but I could coax him to be more sensible and make sure he received the best care." An idea grew from seed to bloom in a moment. Hermione turned back to her sister. "Polly, I'd like to stay."

"Of course. Where else would you live?"

"Not with you. I'd like to stay here, with Great-uncle Edgar."

"What? Why?"

"Because we're the only family he has left. It would be wrong to abandon him."

That was true, but Hermione was seeing another benefit. William had faced the dreadful choice of attempting to rescue her or leaving his wife and children unprotected, and all because she'd put them in danger. Until she was sure all was safe, she'd rather be apart.

"You'd be abandoning me," Polly protested.

"You're eager for me to marry. I'll have to abandon you then."

"That's different."

Hermione brought out a trump card. "It's our Christian duty."

Polly pulled a face. "I'm sure the horrid man had that in mind, and he probably doesn't have a fortune as reward. Are you sure, Hermione? He'll not be an easy patient."

"Father wasn't easy, either. Perhaps dying people never are. At least here there are ample servants to do the hard work."

"Then you're not needed," Polly argued.

"I can do things that the servants can't,

such as tell him more about the family. He's hungry for that."

"That would be charitable," Polly admitted, "but how will you get home when he dies? William can't return for you."

Hermione hadn't considered that. "I'll travel by stage."

"Hermione!"

"Women do it all the time."

"Not ladies."

"Sometimes ladies of limited means. But think. When I leave, we'll know how much money we'll inherit. I'm sure there'll be some way to get enough of my share to hire a companion for the journey. Though that seems silly when I think on it. How is she to get back here?"

"She'll be a servant. There'll be no difficulty about her traveling by stage alone."

"And no more about my doing so."

"You say that simply to be irritating. What if he lingers for months? He's clearly very ill, but I'm not sure he's on his deathbed."

"No," Hermione said thoughtfully. "I wonder if he's having the best possible treatment. Didn't he say he'd stopped taking his medicine?"

"Yes, but . . . Hermione, are you going to try to keep him alive?"

"We can't wish him dead before his time."

"No, but . . . Come home with us and I'm sure he'll be dead within weeks."

"All the more reason to stay here."

"You're *impossible*!" Polly flounced out of the room and Hermione sat hard upon the sofa wondering what had come over all of them. Money — that was it, souring everything, but she couldn't hasten the old man's death, not even by neglect.

She needed fresh air, but . . . No, she would not be pinned here by fear. Without bonnet or shawl, she went downstairs and out into the small garden.

CHAPTER 18

The air was chilly, but the sun was shining. The land sloped downward away from the house, but the garden had been cleverly designed with shallow terraces and horizontal, winding paths. From the lower levels occasional bushes and small trees broke the openness without entirely blocking the view of the river.

She wandered the paths, feeling soothed by nature until she sensed someone nearby. Heart pounding, she whirled — to see Mark Thayne. It *had* been him she'd seen watching the house!

Hand to throat, she demanded, "What are you doing here?"

"Seeking a word with you," he answered.

She looked around. "Is that man here? Has he escaped?"

"No. He's safely dead."

"Thank God," she said. *Safe.* But then she comprehended all his words. "Dead?

From the shot you fired?"

"Yes."

"You *killed* him?"

"I was a soldier," he said patiently. "He's not the first."

She remembered the explosion of gunfire. Had the villain died then — been dead as she'd fallen to the ground with him?

Thayne touched her. She swatted him away. "Don't!"

"Then don't faint."

"I never faint." But she felt close to it. She breathed deeply and commanded her body to behave. "What are you doing here?"

"Keeping you safe."

"If that brute's dead, I'm safe as could be. You're up to some other devilment and you won't involve me. Go away."

She suddenly looked back at the house, concerned that Polly or the children might see her talking to a strange man. The children *were* looking out and they waved. She waved back, but as she did so, she realized that they wouldn't be able to see Thayne. He'd cleverly stationed himself behind a trimmed yew that just concealed him from the house. A hardened, practiced reprobate.

"I put you in danger," he said, oh so reasonably. "I must ensure your safety. I'm truly sorry for having given you that letter."

"Which sweetens no tea. I'm safe now, so go far away before you embroil me in some other madness." Something in his silence alerted her. She moved to the side so she, too, would be out of sight of the house. "What?"

"You're not completely safe. The person who sent that man after you could still be a threat."

"I don't have the letter anymore," she protested, but she'd already thought of the problem.

"She might not know," he said. "The danger's slight, but you need to be careful for a day or two and I need to stay nearby. Once the letter arrives in London, I'll receive word —"

"Once your stolen goods arrive in London," she said.

"As you say. Once they're there, the original owner will know there's no purpose to pursuing you."

Her moving out of sight had brought her too close to him, but she would *not* be weakened by that. "I suppose she acquired them by foul means and you think that removes your guilt."

"If you wish. The point, if you'll focus on it, is that you will no longer be in danger. I believe the villains will be too busy for spiteful revenge in the north."

"Revenge? *Villains?* How many are there?"

"Only two of significance. One of them is the woman who wrote the letter — a middle-aged Frenchwoman who can seem respectable. Be on your guard against anyone like that. The other threat is your attacker's brother and very like him in all ways."

"There's *another*?" She grasped the branch of a bush for support. He reached for her, but she said, "Don't!"

He lowered his hand, but his eyes were concerned. "You have reason to be afraid, but I believe he's in London."

"I dearly hope you're right."

"I must also ask you to be cautious with any letters you receive."

"*Letters?* I'm to be afraid of correspondence now?" She was ashamed of the high pitch of her voice, but she couldn't help it.

"I know it sounds odd, but yes, you should beware of letters, especially if they arrive damp. If you receive correspondence that seems to have been dampened by rain, don't open it. Bury it in the ground."

On a breath she said, "You're mad as well as criminal."

"Just remember what I say."

"And if I don't?"

"The letter might explode, injuring you."

Hermione wanted to cling to a belief that his warnings were mad, but she couldn't. "What a world you've dragged me into."

"And I regret it. It should be over soon. I'll guard you as long as necessary, but I won't accost you again. If you're concerned about anything, leave that gate down there open."

She followed his gaze to a head-high wooden gate that opened to a lane. That must be how he'd entered the garden. "Leave the garden open to marauders?"

"A child could climb it. I can see it from my room at the inn. If I see it open, I'll come up. You could leave a note beneath that white rock there."

"Practiced at sneaking and conniving, I see."

"Expert at it. From the inn I can also see this side of the house. Which is your room?"

"Planning another invasion, sir?" Oh, stupid words, especially when they brought a rush of memories. Of talking. Of binding and kissing.

He, damn him, showed no effect at all. "Merely another way of sounding the alarm. If your window faces this way, use the traditional method. Set a lit candle in it."

She gathered her strength. "Don't watch for it, sir, for it will not happen. If that horrible man truly is dead, I expect my life to return to its pleasant, normal path with no further danger or contact with you, and I thank God for it. Good-bye." With that, she walked away and didn't look back.

When she returned to the house, however, she went into a ground-floor room to peer out. She didn't see him, but he could still be behind the yew and she wouldn't know. She resented that, but she particularly resented the irrational regret that had her biting her lips on tears.

Mark slipped out of the garden and walked back down to the Ferry Inn. Too late, he saw Sir William Selby walking up, but the man was too preoccupied to recognize the curricle groom in ordinary clothes. Mark wondered what was worrying Sir William, and hoped nothing would keep the Selby party at Riverview House for long.

Perhaps he could find out.

When he got back to the inn, he bought ale in the taproom, where the barmaid proved happy to gossip. Jilly was a short but well-endowed young woman with dimples and thick, bobbing curls. It didn't take much to turn the talk to Riverview House.

"Poor old Mr. Peake," she said. "Came here from foreign parts to visit his family, but they're all dead and gone. Then afore he could move on, he took sick. Powerful bad he is, from what the servants say, but he's family come to visit him now, which is a blessing. Best not to die with only strangers around, and there are Peakes in Saint Andrew's cemetery to keep him company."

A sad tale, but Mark could see nothing in it to complicate Hermione's situation as long as the old man wasn't too long a-dying. He'd explained his presence here with a story of looking over the area on behalf of a Liverpool merchant who was thinking of leasing a house in the area. The ferries made that possible and increasingly attractive. To support the story, he had an appointment with an agent to look at a house later today.

Now he said, "A rival might come around here, trying to find the right place before I do. A short, muscular sort of man by name of Boothroyd. Let me know if he turns up, sweetheart?"

Jilly smiled, winked, and agreed.

He couldn't take more steps without raising suspicions, and he couldn't linger many days over finding a house, but he shouldn't need to.

Braydon should arrive in London ahead of Solange, and he'd make sure her arrival was watched for. Once she'd joined Waite, she'd present no danger up here, as long as Seth Boothroyd was with her. If Boothroyd traveled north, or even slipped out of sight, Braydon or Hawkinville would send word and Mark would stay here on guard.

He hoped it didn't come to that. The end of the Crimson Band was close, and he wanted to be in London to assist and celebrate.

To Hermione's relief, by dinnertime everyone had their emotions under control. As they sat to soup, William shared good news about the disturbance in Ardwick.

"The Spencean Crusade came to naught and the roads are as safe as normal."

"That's wonderful," Polly said. "I can't wait to be home, but Hermione wants to stay here."

Memory of her encounter with Thayne made Hermione hesitate, but it was the right thing to do and she explained her reasons to William.

"I agree. I wasn't comfortable with the idea of abandoning the poor gentleman to his plight."

"I intend to look into his medical care,"

231

Hermione told him. "To see if he can be improved."

"If there is an effective treatment, it should certainly be sought."

Polly rolled her eyes but seemed resigned, probably because she'd accepted that there was no grand fortune involved.

Hermione mentioned the hillside garden and talk flowed into plans for the garden at Selby Hall, where one area sloped. The meal passed pleasantly enough. Afterward, Hermione realized that she'd not told Edgar Peake of her plans, so she knocked again on the old man's door. She was let in and found him in a white nightcap in place of the red velvet.

"What now?"

"I've come to ask if I may stay with you, Edgar."

"Stay with me? Here?"

"Yes. You should have family with you."

"Why would a pretty girl like you want to be stuck here with me? I don't entertain."

"I never imagined that you do. If you want the honest truth, I fancy a lazy life."

She said it with a smile, and his lips twitched. "I could dismiss all my servants and let you do everything."

"And I could leave."

"Humph. Too bold for your own good."

"You're probably right, but I may stay?"

"Don't suppose I can stop you."

"Your servants might throw me out if you ordered them to." She saw the manservant struggling with a grin. "If I stay, I'll read to you, play cards, and tell you all about your family during the years you were away. You'll feel better for it."

"You're a saucy piece and you tire me out. Go away."

"But I may stay?"

"If you insist."

She curtsied. "Good night, Edgar."

When he smiled, she was able to take her leave knowing she was doing the right thing. She entered her bedroom and was even happier to remember that she now had it to herself. William and Polly were back together and the boys and Henrietta were in a room of their own, attended by two maids. Peace, quiet, and *Guy Mannering.* However, she soon found that the tangled misadventures of a stolen heir no longer thrilled. Instead, his constant peril seemed too close to her own situation.

Two days ago she would have berated herself for a wild imagination, but now it seemed there truly were villains in this world who wanted to harm her, and one was almost a twin of the brute who could still make her shudder. She couldn't shed the memory of being snatched from her family and carried off by that man, who had been ready to kill her on the spot.

Take the papers.

Break your neck.

Despite the ample fire, she hugged herself and for a weak moment thought of leaving with William and Polly. Perhaps she'd be safer in Yorkshire. But then she loosened her arms and walked around to shake off idiocy. She was safe enough in this house, with an abundance of servants, and Thayne had said that those concerned would soon know that she no longer had their papers.

Dangerous damp letters. Perhaps he was mad, poor man.

To counter her melodramatic thoughts, she'd write to one of her Hampshire friends. Margaret Millhouse was a levelheaded member of that orderly, tranquil world, now married with a child. There was writing paper in the drawer of a small desk, so she sat to relate her journey and the reason for it and the brush with drama in Ardwick. She said nothing about truly dangerous events.

Margaret had been at that ball. She might remember Thayne. Hermione was tempted to slip in a mention. *Can you imagine who I bumped into in Warrington?* No, the less she thought about the man, the better. She filled the page with weather and fashion and all the things that used to occupy conversation back in those leisurely days. It seemed rather dull, but dull equaled safe, and that was what she wanted. Despite the awkwardness of being the daughter of the Moneyless Marquess, her life in Hampshire had been pleasant, comfortable, and ordinary.

If only her father hadn't died.

If only her father had thought to explore for coal.

She could blame herself, too, however. Her father had been an indolent man who never had a new idea in his head, but he'd have acted if she'd urged him to. She'd known that people had prospered from finding coal in other areas of Northumberland. Their land was unpromising, but they could have hired people to look. Carsheld had been so far away, however, and her father would have resisted spending any money on it, and it was all in the past. No point in crying over spilled milk.

She folded, addressed, and sealed the letter, then went to draw the curtains. She looked down at the lights of Tranmere. Thayne had said he could see this side of the house. That meant one window down there was his. Was he looking up, watchful for a candle in the window? She drew the curtains firmly together and went to put more wood on the fire. No more folly!

CHAPTER 19

The next day Hermione saw Polly, William, and the children off in the coach. The children were already in a whiny mood, so she didn't regret the parting. She might enjoy being on her own for a while, with no one to take care of and no one who felt the need to take care of her. As she turned to go back into the house, however, she realized it was full of servants who would expect the master's female relative to take charge. She'd run her father's house for three years, so she was accustomed to it, but how would Mrs. Digby and the other servants react? She considered the situation and then summoned the housekeeper to the drawing room, inviting her to sit. The housekeeper did so, but warily.

"Everything here seems in excellent order, Mrs. Digby, so I don't mean to disturb the management, but are there any improvements you would like?"

The woman relaxed a little. "No, milady, but you must ask for any additions to the menu you want. We've grown used to providing for an elderly invalid."

"The food I've eaten so far has been good, but we've not been served fish. Is it not good hereabouts?"

"It's excellent, milady. It's that Mr. Peake doesn't like it."

"I do if it's fresh and well cooked."

"Then I'll see to it, milady."

"Does Mr. Peake get a newspaper?"

"He did in the beginning, milady, but then he lost interest."

"I would like us to receive one. Which ones are there?"

"There's the *Liverpool Mercury,* milady. He used to get that over on the ferry once a week."

"That will do for now. I'll find out about others. I intend to read to him about what's going on in the world."

"Very well, milady," the housekeeper said, perhaps doubtfully.

"I would also like to speak with his doctor."

"That'd be Dr. Onslow, milady, but he's not been here for nigh on a month now."

"Please send for him to come and call on me."

"I'll see if he will, milady, but the master was right sharp with him the last time."

Hermione wasn't surprised. She enquired about Edgar, but Peter said he was sleeping, so she decided to go out in the sun again. This time, however, she provided herself with a large, warm shawl, and kept to the upper paths, far from concealing trees.

Mark watched from the inn as the ancient Selby coach came down the hill and turned toward Chester, surprised but pleased that they were leaving so soon. Perhaps Hermione had seen sense and persuaded them to it. Two young boys had faces pressed to the window. He waved to them. Rather hesitantly, they waved back.

Now to follow. He'd watch over the Selby coach as far as Warrington. If they hadn't encountered any trouble by then, he'd feel free to go to London. He went in search of the innkeeper to enquire about hiring a horse, but met Jilly crossing the hall with fistfuls of flagons.

"Old Mr. Peake's guests are gone, then," she said. "The servants'll be right pleased about that. Not used to extra work, they aren't."

"Lazy?" he asked.

"Not with Ella Digby in charge," she said with a chuckle. "But a sick old man don't make much work."

"Do you know where I might hire a horse for a day or two?"

"Bill'd know. Bill!" she called.

A bowlegged groom came in, one Mark had noticed always looked as if he carried the weight of the world on his sinewy shoulders. "What d'you want now?"

"Gentleman wants to know where to 'ire an 'orse."

"Povey's livery in Birkenhead, sir. I could ride there and bring one back for you."

For a coin or two, Mark understood. "Thank you."

"Where you off to, then, me 'andsome?" Jilly asked.

He laughed at her sauce. "Merely Warrington. A bit of business."

"If you wanted to go to Warrington," said the groom, "you should have seen if you could go with that lot from Riverview. They're off that way, back to Yorkshire."

"That's Bill for you," Jilly said. "Always knows everythin'."

"So would you, lass, if y'kept your eyes and ears open and blathered on less."

"Tell me this, then — is old Mr. Peake dead? Their coachman said as they'd come to his deathbed."

The Selbys' coachman had visited the inn? Mark wished he'd encountered him.

"Course not," said Bill. "There'd be things 'appening, wouldn't there? Doctor. Undertaker. Armbands and black ribbons. And his relatives would've stayed for t'funeral. As it is, just one lady's stayed. Lady 'ermin or something."

" 'Er-mi-on-e!" Jilly said triumphantly, pronouncing the four syllables with care. "Georgie told me that. A bit too square in't chin and bold in't manner, he said."

"Bold?" Bill snorted. "That from you? There's a pot calling a kettle black."

"My chin's not square. Reckon it's that name. Lord knows where it comes from."

"Hermione was a Greek princess," Mark said, disturbing the squabble. "Lady Hermione? She must be very highly born."

"Don't know about that . . . ," Bill said.

"Fancy that!" Jilly taunted.

". . . but she's staying to nurse the old man, and rather her than me, 'im with some nasty foreign plague on 'im. I'll be off, then, sir."

Damnation. "I've reconsidered. My business in Warrington can wait and the weather looks fine for more explorations of this area today. Thank you."

The groom sighed and slouched away.

Jilly eyed Mark, hip cocked. "Sweet on this Lady 'ermione, are you, sir?"

"Why think that?"

"I've eyes and ears, never mind what Bill 'orrocks says, and there's a fair view of that garden from the front here. You were up there talking to 'er yesterday and it looked like you didn't want anyone in the 'ouse to see you. Proper Romeo and Juliet, are you?"

Devil take it. He'd survived the war by never underestimating the common people, but he'd thought only of what could be seen from the house, not from the town. The lovers' tale could serve, however.

"Something like that. I'm not a suitable husband for such a lady."

"But she'll have you anyway?"

"Alas, she has more sense than Juliet."

"Good for 'er, but she's sweet on you, too."

"She is?" he asked, ridiculously pleased.

"Could tell by the way she stood at times. You'll have to improve your circumstances."

"Do you think I can?"

She assessed him. "Strong man. Clever. Have t'manners of a gentleman. Reckon you could go far if you tried."

"Perhaps you're right. There's a good position waiting for me when I've done with what I'm about."

"Then get about it and get on to t'other. A pot can boil dry, you know."

He kissed her dimpled cheek. "That's very good advice."

"See that you take it, then," she said, and sauntered off to the taproom, her ample buttocks swaying.

Mark's smile faded. He'd love to get on with his task, but that was in London and Lady Hermione Merryhew had not left with her family for the safety of Yorkshire. He went to the window that gave a view up the hill. Could Bill the oracle be wrong? Why would she stay when he'd warned her of all the dangers?

He was beginning to convince himself that she'd gone when he saw her emerge and stroll along a path. Today she had a large shawl wrapped around her shoulders, but no bonnet. Her chestnut hair glinted warmly in the sun.

He left the inn and was heading toward the lane when she turned and went back into the house. He returned to the inn to watch from his window as he thought the situation through. No matter how he twisted the threads, he couldn't stay here for much longer. If he heard that the whole Crimson Band was under arrest, perhaps.

Was Hermione really drawn to him? She'd sent him to right-abouts twice, but in her room at the King's Head she'd been warmer. Much warmer. He'd never forget that kiss. Both those kisses, for the sweet one had been as potent as the fiery.

He smiled wryly at the thought of that good position waiting for him. What would Jilly say if she learned it was a viscountcy? That he was a moonling not to be on his estate, surrounded by servants, living a life of ease. Anyone would. It should be so easy. He merely had to step out of the shadows to become Lord Faringay, returned from Mauritius, an eligible gentleman who could aspire to the hand of a marquess's daughter.

He inhaled, startled to have gone so far even in his thoughts.

Marry Hermione Merryhew? A leap of excitement told him the answer, but it couldn't be. The Crimson Band were finished, but there were other Spenceans with the same purpose. How could he loll around at Faringay with his country still in peril? With innocents like Hermione and her family in danger of being dragged to the guillotine?

He was committed to his cause until every danger of revolution was over.

■ ■ ■ ■

Dr. Onslow came in the afternoon, all smiles until he realized that Hermione wasn't the patient. "Mr. Peake made it perfectly clear, my lady, that he did not wish to use my services."

She coaxed him to take a seat and sent for tea. "He may not know what's best for him, Doctor."

"He most certainly does not." The doctor was a thin man with a fringe of gray hair around a bald dome of a head, and a chilly demeanor, but he seemed the sort to know his trade.

"What ails him, Doctor?"

"A virulent ague brought back from the Orient."

"Yet he's not fevered now."

"As with most agues, it is intermittent."

"Does ague explain his other symptoms, such as his gray skin?"

The doctor's face pinched. "Are you an expert on symptoms, Lady Hermione? His major organs are affected so that a general debilitation has set in, yet he refuses treatment."

"What treatment did you prescribe?"

"Bark, calomel, and James's powder, with

blistering to help draw out the poisons. Living close by a large port, I do understand something of tropical diseases."

"I'm sure you do, Doctor, and it's to Mr. Peake's advantage that you are available. Peruvian bark is for fever, is it not? What is James's powder?"

"An antimonial, and very effective." He was using complicated language to confuse her, but she kept her temper.

"What is an antimonial, Doctor?"

"An elaboration of antimony."

She was irritated with herself. She should have been able to deduce antimony from antimonial. It was a purgative considered effective against many complaints. Her father had taken it at one point.

"You need not concern yourself with these details," Onslow said, reminding Hermione of similar tussles with her father's doctors. There she'd had a marquess's stature and authority behind her, but here she'd have to step more gently.

"I'm sure you're correct, Doctor, but I do like to understand the words I use. Did Mr. Peake show improvement under your treatments?"

"His fever reduced and then ceased and his organs improved. Considerable toxins were discharged. You would not wish to know details of that, ma'am."

"I nursed my father in his last illness, Doctor."

"Ah, I see. All the same, suffice to say that I saw hope until he dismissed me."

The tea came and she busied herself with it, remembering how ineffective her father's treatments had been, despite sweating, vomiting, and loose bowels.

"I wonder how the toxicity got into his body," she said as she passed over his tea.

The doctor sipped before replying. "Undoubtedly miasma, my lady, caused by decaying animal and vegetable matter in a hot climate. That is why the commonest affliction of those who venture into such climes is called malaria, which means 'bad air.' "

She smiled as if she'd no idea what "malaria" meant. He doubtless thought "miasma" beyond her feeble brain.

"My great-uncle speaks of something called kala-azar."

He tutted. "Some Indian superstition. He admitted that the words merely mean the 'black sickness', which is descriptive of symptoms, not causes, and he could offer no suggestion of treatment. He believed it to be fatal and gave that as his excuse to refuse treatment."

Hermione drank some tea, considering the medicines he'd mentioned. "Calomel is mercury, is it not?"

He inclined his head.

"The side effects are somewhat drastic."

"That is proof that it is effective, my lady."

"And the antimonial powder? How does that work?"

"By cleansing the body of toxins."

Sweating, vomiting, and all the rest. That would be hard on Edgar, but she couldn't sit by and watch him die, especially not when she might gain by it. According to the doctor, he'd improved under treatment.

"Perhaps we could try James's powder on its own, Doctor. If that brings about improvement, it might coax him back into other treatments. If opium was added to give relief to his symptoms, might he not be quicker to admit the benefit?"

The doctor put down his cup. "You are now the physician, Lady Hermione? Opium is too often a prop for constitutional weakness upon which a patient comes to depend."

Hermione put down her cup in turn. "Addiction is not an issue if he is dying, Doctor. I wish my great-uncle to resume treatment and if opium is part of achieving that, I wish him to have it. I can easily obtain it for myself."

He rose, flushed with anger, but said, "I would not like to see any patient in amateur hands. I will send up a preparation. Good day to you."

And good day to you, Hermione thought, picking up her cup again, wondering whether she'd done the right thing. But she couldn't help questioning the man. Her father's last weeks had destroyed her faith in doctors. He'd endured any number of unpleasant treatments, all to no purpose. Even the doctors who'd seemed honest had felt obliged to prescribe something, especially if it had a dramatic effect. She'd lacked the courage to challenge them, but she'd do better for Edgar Peake. No mercury.

Yet she'd agreed to the antimonial powders, which would also be drastic. Perhaps she was as bad, willing to try anything, in blind hope. Not blind, no. Something had worked before, and the antimonial seemed the most likely.

She had the notion of a cure in her head now and couldn't let it go.

A cure, or even a miracle. She had to try.

CHAPTER 20

The next morning Mark waited impatiently for the postbag to arrive. No letter arrived from Braydon.

That meant another day here. As the locals now thought him a lovelorn suitor, he didn't hide the fact that he was watching Riverview House. Of course, he was also keeping alert for Seth Boothroyd. He saw nothing but a rider on a slow horse who paused to nail up a poster by the inn door. He went to read it. A five-shilling reward was offered for the identification of a gentleman foully shot during highway robbery near the Chester road. Anyone with information was to communicate with Sir Peter Jarvis, coroner, Chester. The description fit Nathan Boothroyd too well, though the term "gentleman" could throw some off the scent. Dead, his clothes gave that impression, but no one who'd encountered him alive would think him that. All the same, the coroner's attention to duty was inconvenient. Mark hoped he wasn't going so far as to make extensive enquiries.

Even the notice was a problem. If one had reached Tranmere, the posters were being nailed up over a wide area. If Seth Booth-royd had come north to find his brother, he might see one and go to Chester. Once he confirmed that Nathan had been shot, he'd be after someone's blood. Whose would depend on what Solange had told him. If he knew about Hermione, she could be in great danger. Seth wouldn't care about true responsibility. He'd want someone to "scrag." Mark needed to know that Seth was in London and preferably arrested with the rest. Why the hell had he not heard from Braydon by now?

He took a seat in the taproom that evening, chatting to Jilly and a few local men mostly out of boredom. The clock was striking nine when a Riverview servant came in. This turned out to be Georgie, a local man who was courting Jilly. Mark listened, but learned nothing about what was happening in the house except that Lady Hermione took her meals with the old man, so there wasn't the dining room to bother with.

Hermione had just finished supper with Edgar, though he'd eaten little, despite her encouragement. The cook was preparing easily digestible dishes for him, but he pushed more around his plate than he ate. She'd been waiting for a good time to tell him about her discussion with the doctor, but it seemed there wouldn't be a better, so she explained and produced the bottles of medicine.

"I told him. No more quackery!"

"It's not quackery, Edgar. You've no need of bark, but James's powders are well-known and effective."

"What do you know about it?"

"I nursed my father."

"He died anyway, didn't he?"

"Yes, but his heart and lungs were failing. We all knew that. We should have let him go in peace."

"See!"

"You're not in such shape. You're merely . . . afflicted."

He grunted.

"Please try the powders with some opium. I'm sure you'll feel better, and that will be something, won't it?"

"You want me addicted."

"Plenty of people take opium without becoming dependent on it, but if you're dying anyway, why would it matter?"

"You've a nasty twisted way of looking at things," he grumbled, but then added, "Oh, very well. If it'll make you happy."

"Thank you," she said with a big smile. "Peter, please prepare the dose."

Still scowling, Edgar drank it, grimacing at the taste — perhaps more than was called for. "Now I've done as you want, read me some more from that issue of *The Gentleman's Magazine*."

She'd searched the library for books that would interest him, but found nothing. In one drawer, however, she'd found some old magazines and yesterday she'd begun to read to him from a copy of *The Gentleman's Magazine* from January 1815. Now she brought it from the sideboard, but flipped past the earlier pages, saying, "More affairs of Parliament and such."

"Read 'em. I like seeing how foolish they sound with hindsight."

"Is current opinion always wrong?" she asked, turning back to the second page. "Today everyone's in a panic over riots and in dread of revolution. Will we chuckle over our folly a few years hence?"

"Probably. Back in 1799 there were many as thought the world would end."

She picked up an analysis of the state of Europe in early 1815, when Napoleon had been in exile on Elba and everyone thought him defeated.

"Everyone was certainly wrong then," Edgar said, "but enough of that. Find something else."

She flipped some pages. "Here's a recollection of the Frost Fair. I wish I'd been in London then."

"You've been there?"

"A few times. We went there for the premature victory celebrations in 1814. They were wonderful. Visiting monarchs from around Europe, naval reenactments, concerts, fireworks. Everyone was so happy." No more fear of invasion. No more casualty lists. No more families cast into mourning.

And then came Waterloo.

She returned to the magazine and read the recollection of the frozen Thames, and then an article about the shortage of timber. That seemed to bore Edgar, so she flipped over births, marriages, and deaths, seeking something better. "Here's an article about the increased production of coal gas for London illumination."

Edgar did perk up. "I'd like to see the city

streets bright at night."

"You will as soon as you're well. It's even in the theaters now. How splendid that must be. I never thought about how the gas gets to the pipes that feed the lights, but it explains it here. *'The gas is provided in stations owned by various companies, and gathered in mighty gasometers, from which it is delivered by pipes to the area thereabouts. The gasometer at Great Peter Street illuminates the illustrious buildings of Westminster.'* It says there are already fifteen miles of pipe."

"A modern miracle."

"Gas does give a brilliant light," she said, "but it smells. I never noticed the smell from the streetlights, and generally shops lit by gas keep their doors open, but I remember going into one that had them shut. I left very quickly."

"How do they manage in the theaters, then?" he asked.

"I don't know. Perhaps it isn't so noticeable in a large space."

"Didn't a pagoda somewhere burn up when lit with gas?"

"It did. I think it's dangerous." She looked for other interesting items. "An improved way of bleaching using charcoal. Black into white? That makes no sense."

"Chemistry's descended from alchemy. There's still a lot of mystery about it, though no one's found a way to turn lead into gold."

"They've found a way to turn coal into gold." When he looked a question, she told him about Porteous's successful development of coal mines.

"Good for him. Your family had the chance. No point resenting him."

"You're right, but it's galling to think of Porteous as cleverer than I am."

Edgar chuckled. "Don't like him one bit, do you?"

"I try to have no opinion of him at all."

"He must be a miserly sort of fellow not to be sharing his wealth with you and your sister."

She couldn't tell Edgar about Porteous's proposal, because it would touch on money. That would lead to his will, and from there to his death.

"I'm no pinch-purse," Edgar said abruptly. "You deserve a gift. Where's Peter?"

"Eating his meal."

"Bottom drawer over there. Rosewood box inlaid with mother-of-pearl and other bits."

She went to get it, noticing that the drawer contained a number of boxes and packages, but that the rosewood one was the finest.

"It's beautiful," she said, stroking the gleaming wood.

"The gift's in the box. Open it!"

She did, and the slight spicy perfume told her the fan inside was made of sandalwood. She took it out and slid it open, smiling at the prettiness and the perfume. "Thank you."

"A nothing."

"Any gift is something," she said, sitting back down but continuing to waft the fan. "This is something I'll always value."

"Good."

An oriental artifact at last, she thought. Polly would have loved to see it and all the others in that drawer, and probably build much from it, but neither box nor fan was sign of great wealth.

"Where did you acquire it?" she asked, hoping for more about his travels.

He screwed his face in thought. "Goa, I think. So many places. Read me some more."

She put aside the fan and picked up the magazine, scanning the pages for something that would interest him. She certainly found it.

"Edgar, there's an article here about tropical diseases! Malaria and cholera and . . . Listen to this. '*Dr. Theophilus Grammaticus*

257

gave a presentation to the Society of Curious Creatures' — what an odd name — 'on a new regime of treatment for the Black Disease, sometimes called kalyzar in the East.' "

"Kala-azar!" Edgar corrected, but his gaze was sharp. "Go on, go on."

" 'Dr. Grammaticus is lately returned from North Africa, where he claimed to have treated a number of people who were suffering from this generally fatal disease with a preparation of antimony' — antimony, Edgar! — 'combined with the essence of Fungus Mirabilis. He gave accounts of a number of cases but disagreeably refused to identify the fungus, admitting that he had concocted the name so as to keep his secret, which he hopes to sell to the government for use in India, where this disease is also prevalent.' Disagreeable indeed, but now you see why the antimony has helped you."

"But never enough." Edgar Peake had slumped back.

"We need that mushroom."

"It'll be pure invention. Look at the name. What honest doctor would be called Theophilus Grammaticus?"

"If I were a charlatan, I'd call myself Brown or MacKay."

"That's because you have sense and he

258

doesn't. What's the date, 1815? If anything had come of it, I'd have heard of it. Out in the East there were rumors that antimony helped, but out there they think antimony's a panacea. That's why I suggested it to Onslow, though."

"He made it appear to be his suggestion."

"Because he's a charlatan, too. Stop hoping for a miracle."

"But you'll keep taking the medicine? Please?"

"Very well, very well, but it'll do no good in the long run."

Hermione wouldn't give up hope. She put aside the magazine. "I'm going to the library to look for information about mushrooms likely to be the ones Grammaticus used."

"If he used anything. You're a dreamer, girl!"

"Dreams sometimes come true!" she called back.

CHAPTER 21

When the postbag arrived the next day and brought no letter, Mark became concerned. Beau Braydon had survived the many dangers of the war, so Mark had never considered that he might fall victim to Solange. Had she discovered Braydon was his ally and had him killed? It seemed impossible, but she'd learned enough of Hermione's involvement and movements to send Nathan Boothroyd after her. Braydon wouldn't be easy to kill, but as he'd said, a pistol or a rifle could dispose of a strong, well-guarded man with ease. If he was alive, Mark should have heard from him by now.

Mark wrote a hasty letter to Hawkinville explaining the situation and asking for news. He sent it by ferry to Liverpool, which would get it to London at best speed. It would still take at least a day, and any reply would take as long to get back. If only he had messenger pigeons.

If Braydon hadn't survived, he hadn't passed on the knowledge Mark had poured into him. That meant he should set out for London immediately, but Seth Boothroyd could already be in the area, seeking those who'd killed his brother. Damn it all to Hades! Why couldn't Hermione have returned to Yorkshire with her family?

He pulled himself together and forced his mind to calm assessment. Even if Braydon had gone astray, his own letter would have arrived in London. That should have put Solange and Isaac in prison. Without habeas corpus they could be held there indefinitely. Seth could be with them. If not, perhaps Solange hadn't had time to spill the whole story into his mind. Perhaps, perhaps, perhaps. He'd stay one more day and then he'd have to leave for London.

In the afternoon he saw Hermione in the garden. He didn't wait for an invitingly open gate. He went up and accosted her.

She got in the first word. "I commanded you to leave me alone."

"You should have returned to safety in Yorkshire."

She raised her chin. "I have remained to care for my elderly relative."

"At risk of your life."

"That again. Nothing has happened, sir.

261

Nothing. And may I point out that I'm no closer to London here than in Yorkshire. I see you hadn't thought of that."

"In Yorkshire you'd be safely with your family."

"Which would put them in danger. If there is still any danger, which I greatly doubt."

"There is."

"You have proof?" It was a challenge and not at all fearful. Despite everything he fought a smile.

"I don't have proof against it."

She rolled her eyes. "On those grounds we'd all live in fear every day everywhere."

"Not everyone is abducted on the road," he pointed out. "And Nathan Boothroyd knew which road your party was taking. He might have known your destination."

Her face twitched, but she rallied. "If anyone wanted to harm me here, they've had time. I won't live under a sword. I won't."

"I understand. The truth is, I haven't heard news from London and it worries me."

"The woman might still think I have your letter? I can't believe she'd send her other brute all this way for it. If she exists at all."

"Would I be haunting you like this if she

didn't?"

She glared at him. "If she exists, name her."

"Which proves what? Very well, she's a Mrs. Solange Waite, a Frenchwoman married to an Englishman."

"The decent, middle-aged one?"

"Only in appearance. Hermione, you have reason to be angry, but don't let your anger at me lower your guard. She's a dangerous woman in her own right. She's killed in the past, during the revolution in France. These days she uses others, but she's without conscience or mercy."

His sober words melted Hermione's resistance. She could see that he truly did regret involving her and was genuinely worried. "Others such as that Boothroyd man who abducted me," she said. "But he's dead."

"And has a brother, remember."

She did remember. "Who's like him."

"Close to identical."

"I can't get that man out of my head. Last night, I had a dream. . . ."

He took her in his arms.

She allowed it. She shouldn't, but she needed comfort and strength.

"I'll keep you safe," he said.

She was sane enough to snort at that. "It

wouldn't be necessary if I'd never met you."

"Don't sound so hopeless." She felt his kiss on her hair. "I prefer you spicy, as in the bedroom at the King's Head."

That gave her strength to push away from him. "Your preferences, sir, are nothing to do with me."

"Alas."

"Reprobate."

"Undoubtedly."

"You seemed such a hero once," she protested.

"It was mostly the regimentals. I was wet behind the ears, part brash confidence and part terror that I'd not stand up to fire and battle."

"Did you?" But then she winced. "I'm sorry. Of course you did."

"Yes, thank God, though it's easy to understand how some men's nerves break. After a couple of years I was moved to other work, which meant less time directly facing enemy fire and blade."

"What work?"

"Organizational duties in the Quartermaster's Division. It sounds less useful, but it's not."

"You'd rather have been in the thick of the fire." She knew it. She knew him.

We've fallen again into intimate conversa-

tion again, and I'm powerless to resist.

"It would have been easier at times," he said. "Simpler, at least." But then he shook his head. "I didn't come up here for this. I came to tell you I must leave tomorrow."

The shock was a good part dismay. "You just said you'd keep me safe!" She recovered. "No, it's good news. I'll be safer with you gone."

"I hope so."

He sounded calm, but she knew he wasn't. Her heart told her he felt exactly as she did, that parting was painful and unfair. That life was cruel.

"*Why* is there danger?" she demanded. "Why are these people so desperate to retrieve that letter? If it's only a letter, why did you steal it?"

"Better you not know."

"Ignorance hasn't kept me safe thus far."

He gave a short laugh. "Always to the point, but truly, there's nothing more for you to know. Be on your guard. Stay in the house and gardens. If you must venture further, take an armed servant."

"Armed? I'm not sure the footmen here know how to use pistols."

"I don't suppose you do, either."

"Of course not."

He sighed. "Do your best." He touched

265

her cheek. "Farewell, Lady Hermione."

The use of her title was like a step away. "You're going into danger, aren't you? Those people might not pursue me here, but you're going to them. The brute's brother will want to slit your throat." His only response was a wry reaction to her use of that phrase. "Will *you* stay safe?" she demanded with exasperation. "Will *you* take an armed guard?"

"Luck's favored me so far."

"Luck!" She turned away to hide her tears. "Oh, go away, you wretch, and good riddance."

But when she heard the gate creak, it broke her heart.

Hermione stayed where she was until she'd conquered her tears and then hurried into the house. She tried to find the anger she'd used as a barrier against him. Spicy indeed. Only a wretch would refer to her folly like that. Anger turned irreversibly to worry, however, even dread. She remembered his throat-slitting gesture back in Ardwick. She'd doubted it then, but no longer. He could be going to his death, and there was nothing she could do about it.

She took refuge in her room, looking down at the Ferry Inn as if doing so could keep him safe, trying to think of some way to avert fate. Why was she always so powerless in her life? She'd not been able to prevent Roger dying, or Jermyn, or her father and mother. She'd failed to discover coal. She'd probably fail to cure Edgar. . . .

She pulled herself out of her dismal mood. "Spicy" gave her an idea of something that might help. The cook here, Mrs. Kenwick, was an amiable woman who produced good, plain food, but Hermione was worried by Edgar's poor appetite. The antimony with opium was improving him, but he needed nourishment. She went to the kitchen.

"Do you know any spicy dishes, Mrs. Kenwick?"

"Cinnamon cakes, milady?"

"No, I mean pepper or Eastern dishes."

"Sorry, milady, but I can't say as I do."

Hermione smiled to reassure her. "And why should you? But I think we should try to add some stronger flavors to Mr. Peake's food. I'm sure oriental food is spicier and he may have become accustomed to that."

"I'll see what I can do, milady," the cook said, "but it's not what I'm used to for an invalid."

"Perhaps we can find advice in Liverpool, with so many vessels there from around the world."

Hermione went to Edgar's room to ask him, but also to check that he was out of his bed. She'd coaxed him into spending time in a chair yesterday, and even walking around the room a little. She suspected some of his weakness was from lying in bed all the time. Now he was taking his medicine again, he had a bit more strength.

He was sitting in his big chair, watching the river. She wasn't sure watching the river was healthy for him, but he had to look at something.

She went to sit nearby. "Do you have some favorite Eastern dishes?"

"Don't care if I ever eat again."

"Well, I do. I'm going to send George to Liverpool to seek out an Indian cook."

"I keep telling you, I didn't spend much time in India, and I don't like curries, so stop this."

"Where did you spend much time?" she persisted.

"Here and there. Stop pestering me."

She did, but she returned to the kitchen to pore over the few cookery books. She found some recipes for curry, but little else except a few using ginger and cayenne.

"Very well, Mrs. Kenwick, we'll improvise. I want you to add cayenne to your excellent ragout of chicken. Ginger, too. Then for a sweet, make an especially rich cinnamon pudding with rum sauce."

"For an invalid, milady?"

"We can only try. He's not eating much as it is."

Hermione had taken to eating her dinner with Edgar in his room. That night he didn't comment on the ragout or the pudding, but he ate a little more of both and drank some claret she'd had opened.

Then he surprised her. "What if we went in search of that Grammaticus?"

"In search? How?"

"At the last place we know of. The Curious Creatures in London."

"London! You can't travel there."

"I can sit in a chair, so I can sit in a coach."

She hated to mention it, but said, "The medicine will make it difficult."

"Spewing and liquid bowels? I'll stop taking it before it gets a hold on me."

"You can't do that."

"Don't tell me what I can and can't do. You can watch me die here, or you can take me to London." He had on his stubborn face, but it relaxed into wistfulness. "I've not seen London for fifty years. Sailed into Liverpool nigh on a year ago, and I've been stuck here since. I want to see the gaslit streets and all the fine new buildings. The London Docks."

"Docks?" she said, bemused by anyone wanting to see those, but she couldn't resist the yearning in his voice. He'd been a man of action all his life. No wonder he wanted to take action now. Instead of lingering here until he died, he wanted to embark on another adventure — a quest that might kill him but that held the slim hope of a grand reward.

"How would we travel?" she asked.

"The same way anyone does. Hire a chaise."

"Just the two of us? Edgar, I'm sorry, but —"

"You're right, you're right. I'll need Peter. You'll need a maid. A coach, then. Not hired. Buy it."

"*Buy* a coach?"

"Hard to hire a coach for a long journey. Probably only get it for a stage or two, then have to settle into a new one. Buy one. Sell it in London. I've done that sort of thing before."

"I suppose it's possible, but it would be very expensive." He'd never given a hint about how much money he had.

"I've money enough for that. Peter! My writing desk."

Edgar was suddenly full of vigor and she could imagine how he'd been in his prime, but she could also imagine this burning him into a collapse.

His servant arranged his writing things, but when Edgar picked up the pen, he dropped it. "Plaguey hands too weak. You write for me."

Hermione arranged the desk on her lap and at his dictation wrote a letter to his solicitor in Liverpool requesting him to purchase a comfortable traveling carriage for him at whatever cost necessary, and to have it delivered here with four post-horses as soon as possible along with four hundred pounds, transported securely. The sum made her stare, but she wrote it before commenting.

"That's a great deal of money, Edgar. Will it be safe?"

"Should be, unless you or Peter decide to run off with it. New letter. To my bank." That was authorizing his solicitor to draw the funds to cover the purchase and the hire of the first set of horses, plus the money.

Hermione sanded the letters, wondering whether she should try to prevent this extravagance. She'd seen no evidence that Edgar Peake had huge wealth, so he might be spending the last of his money on this wild venture, leaving nothing for Polly. It was his money, however, and if he wanted to spend it in pursuit of a cure for his disease and to enjoy illuminated streets, it was his right.

She took the letters to him for his signature, which he made carefully. "Want them to recognize it."

As she folded the letters, he picked up his seal. She dripped melted wax over the edge and he stamped it. The design was some kind of oriental letter.

"On the journey, you can tell me all your adventures," she said.

"Not all of 'em," he said with a chuckle, eyes still bright with pleasure at their enterprise. "Send the footman across to Liverpool at first light tomorrow to deliver those. We might even have the coach by the end of the day."

"You're used to action, aren't you?"

"Always have been. Hate lolling around. It'll be good to be doing something, even if it kills me."

She had to accept that. It was only as she went up to her room that she realized that she'd agreed to go to London, where, if Thayne was to be believed, enemies lurked. His, not hers, she told herself, but it was a good thing he was leaving tomorrow or he'd be back up to berate her.

CHAPTER 22

The next day Mark packed his valise and went down to pay his bill. The postboy came by to leave a bag for Tranmere and Mark paused in case the letter had come at last. It had. Braydon had made it to London! Thank God he was alive, but as Mark broke the seal, he cursed him for being a slow correspondent.

He scanned the crisp writing until the important part jumped out at him:

Julius Waite returned to his London home along with Seth Boothroyd. Tregoven and Durrant returned to their separate lodgings at the same time. Solange Waite and Isaac Inkman have disappeared.

Though the words were clear, Mark reread them. How the hell had they been allowed to disappear?

He read on:

They arrived at the Swan with Two Necks two days after leaving Warrington and were observed, but by switching hackneys they gave the inept watchers the slip. The next day Seth Boothroyd disappeared from Waite's house.

"Damn them all to hell," Mark muttered, with the inept watchers particularly in mind. Clearly he hadn't impressed upon anyone how clever Solange could be, but he'd not expected this twist and it alarmed him.

If Solange had broken free of Waite, she was embarked on some plan of her own, and it wouldn't be mild or cautious. The urgent question was, had Solange summoned Seth Boothroyd to guard her, or to send him north to find his brother? Mark tossed the letter on the fire and watched it burn, caught between two imperatives. He was needed in London. Braydon was safely there, but he had only facts, not familiarity. Mark knew he'd have better insights that could be crucial in this emergency.

However, Hermione still wasn't safe. Seth could be approaching Tranmere now, so how could he leave? Perhaps he was a traitor to his country, but he couldn't leave Hermione unprotected under such an imminent threat.

He wrote to Braydon explaining the situation.

As for finding Solange and Isaac, he'll need a laboratory. Investigate establishments that sell chemical equipment and supplies. Solange could disguise herself in many ways, so she is unlikely to be spotted by searchers. Isaac would be easier, but he'll be happy to stay in whatever rooms they're using. He likes a whore now and then. They'll be brought in to him, but with his distinctive appearance, you might pick up a trail that way. Boothroyd won't stay inside and is distinctive. Hawkinville should set people to search for him. As soon as I hear from you that he's in London, I'll travel south with all speed.

He sealed and sent the letter, telling himself that Solange, Isaac, and Boothroyd could be anywhere in the vastness of London, undetectable amid a million people. His being there to prowl the streets wouldn't help.

He doubted anyone else would see it that way.

276

Hermione woke to her fifth day in River-view House, determinedly not thinking about Thayne having left. It was better so. The footman set out on his errand to Liverpool and they could only wait for the results. In the meantime, she tried to persuade Edgar to take the medicine for one more day.

"Why? We're going to London to find Grammaticus."

"It might take days for us to begin our journey."

"I'll have someone's guts if it does."

"I can see you're accustomed to being a tyrant."

"When necessary."

"At least continue with the opium. Remember how your joints ached? That will make traveling hard."

"Trying to addict me? Then you'll have me dancing to your tune."

"If you can dance, I'll be delighted."

That won her one of his dry laughs. "You're a saucy piece. So like my Anne. Stupid woman to marry a man who'd lock her in a box."

"Perhaps she didn't realize until too late."

"You watch yourself, then. Suitors are tricksy."

"I'll be careful — if I come across any."

"You will in London."

"Seeking an eccentric society and a quack doctor?"

"Some eccentric gentleman might take a fancy to you. Peter!"

"Yes, sir."

"The brown box in the bottom drawer."

As the servant found the box, Hermione wondered what new wonders might appear. She'd been tempted to explore the drawer that had contained the sandalwood fan.

This time the box wasn't a work of art. It was long, shallow, and made of plain dark wood with a solid lock. The servant also brought something else, an ovoid wooden shape. Despite his darkened and gnarled fingers, Edgar manipulated the shape, sliding pieces in and out and around in a pattern she couldn't follow. Then it opened like a flower revealing several keys nestled within. He chose one and unlocked the plain box. When he opened it, she saw a slender dagger settled in red silk.

"It's beautiful," Hermione said, because it was, in a lethal sort of way.

The hilt was of gold, or a gold-colored metal, set with tiny plates of jewel-colored glass. They might, perhaps, be paper-thin jewels. The blade was about eight inches long and slender, with an unusual rippling form. A design of silver and black followed the ripples all along it.

"Pick it up," Edgar said, "but respect it. It's sharp."

Hermione obeyed. She'd never expected a weapon to feel so comfortable in her hand. She'd held pistols, which were too heavy, and a sword that had felt unwieldy. This felt . . . right.

"It's a kris, from Java," Edgar said. "A lady's kris."

"Women go armed in Java?"

"Some of them."

"Why do you have a lady's weapon?" she asked, turning her hand so light played on the subtle patterns in the metal of the blade. They reminded her of watered silk.

"I forget," he said. She didn't believe him. "You might as well have it if you're to be dealing with suitors."

"I've never found them as dangerous as that."

"London suitors," he said, but he meant something else.

"You're being mysterious, Edgar. Why?"

He shrugged. "You're worried about things, and not all of them my health. Paying attention to worries has kept me alive a time or two." He paused, perhaps hoping for an explanation. When she didn't give it, he said, "We're going to the wicked city. Won't hurt to have a weapon there."

It certainly wouldn't. Trying to hide her reactions, Hermione touched the blade with a finger and cut herself. It was too shallow a cut to bleed, but then, she'd hardly touched it. "It will hurt to have this one," she protested.

"There's a sheath in the lid."

There was, of something hard and light covered with red velvet on the outside. She slid the blade into it, feeling softness inside.

"Silk wool. Find a way to wear it beneath your clothing. It'll do you no good in a drawer."

She thought of the abduction. It wouldn't have helped at first, but perhaps when the brute had dropped her on the ground like a sack, she could have got the weapon out. "I don't know how to use a blade."

"We're not talking about fencing. If you're in danger, don't fiddle around threatening someone. He'll take it off you. Stick it in, and stick it in hard. A kris is strong and sharp. It goes through clothes and flesh like a knife through soft cheese, and it'll go through some bones, too."

She drew the blade out again. It looked so delicate, but she could sense its lethal power. "I don't know. . . ."

"Don't be a milksop. Traditionally, it's worn at the back, tucked into a belt. Find a way to wear it. I'll not go to London without."

"You're the one who wants to go."

"But you want me to."

"You're a scheming, conniving old reprobate."

He showed his long teeth. "And more than a match for you. Go and sort out that blade."

She took the box up to her room, imagining what Polly would say to the idea of her sister going armed. Polly wouldn't be happy about any part of the enterprise. She wasn't heartless enough to wish the old man dead before his time, but she hadn't spent enough time with Edgar Peake to become fond. Polly had been soothed by the belief that Edgar didn't have more than a comfortable income, but when Hermione thought of his cavalier decision to buy a coach and the way he was ordering lawyers and bankers around, she wasn't so sure.

That puzzle box held quite a number of keys and each could unlock a treasure. It was his money, she reminded herself, earned through a lifetime of hard work and danger. It wasn't hers or Polly's to pine over.

In any case, he wouldn't go to London

unless she was wearing the dagger. In the small of her back? It wouldn't show beneath the fullness at the back of her high-waisted gowns, but it would make sitting in a coach uncomfortable and she couldn't think how she'd get at it there. She had to assume that women in Java wore belted garments and wore the kris in open view. She couldn't do that, but Edgar wouldn't go to London unless she had the kris on her. What about her pockets? In a day dress she wore a pair beneath her gown and could reach into them through a slit in the side of the dress. She put the sheathed kris in the right-hand one, but the hilt poked out.

Then she saw the solution. She took out her small sewing case and unpicked a little of the seam at the bottom of her right-hand pocket. She stitched around it to make it secure and then slid the kris through almost to the hilt. The sheath was trapped, and the hilt would be easy to reach. She studied herself in the mirror. It didn't show. She sat down. It felt a little awkward, but it would do.

Thinking of her abduction, she drew the blade as she might have done that day. Again, it felt comfortable in her hand, but could she thrust it into someone's body? It would slide through cloth and flesh, but could she actually do it? She hoped never to find out, but as she eased the blade back into the sheath, she had to admit she felt comforted.

CHAPTER 23

Mark had resisted the temptation to go up to the Riverview House gardens, even though he'd seen Hermione out there in the afternoon. She would believe he'd left, and it was better so. He went out to walk around Tranmere on his spurious task, but also to check for strangers in the area, but his mind kept drifting to Hermione, even to the impossible prospect of claiming her for his own one day.

When afternoon rain drove him back to the inn, he had no distraction from his thoughts. Marriage required a home. Even when his duties were over, what home could he offer?

Faringay had never been idyllic despite his parents' devotion to each other. From his earliest memories he'd been warned to be quiet and avoid all alarms, and to never "disturb your lady mother, young sir." Only now did he wonder whether one of his father's motives in creating the French Wing at Faringay had been to relieve his son from having to be quiet and avoid all alarms in the rest of the house. Perhaps, and then two years later he'd been sent off to school.

When he'd returned for holidays, he'd rarely seen his mother, but he'd noticed how Faringay Hall was deteriorating. Perhaps his father simply hadn't cared, but more likely he feared that workmen and noise would set his fragile wife into a mania of terror. Mark had witnessed those fits only twice, but he'd never forget them. She'd been plunged back into the riotous attack she'd suffered, seeing violence and death all around and sure it came for her.

He'd joined the army to make sure the French wouldn't invade Britain, but he'd welcomed release from the obligation to spend occasional times at Faringay Hall. Was his private war against revolution yet another way to avoid the place? It held extra shadows now because of his mother's suicide two years ago. He knew that his being there wouldn't have helped — quite the contrary — but that didn't save him from guilt.

He had a duty to Faringay, however, and if he took a wife, she would want a home.

Take Hermione there? She'd had enough

of loss and privation. He wanted better for her, and he couldn't marry as long as there was work to do. He had only to remember his mother to know why it was important.

He went down to the taproom in the evening, hoping the amorous footman would come down to flirt with Jilly and let slip a mention of Hermione. He was in luck, or so he thought until he overheard what the man had to say.

George arrived late and in a gloomy mood, complaining of a trip over to Liverpool in the rain to visit a lawyer and a bank. "Taking the old man away, she is. That'll be the end of a cushy job."

"You mean he'll die?" Jilly asked, handing him a tankard of ale.

"Don't know one way or t'other on that, me Jilly, but he won't come back. We'll all be dismissed."

"That's a shame, then."

Mark had become familiar enough at the inn to ask a question. "Where's Mr. Peake going? Bath, perhaps?"

"London. Wouldn't mind going to London, but they're only taking Mr. Peake's man and one of the maids for the lady."

London. What madness was this? Hadn't he made it clear that the people who might hurt her were there? Ignoring Jilly's amused eye, Mark asked, "When do they leave?"

"Likely be tomorrow, sir. The old man's bought a coach."

"Hired, you mean."

"Damned if I do, sir. Bought."

"That'll cost a pretty penny," Jilly said.

"Aye, but we've always reckoned he's warm. Come back from t'Orient with chests of rubies, they say. Not that I've seen any."

"Pity," said Jilly, sidling up against him. "I wouldn't mind a ruby."

They settled to flirting and Mark went up to his room to stand glaring at Riverview House. How could the stubborn woman not grasp how dangerous London would be for her?

He knew which room was hers. Her curtains were drawn, but light shone through a chink. He left the inn and made his way up the dark lane without a lantern, going on memory of the lay of the land, grateful that the rain had stopped. He easily climbed the gate and there was enough moon to show the gray stone paths of the garden, which took him to the house. On the ground floor open curtains showed a bedroom where an old man in a nightcap slept propped up in a bed. Old Mr. Peake, who was going to get Hermione killed if Mark couldn't talk sense into her.

All seemed quiet, and George's arrival at the inn showed that the day's work was done. Some of the servants would be in bed. Any others would be taking their ease in the servants' hall or the kitchen. Presumably a back door was still open, but he'd be detected immediately. He first tried the obvious, but the front door was locked. The windows were closed for the night and the house was inconveniently clear of helpful trellises or climbing plants that could support a man.

There had to be a way.

He worked his way around, checking for other entrances, and came to a patch of grassy garden and glass doors. They were locked, but in a far less substantial way. He wasn't skilled with locks, but three years ago, in preparation for his mission, he'd taken instruction and acquired some tools. They'd do for this one.

After a little fumbling, the lock turned and he entered a silent, dark room. Moonlight suggested the position of furniture, so he took off his boots and left them by the closed door, then made his way carefully out into the entrance hall. It was equally dark, but he could hear a mumble of conversation from the back of the house. That presented no danger to him. His target was upstairs. He climbed the stairs, taking his bearings. Hermione's room should be to his right. When he arrived at what he thought was her door, he turned the knob and entered.

The room was firelit, as her room at the inn had been, but the bed-curtains were drawn fully back. She wasn't here, but her nightgown was draped over a rack near the fire, as it had been at the King's Head. Such a promise of domestic pleasures. He liked the propriety of nightgown and nightshirt, warming by the fire. It spoke of settled domesticity and a comfortable home.

He realized he could smell her as well. Whatever perfume or toilet water she used was light and subtle, but he knew it, and the underlying essence that was her. He touched her nightgown. . . .

But then he put aside folly and left the room. Where else might she be? If she was passing time with the servants, he was sunk, but he doubted she was. She wasn't haughty, but the servants wouldn't be comfortable with a marquess's daughter sitting in the kitchen with them, so she wouldn't do it. She'd be sensitive to such things.

Drawing room or library? A library was probably on the ground floor and there'd been no candle there, ready for her use. The drawing room should be up here, so he went in search of it. He opened doors as he had that night at the King's Head, but with much less risk. No one was hunting him tonight and Hermione was the only guest.

He found two other bedrooms, both unused, and then the drawing room. It was a large corner room set with two sofas, a number of chairs with upholstered seats, and some small tables. A large, screened fire burned in the hearth and Hermione sat in a green gown on a gold-striped sofa, reading a book by the light of a modern reflecting lamp set behind her. She seemed haloed like a saint, but a startled one.

He stepped in and closed the door behind him.

She put the book aside and rose, but with a semblance of calm. "At least I'm not in my bedroom this time. Who's hunting you now, Thayne?"

Despite the calm, she'd flushed with color and he hoped it wasn't all anger. She wore a small flowered pin in her thick mahogany hair and everything about her delighted him. He'd come here to berate her but realized he was smiling. He made himself sober. "No one, but you're a mad fool."

Instead of protesting, she grimaced.

"London."

"London," he agreed. "What possesses you?"

She raised her chin. "Necessity. Why are you even here? Your necessity was to leave."

"So that's why you thought you could get away with this."

"I'm not getting away with anything. You do *not* command me, sir."

"I wish I did."

"I'm sure you do. Stop looming over me. If you intend to stay, sit." She sat back down, hands neatly in her lap.

Keeping a stern face was almost impossible, but he managed as he took a chair facing her. By God, this must be love. A damnable, insane ecstasy simply to be in her presence, despite folly and danger.

She frowned. "Are you all right?" Then, alarmed, she asked, "Is that Boothroyd here?"

"No," he quickly assured her. "There's no new threat. Unless you go to London, that is."

"I must. There's someone there who might have a cure for Great-uncle Edgar. I can't put my safety ahead of his life." Her resolution was infuriating, but such honor was part of why he adored her.

"What cure?" he asked.

"It's complicated, but we hope to find a particular doctor there. I won't be deterred."

"Very well. I must go to London tomorrow, and this time it's certain. I'll find him for you."

"Why?"

"To keep you safe."

Why it should stun her, he couldn't understand, but she became less prickly. "It's not just a matter of the medicine, Thayne. Edgar wants to go to London. He's not been there for fifty years and there are things he wants to see. It will do him good to get away from here."

"Zeus! Then I'll take him. I'll take him and find the doctor, and even make sure he takes his medicine. And you can return safely to your sister."

"No," she said, her square chin infuriatingly resolute. "And don't glare at me like that. I will be perfectly safe."

"Safe? You're a complete idiot."

"Am I, indeed? No," she said, raising a commanding hand, "listen to me. I'm not a simpleton and have given this considerable thought. First, London is a very large city. The chance of my encountering the Frenchwoman or the brute's brother is remote, especially as they won't be looking for me there. You admit they might possibly come looking for me here."

"Which is exactly why you must return to Yorkshire."

"Where they *also* might know to look for me. Can you deny that?" Before he could attempt to, she swept on. "More to the point, those people wouldn't recognize me if they passed me on Bond Street."

"You're planning a disguise? Perhaps there's some sense —"

"I don't need one. The first brute saw me, but the Frenchwoman didn't, and his brother's never been near me. You see? I'll be safer in London than here or at Selby Hall."

He opened his mouth and shut it again.

"Unwilling to admit I'm right?"

"I'm seeking the flaw in your argument."

She waited, like a cat watching a cornered mouse.

"You are a damnable woman."

"You mean I'm right."

He laughed. "Yes, I mean you're right. I'm not convinced you'll be safer in London than here, but your points are valid."

"Grudging, sir, grudging."

"Don't count it against me that I want your safety."

"I don't. But what of yours? May I command you not to take risks?"

"Would you want to?"

Her eyes slid away for a moment and he waited, breath shallow. Finally, she looked up at him. "Yes."

He crossed to sit by her on the sofa. "So we can talk more quietly," he said, but that wasn't the reason, and they both knew it. Her brows rose, but she smiled. The damnable woman was ready to be kissed.

CHAPTER 24

"A sensible lady would fend off an amorous gentleman," he pointed out.

"Are there no times when a gentleman needs to fend off an amorous lady?"

"Are you determined to score points in every round?"

"I've always been competitive, and I like to win." She leaned forward and kissed him. It was a decorous kiss, but dangerous as lips lingered against lips. He drew her closer, but her hand on his chest stopped him and then gently pushed him away.

"Well fended," he said. "Are any servants likely to come up here without being summoned?"

"No, and they won't expect to be summoned. My maid left washing water an hour ago and put it by the fire to keep warm. I can get into and out of my simple clothing by myself."

With some women that would be an

invitation and his line would be, *"All the same, allow me to assist. . . ."*

He might have said it if she'd not continued, "It's time that you tell me how you sank to thievery, my friend."

My friend. He wanted to be far more than a friend, but she was fending wisely. He shifted back so there was clear space between them, deciding what to say. She still thought him a thief and she worried. If he told her the truth, she'd worry more, but she wouldn't be fobbed off with nothings.

"Is it because of your mother?" she asked.

Witch to put her finger on it. He should leave before she guessed all of it, but this could be the last time he'd ever sit and talk to this woman, this friend, this enchantress. Perhaps she was a potion — an irresistible one, especially when close and by firelight, or moonlight, or in a garden by bright light of day.

"How she was harmed by the French Revolution," she probed. "How she lost her wits and didn't know you?"

As he feared. He could give her part of the truth and he wanted to. He took her hand, stroking her fingers with his thumb. "Yes. I do what I do for her sake." He spun out the story in his head. "I can only steal from the French, you see." No wonder she looked puzzled. "The French drove my mother mad, so I can steal from them with a clear conscience."

She probably thought him half-mad, and she'd be right for the wrong reasons. If it squashed any growing tenderness, he must be pleased.

"Not all the French were Jacobins," she pointed out gently.

"I know my feelings aren't reasonable, but I can't help them. If I meet a French person who's over forty, I can't help wondering if they were Jacobins. If they took part in the mobs and terror, if they slaughtered innocents simply for their birth. I was obliged to spend some time in Paris in 1814 and I looked at everyone of that age and wondered if they'd cheered as people's heads fell into the guillotine basket. As the heads of my uncle and cousins and my parents' friends fell into the basket. I wanted all such people sent to the guillotine in turn."

Too much of the truth. He'd tightened his grip on her hand. Instead of protesting, she matched that hold. "It was a madness, Thayne. They are probably normal people now and ashamed of what they did."

"That doesn't make them innocent."

"No, but such hatred could destroy you. You could hang if caught for theft."

297

This felt like a confessional. His mother had retained her Roman faith and when he was young, she'd insisted on him being trained to it and taking its sacraments. It had been one of many performances he'd enacted to keep his mother sane. At the same time his father had taught him Protestant ways, making the papist ones seem like playacting or a game. Once he went away to school, he'd left the papist ways behind him.

His mother had never commented. Either she'd forgotten or she was sane enough to see how it must be in a country where Papists were still burdened with many restrictions.

Now, in this new, golden confessional, he told what truth he could. "The thievery is recent. My feelings led me to being a soldier, to fighting to ensure that the French would not trample Europe or invade Britain."

"You weren't alone in that. If Napoleon had invaded, I would have taken up arms, for he brought misery everywhere he went. But we're at peace with France now, Thayne. The battles are over."

"My mother's cause remains." He escaped for the moment by putting more wood on the fire. "No one burns wood in London anymore. I like the way it crackles, and the smell of it." As he replaced the screen, he said, "It reminds me of campfires. Good times and bad."

Light dimmed, and he turned to see she'd extinguished the lamp. It removed her halo, but now she was warmly lit by the flaming fire. She held out a hand, inviting him back. He shouldn't respond, but he turned down the two small lamps burning on the mantelpiece, took that welcoming hand, and sat down again beside her.

"Mention of the army makes me think of my brother Roger," she said. "What would he be now if he'd survived?"

"Marquess of Carsheld?"

She smiled. "True, but what if Jermyn had lived? Would Roger have stayed in the army? If not, what? And what would the army have done to him?"

"The army didn't create my problems."

She leaned toward him, and he took her into his arms. Her head nestled on his shoulder, her pinned-up hair tickling his chin. He remembered it escaping pins in the inn and was tempted to set it free. Too dangerous by far.

"But you were so young," she said. "You're not close to old now."

He blew at that hair. "Hoary with age after

becoming tangled with you."

His joke was rewarded by a chuckle and she turned up to him. "Then you'd better kiss me before you crumble to dust."

They'd known so few kisses and this was a new one. She offered understanding and comfort, but it instantly grew into more. He tried to draw back, but she held on tightly.

"Give up your criminal life, Thayne."

Delilah's kiss? "I can't."

"And I can't bear to think that you might hang. There must be other ways to earn money. Become a Bow Street Runner."

He sipped at her lips, smiling. "No one's tried to cosset me before."

"Cosset?"

"You'd wrap me in flannel and keep me by the hearth if you could."

"You want to do the same to me."

"I admit it, but that's the natural order."

"Not in my heart. I can't bear the thought of you in danger."

She kissed him then with a fear-filled desperation and he couldn't resist it. He tumbled her back to sprawl on the sofa as he consumed her with kisses beyond control. This indeed was truth. There was nothing moderate about his need for this woman, and nothing orderly about her response.

He'd known she could be passionate, but not that she'd discard all sensible restraint and fight any attempt of his to be wise. When he tried again to retreat, she urged him on, hands tight on him, entwined and moving with him, under him. Helping him explore her leg, her skin, her wet inner heat. . . .

Hades!

He dragged himself free and tugged her skirts back down with shaking hands. "We mustn't."

"No." But she said it on a breath, wide eyes on his.

Above everything in the world, he wanted to satisfy her clear desire. But he could offer her nothing, not even that he'd live. He wouldn't leave her ruined and alone.

He tried to move off the sofa, but she held on to his jacket and then coaxed him back down, shifting so they lay in each other's arms, his head on her shoulder, her arm around him. He ached as he knew she did, but to be cosseted in her arms like this was another sort of heaven.

Her gentle perfume spoke of simple days and rural tranquillity, and the fire glowed, occasional flames licking over the logs, giving off that soothing tang. This was a peace such as he'd never known before in his life.

CHAPTER 25

Hermione stroked his hair, her body regretting their good sense, but her mind content, loving having him in her arms like this. In her protection, for this brief moment at least. He was right. She wanted to protect him all her days, but she tried to show him that she understood his choices. "It's noble to care so much for your dear mother's plight."

"Confessional again?" he murmured. "I never loved her, and she never loved me. I was her only child because giving birth was too dramatic and bloody for her. It took months for her to recover in her mind, and she only ever treated me as a child who happened to live in the same house."

Wordless, she kissed his hair.

"I don't remember minding. I had a loving nurse."

All the same, she wondered whether an infant knew when something was so adrift.

"To complete the confession," he said, "I didn't love my father, either. He was more attentive, but his main focus was always my mother and her needs. When I visited before joining my regiment, he apologized for not considering children when he married, but I know he'd have done the same again. She was everything to him. So once I was in the army, I hardly gave them a thought."

"You have nothing to reproach yourself with."

"The Bible commands us to honor our parents."

"Probably because it was written by hoary old men."

She delighted in his chuckle. "Not a chess player, but sharp debater," he said.

"Too sharp to be ladylike."

"A warrior lady."

"Not at all." As was clear by the fact that she'd taken the kris out of her pocket before coming here to read. If he'd been a villain, that could have been a fatal piece of carelessness.

"You said you'd have fought if Napoleon had invaded," he said.

"When it came to it, I'd have probably hidden in a corner, quaking."

"A kiss for courage," he said, turning up his head. She provided it, but lightly.

Anything more would be too dangerous.

"Your turn to confess," he said, settling back. "Do I gather you were stretched to honor your father?"

"Extremely. He did nothing to deserve it, and didn't have your parents' excuse. He avoided us when we were children. By the time we were old enough to be worthy of his interest, we all knew he was lazy and selfish to the bone. Money was always short and he flew into tantrums at talk of any spending on us or the house, but he denied himself nothing. Fine horses and clothes, and fine women in London, I'm sure. Once, when we were in London in the spring, he ate a whole dish of new peas, the first of the season, without thinking anyone else might want some. I didn't love him and I feel no guilt about it."

"I grant you absolution."

"Perhaps the papist confessional has a purpose," she said, looking at the fire, which would soon need another piece of wood. The supply in the box was getting low, but she couldn't ring for a servant to bring more. Perhaps she'd end up cold again, but for now Thayne would keep her warm. "I've never been able to talk this way before. I'm sure Polly feels the same about Father, but she'd be distressed to tears to say it."

"People cling to convention."

"Thinking as they ought," she agreed. "The world would fall into chaos if we didn't, but here I can say I didn't grieve for my older brother's death, either. Jermyn was exactly like my father. Roger was a better brother, but just as selfish. I blame my mother for that. She thought sons so much more important than daughters." She found she wanted to talk about Roger, something else she'd been unable to do honestly. To Polly he had to be a perfect hero in every respect.

"He went into the army because he needed a profession and Napoleon needed to be stopped, but I think the action appealed to him. He loved riding and shooting and any sort of sport. At Harrow, he excelled at cricket, but I doubt he excelled at his studies. I never saw him with a book. He was rarely home once he went to school. We lived on a tight purse, but he had wealthy friends. One was the heir to a dukedom with access to fabulous horses and hunting. Another was an Irish boy and Roger spent a summer there on a horse-breeding estate. There was another duke's son who seemed to be full of fun and many others. When Roger's death was reported in the papers, we received letters from so many people who clearly felt his loss."

"That must have been a comfort."

"Perhaps, but I found it unsettling. The letters were heartfelt, but they were from strangers. One even offered assistance if needed."

"Your father was the Moneyless Marquess."

"You think he was offering *money*? That's even worse."

He shifted again to look at her. "The sin of pride?"

"Dignity," she protested.

"But if the letter was from a friend, the writer was probably as young as your brother. It could have been well-meant."

"I hadn't thought of that. At the time I was in no state to think clearly at all. I was torn apart by Roger being gone, far away and violently." That brought his danger too close. "Can you not give up crime?"

After a moment he said, "Not yet."

That was something. "Soon?" she persisted.

"I don't know, love."

"Love?"

He moved them both to sitting. "I shouldn't have said that."

"But did you mean it? If you loved me . . . No, I won't say it."

"If I loved you, I'd choose the safer ways? Perhaps you're right."

"I don't understand. I don't think you're telling me the whole truth. Are you in debt? Did your father leave you in debt?"

He put fingers over her lips. "I haven't told you the whole truth, and I can't. It's true, however, that my path is dangerous and I can't leave it yet. There's nothing for us until I can."

She wanted to fight his sober words. She wanted to beat against his will until he told her everything, because if she understood the problems, she could solve them — she'd be able to sweep away the danger and have the prize. But some instinct stopped her. Her fighting and beating could shatter everything. "At least promise to be as careful as can be."

"I can do that."

"And promise to come back to me."

He grimaced at such an impossible demand, but said, "If there's any way on earth." He kissed her forehead. "I begin to understand my father, but I must be stronger than he."

She wanted him bound to her needs in the same way. That was probably unworthy, but she wanted it all the same and was desperate enough to say it. "I need you alive and with me, Thayne. A week ago I didn't know it, but I think I've needed you ever since that ball."

He cupped her face with one hand. "And I you. I vow to do my utmost to be safe and to return to you."

His kiss was so gentle it felt almost sacred, and he held her as if she were made of spun glass. She'd not been cherished like this since she'd been a child. She'd never been important to anyone like this, or felt this way about another. It was painful and precious and she ached to find a way to chain him to safety.

He needed something different, however, and she loved him enough to try to give it.

She moved back to smile for him. "Don't think me fragile. I'm not bold or brave, but I believe I'm strong in the mind. I stay on the level. I don't fly high and low. I cope with what happens." *I won't run mad, no matter what happens.*

It worked. She saw his lopsided smile again. "As when a rascal invaded your room."

"Polly would have screamed, then and there, but I didn't."

"For which I burn incense at your altar."

"What I'm trying to tell you is that you don't need to fret about me."

"Can you not fret about me?"

"No, because you're a thief with horrible people wanting to kill you. I'm an ordinary woman living an ordinary life. Why couldn't you be a . . . a shopkeeper?"

His smile broadened to a grin. "What shall we sell? Candles or cups, books or bodkins?"

"Soap, always wrapped in a pretty package."

A log collapsed in the grate, bringing them back to reality. The fire would soon be out. How long had they been here, illicitly alone and intimate, lost in passion, longing, and whimsy?

He stood, straightening his clothing, but then he looked at her. "My Hermione, relaxed in the glow of firelight, disordered and dangerous to all my righteous intentions."

She should have straightened, stood up, and perhaps even protested, but she could only smile back at him, so handsome and strong in the dying light, despite his scruffy trimmings.

He knelt by the sofa to kiss her. "I want to stay here with you more than I've wanted anything in my life."

So tempting to grasp him and hold him. Instead she smiled. "One day you will."

One day, if it was within her power, a

fireside conversation and kisses sweet and spicy would lead in due course to a lawful bed and thence to heaven. But where? In a cottage? In some tenement? Reality crept into the idyll, but she felt sure now that he wasn't a common thief. A good life must be possible.

"You truly must go to London?" she asked.

"Yes."

"Into danger?"

"Perhaps."

"Then go in disguise."

"A wig and fake mustaches?"

"A woman would be better. A long wig and a fake bosom."

"No."

"Infuriating man. I wish I could give you a talisman."

"You already did." He rose and took a bit of dirty white out of his pocket. She recognized the silk rose.

"You kept it," she said, and tears threatened.

"Treasured it. It's sadly battered and grimy, but it's kept me safe."

"Then don't lose it." She reached into a pocket and took out a brass button. "I still have this."

"Polished, even."

"Of course."

"I'd kiss you again if I dared. May that talisman keep you safe. Don't forget that you could be in danger, too. Be as careful as you pray I will be."

He was finding it hard to leave, and she wished he need never do so, but he must. She rose and lit a candle at the dying fire. "How did you get into the house?"

"Through the glass doors into the garden."

"They were unlocked?"

"I had the means to unlock them."

That shook her. Was he a common thief after all? A housebreaker? She'd leave all that for daylight and sanity. "I'll go ahead to be sure the way is clear."

She opened the door and looked out into the dark house. All quiet and clear. She led the way downstairs and to the side door, where he put his boots back on. Again he lingered. Again, despite all good sense, she longed to beg him to stay.

"God go with you," she said.

"And with you. Till we meet again."

"In London?"

"Remember, my enemies won't recognize you, but if they see you with me, you could be in danger. Stay away from me, Hermione. I'll come to you when it's safe." Perhaps he saw her doubts, for he added, "On my honor, I will."

Hermione watched as long as his shadowy form was visible, but in time she had to admit that he was gone. Her beloved was gone.

Her beloved. Her tender emotions grew from the gallant young officer of that ball and seemed able to overwhelm the reality now, but reality lurked like a shadow. She was in danger of falling in love with a man who could offer her nothing but poverty and fear.

And yet, now, at this moment, she was powerless to be sensible.

Her beloved was gone. *Forever,* said the dread in her mind, but "For now," she said out loud to fight the dark. They would meet again and somehow she would find a way for them to be together. She remembered Edgar's money. She hoped it would be a long time before he died, but perhaps if there was a fortune, he'd give her a dowry. It might be enough for a simple, decent life. There had to be a way!

She locked the door and went back upstairs, reliving the encounter. Reliving all their encounters. How extraordinary that they meet again after all these years by happenstance, but somehow she felt it had always been inevitable. Why else had she kept the brass button and even polished it now and then? Why else had she found reasonable offers of marriage lacking?

She returned to the drawing room to make sure the fire was safe and then went to her bedroom, where her nightgown hung before the fire. As it had at the inn. If she'd been in her bedroom earlier, he would have invaded here. Would their encounter have tumbled even further out of control? Propriety and good sense said no, but propriety and good sense seemed to be a small part of her these days and the rest of her ached with *What if?* What if they'd lost all restraint? It would have been glorious. What if he died and they never had? The cold, sensible parts of her mind shouted how wise it had been not to commit herself, and how she mustn't let passion overrule them.

But it's so much more than passion.

She walked past the bed, sliding a hand over the smooth wood of a post, to the window, where she peered out through a gap between the curtains. There were few lit windows at this hour and none not covered by curtains or shutters.

It's love. Even apart. Even if we were apart

forever, love would rule.

He had a room at the Ferry Inn, and she knew where that was, even in the dark, but she didn't know which window and couldn't stay staring at the building forever, as if that would protect him.

She turned away and poured lukewarm water into her china bowl, but as she did so, she offered a simple prayer. "Keep my beloved safe, dear Lord. Bring him back to me."

CHAPTER 26

Mark left Tranmere the next morning by boat for Warrington. At the Nag's Head he commented on the poster about the corpse by the road. No one seemed to have connected it to a man who'd hired a horse there, nor did he hear any suggestion that Seth Boothroyd had been there asking about Nathan. Hermione should be safe — unless Seth was still on his way. Or if Seth was going directly to Riverview House.

Mark climbed into the London coach trying to persuade himself that Solange couldn't possibly have discovered the exact address, but worry was agonizing. He prayed Hermione would set off for London today or tomorrow, because she'd been right, his clever lady. She would be safest there. As the coach rolled out into the London road, he hoped he'd arrive to the news that Solange and Isaac had already been found and jailed, and that Seth Boothroyd was with them.

At the first stage he considered leaving the coach and riding back. He could ride guard on Hermione and her party as they traveled to London. They'd travel slowly, however, with an elderly invalid, and he must make speed.

She should be safe.

"Should be" wasn't good enough, but it had to be.

After a twenty-five-hour journey, he left the coach in London, stiff, tired, but ready to put his plans into action. He went first to Hawkinville's house to report and get the latest news. He'd never visited the Peel Street house, but he knew the way of it. He entered by the back of a house three doors down and passed through the cellars into number 32.

Major George Hawkinville was a tall, lithe man with an appropriately hawkish face and a fierce intelligence. Though not much older than Mark, he'd been awarded a baronetcy for his organizational work during the war.

"Have you breakfasted?" he asked. "No? Then do so as we talk. We had Braydon's report — clever, that — but I need to hear of recent events from you."

Mark was glad enough to settle to excellent food and coffee as he told the tale, or most of it, and then asked for the latest news about Solange.

"Damn all," Hawkinville said. "Your suggestion about chemical suppliers hasn't borne fruit as yet, nor the one about whores. Waite's house is watched, as are the lodgings of the other Crimson Band members, but there's no sign of the errant three. They could be in Timbuktu."

"Solange won't be far from London. She's a city woman and London is her target. Unless Paris has become possible again?"

"The French are too weary for such passions. They'll erupt again, but not soon enough to affect this. We need you to find the damn woman before she does anything."

"Have people been warned about the explosive letters?"

"Key people, yes."

"And the gas?"

"Those notes weren't specific, so we don't know what to warn against. Sidmouth refuses to create panic." The Home Secretary was notoriously both worried about the threat of revolt and determined not to feed the fire. "Our chemists don't believe there's any danger. Coal gas needs to build up to explode. How can it do that when burning in the street? Inside buildings the smell would alarm people before an explosion became possible."

Damnation. Hermione's arguments about why she'd be safe in London had been sound, but he'd rather have the entire Crimson Band behind bars. "So there's not enough to arrest Solange and Isaac, even if I find them."

"We'd jail them anyway. But I can't deploy many resources on the search without more purpose. There are other targets, especially Thistlewood and his gang. Which is why you'll be useful, Faringay. I assume it is Faringay now?"

Mark shrugged. "It seems so."

"I gather Braydon has offered Faringay a temporary home. Useful of you to draw him in."

"None of my doing. He threw himself in. You're making full use of his talents?"

"Of course, though he doesn't have your remarkable inside knowledge."

"Except all that I told him." Curious, Mark asked, "Did you, too, tire of a tranquil life?"

"Never had chance to find out, but I wouldn't mind doing so. This keeps me away from my wife and child too often."

Mark hoped he hid his surprise. Hawkinville, like Braydon, was not obviously domestic. "Congratulations," he said, wondering what sort of woman had caged a hawk.

Hawkinville nodded his thanks. "Will you marry now your hidden life is over? There's inheritance to consider."

"I'll have to think about it. For now, I must be off."

He left then, having avoided telling Hawkinville that Ned Granger was going to live another day. He'd had plenty of time on the journey to assess the risks, and he'd decided that if Solange hadn't been located, he should visit Waite to find out what he knew. Hawkinville might try to stop potential waste of valuable talent. He'd fail, but why invite discord?

He took a hackney to Waite's Bloomsbury town house, unable to ward off thoughts of Hermione's reaction to this. He smiled at how vigorously she'd point out his folly, and took out the scrap of grubby silk. Perhaps he should try to wash it, but he was afraid of its disintegrating.

Everything about her could so easily disintegrate. She thought him a common thief pursued by vengeful victims and demanded that he change. She might feel more kindly if she knew he was working for the government, but she had too much sense to imagine that made him any better a man to love and marry.

When they were together, anything seemed possible, as if they'd fallen into a fairy ring, but reality was harsher. He lived a dangerous life impelled by a cause he couldn't abandon. On the other hand, circumstances seemed likely to compel him to take on his true identity, and if the Crimson Band was destroyed, he might be able to take a less active role.

Unless he was addicted to danger and action, as Braydon seemed to be, and perhaps Hawkinville as well. What sort of life was that to offer any woman?

The hackney halted. He put away the rose, climbed out, and paid the driver. He'd asked to be let down around the corner from Waite's house. He'd normally knock on the front door, but his story required him to be cautious, so he went to the back and entered by the steamy, aromatic kitchen to be stared at by a plump cook, a scrawny footman, and some sort of scullery maid.

"Who are you?" the cook demanded, chopping knife in hand.

"He's been here before," said the footman. "Visiting the master." His narrowed eyes were suspicious, but only in a general way. Mark doubted any of the servants knew Waite was more than a reforming orator.

"I have indeed," Mark said, "and he'll want to see me now."

The footman sniffed. "I'll take you up, then. Come on." No "sir." Not surprising that the footman thought little of him. Nor did it matter. Mark's main concern was that Seth Boothroyd be here, or a new bodyguard of the same type. Waite wasn't a man of violent action, but he was capable of ordering it.

The house seemed as calm and elegant as always, furnished tastefully with fine furniture and ornaments. Mark had never understood how a man who owned and enjoyed such a home could seek a chaos that would destroy it, but there had been wealthy men, scholars, and even aristocrats on the side of revolution in France. It hadn't saved them from a grim end once the mob ruled.

The footman knocked on the door to Waite's study and was told to enter. He did so and announced, "Mr. Granger, sir."

Waite was behind his desk writing a letter, but he jerked to his feet, eyes wide. "Granger?" He was afraid. Solange had told him something. Unfortunate, but that might mean he knew where she was.

"Yes, sir," Mark said soothingly. "Please don't be alarmed, though there are alarming matters."

He slid his eyes toward the footman and after a moment Waite said, "You may go." When the door was shut, Waite demanded, "Where have you been?" He'd recovered some of his patrician manner, but for a moment there he'd feared Mark had come to harm him.

"Here and there," Mark answered, alert for sounds in the house that might indicate trouble. He heard none. All well so far. "May I sit, sir?"

Waite settled back in his big chair. "Yes, yes, of course."

"You ask where I have been," Mark said, sitting in the plain wooden chair that faced the desk. "The answer is, sir, in hiding whilst at the same time on the hunt."

"You speak in riddles. I must tell you, Granger, that my wife believes you the traitor in our midst."

"Believes" implied current communication. There was nothing for it. He'd have to try the bold move he'd devised. "Does she, sir? I regret to tell you that she is the traitor."

"Solange? What madness is this? She is the one most ardent for our ends."

"Precisely, sir. If I may explain."

"Do so, but I fear you're fit for Bedlam."

Many would agree. Mark hoped that Waite would follow his lead on the next, crucial question. "May I ask why Mrs. Waite claims I'm a traitor to the cause?"

"Because she came across you in Warrington, where you should not have been. She wrote to me from there, telling the whole tale."

So that was it. The Crimson Band had a policy of putting as little as possible in writing, but he should have realized that Solange would ignore that. On the other hand, Waite's words might mean that he'd heard nothing from her since.

"She sent Nathan Boothroyd to demand an explanation of you," Waite continued, "and you fled from him. That proved that you were the person who stole some vital papers from her in Ardwick, and therefore the traitor we suspected was among us. I was both shocked and hurt, Granger. Deeply hurt."

Mark simply asked, "What vital papers?"

"You claim innocence of that?"

"I claim *ignorance,* sir, but I'm also puzzled. I thought it our policy to avoid putting anything of importance in writing."

"Yes, yes, but the subject was complex and my wife believed it essential to record it. The papers were stolen from her room. We believed you innocent because you were already on your way to London, but then you were discovered the next day in Warrington."

"Which looked like proof of guilt. I see. Permit me to tell you what really happened, sir. As instructed, I purchased a seat on the night mail from the George and Dragon, but then returned to the King's Head with an idea that Durrant could incorporate into a speech. Passing Mrs. Waite's bedroom, I heard her speak. You'll remember, sir, that the walls and doors were thin."

"Yes, yes, go on."

"She said — your pardon, sir — 'Waite is weak. I'm done with him, but I'll sow discord before I leave.' "

Waite's cheeks flushed with anger. "What? I don't believe you." But was there a hint of doubt?

"I found it hard to believe myself, sir, but the words were clear. A man replied, but in too low a voice for me to catch the words. I thought it was Tregoven." If Mark had to cast lethal suspicion onto anyone, best it be Tregoven.

"Even more unbelievable," Waite said, but he was frowning now.

"It has seemed to me, sir, that Mrs. Waite has become impatient over our lack of progress. She took the failure of the assassination attempt hard, and then the Blanketeers' March failed to reach London, and the Crusade came to nothing. Her enthusiasms have perhaps become a little rash. The exploding letters," he added, and saw it find its mark. "At that moment in the inn I faced a dilemma. I needed to travel to London in case the Crusade bore fruit —"

"Which it did not."

"Indeed, sir, but I didn't know that at the time. I also needed to do something about this new problem."

"Why not come to me?" Waite demanded. It seemed he was swallowing the whole line.

"You don't believe me now, sir. Would you have believed me then? To be honest, I feared deadly reprisals."

Waite didn't respond, but he looked away. He'd never been at ease with the sort of violence Solange took as matter of course.

"By then I'd missed the London mail," Mark continued, "so I decided to linger in Ardwick in hope of learning more. Of learning that your wife was innocent and I had misinterpreted."

"Which I'm sure is the case."

Mark nodded, but went on. "Mrs. Waite planned to take a coach early in the morning, so I stayed the night at another inn, rose early, and found a place from which I could observe. You'll remember that there was much disorder that morning because of the Crusade, so when she chose to travel by way of Warrington, I didn't see that as suspicious. I watched her set out, then hired a horse to ride ahead. Once there, I waited to see if she'd continue to London, in which case I, too, would take a coach for London. I would arrive ahead of her, as I would travel through the night. Then I'd observe her again."

Waite was taking in every word and weighing it. "What we have here is a series of misunderstandings, Granger. When my wife arrived in Warrington and saw you there, where you should not be, she was naturally alarmed. You were supposed to be in London, and her papers had been stolen."

"Or so she said."

"Of course they were! And of course she sent Nathan Boothroyd to discover what you were doing. Whereupon you fled."

"So she said."

"This is insanity!"

Mark played a trump. "Has Nathan confirmed her story?"

Waite stared, and then admitted, "Nathan has disappeared."

"Ah," Mark said, loading it with meaning.

"I will not believe that my wife concocted such a story and then sent Nathan away so he could not correct it. Nathan would come to me."

"If he was able to, sir."

"What are you suggesting now? That he's held prisoner?" After a moment, he shook his head. "No. No. This is all impossible."

"It's alarming, sir, but consider. You only have the letter your wife sent to you as evidence of her story, and here I am, with a different explanation. I'm willing to confront Mrs. Waite with my suspicions."

It was the key play. Mark watched as Waite rose from his desk and went to the window, presenting his back. A longcase clock ticked many seconds before he said, "She is not here."

"I feared as much, sir."

Waite turned back. "Why?"

"I arrived in London and watched for Mrs. Waite to arrive at the Swan with Two Necks. When she did so, I heard her give a direction that was not here, to her home."

"Where did she ask to go?" Waite asked sharply.

"The Cock near Temple Bar, but when I arrived there, she'd already taken another hackney to who knows where. As you can imagine, sir, I was deeply disturbed by this suspicious behavior."

"Yet still you didn't come to me."

"You would have set me to finding her, sir, and I judged it best to do that directly." He lowered his voice. "We can't disregard the possibility of a spy in your household."

"A government spy, *here*?"

"A spy for Mrs. Waite," Mark said gently. "Does she have a maid?"

"Yes," Waite said, pale now. "She doesn't take Jeanne when traveling, but they are close. I shall demand answers."

He walked toward the bellpull, but Mark said, "Not yet, sir. We may wish to keep my part in this secret."

Waite drew back his hand. "I can't believe this. My wife. Her maid. Under my roof." Yet his hand had been shaking. "Have you found her?"

"Alas, no, sir. Not yet, and I'm deeply concerned. What is she planning that she chooses not to share with you?" When Waite didn't answer, Mark prompted, "What of the exploding letters? If she pursues that on her own, it could turn all Britain against our cause."

"We must not quail before the cost."

"Think not of cost but of consequences, sir. As I said, the likely victims will be clerks or servants, perhaps even women. Also,

Isaac let slip a mention of gas."

"That will come to nothing. I've learned that the government received warning. And what other warning, Granger, than the papers my wife had, which you say were never stolen?"

Damnation. He'd asked via Braydon that word be let slip that the government had evidence of a plot to do with gas. That had been to deter Solange from continuing any pursuit of Hermione, but now it undermined his story.

"If you say the papers existed, sir, and have arrived in government hands, then I apologize, but I'm still worried that Mrs. Waite seems to have gone into hiding. Can you guess what she might be doing?"

"I thought we were completely of one mind, but now . . ."

"Might she pursue the gas plan even now?"

"Surely not." But Waite sounded sure of nothing.

Mark risked a direct question. "What is the plan?"

Waite blinked at him. "I'm not sure. She told me something about a great explosion, but I had other things on my mind."

"Does she know the government is aware, sir?"

"Perhaps not. I had word by private means." Waite paced the room, heavy with concern. "To implement any plans without careful preparation would be madness, especially with no uprising to increase the effect. Surely she cares too much for our ultimate triumph to do such a thing."

"We must hope so, sir, but she must be found. Does she have some other place, or a special friend?"

"No, no. Would I not have thought of that?"

"Of course, sir. My apologies."

"Put your mind to this task, Granger. Find her for me. And the Boothroyds."

"Seth, too, has disappeared?" Mark asked.

"He left my house without permission three days ago and I've heard nothing since. The Boothroyds, my wife, Isaac." He collapsed back into his chair and sank his noble head in his hands. "Never was a man so vilely betrayed."

Mark allowed himself an eye roll at that hyperbole, but said, "It is certainly a serious situation, sir."

Waite emerged, surprising Mark with a glint of tears. "My wife is passionate and can act unwisely, but she is a noble creature. Find her, Granger, before she puts herself in mortal danger. I'm sure I can persuade her to be wise."

"I will do my best, sir." Mark rose, pleasantly surprised by the success of the visit.

He'd retained his place in the Crimson Band and shattered the suspicions Solange had created. He'd also strengthened Waite's distrust of his wife, so if Solange turned up repeating her suspicions, she would at least be doubted.

He'd failed in his main purpose, however, because he still had no clue as to where Solange was or what she might be doing. Waite was right about one thing. She wouldn't tear apart what she'd built for any petty reason. She was intent on some cataclysmic enterprise.

"Are any of the others available to assist me?" Mark asked.

"Tregoven and Durrant? They're in London, but they don't know that my wife and Isaac are missing."

"One might," Mark reminded him.

"Tregoven dined here last night!"

"Judas ate at the Last Supper. You may wish to have him watched."

Waite liked the biblical reference that suited his grand view of himself. "I'll set some of the Brotherhood to that. Should Durrant be watched, too?"

"An excellent idea, sir, and Mrs. Waite's maid. When I overheard Mrs. Waite at the King's Head, she said she'd sow seeds of discord. Other than casting suspicion on me, what did she do?"

Wearily Waite said, "She harangued Durrant and Tregoven interminably, insisting one of them stole her papers. Someone took them, Granger, for they ended up in the government's hands."

"There are many working against us, sir."

"I fear I was most impolite to Durrant when he protested to me. Tregoven seemed less upset." He looked at Mark. "He was with my wife? In her room?"

Mark hadn't intended to suggest an illicit relationship, but he said, "He was, sir," in a tone he hoped would spread the rot.

Waite sat straighter. "I will not tolerate betrayal. I shall summon Tregoven here and question him. I will know truth and deception when I'm face-to-face with it."

Mark had to fight a smile at that.

"Will you stay for that?" Waite asked.

"I'd rather pursue my enquiries, sir."

"As you will. Thank you, Granger. This can't have been easy for you."

Mark inclined his head and went toward the door. All in all, very satisfactory.

"Ah . . ."

Mark turned back. "Sir?"

"You must live a charmed life, Granger."

"Why?"

Waite was fiddling with an amber-handled penknife. "In my wife's letter from Warrington, she urged that you be declared a traitor. From what she said, it seemed reasonable."

Mark knew what that meant. "The Brotherhood has been told to watch out for me?"

"Rather more than that, I'm afraid. They've been told to kill you. I'm surprised you've wandered the streets of London for days without injury."

Damnation. His position in the Crimson Band was over after all.

"I will rescind the order immediately, of course," Waite said, "but that may not reach everyone."

"I take comfort that few know me on sight."

"As for that, Tregoven produced a sketch." Waite opened a drawer and took out a print. "Quite a good likeness."

Mark took it. A damnably good likeness of a bristle-chinned man in a low-crowned hat. Apart from the style of hat, it was himself at the moment. "He applied himself to the task with enthusiasm. But then, he would have his reasons."

"Could Tregoven truly be in league with Solange against me and still dine at my table?"

"There is no limit to the depths, sir."

Waite was losing his noble demeanor and looking more a confused old man.

Mark folded the print and put it in his pocket. "I must go, sir. I'll report to you on any progress. Please take care."

"You think *I* am in danger?" Waite tried for disbelief, but fear shivered beneath the question. "I have no one to stand by me. Stay here, Granger. You will be safe here."

Be your new Boothroyd? "I can't search for Mrs. Waite from here, sir."

"You can't search for her when in danger."

"Now I'm warned, I'll assume some disguise."

A wig and mustache, or bosoms? But it was no longer humorous speculation.

Waite unlocked a drawer and took out some banknotes. "Take these to help you get by."

Mark didn't want to take money from a man he meant to destroy, but to refuse would look odd. He put them in his pocket. "Thank you, sir."

"God go with you. Find Solange and Isaac for me. Bring them home." The words were sincere and pathetic.

Mark bowed and returned to the kitchens to leave by the back door. The thin footman still eyed him suspiciously and now Mark wondered whether he was a member of the Brotherhood. Had he already sent word that the traitor had been found? He left the house and walked down the back lane feeling as if he had a bull's-eye painted on his back.

Devil take Solange. Well, he was sure Lucifer would in the end, but not perhaps before she got him killed. He needed a safe haven and a transformation.

CHAPTER 27

He hired a hackney cab at the first stand and traveled in its concealment to Braydon's rooms. He was relieved to be inside.

"A damnable situation," Braydon said when he'd heard the tale, "but insane of you to think of trying to keep up Ned Granger. What disguise will you assume now?"

"It's time for Lord Faringay to return from Mauritius."

"That won't change your appearance sufficiently. What if you come face-to-face with the Frenchwoman, or anyone else from the Crimson Band?"

"I'm hoping they'll remember that Granger was a nobleman's by-blow and come to a desirable conclusion."

"Jupiter! That you're a half brother? Did you have this in mind when you devised your story?"

"I'm not that farsighted. I merely wanted an explanation for my manner. I didn't think I'd be able to hold to a lower style."

"You didn't think ahead to when the masquerade would end? That's not like you."

True enough, Mark thought. Perhaps he'd avoided the subject. The end of the masquerade had always meant returning to Faringay Hall.

"Most of the Brotherhood don't know me," he said briskly. "They'll never imagine an elegant lord is the man in that drawing."

"True, but an elegant lord? I don't remember you ever being a beau."

"Amazing the effect a couple of years in the south Indian Ocean can have on a man. Desperate for civilization, I have returned via Paris, where I embraced good barbering and tailoring, all the latest styles."

Braydon let out a laugh. "I'm to achieve this miracle?"

"If you will, kind sir."

"The barbering will be easy enough and I'll be glad to see the end of your shaggy hair and bristles, but clothes? Clothes take time, especially the finest."

"Time I don't have. Secondhand?"

"A *rag shop*?"

"Don't faint. Then is there anyone of my size who will sacrifice in the cause?"

"Better," Braydon said. "Let me consider.

As I do . . . Johns!"

An impeccably neat, gray-haired valet entered. "Yes, sir?"

"You'll be pleased to know that this disreputable gentleman is no more. He needs a bath, a shave, and a short but stylish haircut to begin the transformation into Viscount Faringay."

The valet accepted this with enthusiasm. "Yes, sir."

"I assume you have answers to my other quibbles," Braydon said to Mark.

"I hope so."

"Then I'll quibble later."

Mark had no objection to baths, but wasn't sure how he felt about short hair. As Braydon said, he'd never been interested in his appearance, and in the army he'd done without the fuss of shaving and barbering as much as possible.

Braydon's bath was large and the filling of it efficient, so he was soon lounging in it, going over his plan, seeking weaknesses. There were dangers, to be sure, but he'd no mind to creep about London dressed as a beggar, never mind as a brawny woman.

The valet shaved him and then snipped away at his hair with scissors.

"Do you cut Braydon's hair?" Mark asked, hiding nervousness.

"Definitely not, my lord, but I am quite competent. I assumed you would not want a gossipy barber to engage in the primary transformation."

"True enough."

There was a knock on the door and the valet went to it. After a murmured conversation, he returned with a small bottle.

"What's that?" Mark asked.

"Venables Hair Tonic, sir. It can change the color somewhat."

"My hair is black," Mark said warily. "What can you change about that?"

"Not quite black, my lord. This will enrich it."

Mark surrendered. When the valet was satisfied with the haircut, he massaged the contents of the bottle into it. "Before coming to work for Mr. Braydon, I was employed by a gentleman who favored Venables. He was not so dark as you, but the tonic gave an interesting hue to his rather undistinguished hair. It did no harm, I assure you."

"As long as you don't turn me orange."

The valet gave a polite chuckle and rinsed. "If you will rise from the bath, my lord?"

Mark did so and was rinsed again, then swathed in an enormous towel. He'd have a few of those for his own, he decided. A glance at the mirror showed his hair to be alarmingly short but still normally dark. Once he was dry, he put on one of Braydon's banyans — an excellent garment of soft brown wool lined with silk. He might get a taste for some aspects of dandyism. The valet steered him to the chair in front of the dressing table and combed his short hair this way and that.

"To have it dry just so, sir. It is the fashion. Now, if you will oblige, your nails?"

Mark surrendered to having his nails and cuticles pared and lotion applied.

When Braydon came in, Mark said, "I've been right all along. Dandyism is a dead bore."

"It might yet keep you alive. I've thought of the very person. Right build and just back from Paris with a new wardrobe. I need to go in person to persuade him to surrender some to the cause."

"I can't imagine why he should."

"He's a kindhearted fellow. Your plight, returned from pagan lands in such a state, will touch him."

"And my story of having acquired my clothing myself in Paris?"

"I'll persuade him to support that. Even mention encountering you there if that seems necessary."

"You must be very persuasive."

"He yearns for my approval."

"Don't tell me — you're the new Brummell."

"Gads, no. That would require hobnobbing with the Regent. Adieu."

"Adieu," said Mark with a laugh as the door closed. "How did you come to be employed by Braydon, Johns?"

"He employed a gentleman in the army, my lord, where I assume there were not quite such demands. That individual wished to return to his home area, so Mr. Braydon persuaded me to take his place."

"Persuaded. Was your previous employer much put out?"

"I believe there were words, my lord, but I am not a slave and the change suited me. Mr. Braydon wears his clothing in a most exemplary manner and he does not seek a rural life."

"You prefer Town?" Mark asked.

"Infinitely."

"I'll need a valet. Can you find me one who comes close to your excellence?"

"Probably not, my lord, but I will do my best."

"One who won't object to rural life. I have an estate to take care of."

"Very well, my lord." Mark noted the

silent commiseration with amusement. The valet and Braydon were lucky to have found each other. There wouldn't be many rich dandies without estates of any kind.

He had an estate, but he needn't spend much time there. Faringay Hall had survived without his presence. After his father's death and then his disastrous visit he'd never returned, but he'd appointed good people to manage the place and correct the decades of neglect. There was no need to return there at all. He could serve his country from bachelor rooms such as this.

If he didn't love and desire Hermione Merryhew.

They could be a Town couple, but he knew that wouldn't work over time. There would be children, and children should be raised in the countryside. As well, he suspected that was the life she'd prefer. She certainly wouldn't want him to continue his dangerous work, but could he abandon it when the threat continued?

What would she think of Viscount Faringay? He assessed his appearance in the mirror, rubbing a hand over his remarkably smooth chin. It would take at least two skilled barberings a day to keep it that way, but it did alter his appearance, especially with his short red-tinged hair. It was even curling a bit as it dried.

A handsomer fellow than poor old Ned, but Ned was the man she knew.

He glanced to where Johns was sweeping up a remarkable amount of hair, and thought of some men he knew who even at his age bemoaned the way their hair was abandoning them and called for the return of wigs. A fashion for wigs would certainly help with disguises.

The valet persuaded Mark into the parlor and provided coffee and the day's newspaper before returning to clear up the bath. The newspaper made interesting reading, for he'd been out of touch with events for a while.

His eye was caught by an item on lunatic asylums. If not for his father's care and sacrifice, his mother could have been in one. Perhaps he should take an interest in such places. A peer of the realm was supposed to have his benevolent interests. He'd definitely do what he could for wounded soldiers. The neglect of their needs was scandalous. Perhaps he'd be able to employ some, or even give them small pieces of land on his estates.

Lord, was he turning into a Spencean? Why not? The man had had some sound ideas among the nonsense.

Then he noticed something. The conscientious Chester coroner was making enquiries in London! A small notice sought assistance in identifying the body of a man found foully murdered, a man wearing clothing purchased in London. The description was clearly of Nathan Boothroyd.

When Braydon returned, Mark showed him the item. "I suppose the man wrote to you for information."

"He did. Of course I had nothing to add, but it gave me the opportunity to drop in my grandmother's name again."

"And put you above suspicion. All the same, it's a pity we couldn't have left him naked."

"Would have undermined the footpad thievery somewhat. The clothing could have led to identification, which could have been useful, but it turns out to have been purchased secondhand. The jacket had been skillfully altered, but who's likely to find one particular tailor in London?"

"Useful?" Mark asked.

"We need to flush out Seth Boothroyd. Hence the item in the paper. We've had no luck with the woman or the chemist, but if Seth goes north to identify his brother's body, we'll have him."

Mark rose to his feet. "You and Hawkinville *sent* him north?"

Braydon raised a hand. "Calmly, calmly. If Seth Boothroyd goes to Chester, he'll be arrested. He'll be no danger to your lady."

"No? If he goes to Solange with the news, she might suspect a trap. She'll certainly stoke Seth's fury. Toward whom? Me, but also Hermione. Remember, Solange might know Hermione's precise location."

"And you have left guard duty," Braydon said, inhaling. "We'll send someone posthaste."

"Fortunately that's not necessary," Mark said, not one whit less angry. "Unless anything's gone seriously amiss, Lady Hermione is on her way to London."

"To *London*?"

"Where, she explained to me, she'll be safer than anywhere else."

"She's deranged!"

"As it happens, she's not." Mark laid out Hermione's arguments.

"She's right," Braydon said, but shook his head. "I apologize for the lack of foresight. We couldn't let the opportunity go, but we should have taken additional steps to make sure Lady Hermione came to no harm."

"It's the government and military way, isn't it? Always the broader picture with no consideration for individuals trampled underfoot."

"Would you let the revolutionaries have their way in order to keep Lady Hermione safe?"

"Yes. No . . . Devil take it! I pray God it never come to that."

"Amen. The main thing is to find Solange Waite and her chemist and make an end of her." Braydon broke off as his footman entered with a small trunk. He dismissed him and opened it to extract two complete outfits. "I could have persuaded Troughton to part with more, but these are the only two he hasn't already worn."

"Good God."

"Don't tremble on the brink."

The two of them had trembled on the brink of an argument and even a fracture, and though Mark still simmered with fury at the careless risk, continuing it would serve no purpose. He accepted the lighter tone, but he'd remember from now on that his purposes and the government's might not always be in accord.

"That jacket is pea green," he objected.

"Not quite, and it's the latest thing. Not, I grant, what I would have chosen with your coloring, but a vast change from Granger. Short, your hair seems a different color."

"Venables Tonic." Mark went to a mirror to inspect it. "Less ebony, more dark mahogany."

"A nice touch. I'll congratulate Johns. And you're ready in good time. I dropped by Hawkinville's and there's been an exploding letter."

That turned sharply. "Where?"

"The Home Office."

"Addressed to Lord Sidmouth?"

"No, to a subdepartment to do with criminal transportation. It came into the hands of a minor clerk, too lowly to have been warned."

"Damned devious Solange! Was he hurt?"

"No, thank God. It was damp, so he put it aside to dry. A few hours later there was a popping noise and it burned up, leaving a scar on his desk. People are alarmed, but if that's the worst of it . . ."

"It was a test, and I hope it was a disappointing one." Mark considered it. "But not without purpose. Solange will need to know the results. There'll be a Brotherhood member in that subdepartment."

"So there will."

Mark sat and wrote a letter to Hawkinville, and Braydon sent his footman to deliver it. "See how you're needed. That hadn't leapt to my mind."

"Hawkinville may have realized, but best to be sure. If she's testing the explosives and our reactions, she's nearly ready to act."

"How do we find her?" Braydon asked. "Hawkinville's people have made enquiries at every place favored by the French, especially those with any taint of revolution."

"For God's sake, she'd never go there. We're more likely to find her knitting mittens for the poor in a Methodist church society."

"Knitting?"

"Don't leap at that. It was only an indication. By inclination she's more likely to be honing blades and checking pistols."

"She goes armed?"

Mark reined in his frustration. Even in the throes of war he'd been able to take a cool eye to pressing problems, but it was eluding him now. Crisis was imminent, but it was the danger to Hermione that had his nerves on edge — that and an awareness of how little Braydon and the others understood about Solange. If he'd come to London sooner . . .

There was no point to what-ifs.

"She probably does carry weapons," he said, "but I was sketching her personality. She's determined, ruthless, clever, and well able to present any appearance to the world in pursuit of her aim, including dull and respectable. However she appears now, it will have no connection to her true nature."

"No idea what disguise she might have assumed?"

"It could be anything, including male."

"The searchers are alert for a woman with a French accent. Will she be able to disguise her speech?"

Mark considered. "I don't think so. Good work. There can't be that many French people here, and French accents are generally noted, with suspicion."

"It can't be long, then, and you need to be able to move around London. Let's complete your transformation. Into your bedroom."

"My bedroom?"

"Where else is Lord Faringay to stay? You have a town house?"

"I do, as it happens, but it's been leased for years. Thank you."

"Reparation, perhaps, and gratitude for enlivening my life."

It was a peace offering and Mark accepted it with a nod.

"Johns!" Braydon called. "We are to dress Viscount Faringay."

Soon Mark was in fawn pantaloons, a

fawn and cream striped waistcoat, and the green coat, which was a very snug fit as well as being puffed up at the shoulders and pinched in at the waist.

"What happened to Brummell's style of black, black, black, and perfectly white linen?"

"Man craves variety."

"You'd never wear this."

"I don't have to deceive the eye. Sober colors and style would be too close to Granger."

Mark rolled his confined shoulders. "I'd rather be back in the Crimson Band."

"You've become too accustomed to that low milieu. It was never your destiny."

"Poor Ned. It's as if I'm killing him off."

"Requiescat in pace."

"Do I truly have to wear a starched shirt collar that comes up to my ears?"

"Yes, because Granger never would. Johns, a neckcloth."

This was also starched, but less rigorously, and cream rather than white. It was soon arranged in a crisp set of folds and secured with a green jade pin. Mark had to admit that the frame of white collar and cream neckcloth altered the look of his smoothly barbered face even more.

He wondered again what Hermione would

think of this new man. She should approve, but what did a person fall in love with? Appearance, character, or something less tangible? What part of her did he adore?

All of her.

"You see a problem?" Braydon asked.

Mark snapped out of daydreams. "No. Where are my boots?"

"Those boots would destroy your transformation. They've been discarded along with the rest of your rags."

"I go about in stockinged feet?"

"My footwear, alas, is the same size as yours. Hessians, Johns."

The valet presented a pair of glossy black boots, complete with golden tassel at the front. They did indeed fit, but in the slightly uncomfortable way of another man's footwear.

"I'll ruin these for you," Mark said.

"They're my third-best pair. I'll survive."

"You have *three* pairs of Hessians?"

"Don't be provincial. The hat, Johns. My fourth best, note."

The high beaver hat also fit, but a pair of Braydon's tan gloves was too tight.

"We'll have to buy you some ready-made," Braydon said, circling Mark. "Johns, you have Lord Faringay's size?"

"Yes, sir."

"Off to purchase them, then."

The valet went, and Mark considered himself again in the mirror. "Even members of the Crimson Band wouldn't easily see Ned Granger in this, so some random member of the Brotherhood with Tregoven's picture in his pocket won't even consider me."

"Good. We can get to work."

Mark turned away from his reflection. "Tempting though it is, there's no point to my prowling the streets. Isaac prefers to stay indoors as long as he has peace to think and his chemical toys to play with, and Solange won't want to show herself, no matter how she's disguised. She'll also need to keep Isaac's mind on her purpose and make sure he doesn't blow up their lodging in an experiment."

"What, then?"

"We find Solange's contact in that department of the Home Office."

The valet returned with a pair of ready-made leather gloves, though it clearly pained him to offer such inferior items.

Mark thanked him and put them on. "Excellent. Viscount Faringay is about to visit his old military acquaintance Sir George Hawkinville. All I need is my money."

He looked around for his clothing, but then remembered it had been discarded. Foolish to pine for Ned and comfort. The banknotes and coins had been preserved and were being offered by the valet on a silver tray.

Mark was in the carriage with Braydon on his way to Peel Street when he remembered the silk rose. He thought of turning back for it, but it would still be there when he returned. He had urgent business, and in truth he wouldn't like to have to explain his devotion to a frayed, silken scrap from his past.

Solange read the report of the explosion. *Satisfactory.* She'd told Isaac not to create a grand effect this time, because she didn't want to alarm the government too much at this point. He'd accepted that with surprising indifference, and also the limits she'd put on his experiments. His mind was clearly on their grand plan, which was as well. She had no intention of disturbing the residents of Great Peter Street. Yet.

Here she was Mrs. Truman, a sad case. She was a widow who'd come to London from Essex to seek help for a painful disease of the mouth that meant she could only mumble. Thus, so easily, her accent disappeared. She was further burdened by a simple son. The curious neighbors had easily believed that, for Isaac was presently content to lurk indoors with his gin, his favorite foods, and some books. He'd probably want a whore soon, but that should present no difficulty.

She acquired Isaac's necessities with the assistance of the Sisterhood. There weren't many female members of the Three-Banded Brotherhood, and most were complaisant wives, but over time she'd identified some who were true believers and formed them into a secret society of her own. Women embraced revolution less readily than men, but when they did, they were wholehearted. No wonder, given the cruel way the unreformed world treated them. Her revolution offered them true equality, so she could trust the members of the Sisterhood more than any man.

One, Betty Logan, was acting as her maidservant, going out to the shops and gossiping with neighbors, collecting news and reinforcing Mrs. Truman's sad story. Two others, Sarah Lawrey and Maria Hadstock, acted the part of friends. They visited, bringing along anything unusual that Isaac wanted. Maria also served as intermediary with Jeanne back in Waite's house.

Maria had brought the news that Granger had visited Waite and left alive. More signs of Waite's weak folly. Hadn't she sent proof that Granger was the spy in their midst and knew too much? Hadn't she suggested the picture, and that he should be killed?

She paced the room furiously, skirts swishing against the furniture in this confined, shabby room. She would not have chosen to rent this small house if not for its particular advantages. She'd had this plan in mind for some time, waiting for a property like this to become available. It had, not long before she'd had to go north for the Ardwick meeting, and so it had been ready for her on her return.

Granger had outwitted her in the most unbearable way, and probably killed Nathan Boothroyd. However, his theft of the papers had spurred her to this, which was coming to fruition at just the right moment. She would be victorious, but she wouldn't thank him. When she'd heard he'd visited Waite, she'd sent Seth Boothroyd to his lodgings to kill him, but he was too cunning to be there.

How had he escaped the London Brotherhood?

Waite would have warned him now, so he'd be in hiding, in fear for his life. The satisfaction of that would have to do for now. He could do nothing to thwart the plan. No one could. And then she'd arrange the death he deserved.

CHAPTER 28

Hermione arrived in London after a journey that had been both better and worse than expected.

On the day after she'd parted from Thayne, a handsome traveling coach had arrived at Riverview House as ordered, drawn by two pairs of horses, each with a postilion. It had carried a clerk bearing the money, and an armed man to escort the clerk.

Hermione had had a few hours' warning and so everything had been ready. A trunk had been packed for Edgar along with blankets, pillows, and nostrums to go with him in the coach. Hermione's valise and the luggage of the servants had joined the trunk in the boot and they'd all settled into the smart and well-upholstered vehicle with a hamper of food and drink for the journey.

Nolly Forshaw had always seemed levelheaded, but she'd perched on the edge of her seat vibrating with excitement as they left. She'd remained excited during the journey, for she'd never gone farther from home than Liverpool, but she'd proved practical and useful at the same time.

Peter was stoically anxious. He'd visited London, but only once, in service to another gentleman, and he emanated forebodings about Edgar. Hermione could only hope his instincts were awry.

She'd visited London three times, but always with her father and restricted to the fashionable West End, which seemed unlikely to house Dr. Grammaticus or the Curious Creatures. Where were they to stay, and how would they search for the cure? She had put that aside to be dealt with when they arrived, just as she'd tried not to think of Thayne and any danger he might be facing. She managed that during the day, but fears disturbed her nights.

At least the weather had been pleasant and Edgar had enjoyed the varied countryside and places they'd passed as well as marveling at the excellent condition of the toll roads. Their slow speed seemed astonishingly fast to him. All the same, the journey had proved a strain on him and they'd had to increase the opium for the pain in his joints.

In the afternoon of the second day he'd begun a fever. Hermione had been alarmed by his heat and shivering and ordered a stop at the first inn they came to. Then she'd had to plead with the innkeeper to let them stay. She'd managed to persuade the woman that it was a tertian ague and not infectious, but as the fever continued through the night, she'd been terrified that the old man would die.

"Don't fret so, milady," Peter had said. "He has these fevers now and then and the bark deals with them. I have some here."

It had helped, but if she'd realized how frightening the fevers could be, she'd never have supported this journey.

By morning Edgar's fever was down, but he ate little breakfast and seemed weaker as he was carried out to the carriage for the third day's journey. Hermione had chosen a slow pace thus far, allowing for frequent rests, but now she ordered the postilions to greatest speed. Once they were in London, Edgar could start the antimony again and there would be excellent doctors.

It was evening by the time they left open countryside behind and drove though the market gardens that provided food for the city.

"Where are we staying?" Edgar asked weakly.

"I told the postilions to stop at the first good-quality inn."

Edgar shook his head. "Peter, call out to them to take us to the Cross Keys Inn, near Cheapside."

That would be some distance, but Hermione didn't want to distress the old man more than she must.

Peter opened the window and called the instruction.

"Why the Cross Keys, Edgar?" Hermione asked.

"Stayed there when I came to London back in 1770, ready to make my fortune."

Nearly fifty years ago! As they traveled into the City of London, an area she didn't know, Hermione prayed the inn was still there and still respectable. Streets became narrow, but many were lit by gas. Edgar revived enough to marvel at that and at the brilliant shop windows, full of tempting items. They had ample time to study the scene. The press of vehicles and pedestrians kept them to a snail's pace.

Edgar said, "Last time I was here, people kept to their homes after dark, or went about in groups, well armed. What a sight. What a sight."

It was, but Hermione exhaled with relief when they turned into the innyard at the Cross Keys. It was respectable, but busier than she liked. Coaches of all sorts were coming and going and messengers dashed in and out with letters and packages, even at this late hour. It might have suited a young, healthy adventurer, but it was no place for an old, sick one. Tomorrow she'd find somewhere quieter, but it would have to do for now.

Edgar looked gray and haggard enough to be a corpse and again she had to persuade an innkeeper that he didn't carry a pestilence. She wielded her title ruthlessly, and the grand manner she could assume when she wished. Eventually they had a fine suite of upstairs rooms with two bedrooms and a parlor between. Fires were already lit there and were quickly built up by willing servants. The beds seemed clean and free of damp.

As soon as Edgar was settled in his bed, Hermione said, "You must start Dr. Onslow's medicine again."

"Left it in Tranmere," he muttered, clutching the covers to his chest.

"*What?* Why did you do that? We'll have to find a doctor here."

"James's powder. Can buy it anywhere,

but we don't need it."

"Yes, we do. *Please,* Edgar. How else are you to get about and enjoy London?"

"Brought my antimony cup."

"Your what?"

"Common enough with travelers. Show her, Peter."

The servant brought over a small, square box and opened it to take out a metal cup.

"Antimony and tin," Edgar said. "Steep wine in it for a few hours and drink. Most travelers have one. Good for all kinds of tropical ailments. Probably kept me alive."

"Then why were you taking Dr. Onslow's James's powder?"

"Seemed you'd prefer it that way."

"Oh, Edgar. I only want you to be as well as possible so that when we find Dr. Grammaticus, he can cure you."

"Mare's nest. But I'll take the antimony and the opium. I do want to see some sights now I'm here."

Peter poured wine into the cup and put it aside.

"What would you like to eat?" Hermione asked. "I'm sure now we're in London, you can have anything."

"I'm not hungry. My bones are torture and I have a headache. Give me some laudanum and let me sleep."

There was no arguing with him in this mood. Hermione nodded to Peter and went into the parlor. Nolly was in Hermione's bedroom putting away their clothes, so for the moment she was alone with her anxieties, fears, and doubts. Edgar was worse, the inn was too noisy, and she hadn't been prepared for the bedlam all around her here. She remembered the mob. The London mob was notoriously violent and could form in an instant over nothing.

She sat by the fire rubbing her chilled hands.

Peter soon came into the parlor. "He's settled, milady. I'll give him the antimony when he wakes."

"I hope that form of antimony will help."

"I'm sure it will, milady. He told me that he started taking it onboard ship as soon as he realized he was ill, and he took it for weeks after he landed. But it's never cured him. He took Dr. James's powder in the hope that it'd do better, but it was the same. Some improvement at cost of great discomfort, but no true progress. And the opium, it just eases him." There was criticism behind the words. Peter was fond of the irascible old man and he'd not liked the hardships of the journey.

"He wanted to come," Hermione pointed

out, "and once he's stronger, he'll enjoy seeing London."

"As you say, milady." Peter returned to his charge, leaving Hermione even more dismayed. If only she had someone to advise her. She doubted Edgar knew any more about today's London than she did and he was in no state to advise her on anything at the moment. She sat up straighter. She'd have to cope alone. Tomorrow she'd find a quieter inn, and set about finding Dr. Grammaticus. She knew that lawyers congregated around the Inns of Court and merchants around the Bank of England. Did doctors have their own area? How could she find out?

A tap on the door brought the innkeeper. "I beg your pardon, milady, but what are we to do with your coach?"

"Do?" Hermione asked.

"Do you wish us to house it for you, or is it to be sent to some establishment?"

Another decision seemed too much, but she had no choice. "Yes, of course I wish you to house it," she said with a grand air. "I suspect we will sell it shortly."

He bowed. "Very well, milady."

How on earth did one sell a coach? She knew gentlemen bought and sold horses at Tattersall's, but not how and when, and did

Tatt's also deal with vehicles? How much did it cost per day to house a large coach? She was going to have to broach the subject of finances as soon as Edgar improved. She'd constantly put off asking how much money he had, but if they couldn't pay their bills here, they could be dragged off to debtors' prison. She sat down on a hard sofa and shocked herself by crying. The trickling tears came from weariness as much as worry, but she hated feeling so weak.

Nolly came in and clucked her tongue. "Tired out, that's what you are, milady. You need some food and a good cup of tea." She whisked off, not seeming intimidated by bustling London and a grand inn. Hermione started to laugh, and it bubbled away her doldrums.

Nolly was soon back with an inn servant bearing supper dishes, and another carrying the tea tray. She supervised the spread of food on the table as if born to command, with much play of "her ladyship."

There was plenty of food, but only one setting. "Bring another setting," Hermione told one inn servant. "My maid eats with me."

Nolly almost protested, but kept it back until the inn servants had left. "That in't right, milady."

"It is if I request it, and I need company."

The maid bobbed a curtsy, and said, "Very well, milady," but she still seemed dubious.

Hermione had become fond of Nolly on the journey. She was a cheerful soul with excellent good sense. She'd coped with every necessity and clearly relished new experiences. She was rather plain, with a sallow complexion, a snub nose, and mousy hair, but a good companion.

Hermione remembered Peter and went into Edgar's room to tell him to order whatever he wanted; then she returned to sit on one side of the table and waved Nolly to the other. The inn servant returned to set the second place, his face rather pinched. Of course, Nolly's clothing marked her as a lowly servant, but it was no business of his how Hermione chose to eat. Once he'd left, Hermione served herself from a dish of pork cutlets and another of cabbage and potatoes. She urged Nolly to do the same.

Pouring tea for them both, she asked, "What do you think of London so far, Nolly?"

"It's very big, isn't it, milady? A person could get lost here right easily."

"They could, so please don't wander."

"But you'll be wanting me to run errands and such." Clearly this was already a worry for the maid.

"No, I won't," Hermione assured her. "I'll use an inn servant. I will want you to accompany me, but then we can get lost together." Seeing that her joke had alarmed, she added, "My first purchase will be a guidebook, and we'll take hackney carriages if we go any distance."

"If you say so, milady," Nolly said, but she was picking at her food.

"Eat up. We'll need our strength."

Nolly did settle to eating, with increasing relish, and then drank two cups of tea.

"My, that's a grand brew, milady." She drank some more and then asked, "Begging your pardon, milady, but you seem out of sorts. Has something gone amiss?"

When Hermione thought of her recent life, she could laugh, but she said, "Nothing in particular, Nolly, but I worry that even if we find Dr. Grammaticus, his cure won't work. Then I'll put Mr. Peake through more suffering for no purpose."

"Doctors do like to dose a person, don't they?" Nolly said. " 'Cause that's how they get their fee."

"How true. My father suffered that way. I doubt any of the potions did him any good."

" 'Appen things'd be better if doctors were only paid for stuff what worked."

Hermione stared. "That's very true. We'd never achieve it, though."

"It'd be a right revolution, wouldn't it?" Nolly said with a chuckle. "Never you mind, milady. You'll find this doctor, and he'll have a true cure."

"I do hope so. And in the meantime we'll explore London. Have some of this pear tart."

Nolly took a big slice and then poured cream from the jug onto it. "This cream's a bit thin."

"City cows rarely see grass."

"Well, I never!" Nolly tucked in all the same.

Hermione ate some, but her own words unsettled her. Wealthy Londoners ate wholesome food brought in from the countryside, but the poor must often make do with paltry stuff, or even no food at all. The London rich spent thousands on gewgaws while the poor scraped for pennies. Bread was their staple food, but the Corn Laws were keeping the price of wheat high in order to support the living of people in the countryside.

No wonder London smoldered with resentments and the poor en masse so easily formed a violent mob. When she remembered how a minor event had caused such chaos in Ardwick, she shuddered at what might happen here. The Ardwick event had been called the Spencean Crusade. The man in the inn had been stirring trouble with talk of Magna Carta and crusades. His waistcoat had been striped in black, red, and green.

The colors of Thayne's neckcloth.

No, she would never think Thayne a revolutionary. Thief, sadly yes, but nothing worse. Where was he now? *How* was he? He must be safe or surely she would sense something amiss.

If all had gone to plan, he was here in London. So tempting to seek him out. He'd warned her not to, but the address on that letter was clear in her mind. Sir George Hawkinville, 32, Peel Street. That was in the West End of London, but only a few miles away.

Sir George. A knight or a baronet at a fashionable address. It was odd, but for all she knew, there could be a gang of gentleman thieves. She'd read scandals of criminals in high places. Whoever Sir George was, she could write to Thayne care of that address in order to tell him she was safe and had arrived in London. She'd treasure such a message from him.

He'd been serious about her not trying to meet him here, however, and she couldn't be sure Sir George was a person to be trusted. She'd only just arrived in London. In a day or two perhaps everything would be clearer. She drank the rest of her tea, concentrating on Edgar.

As soon as they'd begun to plan this journey, she'd glimpsed the vigorous man who'd traveled the world and survived adventures. Even unwell, when they'd entered the noisy bustle of London, he'd sparked again. She touched the kris in her pocket. She didn't expect to have to use it, but it had become a talisman. It would guide her safely to the cure.

She touched the brass button that lay beside the hilt. Thayne *had* arrived in London and he *was* safe. Perhaps believing that would make it so.

CHAPTER 29

The next day Hermione found Edgar improved, so she felt able to set off with Nolly to find a bookshop. A nearby one provided an excellent guide to London, and she also purchased two newspapers. Ones printed that very day. What a luxury!

She couldn't help looking for Thayne in each passing man, but she also kept alert for the brute's brother. He'd never seen her, but if she saw him, she'd have a valid excuse to use Sir George Hawkinville's address. Alas, she saw no one with even the slightest resemblance.

When they returned to the inn, she described their little outing to Edgar, who was drinking some spiced ale that the innkeeper had recommended. He seemed to be enjoying it, which was a good sign. He enjoyed her account, too, and later, a spicy stew. She read one of the newspapers aloud as he ate, relating matters of national interest.

In a few minutes he growled, "Duties on rice, naval stores, and pursers. Twaddle. Isn't there anything *interesting* going on?"

"Lunatic asylums?"

"No."

"Window tax?"

"Rubbish."

She reminded herself that he still could be in pain and looked ahead. "An elephant is dead in France."

"What? Why?"

"It doesn't say. It was forty years old."

"No age for an elephant. Poor thing."

She skipped over the list of performances at theaters, as he wasn't well enough to attend, and spotted a long piece about American shipping and trade. Edgar seemed interested in that, but eventually he dozed off.

She took the papers with her into the parlor and ate lunch there with Nolly. Afterward, she set to searching the paper for advertisements or items to do with medicine. It would be miraculous to find mention of Dr. Grammaticus, but perhaps there were associations of physicians. She also looked for mention of the Curious Creatures. They might know Grammaticus's whereabouts. There were many nostrums on offer: Ching's Worm Lozenges, Dr. Fothergill's Nervous Drops, Nelson's Mixture for Diseases of the Lungs. Nothing about Dr. Grammaticus's cure for the Black Disease.

As she continued to scan down the column, her eye was caught by Dr. James's powder. It was among a long list of products available from F. Newbery and Sons, who warned the public to be wary of imitation products. Lawrence's Powder. Dr. Steer's Convulsion Oil. What on earth was Cephalic Snuff?

Never mind that — Newbery and Sons sounded just the place to find Dr. Grammaticus's cure. It was located to the east side of St. Paul's, which wasn't far away. She summoned Nolly and they set off to walk the few streets. The tall brick building must be the warehouse, but the public could enter only a small shop. The glass-fronted shelves were full of bottles and boxes and the counter spread with more of the same, some open. They must provide the odd mix of smells. A gray-haired clerk stood eager to assist.

Hermione went straight to the point. "Do you carry Dr. Grammaticus's cure?"

The man blinked. "I don't recall it,

ma'am. If you will allow me a moment?"

He went to consult a thick ledger, but Hermione was prepared for the result. He returned to say that they didn't. "I must admit, ma'am, that I've never heard of it. What ailment does it assist? Perhaps we have something else."

"It's for kala-azar, a tropical disease." From the look on his face she feared the man would be offering her a cure for insanity, so she came up with an explanation. "A friend living in India has written to ask me to procure Dr. Grammaticus's cure for her. Can you suggest where I might find it?"

His nose went up. "If Newbery's doesn't carry it, ma'am, I doubt any other establishment will."

Hermione was very tempted to wield her title, which would bring down those hairy nostrils. Instead she spoke mildly. "Pray, sir, do you know an association called the Curious Creatures?"

She expected another flat denial, but the man responded with a smirk. "Is *that* where you heard of the so-called cure, ma'am? Just the sort to rattle on about nonsense."

Irritation building, Hermione said, "You may be correct, but where will I find out more about them?"

"You will be better advised to avoid them,

ma'am." Under her stare, he wilted. "I believe they meet at the Green Man in New Bond Street."

"Thank you."

As Hermione left, he called after her, "There'll be nothing to anything coming from there, ma'am — you mark my words!"

"Infuriating man!" Hermione exploded once they were outside again.

"They do sound an odd lot, milady."

"Don't be impertinent!" Hermione immediately apologized. "Please, continue to question my actions, Nolly. I truly don't know what I'm doing."

"You're doing fine, milady. You've learned a lot in one day."

Hermione smiled. "I have, haven't I? And New Bond Street is in the fashionable part of Town. We'll need a hackney to go there, but I'm familiar with the area. We'll go there now."

"Are you sure, milady?"

Nolly's nervous question made her hesitate. She'd never taken a hackney carriage without a gentleman as escort. But if she stuck to that, she'd go nowhere. "A hackney is perfectly safe," she said, "and New Bond Street is a safe part of Town."

It took some time to cover the distance, but the journey took them through interesting older parts of London, and then into Mayfair. Nolly was agog, particularly at the way streets of buildings went on and on and on in all directions.

When they climbed down, Hermione paid the fare but looked dubiously at the Green Man. It seemed little more than a tavern, but the area was as respectable as she'd thought. Just up the street she saw the Blenheim Hotel, which she and Polly had visited once with their mother to take tea with an old friend.

Surely it was safe, but there was one hazard she'd not foreseen. It was gone midday and the tonnish sort were out and about. She might encounter someone she knew and she wasn't dressed for fashionable society. They'd think the Poor Merryhews had fallen into even deeper poverty. She hurried inside the low-ceilinged building.

The small entrance hall reminded her a little of the Lamb in Warrington, but it wasn't used as a taproom and the prevailing smell was of tasty food. Through a door she glimpsed a common dining room with long tables, but some of the diners were well-dressed gentlemen. Respectable, then, but she saw no women.

A sturdy man came forward in polite

curiosity. He was neatly dressed in a dark suit, so she assumed he was the innkeeper.

"I've come to enquire about a group called the Curious Creatures," she said, in as tonnish a manner as she could. Alas that her clothing didn't suit.

"The Curious Creatures?" he echoed, oddly guarded.

Heavens. It had never occurred to her that it might be some sort of secret organization. She was here now, though, so she'd plow on. "I was told they meet here, sir, and I wish to speak to someone from that group. It is a matter of some importance."

"Um, well, they have met here, yes, ma'am, but there's no one here right now."

"I didn't suppose there was," she said, letting her irritation show. "You must know the address of someone."

"Well, as to that . . . Tell you what, ma'am, why don't you write a letter about your business and I'll see if I can think where to send it."

Hermione gave him her haughtiest stare, but it didn't move him, so she sat at the table he indicated and drew off her gloves as she waited for pen and paper.

" 'Appen he don't want you to know, milady," Nolly whispered.

Hermione echoed the Northern term.

" 'Appen. But they do meet here and I will make contact."

When the materials came, she wrote her note, keeping her request vague. After a moment's hesitation she signed it with her title, Lady Hermione Merryhew. If the innkeeper opened it to see what it said, that might give him pause. If he sent it on, it might spur the recipient to a rapid response. She sealed it with a wafer and gave it to the innkeeper. "Thank you. If I don't receive a reply in the next day, I will return."

"I may not be able to get it to anyone in that time, ma'am! Not everyone's in Town."

Hermione had to accept the justice of that. She could only say, "I'm sure you'll do your best," and hope it was true.

They left the inn and she looked around for a hackney to take them back to the Cross Keys. None was passing, so they'd have to find a hackney stand. She thought there was one at Oxford Street that she and her mother had used. She was still uncomfortable in the fashionable throng and would have gone there briskly, but Nolly paused to stare in wonder at a window full of fruit of all varieties.

Well, why not? The beau monde would assume she and Polly were poorer now their father was dead, whether she dressed in silk or fustian, and they'd be correct. So she ambled along at Nolly's pace, enjoying all the shop windows and introducing the maid to the pleasure of imaginary purchases.

Over three days as the dandified Lord Faringay, Mark had joined in the hunt for Solange without success. Though he resented the waste of time, he'd also had to take his place in the beau monde and even attend a couple of manly evenings with Braydon, where old friends had teased him about his transformation. None, however, had seemed to doubt his Mauritius story.

When not wasting time on such matters, he'd sought new ways to find Solange. At his suggestion, the notice in the papers about Nathan's body had been made into posters that were nailed up all around London in hope Seth Boothroyd would see one. He was barely literate, but someone might catch the resemblance to Seth and report that. The posters urged people to go to Bow Street with information, and to claim their reward. Still nothing, and every day increased the danger.

They'd failed to find Solange's contact in the Home Office. The enquiries had been discreet but thorough, but they'd uncovered no suspicious person, and certainly no one with a taste for black, red, and green in even the most subtle form. Hawkinville had been inclined to dismiss the idea, but Mark had looked at it from all angles and decided they were looking for an innocent gossip.

"A flapping tongue," he'd said. "It has to be. A man in that department gossips with someone who reports back to Solange."

"A woman."

"Yes, of course, and the man himself will be innocent of anything but gossiping about his work with a beguiling lady."

"But guilty as hell anyway," Hawkinville said. "If the connection's illicit, he'll not easily admit it, but people in the department will know who fits the mold and we can apply force if necessary. What female friends does Solange Waite have?"

That question stumped Mark. "I'd have said none, but it's clear she's been playing a deep game. I blame myself for not realizing that sooner. I remember a few times when she paid attention to some of the wives of ardent Brotherhood members, but I saw that as her playing the good wife to Waite. Now I believe she'd watch him drown without raising a finger unless it suited her needs."

Hawkinville had demanded names and Mark had supplied them, but he hadn't believed that the wives who came to mind could be complicit in explosions. However, Solange might have detected a few women who thought as she did. In this case, it would need only one.

He wasn't surprised that the enquiries thus far had achieved nothing, but the need to play the returned Viscount Faringay was an irritating waste of time. He had to do the minimum, however, and today he was traveling by hackney to the City to visit his bank. He could have summoned his banker to Braydon's rooms, but the journey gave another chance to watch for a glimpse of his targets and to assess the mood of the people sporting black, red, and green.

As always, London was raucous and chaotic, but the mood was no more fractious than usual. When he saw people sporting the colors, he wondered whether they'd seen Tregoven's picture and were ready to stab or shoot Ned Granger on sight. When he stepped out of the carriage, a nearby shopkeeper wore the colors, but paid no attention to him other than to hope for a customer.

At his bank he found he was more comfortably off than he expected or deserved, for he'd not paid close attention to the people chosen to oversee his property and investments. As he left, he decided they should have a bonus, perhaps at Christmas. A fleeting image of a jolly Christmas at Faringay evaporated in face of reality. The place held too many dark memories. A letter would do. . . .

He was pulled out of his thoughts when a man said, "Thayne? Gads, man, you're buffed to a fine polish."

It was Hal Beaumont, an excellent fellow who'd lost an arm in the war.

"Comes with being Viscount Faringay now," Mark said, shaking hands. At least it had been Beaumont's left arm.

"Surprised even that led to a green coat."

"Passed through Paris on the way home and thought I'd try dandy ways for a while."

Beaumont laughed. "Rather you than me. Are you fixed in Town now? Be pleased to have you round to dine, but it can only be certain nights. Mrs. Beaumont's engaged in the theater four nights a week at the moment."

A deft way of revealing that he'd married an actress. The world was full of surprises.

"I'd be pleased to," Mark said, "though I'm heavily engaged in gathering up the pieces. Went from the army to some business in Mauritius. I'm staying with Beau Braydon at the moment. Twenty-three, Parsifal Street."

They exchanged cards and went their ways. Mark had grown used to such encounters, but at the moment the fashionable world was like a cheery gathering seen through a window, while he stood out in the cold because he was aware of the darkness threatening them all. Having fought in the war, having been maimed in the war, wouldn't save Beaumont and his wife from being seen as enemies by people like Solange.

He remembered the story of Nell Gwyn's carriage being attacked by a London mob angry at many things, including Charles II's French mistress. She'd let down the window and called out that she was the English whore, and the mob had cheered her. The ever-unpredictable London mob.

He returned to the West End to visit a coffeehouse in Brook Street, which he'd set up to receive correspondence. There were some letters there — sent on, he saw, by his London solicitor, whom he'd neglected to visit because old Dellarfield would lecture him on his duties to the estate.

He shoved the letters in his pocket and went on to the glove maker who had Braydon's patronage, where his first pair of new gloves might be ready. He'd thought such fine details ridiculous, but he'd seen how those who cared about such matters had noticed the quality of his ready-made pair, and a man couldn't wear York tan for every occasion.

Then, as he walked down Bond Street, he saw Hermione across the road.

He turned away in case she recognized his face, but his heart was pounding and not from alarm. The need to turn, to cross, to speak to her, was almost too much for his willpower. He won the battle, but he did eventually turn to look to be sure it was her. No doubt about it, for she was in the same brown spencer she'd worn in Warrington, though the bonnet was different. Of course, the straw one had been ruined.

He turned away again, relieved to see with his own eyes that she was alive and safe and lodged in an excellent part of Town. It was highly unlikely that she'd stumble across Solange or Seth Boothroyd in the West End.

He chanced another look and found that she was walking away, which meant he could indulge in watching her. She was light on her feet but straight-backed and held her head high. She might be the victim of pity as the daughter of the Moneyless Marquess, but there was nothing meek about her. She and her maid paused at a milliner's shop, but didn't go in, then again at a perfumer's. Wistful? With his newfound prosperity in mind, he longed to dash over there and purchase whatever she desired.

One day he might have the right.

Then he saw black, red, and green stripes on the neckerchief of a messenger of some sort, whistling as he wove through the beau monde, doubtless anticipating gory deaths for all the "swells" around him. The man might not think of plainly dressed Hermione that way, but if revolution exploded, her title alone would condemn her.

Nolly said, "A fine gentleman gave you the eye, milady."

"What? Who?" Hermione looked around. Not someone she knew, she hoped.

"Walking away over there, in the green coat. Handsome young fellow."

"Such an odd shade for a coat, and the cut! I very much doubt such a frippery dandy was interested in me dressed so dully."

Hermione turned forward again and almost bumped into a man. He stepped back and apologized, but his neckerchief startled her. Black, red, and green stripes.

The man in the inn had been attempting to stir revolution, no doubt about that.

However, the woman in Ardwick wearing the gaudy knot of ribbons had been fleeing a riot, not inciting one, and Thayne would have nothing to do with revolutionaries. Not with his mother's sad story. All the same, she'd seen no sign of a new fashion for black, red, and green stripes. None of the tonnish shoppers wore them.

She went back to the beginning. Thayne had stolen papers from someone in Ardwick, and that someone had tried to kill both him and her to get them back. A woman, he'd told her. A Frenchwoman called Mrs. Solange Waite who dressed soberly. Had she been the woman wearing the gaudy ribbons?

Pieces wriggled into some sort of pattern, but still made no sense.

Thayne would never be a revolutionary, but he'd worn the colors.

Colors.

"Milady?"

Nolly's query made Hermione realize she'd stopped dead. She quickly walked on, but her head was buzzing with a tangle of ideas. Roger had been so excited when Grandfather Havers had purchased a pair of colors for him — a commission in the army. Could Thayne still be in the army, but working secretly?

There'd been stories in the papers of government agents pretending to be revolutionaries in order to discover the villains' plans and bring them to trial. One who'd given evidence against Arthur Thistlewood last year had seemed an unpleasant character simply out for gain, but there had to be more noble examples.

But, Lord, that would mean that Thayne had fallen into danger by stealing from people who plotted riot and revolt, and Sir George Hawkinville fit better into that picture. The air seemed a little thin. This was danger of a whole new dimension, especially when she saw how important it would be to him, and how he'd take any risks to bring revolutionaries to justice.

Peel Street must be nearby. She could go there and demand answers. Find out whether he was safe.

No. She knew nothing for sure and must do nothing that might put Thayne in greater danger, but it was hardly bearable when his danger might be so much more acute.

CHAPTER 30

Mark returned to Braydon's and found Hawkinville there.

"Glad to see you're still safe, Faringay."

"I wish someone would recognize me and shoot me. Chances are they'd miss anything vital, and if he was caught, he might have something useful to say."

"Unlikely, and even a minor wound can kill if it festers. Keep a level head, man."

A just rebuke. Mark knew the mere glimpse of Hermione had rattled him.

"Look. If I became Ned Granger again, I might learn more. Waite will have spread the word by now that I'm true to the cause."

"How would you explain your hair?" Braydon asked.

"I'll shave it and talk of having been confined by a fever."

Hawkinville said, "You're becoming unbalanced, Faringay."

"Where's the balance in any of this? Parts

of London could blow up at any moment. The mob could ignite."

Mark expected to again be told to calm, but Hawkinville said, "As it happens, there is new urgency. Four days from now the Regent plans to attend a special performance of *The Surrender of Calais,* which is expected to be particularly splendid now Drury Lane theater is entirely lit by gas."

Gas. "Dear God."

"The theater has been thoroughly inspected — normal concern about any gas installation, you see — and we've placed people among the workforce there. The chemists don't see how it could be done. All the same, I would prefer to have the woman and her chemist secured before the event."

"The Criminal Transportation Department?"

"Is being mined as desperately as you could want."

"Nothing from the posters about Nathan's death?"

"Not a nibble. Extend your mind to other leads."

Mark only just stopped himself from saluting. He now outranked Hawkinville by a considerable margin, but it never felt that way.

"Gas in Drury Lane," he said to Braydon when Hawkinville had left. "What the devil can Isaac do with that? Gas flames could cause a fire, but fire's been a danger in theaters forever."

"If confined, gas becomes explosive," Braydon said, "but how could it be confined in the vastness of a theater without poisoning the audience first? No point in mangling your neckcloth over it."

Mark had been trying to free himself of his. "Damn all neckcloths and those who tie them," he said, wrenching it off and opening his collar. It crunched slightly as he rolled his head against it.

Braydon chuckled.

"And men who laugh in dire times."

"It's the only way. Sit and we'll drink claret and seek wisdom from it." He poured some, but Mark paced the elegant study. "Poison the Regent with accumulated gas?"

"Can't see it. Audiences are already complaining of the smell and how it stings the eyes. If the density increased, no one would linger."

Mark took the wine and sipped. "But blowing up the Regent would be exactly the sort of drama Solange would love."

■ ■ ■ ■

"Where's Nathan?" Seth Boothroyd asked, as he did with increasing frequency. "I should go north to find him. He could be in trouble."

He's dead, you numskull. Solange couldn't say that. Thick-skulled though he was, she needed the remaining Boothroyd close. She did regret Nathan's death, for he'd been the sharper of the two. She'd never expected Granger to be the one to survive a confrontation. She had to say something to Seth. "I'll send someone to make enquiries."

"Who?" he persisted. "When?"

It could be useful to know exactly what had happened and she could afford to send Sarah north. "I'll send Miss Lawrey. She can be searching for her missing brother."

"I'll go with her."

She very much wanted to shoot him in his pea-sized brain. "A dangerous man like you would ruin her story. I promise you, if anything has happened to Nathan, the villains will suffer for it."

He nodded, but his spatulate fingers were working. "I'll scrag 'em slowly," he said. "Very slowly."

A torture chamber! Why hadn't she

391

thought of it before? "As is your right, Seth. As is your right."

"Seth Boothroyd," Mark said as he and Braydon sat for dinner. They'd spent the past few hours at a meeting convened to discuss the Drury Lane situation, but he couldn't feel any progress had been made.

"The best lead," Braydon agreed. "If he's like his brother, his appearance is distinctive."

"A bit heftier, a bit lower in the brow, and significantly more stupid, but close enough and I can't imagine him staying indoors or assuming a disguise. This soup is excellent. You have the art of living well."

"Why not when I can afford it? You can, too."

"I'm wriggling slowly into my new skin."

"It's not new. It's reality."

Braydon kept making that point. He couldn't seem to understand how ill-fitting Viscount Faringay was to Mark.

"Someone should have seen a resemblance to the description," he said.

"Perhaps it isn't as clear as we think. Or he's not in London. None of them are here."

"In that case we're looking for a needle in a haystack, but I doubt it. If Solange is planning to blow up Drury Lane, she has to be nearby."

"If. There's no real evidence, but I see it can't be ignored."

"And the royal family can't be locked up, more's the pity."

Braydon gave him a look. "Now you're sounding like a revolting specimen."

"I don't have to admire the Regent to work for stability. I'm aware of the many flaws in society and may work to amend them in time, but not by blood and fire."

Braydon raised his hand in a *pax* gesture and they settled to finishing their soup.

As Braydon put down his spoon, he said, "We could take a leaf from the Crimson Band's book and produce a likeness."

Mark smiled. "A brilliant idea! You could draw it?"

"I'm afraid not. My talents are limited to memory and description."

"And excellent ideas. How do we get a recognizable likeness?"

"And where do we post the picture for greatest effect?" Braydon rang for the next course. "The description's been nailed up in post offices, inns, and such. Where else might Seth Boothroyd visit? Taverns? Shooting galleries?"

"Think lower. Cockpits, dogfights, and cheap brothels. I wonder if we could recruit

Tregoven. I've always suspected he'd sell his mother for money."

"True or not, he's gone."

"Gone?"

"Hawkinville mentioned it before you arrived. He's slipped away, perhaps sensing a sinking ship."

"A rat to the end."

The footman came in with beefsteaks and roast potatoes. When the man had left, Braydon poured claret. "Who else has had a good look at a Boothroyd and has artistic ability?"

"No one I know of."

"Someone in Waite's household?"

"Whom we could trust? If Solange learns of the picture, she'll get rid of Seth one way or another."

"Charming lady."

They both settled to eating, but delicious food didn't bring inspiration.

Until Braydon put down his knife and fork. "Most young ladies learn to draw, don't they?"

"Do they?"

"They generally seem to have a small collection of sketches and watercolors for gentlemen to admire."

It seemed a diversion, until Mark saw where Braydon was going. "No," he said.

Braydon sipped. "It wouldn't endanger Lady Hermione and it could be the key to victory."

"Any contact with me could endanger her."

"Then I'll approach her. Is she in London yet?"

Mark thought of lying, but if a drawing by Hermione could avert the death of hundreds or more, he couldn't. "I saw her today. In Bond Street."

"Did you speak?"

"That would endanger her."

"So you don't know where she's lodged."

"No."

"What part of Bond Street?"

"Near Oxford Street."

"You feel qualms," Braydon said, "but you have no choice."

"You had a good look at Boothroyd and he must be imprinted in your magical memory. Can't you at least attempt the drawing?"

"I would if I could, I assure you. There was an officer who'd do rapid sketches of the men and catch their essence. Vandeimen, that was the name. He made it look so easy that I tried it myself. The best that could be said was that the eyes, nose, and mouth were in approximately the right places for a human being. No one would recognize one from the other."

"The same could be true of Hermione."

"But we must try. She shouldn't be hard to find if she's using her own name."

Braydon was right. Mark wanted to shield Hermione in every way, but he could think of no one else who'd seen one of the Boothroyds and might be able to draw a likeness.

"She'll be in the party of Mr. Edgar Peake," he said.

"Excellent. Hawkinville can alert the magistrates, and even recruit the military to locate her."

"Dammit, no! We don't know where members of the Brotherhood lurk. It could sign her death warrant."

He saw Braydon fight the urge to argue. He was probably right, but Mark couldn't permit such dangerous drama. "Then we'll check the inns and hotels around Bond Street ourselves," Braydon said. "I'm willing to trust Baker and Johns to help if you are."

"Of course; it's Hawkinville and those he'd recruit that I don't trust. They're all fine fellows, but any or all of them might decide a sacrifice is necessary for the greater good."

Braydon didn't protest that. They both had long experience of war, where no general could succeed if he worried about individuals. He rose. "If it's just the four of us, we should start immediately."

CHAPTER 31

Hermione tried to act normally for Edgar's sake, but by the next morning she felt caged. Her night had been troubled by wild notions of all the dangers Thayne might be in even now. She could never forget the brute who'd abducted her. He was dead, but he had a brother. Thayne was much stronger than she was, but she wasn't convinced he could win in a fight against such a man.

She longed for a word, a glimpse, to reassure her that Thayne was at least alive. The address in Peel Street begged to be used.

She couldn't bear to do nothing, so she went out with Nolly for a brisk walk. It would be the wildest chance to see Thayne, but she looked anyway. She had no success there, but she did see a few more people wearing the suspicious colors. The sightings confused her rather than clarifying her thoughts. The man cleaning gas lamps had a surly look to him, but the young mother carrying a toddler didn't, nor did the ballad singer selling the words and music of a patriotic song about Princess Charlotte's coming baby as a new hope for Britain.

Perhaps she'd let her imagination run wild and the colors were a fashion, but one restricted to the lower class. In that case Thayne was a common thief who'd stolen money from someone angry enough to pursue him over it. She couldn't believe he enjoyed that way of life, so as soon as she inherited Edgar's money, all would be well.

No, that didn't help. She wanted Edgar to live for decades.

"Oooh, milady. Look at those blue boots!"

They were outside a shoemaker's shop where the window displayed a pair of half boots in a dashing sky-blue cloth with cream silk ribbons. A sign offered to make the same in a day in a lady's choice of color.

"They wouldn't be suited to wet days," Hermione said.

"But grand for dry ones."

"I don't have a gown to suit them,"

"Perhaps it's time you had new gowns, milady."

"I don't have the money for them, Nolly."

"Mr. Peake's your great-uncle, milady.

Surely one day you'll have what's his."

"I hope that will be a long time away."

"But he wouldn't begrudge you new boots. They're very pretty."

They were, but she wouldn't be tempted. She still didn't know how much money Edgar had, but regardless, it was his money and not to be spent on indulgences for herself, or in providing for a rascally husband.

Or even a noble one, serving his country in the most dangerous way.

She walked on, having to accept that the latter was more likely. She couldn't truly say she knew Thayne's nature from evidence except that he'd once been an enthusiastic and idealistic military officer, but her sense of him was so powerful that it made base thievery impossible.

Money wouldn't turn him from such a cause, but in that vulnerable moment she passed a shop where lottery tickets were sold. She had three shillings in her purse that were her own. She went in and purchased a share of a ticket. People won large sums in the lottery and surely with money of her own she could do something. However, she left feeling ashamed of the waste of the shillings and weighed down by lack of hope.

Perhaps they would find Dr. Grammaticus, and perhaps his cure would work, but Thayne would still be in danger and out of reach. Grammaticus would probably turn out to be exactly the sort of quack they suspected and Edgar could be dead within months. Which would mean . . .

Horrified by the direction of her thoughts, Hermione hurried back to the inn, doubly determined to do everything possible to make him well. As if to emphasize her wickedness, it started to rain. Her hat and shoulders were soaked and her hem was muddy by the time she dashed in. She had to change before going to Edgar.

"I was hoping to take you around London, but the rain's spoiled that plan." She noticed that he'd put the newspapers aside. "Shall I read to you?"

"No. No news from the Green Man?"

"Not yet."

He hunched down. "I've a headache from all this racket. Go away."

It was particularly noisy at the moment, and his room showed nothing but the wall opposite. Very well, that was something she could do. She sat in the parlor to consult her guide to London. Nolly sat nearby stitching a shift. Rain splattered against the window and clouds had gathered to such an extent that they both needed candles. Alas, the inn didn't have the ingenious reflector Hermione had used in Riverview House.

The book was little use. It listed all the principal hotels and inns but with no indication of their nature. Was she going to have to inspect them all? Moreover, she still hadn't done anything about selling the coach and had no idea how to go about it. She felt a headache of her own coming on and could easily become as blue-deviled as Edgar.

Someone knocked at the door and Nolly hurried to open it.

"A gentleman for Lady Hermione," a maid said, and handed a card.

Nolly brought it over.

The Honorable Nicholas Delaney. The name seemed slightly familiar, but Hermione couldn't pin down the connection. She turned the card, and on the back was written, *The Curious Creatures.*

Thank heavens. Something was turning out right.

"Send him up," she told the inn servant, and went to the mirror to be sure she was neat. Prepared, she turned to greet the visitor and had a moment of surprise. This was no eccentric natural philosopher. Of course not. He was an honorable. He must be the son of an aristocratic family. But he wasn't typical of that sort, either. There was an easy, relaxed grace to him, and his jacket, breeches, and boots looked comfortably well-worn. His blond hair was a little long and his complexion accustomed to the outdoors. With a pang, she realized he reminded her a little of Ned Granger. But he'd come about the Curious Creatures.

"Mr. Delaney, thank you for coming. Won't you be seated?" She took her chair near the fire and he sat in the one opposite.

"I could hardly resist," he said with a smile. "Being a curious creature."

His manner unsettled her. It seemed overly familiar. She wasn't accustomed to being nervous in men's company, but she was glad Nolly was present as chaperone. "You're a member, sir?" she asked.

"Founding member. I happened to be in Town, so Tenby of the Green Man sent to me to deal with what he saw as a troubling enquiry."

"Troubling?"

"We do have women in the Curious Creatures, but not many, so he thinks of it as a gentlemen's club. An enquiry from a lady — in both meanings of the word — alarmed him. No matter. How may I help you?"

He seemed to have settled to a more normal manner, so she relaxed. "I read a reference to a meeting of the Curious Creatures, sir, where a Dr. Grammaticus spoke on the subject of antimony in the treatment of a disease called kala-azar."

His brows rose a little. "Intriguing. What's kala-azar?"

"You don't know?"

"I must have missed that meeting."

"It's a tropical disease caused by miasma, but it's not malaria, so doesn't respond to the bark. A relative of mine is afflicted."

"When did Grammaticus address the Curious Creatures?"

"January 1815."

"I wasn't in Town then, but we do keep records, if that's what you seek."

"I seek Dr. Grammaticus himself, sir. He claimed to have made the antimonial treatment more effective by addition of a fungus, but he refused to reveal which one."

"I see. Have you enquired at Newbery's for it?"

"You know of them?"

"They're quite famous."

"So if it existed, they'd have it?"

"Yes."

The directness of it made her sigh. "You hold out no hope?"

He smiled. "There's always hope. Grammaticus might not have made his cure available for purchase, but he could have set up a hospital to provide the treatment at a high price. Whoever you spoke to at Newbery's might not have known that, or might even have been unwilling to share the information."

"Rivalry. The clerk there had a very low opinion of the Curious Creatures."

"There you are, then."

Hermione considered his suggestion. "I doubt he's set up a hospital in Britain. The disease is contracted in the tropics and sufferers don't generally live long enough to travel home."

"Ah. Then I suspect he hoped to interest the government for use in India. If he's set up a hospital, it will be there."

"India! A letter would take months. That will be too late. I think my great-uncle has only been kept alive this long by taking antimony alone."

Delaney lit with sparkling curiosity. "Intriguing. Perhaps you'd allow me to make enquiries for you — being a Curious Creature of some expertise. If Grammaticus has interested the government, someone at the Foreign Office might know more. Or someone with the East India Company."

His light manner made her uncertain, but she needed help, especially from one who knew London. "Thank you, sir. That's very generous."

"On the contrary, it's obligatory. You don't recognize my name, do you?"

Clearly she should. Hampshire? Yorkshire? "My apologies, sir . . ."

"I was at school with your brother Roger."

"Oh. That was some time ago, and Roger is dead."

"Yes, I know. I wrote to your parents, though it was delayed, as I was abroad in 1810."

He remembered the date. "You were good friends? I was five years younger than he, so I don't know much about his school days."

"We were good friends," he agreed. "We were part of a group who called themselves the Company of Rogues."

"I remember that," she said, spun back to a moment in the past. "We were in the garden and Roger was talking about some jape 'the Rogues' had been involved in and Mother said he was keeping disreputable company. He fell into a tiff, declaring the Company of Rogues the best of good fellows, and wouldn't stand down from that. He and our parents were at odds for days." Tears escaped at the memory and she pulled out a handkerchief to dab at them.

"That sounds like Roger," Delaney said with a wry smile. "Once he embraced a cause, it was his . . ." She knew he'd been about to say "to the death," but had collected himself in time. "The Rogues still exist," he continued, "though down from twelve to ten, and we assist one another as necessary. You've inherited Roger's right to aid, which is why I said my assistance is obligatory."

"Not on me, I hope," she said, suddenly prickly. She remembered all those condolence letters that had seemed inappropriately phrased, coming as they did from strangers. All from "Rogues"?

"No obligation to receive," he said equably, "but if your need is as serious and urgent as you claim, you'd be unwise to refuse assistance. Despite the dire predictions of our masters at Harrow, who often said we'd all end on the gallows, today the Rogues command a wide range of expertise and considerable social power."

Hermione felt as if she'd been swept up into something without any say, but she must remember Edgar. If there was any chance of a cure, he must have it.

"Very well, Mr. Delaney. I'm happy to accept your assistance. And I thank you for it."

He rose. "Excellent. I'm about to go even further beyond the line, but — are you quite satisfied by this location for an invalid?"

She'd risen, too. "I'll accept help there gladly. I do want to move, but I don't know where will be best."

"I'll see to it." He bowed. "Good day, Lady Hermione. I'm pleased to have made your acquaintance."

He left, and Hermione sat down feeling surprisingly shaky.

"Are you all right, milady?" Nolly asked.

"Yes, but it's unsettling to discover that a stranger feels he has the right to intervene."

"Intervene to good purpose, milady. Seems just the type to get things done."

Whether I want them done or not, Hermione thought, rankled by that "I'll see to it," as if he would pick the place and move them, willy-nilly. She kept such ungracious thoughts to herself and went to tell Edgar the good news, omitting the speculation that Grammaticus might have traveled to India.

He did brighten, but then said, "Should have brought this Delaney in to talk to me."

"I thought you had a headache."

"It's gone. Would have enjoyed talking to

a gentleman. You probably chattered nonsense to him."

Hermione left before her temper escaped and ate lunch on her own, brooding on men and the way they treated women. Oddly, despite Thayne's overturning of her life and occasional attempts to order her around, he never treated her as a feeble idiot. He'd been annoyed with her decisions, but he'd listened to reason. No other man had ever done that. But would she ever see him again?

He could be dead and she'd not know it.

The rain had stopped. Before she fell into a complete fit of the blue devils, she'd go out to buy one of the day's newspapers. The air was still cool and damp, and she had to be careful of puddles, but fresh air did raise her spirits. She purchased the newspaper; then on the way back to the Cross Keys she came across a lad tempting purchasers on a street corner to buy one of the broadsheets draped over his arm.

"Family poisoned in Shoreditch! Honest damsel snatched off the streets! Gentleman found murdered in the Thames!"

Nolly said, "Oooh!" which made Hermione think Edgar might be amused by such lurid tales, so she bought a copy of the roughly printed paper. There was even an illustration on the front, presumably of the honest damsel being snatched, already half out of her clothes.

Hermione entered the Cross Keys looking forward to sharing the treat with Edgar, but she heard the innkeeper say, "Ah, here's Lady Hermione now, my lady."

A woman turned to her. She was only a little older than herself and quite plainly dressed, but Hermione recognized the finest quality from the curl of the brim of her black bonnet to her gleaming kid half boots. The quality was underlined by the liveried footman attending her. She had even features and fine eyes that Hermione thought suggested a good brain, but people probably described her as handsome rather than beautiful.

The woman came forward, smiling. "Good day, Lady Hermione. I'm Lady Arden, sent to assist by Nicholas Delaney." Hermione must have reacted, because Lady Arden chuckled. "I know, he can sweep along, can't he? But with the best intentions."

"The road to hell . . . ," Hermione murmured, but then grimaced. "I do apologize, Lady Arden. Won't you come up? Would you like tea or some other refreshment?"

"No refreshments, thank you," Lady Arden said, and they went up the stairs to Hermione's parlor. Once they were there, she said, "I can see why the Cross Keys is not quite suitable for an invalid."

"It's not just the noise," Hermione said, as they sat. "There's nothing for Edgar to see but the wall opposite. He likes people to call him Edgar, but he's my great-uncle, Edgar Peake."

"And suffering from an oriental disease, I gather. Is it infectious?"

"It seems not," Hermione said. "Edgar knows the disease from the East, and he assures me it's caught from tropical air like malaria, not from people. Also, no one he's been in contact with has caught it."

"Then can I persuade you to come to stay with us at Belcraven House while the Grammaticus cure is sought? We have an absurd amount of space, especially as only I and my husband and child are there at the moment."

Belcraven House. Hermione recognized then that this woman was the wife of the Marquess of Arden, the heir to the Duke of Belcraven. She wasn't awestruck by a ducal family, but she was feeling swept up again and by greater power. "It's very kind of you, Lady Arden, but we are strangers."

"It must seem so," Lady Arden said, showing no offense, "but you're part of the Rogues. You won't escape their cloak even if you refuse my hospitality. Don't worry, I understand your resistance — completely."

The "completely" made Hermione wonder about Lady Arden's introduction to that world, but she had other concerns. "I'm not sure a ducal mansion would be suitable."

"You're a marquess's daughter."

"But my great-uncle is a simple man. No, not simple, but he's been an adventurer all his life. And I'm the daughter of the Moneyless Marquess. We never lived in grand style."

"And I was a schoolteacher, so neither of us need weigh our precedence." With a charming smile, Lady Arden said, "Do please come. I'll enjoy your company, your great-uncle can have the best care and a room that looks out over Marlborough Square, and our servants will enjoy having more to do."

Despite the apparent sincerity, Hermione had to object to that. "Coming it too brown there, I think."

"I promise you, it's true. The duchy has great wealth. We dispense huge amounts to charity, but we also employ as many as we can squeeze in, both in Town and in the country. Honest, healthy people prefer employment to alms, but they also prefer to feel useful, not in a sinecure. We entertain as much as possible for the same reason."

Hermione had been about to agree to the plan, but the last sentence made it impossible. "I haven't any clothes. I mean, I only took essentials to Tranmere, without any expectation of traveling to London. I've nothing fancy or fashionable with me."

Out of pride she didn't say that she didn't own anything fancy or fashionable enough for Lady Arden's world.

Lady Arden eyed her. "I think we're close in size."

"You can't lend me your gowns, my lady."

"I believe I can, and don't fear that others will know. To provide employment, I order new garments generously. All British materials, of course. No French silk or lace. However, when I particularly like a gown or outfit, I prefer to wear it again and again, despite what fashion commands. The result is that I've any number that I've only worn once, or even never. You'll be preventing a shameful waste."

Hermione couldn't help but laugh. "I assure you, Lady Arden, I'm not quibbling out of a Puritan inclination."

"Excellent. If any small alterations are

necessary, we employ seamstresses for such work. Will you come?"

Hermione's pride wanted to resist, but that would be idiotic. "Yes, and thank you."

"Excellent. How many are in your party?"

"Only myself, Edgar, Edgar's man, and my maid."

"I'll send a carriage." She rose. "I'll leave and put everything in hand."

Mention of a carriage reminded Hermione. "We have a carriage. Edgar bought it for our journey here. The plan was to sell it, but I've no idea how."

"Nor have I, but I'll make the arrangements. It's probably too large for Town use, so use mine." She took a paper out of her reticule. "I prepared this for you. Knowledge is power." With that, Lady Arden made her good-byes and departed, showing herself out.

Hermione unfolded the sheet of paper.

The Company of Rogues
Nicholas Delaney, brother to the Earl of
    Stainsbridge
Lucien de Vaux, Marquess of Arden, heir
    to Belcraven
Leander Knollis, Earl of Charrington. Ex-
    diplomat
Lord Darius Debenham, younger son of

the Duke of Yeovil

Francis Haile, Viscount Middlethorpe, gentle man

Con Somerford, Viscount Amleigh. Ex-military

Simon St. Bride, Viscount Austrey, heir to the Earl of Marlowe

Lord Roger Merryhew, army, deceased

Hermione paused there, surprised and touched to find her brother listed, but then sad because he seemed like a ghost in the midst of life. What would he be now if he'd survived?

Marquess of Carsheld, of course, and much higher on the list, for Lady Arden had listed the men by their official precedence.

There were four more names.

Sir Stephen Ball, baronet, reforming politician and lawyer.

Was he the sort to incite people to violent rebellion?

Allan Ingram, Royal Navy, deceased.

Did he have family? Had they been swept under the Rogues' protection, whether they wanted to be or not? How prickly she was becoming.

Miles Cavanagh, heir to the Earl of Kilgo-
ran, Irish horse breeder.
Major Hal Beaumont, ex-military.

The list did present a range of power and
influence to draw on, though she'd have
liked to see a physician among them. Then
she noticed something else. The list was in
order of precedence except that Nicholas
Delaney was at the top even though the
younger son of an earl should have been
somewhere in the middle.

She refolded the paper and put it in her
writing case. Lady Arden had said
"Knowledge is power." Perhaps that detail
had been a discreet warning. Nicholas Delaney commanded all these powerful men?

That might be the case, but he didn't
command her.

Neither she nor Edgar would be a rogue's
plaything.

But then she remembered that Delaney
had implied that his Rogues would feel an
obligation to help Roger's sister. Could that
list of powerful men be used to keep Thayne
safe? If he were a common thief, very likely,
but she felt sure he wasn't. All the same,
she wouldn't lose sight of the fact that she
might have influence at her command.
Perhaps tomorrow she would contact Sir

George Hawkinville in hopes of letting
Thayne know.

CHAPTER 32

Lady Arden was efficient. Within two hours Hermione and her party were traveling westward to Mayfair in a very fine carriage. The seats were upholstered for comfort and the springs dealt excellently with the cobbled streets. Hermione had noted the escutcheon on the door and small coronets at each corner of the roof. The coachman and two powdered footman were in livery. Ducal, but this was the state expected of a marquessate and she'd never experienced it before.

Edgar had cackled when he was carried out into it. "If only some of my rascally friends could see me now."

Whatever came of all this, Edgar was better for the new adventure. He watched London passing by, commenting in a sprightly manner on the vast change in fifty years. Nolly, too, was taking everything in, like someone at a play or pantomime.

When the carriage traveled into Marlborough Square, Hermione herself couldn't help being impressed. It was a particularly large square with a handsome garden in the center surrounded by railings. The houses on all four sides varied from terraced town houses to some mansions set apart from their neighbors. Some even had railed-off courtyards in the front in the style of a century ago. From terrace to mansion, all were grand.

They stopped in front of a mansion, though one without a courtyard. The gleaming black front door opened directly onto the street with a flight of steps. An army of liveried menservants and well-dressed maids emerged to sweep them into the house as a tide might sweep loose boats into harbor.

Lady Arden waited there to greet them and soon Hermione saw Edgar settled in a handsome room, which contained a comfortable chair and a chaise as well as a bed. Both chair and chaise were set to give a view of the square through long windows. Everything was ideal, including the adjoining dressing room, which held a bed for Peter and stairs down to the servants' quarters in the basement. Edgar chose the chaise, so the journey hadn't tired him too much. Hermione could leave him to go with Lady

Arden to her own room, which was equally grand.

"You have a view of the garden," Lady Arden said. "I hope that suits."

Hermione looked down at trees, paths, and flowers and realized she'd missed greenery the past few days. "Perfectly."

"There are ways into the garden from a ground-floor anteroom and the morning room nearby. I'm sure you'll find them, but if not, there are servants to guide you. You, too, have a dressing room with a bed for your maid. There should be everything you need, but if not, don't hesitate to request it. There are bellpulls. I'll let you get settled and then we'll inspect my wardrobes."

Hermione had taken off her bonnet and gloves. "I could come now. I'll admit to anticipation."

Lady Arden's smile could almost be a grin. "No matter how practical or high-minded we are, there's something about new gowns that thrills, isn't there?"

"I don't think I'm high-minded at all," Hermione said, "and I'm practical only by necessity."

"And honest, which I value above all. Come, then."

Hermione followed, indicating that Nolly should come, too.

"I'm a bluestocking," Lady Arden said as they went along a corridor, "and a believer in the rights of women, which Arden finds damnably high-minded. Fitting into this world has required adjustment, but I've come to accept the pleasures involved."

Hermione heard Nolly gasp at the curse. Belcraven House would add to the young maid's education in all sorts of ways. How had a bluestocking of that sort ended up married to the heir to a dukedom? She feared it couldn't be a comfortable match, but that was none of her business.

She'd visited grand houses and occasionally the more personal apartments of wealthy people, but the Marchioness of Arden's suite of rooms caught her breath. The proportions were perfect, the art valuable, and the ceiling of her boudoir was painted with a trompe l'oiel of Olympus. "To remind us that we're mere mortals?" Lady Arden suggested. "But one becomes accustomed. No gods and goddesses looking down as I bathe," she added, leading Hermione and Nolly into a dressing room that was lined with armoires and chests of drawers and held a number of mirrors. True, the ceiling here was without deities, but it was beautifully painted with a night sky.

Three additional maids were summoned

and soon Hermione was out of her plain gown, and then out of her light corset.

"Very comfortable, I'm sure," Lady Arden said, "but for these gowns you'll need a better form. I'm larger there than you, especially since having a baby. Do we have any of my old corsets?" she demanded of the room at large.

A low drawer was plundered and three were produced, all beautifully made and one without shoulder straps.

"The style is for exposed shoulders," Lady Arden explained.

Hermione knew that, but she'd never actually worn such a style, as she'd not had a new evening gown for years. She remembered that bare shoulders had been in vogue back in 1811, when she'd attended that magical ball, but her mother had absolutely refused to allow her to display herself. Now she was laced into the strapless corset and then a gown of pale yellow silk was eased on over her head and fastened at the back.

"Just a little taking in at the sides, milady," said a servant, already busy with pins. "The length's good, which is a mercy, for we'd have to raise the whole lot. We'd not want to harm that embroidery."

True. The gown was quite plain, but the

lower part of the skirt consisted of rich embroidery of delicate white flowers set off by seed pearls. Hermione had never worn anything as lovely.

"It's exquisite," she said.

"Yes, but not a perfect color for you. Nor for me, either, which is why I haven't worn it, despite its beauty. You'll wear it, but we need a stronger shade for you to look your best."

It was a general command and the maids set to, producing a deeper green, a bronze stripe, a riot of flowers, and a pink.

Hermione couldn't resist touching that one. "I had a gown of just that shade for my first ball."

"Which brings pleasant memories, I see. Try it. I remember Madame d'Esterville persuading me to order it, but I've never cared for pink. Oh, yes," she added as it was being fastened. "The color's perfect on you."

Hermione looked at herself in the mirror. In 1811 her gown had been demure, with a square neckline, puffed sleeves, and white rosebuds on the bodice, perhaps to remind the gentlemen that she was young and innocent. This gown only just covered her corset, and that rose only just above her nipples, and the sleeves were mere ruffles around her upper arms. The trimming was a complex arrangement of beads designed to draw the eye to her bosom.

"Perhaps a little bold for an unmarried lady," Lady Arden said. "We could add some gauze or lace."

She was probably right, but a wicked spirit had Hermione saying, "I'm hardly a miss in her first season. I like this."

Especially if I indulge in dreams of encountering Thayne when wearing it.

It didn't seem likely, for even when freed from shady duties, he'd never attend a ton event, but a lady may dream.

She was soon in possession of gowns for all occasions along with spencers and pelisses and two fine shawls. Hermione could just fit into Lady Arden's slippers, so appropriate ones were added. For outdoor wear her sturdy half boots would have to do. If only she'd ordered those cambric ones.

"Now," Lady Arden said, "I think we deserve some tea in my boudoir." She sent a maid off with that order.

Hermione realized that Nolly had been standing by, in awe and silence, not knowing what to do. Her simple dress, plain apron and mobcap, and well-worn boots were no match for the clothes of the other maids. What to do?

"Nolly, please return to my room and be ready to assist with putting these clothes away. You know the way?"

Nolly bobbed a curtsy. "Yes, milady," and escaped.

Hermione thought she heard a titter. She addressed the maids. "Nolly Forshaw was a housemaid in a small house before I asked her to accompany me on my journey to London. I needed a maid for propriety's sake, so she obliged, and she's proved to be hardworking, honest, and clever. But no, she's not trained to be a lady's maid or accustomed to a grand house. I'm sure I can rely on you all to be kind to her and help her enjoy her time here."

One maid blushed. They all bobbed curtsies. "Yes, milady."

When they were in the boudoir, Lady Arden said, "That was well done."

"I hope so. I don't want her to be miserable here. She's been enjoying this adventure so far."

The tea tray arrived, and Lady Arden unlocked her tea caddy and mixed leaves. "Now, can you satisfy my curiosity and tell me more about your quest for a cure?"

Hermione did, breaking off only to take her cup of tea when it was ready. However, she left out all the incidents involving Thayne. She'd love to share them, but they would raise other, complex questions. She'd simply love to talk about him, as lovers always do. *Lovers.*

"Is something the matter?" Lady Arden asked.

Hermione realized she'd fallen silent. She couldn't resist. "Something reminded me of a gentleman I know."

"A pink dress, perhaps?" Lady Arden said with a twinkle in her eye. "If we're to talk gentlemen, we should be less formal. My name is Beth. Will you use it?"

"With pleasure," Hermione said. "It's a delight to have another woman to talk to. I've had my sister, of course, but she's so busy with her children and her home, and she flies into alt at the slightest thing."

"I won't do that, I promise. So, the gentleman?"

A part of Hermione was shrieking a warning — that she should keep everything to do with Mark Thayne locked away, but perhaps it was already too late. The longer she went without seeing him, the worse the yearning seemed to be.

"I met him at my first ball," she said, aware of blushing. "Wearing a gown of that shade of pink. But much more demure. We

426

danced twice, and he tried to steal a kiss on the terrace. I fell in love a little."

"Only a little?"

She could chuckle at that. "I was seventeen. Seventeen falls in love so easily, and out of it as well. He was going off to war and I was plunging into an abundance of assemblies, balls, and parties. I remembered him, but I didn't burn candles at an altar for him over five years." The lie came so easily. It was what any sensible lady would say.

"So you're not a romantic."

"I don't think so, but my sister accused me of being one because I enjoy novels and stories of adventures."

"We'll ignore your sister for now. What of the gentleman? I assume you've met him again?"

Hermione sipped her tea, knowing she should lie again, but she could tell part of the truth. "On the journey. In Warrington. Briefly. Then again a few times." Another sip of tea. "That was when I realized I still felt warmly toward him."

"That you're still in love with him," Beth Arden said.

"You're blunt."

"It's often best, but don't answer if you don't want to."

"Perhaps, then."

Beth raised her brows.

"How does one know?" Hermione protested.

"Do you know how he feels about you?"

Hermione felt positively red-faced, and laughed a little. "He's not indifferent, but there wasn't time. . . ." Not true. In the drawing room in Riverview House they'd stolen forbidden time to lie in each other's arms and talk, as they so easily talked of all manner of things. They'd stolen time to do all kinds of things they shouldn't, and even more if their consciences and good sense had allowed. Time enough to confess their love, and to accept that it was impossible. Then, at least.

She pulled herself together and tried to find truth to share. "He's in no position to wed. He has no money, and my portion is very small. I don't even know where he is now. He was traveling to London, but I have no address for him."

"Did he know you were to travel to London?"

"Yes."

"Then he should find you. If he cares, he will."

"Isn't that romantical?" Hermione said. "It sounds like one of those ancient challenges. To win the fair lady, find the magic chalice and slay the dragon. And then, of course, the stableboy is revealed to be a prince."

Beth chuckled. "Which is too romantical by far, and if you met your gentleman at a ball, he's no stable lad." She topped up their teacups. "There might have been something to those traditional tales, you know. It's good for men to be put on their mettle. Otherwise, they don't always value the prize."

"Life presents challenges enough," Hermione said.

"So it does," Beth said, sobering. "Sometimes, in this gilded palace, I forget. But you must enjoy the glitter while you're here. We have a dance party planned for tomorrow, which will be an excellent beginning. Now, if you've finished your tea, may I take you to see my son? In my eyes, of course, he is the handsomest child in creation."

Hermione was introduced to little Long Longridge, who was certainly a handsome toddler, with bright blond curls and big blue eyes, who ran to his mother with delighted "ma-ma-ma-ma" sounds.

She swept him up into a hug. "Good afternoon to you, too, my darling. Here's a new friend, Hermione."

The blue eyes studied Hermione for a moment; then the lad turned behind with most of his body, almost twisting out of Beth's hold. When she put him down, he ran over to a pile of small leather balls and grabbed two to shake them. They seemed to have bells inside, each with a different tone. It was clearly a favorite toy, and mother and son sat on the floor to roll and throw the balls, making music. Hermione slipped away and returned to her room, indulging in dreams of a dark-haired child running to her with such joy.

Perhaps that was more than a dream now. On top of the Company of Rogues, she had Beth Arden as a friend and was ensconced in a center of power. In the grandeur of Belcraven House, anything within the human sphere seemed possible.

She was still afraid of doing something that would trigger disaster, so she wouldn't take the risk of writing to Sir George Hawkinville, about whom she knew nothing. She considered telling the whole story to Nicholas Delaney and taking his advice. He'd irritated her, but he'd been efficient and Beth's attitude to him and his Company of Rogues had been unspoken endorsement. Her instinct said she could trust Beth Arden's judgment.

She wasn't carrying her burdens alone anymore. The relief was so great she had to sit down. She'd keep up her guard, but she didn't have to handle all the problems alone.

CHAPTER 33

That evening Hermione dined with Edgar, despite his protests that he didn't need her playing nursemaid. She wanted to be sure he was eating properly, but also she was somewhat overwhelmed by the large house and the number of servants hovering to fill her every need. All very well to feel grateful for powerful support, but that didn't mean it was comfortable.

She hadn't dared to venture down into the kitchens, so she'd sent a note to the cook asking for spicy dishes, but not curries. The result was a rather fierce soup that she put aside but Edgar seemed to enjoy, and a dish of lamb with spices that she found delicious.

"I taste cinnamon and nutmeg," she said, "and who knows what else?"

"Aye, they're lavish with spices in some parts. Could use more hot pepper. Often used to get a hot sauce to dip food into."

"I'll suggest it to the cook."

He looked at her, chewing some of the tender lamb. "You're good to me, Hermione. Why?"

"Why not?"

"I'm a sick, cantankerous old man."

"Yes, but I like you anyway. It's also my duty, as the representative of your family."

"In the hope of my money."

She didn't know what had set him off in this mood, but honesty seemed best. "In part, but only when you're dead. If you spend it all during your life, I'll have no complaint."

"Your sister will, and her husband."

"Not William, but Polly, yes. Why does it bother you now?"

"Because you belong in a place like this. A marquess's daughter. Really here, dining with the others, not with me."

"An *impoverished* marquess's daughter. The truth is I feel like a fish flapping on the beach. But if you think I've found my place, remember, I wouldn't be here if not for you. I'd have missed so many lovely things if not for you."

The inn, Warrington, that night in your house . . .

"Humph," he said. Then he added, "I've quite a bit of money."

She seized the moment. "How much? I need to know, Edgar. I don't want to overspend."

He laughed. "You won't do that. I've more than I'm likely to use, so there'll be an inheritance when I'm gone."

She put aside all thought of how long that might be. "Thank you. But I don't like to think of your death. I'm not lying, Edgar. I like you, and I want you restored to health and enjoying yourself for years to come. Decades even."

"Think I'll live to be a hundred?" he scoffed, but his eyes looked a little damp.

"People do."

"So rarely the newspapers make note of it."

"Even so. Speaking of papers, shall I read to you?"

"No," he said. "I'm going to give you and your sister some of the money now. No point my sitting on it like a broody hen. I'll get my banker to sort it out."

"From Liverpool?" she asked, startled.

"My main bank's in London. Sent money to London when I started thinking of coming back. Invested in this and that through an old friend who came back before me. He died last year, but it's in good hands. The Liverpool man was just a secondary when I decided to go back there. Bad decision."

"You wouldn't have fallen ill if you'd come directly to London?"

"I was ill when I landed, but there was nothing in the Wirral for me. The past is past. Remember that. Dead and gone and should be buried with the corpses."

"I don't agree. There's value to remembrance."

"Not if it leads to wasted time and folly. Do you pine for your old home?"

She was bewildered by the change of subject and wished he'd said more about the money, but he would give them some now. Even a little, a few hundred or a thousand, would make a significant difference.

"My old home? I'm not even sure what that means. I was born in Carsheld Castle, but I left there when I was eleven. It was damp, gloomy, and crumbling down. We moved to Leyden Hall in Hampshire, but though it was part of Father's property, it didn't feel like a home. Then I moved to Selby Hall to live with Polly."

"Hope to see you in a home of your own, then. Dance at your wedding, even."

She smiled. "I hope for that, too, Edgar."

"Choose a good man, note. One who'll love you for who you are. Should have your pick with ten thousand in hand."

"Ten thousand? *Pounds?*" Stupid thing to say, but she could hardly take it in.

"Pounds, guineas. I don't care. There'll be plenty left for me, so don't fret about that."

Hermione put down her knife and fork before she dropped them with a clatter. "You're going to give us ten thousand pounds?"

"Each."

"Now?"

"As soon as it can be arranged. It's well invested and you'd be wise to leave it so and use the income unless there's great need, but I'll put no ties on it. And of course there'll be the remainder of what's mine one day."

There was wine with the meal, but she'd only sipped it. Now she took a long drink as she let his words settle.

"Edgar, are you sure you can afford to be so generous?"

He rolled his eyes. "Only you would question a man at a time like this. I'm not a fool, girl. I know what I'm doing. Say thank you and have done with it."

She had to laugh. "Thank you, thank you! Such a sum will make all the difference, especially to Polly."

"You fuss too much about that sister of

yours. Think of yourself for once. You'll be a well-dowered heiress, so keep your wits about you and wear the kris."

Oh dear. She'd taken it out of her pocket and put it in a drawer when she'd learned she was to try on gowns. She smiled, thanked him again, and chattered about some boots she'd seen that she could indulge in now. Of course he berated her for not buying them, which carried his mind far from the weapon. She left before he recollected it.

She hurried to the privacy of her room and was able to try to absorb the size of the bounty. *Ten thousand pounds, well invested.*

She flopped flat on her back on the bed to contemplate it. Ten thousand pounds!

It felt like the wealth of Croesus, but she made herself be more realistic. She should spend only the interest, which wouldn't be enough for Belcraven-like luxury, but it would provide a comfortable life. She sat up to hug her knees. A decent, happy life for her and Thayne and their children, even if he never earned a penny.

The next day Hermione hoped for a visit from Delaney and even thought of summoning him, but over breakfast Edgar asked when he could see more of London. The antimony was definitely helping him and the unpleasant effects were moderating, which he took as proof that it wasn't working. So he wanted to see the sights now.

Very well, and it would be a thank-you for his generosity. They weather was clear, so perhaps they could use an open carriage. She sought out Beth for advice and found her in the entrance hall, directing the placement of flowers for the evening party.

"A barouche? Yes, of course. An excellent idea. Ah, Arden, you've not yet met Lady Hermione."

A man had entered the hall from the back of the house. Hermione didn't know what she'd expected of Beth's husband, but it wasn't this startlingly handsome Greek god. He came over smiling pleasantly enough, but she still felt tongue-tied.

"Roger's sister," he said, inclining his head. "He was a good man."

Of course. He was a member of the Company of Rogues. His simple accolade startled a hint of tears. "Thank you."

"It seems a shame that the Rogues didn't keep in touch with your family, in case there was any need."

There it was again. Pity for the Moneyless Marquess's family. "There was no reason why you should, my lord."

"I'm sure Nicholas doesn't agree. A sad lapse."

"Cease sparring with Nicholas, Arden," Beth said, but with good humor. "Hermione is to take her great-uncle out in the barouche to see London. You could escape the chaos here by being their guide."

Hermione didn't know who was more taken aback — herself or the marquess.

"I have pressing business elsewhere," he said, with a look at his wife. Beth had told him to stop sparring with Mr. Delaney, but had been unable to resist challenging her husband herself. Hermione was surprised not to see more annoyance in him.

"In truth, I do," he said to Hermione, "and I wouldn't be the best of guides, as I pay little attention to details outside my sphere. I'm sure there's someone employed here who'll suit." He gave them both good-day and took his hat, gloves, and cane from a servant standing quietly by, then left. Outside, a carriage awaited him, so his excuse had not been a polite fabrication.

"He's right, of course," Beth said, looking around and fixing her gaze on one footman. "Find Kingsley for me, if you please." Soon the butler appeared and was instructed to arrange for the barouche to be brought round and to find someone who could act as guide to London. Then Beth returned to the preparations for her party and Hermione hurried upstairs to announce the outing to Edgar.

He was delighted at the prospect, and so was she. She returned to her room to put on bonnet and gloves, but then changed her mind. "I'll wear one of the new morning gowns," she told Nolly.

She'd be traveling in a grand carriage and had no desire to look like a poor relation, but there was always the possibility of a chance encounter.

"Which one, milady?"

"The sprigged muslin and the straw bonnet. The one with the flowers. I feel like spring, even though it's nearly autumn."

Nolly giggled and Hermione resolved not to act like an idiot in love.

Once she was dressed, she considered footwear. Her well-worn half boots wouldn't do at all, and it was a shame she'd not indulged in the blue half boots, which she could now afford to buy with hardly a thought. Her giddiness over ten thousand pounds had not completely dissipated. Last night she'd written to Polly, so soon she'd feel the same relief and excitement.

Footwear. As she wasn't going to be walking far, she chose a pair of Beth's white kid slippers.

"You look lovely, milady," Nolly said.

Hermione regarded herself in the mirror and had to agree. The bright colors and flowers in the bonnet made her look lighter and brighter. Had she become somewhat gloomy over the past few years?

She smiled at the maid. "You're looking very well, too."

Someone had found Nolly a blue-striped gown and a fancy apron and cap and she grinned. "Not so shabby, am I, milady?"

"Go and find your bonnet, Nolly, for you're coming out for this exploration."

"Thank you, milady!"

Once the maid had gone, Hermione considered a problem. Where could she put the kris? The fashionable gown wasn't made for pockets. Instead, she had a pretty, matching reticule, but it was far too small. Feeling guilty, she tucked the dagger in a drawer under her shifts, and prayed Edgar wouldn't ask. She was going for a drive in the Marchioness of Arden's barouche, after all. She'd be in no danger, from suitors or enemies.

Thayne's button would fit in the reticule. She was about to put it there when she had a better idea. Smiling, she tucked it behind the busk of her corset between her breasts.

Nolly returned, bright with excitement, to say the carriage was waiting for them. They went to the stairs to find Edgar being carried down in a chair with poles, managed by two footmen. Beth was waiting in the hall, supervising.

"Isn't it ingenious?" she said. "Arden anticipated the problem and had the idea of cutting the top off one of the old sedan chairs. One of the carpenters made an excellent job of it."

"That was very thoughtful of him," Hermione said, trying not to show surprise that the mighty marquess had busied himself over such a minor matter.

"Much better, this is," Edgar said as she walked beside the chair to the door.

"Isn't it? Living in Belcraven House is rather like being in a fairy palace. Every wish and need magically fulfilled." She paused before crossing the threshold to make a specific wish of her own. *Let me see Thayne today.*

Perhaps she'd already been too far out of the fairy realm, for she returned three hours later with her wish unfulfilled. Apart from that lack, it had been an excellent outing. A lanky footman called Jeremy had presented himself out of livery to accompany her and Edgar in the carriage. He'd given Nolly a saucy look as he sat beside her in the backward-facing seats. Nolly had turned up her nose, but Hermione could see she was enjoying the attention.

"London born and bred, milady, sir," the footman announced proudly in a strong accent, "and I've always 'ad an interest, if you see what I mean. My grandfather was a rare one for stories, and 'e'd take us walking around on a Sunday."

They'd driven past St. James's Palace and around the old parks, and halted outside Westminster Abbey as Jeremy spoke of the history and curiosities. Hermione had resolved to return one day with a bath chair for Edgar so they could go inside. Westminster Hall followed, and then Whitehall. They'd been following the river, but they'd only glimpsed it through the buildings built all along the banks.

"Best way to see them's by boat, milady, sir," Jeremy told them. "Shame I can't take you to see Waterloo Bridge, 'as opened only a few months ago on the second anniversary of Waterloo, with the Duke of Wellington in attendance, as well as the Regent and all the great men."

By the time they returned to Belcraven House, Edgar was tired, but he seemed to have enjoyed their adventure. He settled in his bed for a rest and Hermione went to her room to take off her bonnet and the slightly tight slippers. For the dance party she'd wear her own, even though they were the worse for wear.

She took out the button, warm from resting against her skin, and buffed it with her handkerchief, but then replaced it. Keeping it close felt like a talisman that would protect Thayne. If only she knew he was safe. But that was silly. He'd survived a war without her hovering over him. And he still had the rose.

Her mind swooped back to that moment when he'd told her he'd kept it. That he'd felt the same impossible connection that she had through the years. The firelit room, his soft voice, the closeness that made it impossible that they be apart for so long, that she not know where he was at this very moment.

She wished Nicholas Delaney would come so she could start her search for Thayne. Why only wish? She could summon him. She didn't know his address, but surely Beth would.

She quickly wrote the note, not explaining the reason but phrasing it as politely as she could while expressing some urgency. Then she consulted Beth, who dispatched it by a footman, without comment.

That done, Hermione was left with nothing to distract her as she waited. She could offer to help with the arrangements for the party, but the abundance of servants was obvious. She'd only be in the way.

She went to her room and attempted a letter to another Hampshire friend, but her account of arriving at Belcraven House seemed too much like boasting. She pecked at a light lunch by the window of her bedroom, trying to read *Guy Mannering,* but fantastical adventures no longer amused her. It was more interesting to watch Beth's son as he toddled into the garden below, accompanied by a maid. Hermione watched him trot around the paths, exploring every little thing as Polly's boys liked to do.

As hers would one day. Thayne's children. She smiled with delight at the thought. Would they be black haired or brown? What sort of garden would they have to play in? She liked the countryside and it would be reasonable to spend some of the capital on a modest estate, but Thayne might not want rural life. He came from an aristocratic family but had clearly been cast off by them, and his life had been in the army and London.

She didn't care where they lived as long

as they were together, but if they had a town house, she'd like a garden.

She sat watching the child, dreaming, until the chiming clock told her an hour had passed. She was turning into a lovesick fool. She'd bring her mind into the moment by reading the newspaper, but when she picked it up, she found the broadsheet beneath it, with promises of poisoning and murder most foul.

The story of the poisoned family was heartbreaking, with ten people dead, including six children, because someone had used rat poison instead of salt in the stew. There was no suspicion of it being anything other than a tragic mistake. The public was warned yet again about the handling of poisons.

The flaming warehouse was reported as a case of arson. An employee was sought to answer questions, and a full description was included. Jack Patchem been caught pilfering and dismissed. He'd left cursing his employer and the next night the place had burned. What if it wasn't him? she wondered. He'd probably be convicted and hanged anyway. The world wasn't always fair.

She read the sad case of a small child killed by a runaway cow that had been fleeing its own slaughter, and about a chicken that was said to be able to count by pecking with its beak.

Friends or family were urgently sought to claim the body of a gentleman found drowned in the river, with evidence of foul play upon him. He was identified by cards in his pocket as . . .

Edward Granger.

CHAPTER 34

Hermione looked at the words, blinking to make them change to something else.

The words still said "Edward Granger." Something about an inquest. Any information . . . Coroner . . . Stirling . . .

Her hands began to shake, but she couldn't put down the paper because her fingers were clenched on it as if the force of her grip could change reality.

Edward Granger. Found in the river, with evidence of foul play.

Did that mean a slit throat? Had Thayne's enemies found him in the end?

Her grip turned limp and the paper slithered away.

She gripped herself instead, as if that might stop the shaking. It couldn't be true. Surely she'd know if he was dead! She'd know in her heart.

She rose to pace the room. Of course it was a mistake. The dead man had one of

Thayne's Granger cards, that was all. Yes! That was it. He'd given the man a card. That explained everything.

She must go and correct the error.

Yes, that was the thing to do.

She found her bonnet and tied it on.

Money for a hackney. She grabbed her knitted purse and headed for the door. As she reached for the knob, the door opened and Nolly came in.

"A visitor . . . Are you going out, milady?"

Hermione tried for a calm, commonplace manner. "Yes. An urgent errand."

"Then you'll need me, milady. Do you want a carriage?" From Nolly's expression, the calm, commonplace manner wasn't working. "You do have a visitor, milady," Nolly said. "A Mr. Delaney."

Delaney. Hermione almost laughed. No point to that anymore.

But Thayne *wasn't* dead!

"Take him to Mr. Peake," she said. "Mr. Peake wished to speak to him. I must go out. *Don't try to stop me, Nolly!*"

The maid backed away. "Of course, not, milady. I'll do just as you say, milady."

She almost ran away. Shame to frighten her, but Hermione couldn't think of that now. She hurried downstairs, pulling on her gloves. *Coroner. Mr. Stirling. Carriage.*

She was aware of servants going this way and that, preparing for a dance party. How could there be a dance party, when . . . ? But Thayne wasn't dead. It was all a mistake. She hurried across the hall to the front door.

"Hermione?"

She glanced to the side. Nicholas Delaney. "My apologies, sir. I must go out."

"Of course," he said, and opened the door for her.

"Thank you." She hurried out but became aware that he was still by her side. "Sir?"

"I'll accompany you. Where do we go?"

"There's no need. . . ." But there was. She didn't know where to go. "I need to speak to a Mr. Stirling. He's the coroner."

"I know where he lives. If we walk in this direction, we'll come to a hackney stand."

His calm tone seemed most peculiar. "Don't you wonder why I need to go to the coroner?"

"Of course, but you'll tell me or not as you wish."

She stopped to look him in the eye. "It's not *true,* you see. I have to tell them that."

"What's not true?"

"That Ned Granger is dead. I mean Mark Thayne. But it said Ned Granger. Of course."

"Of course. We should certainly find out the truth. Come along."

Everything seemed suddenly calmer. Nicholas Delaney would take her to the coroner. She'd establish the truth. All would be well.

"It was in a newssheet," Hermione explained as she hurried along. "Not a proper newspaper. The rough sort boys sell on the street. I'm sure they print nonsense."

"Very likely. What did it say about the death?"

"Drowned. Throat slit. No. Foul play. They only knew him by a card in his pocket. Isn't that ridiculous? He could have given a card to anyone!"

"It does seem flimsy evidence. There'll be an inquest, of course, so the truth will come out."

"Will there? I suppose so. But I must tell them, now."

"Of course. They could have already seen their error."

"That's true. The paper was two days old."

"We'll soon find out. Here we are." He ushered her into the hackney carriage, gave the driver an address, and then sat beside her.

"Thank you. You're being very kind."

"I would assist anyone in such distress."

He offered her his handkerchief and she realized she was leaking tears. She dabbed at them and then blew her nose. "It was a shock, you see."

"Yes."

"My mother's death was unexpected," she said, "because after the carriage accident it seemed she was recovering, but when she died, we weren't completely unprepared. My father took some weeks to die and he was an old man. Thayne's no older than you. But then, Roger was only twenty. Young men die in wars."

"Yes."

She was rattling on, but she couldn't help it. "That was war, though. We're at peace now. Why do people try to disturb the peace?"

"That's too deep a question for now. We're arriving."

"So soon?" she said, suddenly panicked. The truth lay in this ordinary-seeming house before her? A brick house in a terrace of them?

Mr. Delaney eased her out of the carriage. "Come along. You need to know the truth."

"Do I?"

"Yes."

"Lady Arden said knowledge is power. She gave me a list of the Company of Rogues.

Your name was at the top, but it shouldn't have been."

"I'm sure you're right."

He rapped the brass knocker. A serving-man opened the door. Delaney gave him a card. "Mr. Delaney and Lady Hermione Merryhew to see Mr. Stirling if he's available."

They were ushered in, and placed in a small, chilly reception room. The house had a musty smell, and though it was handsomely furnished, everything was in an old style.

"Stirling's an elderly man," Delaney said, "but shrewd and honest."

The servant returned and led them to another room. Hermione's legs began to weaken and she clung to Delaney's arm. She would not faint. There was no need. She was here to sort out a mistake.

It was a study of sorts, the walls lined with books and a brisk fire in the grate, but again a little musty. The man standing to greet them had thin gray hair, but a spare, vigorous body and keen eyes behind spectacles. "Lady Hermione, Mr. Delaney, how may I serve you?" He spoke with a slight Scottish accent.

She was urged toward a sofa and settled there. Delaney spoke for her. "Lady

Hermione is under some distress, sir. Would it be possible for her to have some sweet tea?"

"Yes, of course, of course." The order was given and then the coroner sat opposite them. "Can you explain your mission here as we wait, sir?"

"Lady Hermione read a report in a paper of a body being identified as a Mr. Edward Granger. As she knows the gentleman, she is affected by it. She doesn't believe it can be true."

"She has reason to doubt it?"

"Not that she's shared with me thus far, sir. Hermione?"

She jerked out of a daze. "Yes?"

"Can you explain to the coroner why you're sure the body can't be that of Edward Granger?"

The tea came in then, however, and was dispensed.

Delaney put a cup and saucer in her hands and commanded, "Drink."

She did. It was heavily sugared, which was not to her taste, but it did begin to clear her head. She drank some more, then put the tea down. "It's the card, you see, sir," she said to the coroner. "He could have given a card to anyone. It's no proof of anything."

"I agree, Lady Hermione, but there was

more than one card." The eyes were sympathetic, but the tone was firm. "We are scrupulous in these matters. After some days in the water the contents of the pockets were in a sorry state, but there were a number of cards and they all seemed to have the same name on them."

"Oh." She turned that in her mind. She knew Thayne couldn't be dead, so there had to be some other explanation. "Was there any other means of identification?"

"I'm sorry, but yes. After the notice was circulated, a friend came forward to identify the remains. Mr. Granger was interred yesterday under the supervision of this friend."

Interred?

Buried already?

"The friend's name?" Delaney asked.

"Ah, I do not quite recall. Let me think. Mitchell, I believe. Yes, Mitchell. I do not have his address to hand, but it will be recorded, if you would wish to have it."

Mitchell? She'd never heard the name. "He lied," she said.

"Collect yourself, please, Lady Hermione. With what motive?"

Thayne's enemies. But they would have murdered him, not identified him. But he *wasn't* dead.

Stirling had said something.

"I beg your pardon, sir?"

"No matter, my dear. I fear this young gentleman meant a great deal to you. Naturally you are reluctant to accept that he has gone. I would normally say it was a pity you didn't have the opportunity to see his remains and make peace with the truth, but in the circumstances that would have been no consolation."

"His throat was slit."

"Good heavens, no. Whatever gave you that idea? A severe blow to the head. Lady Hermione, please pay attention to this one thing." His tone was a warning.

"Yes?"

"The inquest concluded that he was the victim of a felonious assault, for there was nothing of value in his pockets, only the waterlogged cards, a handkerchief, and a tangle of white silk which could once have been formed into a rose."

Suddenly she couldn't breathe. "No."

He didn't contradict her, for there was no need. There was no hope. The corpse had had the rose. Thayne was dead.

She broke into sobs and was gathered into Nicholas Delaney's arms. In time, after more sweet tea, this time with brandy in it, she had the strength to stand, to leave, supported by Nicholas Delaney's arm. In the carriage she sat in numb silence until she said, "How do I go on? How does anyone go on?"

"One day at a time. One hour at a time. One minute, even. Do you want to tell me about him?"

She longed to, but she couldn't think yet what Thayne would want people to know about him. She couldn't think at all.

She began to weep again.

CHAPTER 35

"We've given her some laudanum," Beth Arden said, entering the drawing room, where Nicholas waited. "Poor woman. I suspected she was in love, and not quite smoothly, but I didn't expect a tragedy. Who was this Granger?"

"Also known as Thane or Fane," Nicholas said. "A false name implies a great lack of smoothness in their affairs, doesn't it, but which is true, which false? I asked Peake about Granger and Fane or Thane, but none of the names means anything to him. He didn't believe Hermione had any meaningful encounter on their journey to London."

"Perhaps it was earlier, on her way to the Wirral with her family. Warrington. She said she'd encountered the man in Warrington. That must have been when she was traveling with her family, though."

"You're imagining a clandestine affair," he said, "but he could have been known to her family under one name or the other. They could all have shared a jolly dinner."

"Whatever the truth, it's a sorry tale. She spoke of him with such brightness in her eyes, but all the time he was dead. I feel I should put on mourning."

"Instead you have a party to host."

Beth put a hand to her head. "Lord above. Should I cancel? I can't, not within hours. If I attempted it, half the guests wouldn't receive the news in time."

"Beth, I'm shocked. Succumbing to hollow convention? You don't have a corpse in the house, and your connection to the deceased, and even to the bereaved, is tenuous."

"Might she be upset to hear dance music and laughter nearby?"

"Not if she has a rational heart."

"Does anyone?"

"No," he admitted, "but she's suffered the deaths of both parents and two brothers. She must know that neither earth nor heaven weeps for our losses."

"No matter how much we wish they did."

"Because we believe we should be the center of the universe, not mere ants, scurrying busily beneath the surface."

"Don't tell Lucien he's a mere ant."

"I try, I try. The lessons in humility never

stick. Might he recognize the names Granger, Thane, or Fane? As families of importance, I mean."

"He might. He was trained to this life from the cradle and they all seem to know each other, at least by the repute. 'Oh, that must be one of the Herefordshire Fanes,' " she said in a fashionable drawl. " 'I believe my second cousin married a Pulteney Fane-Frobisher. . . .' "

He chuckled. "You have the manner pat, but the details wrong. Perhaps the second cousin married the Earl of Westmorland. Fane's that family's name."

"You remember that sort of thing?" she said with surprise.

"Eventually. I, too, was trained to it from the cradle."

"It's so easy to forget."

"I take that as a compliment. I wish Arabella Hurstman was here. She'd be able to rattle off genealogies on the instant — though I'm not sure how much use it would be. There will be hundreds of Grangers, Fanes, and Thanes who once attended a ball."

"What about Westmorland? If he's a Fane, could he have been Edward Granger?"

He smiled. "The Earl of Westmorland found dead in the river? It wouldn't go unnoticed. He's the Lord Privy Seal. You see? Knowing about him and that he's a Fane is hardly obscure knowledge. I shall try to sort this out."

She went with him to the door. "Will you return this evening?"

"Of course. Eleanor's looking forward to it. By the way, I have news of Dr. Grammaticus. I assumed Hermione's summons was impatience over that and was anticipating her admiration and joy. Last heard of, he was in Tunbridge Wells, dosing invalids of all sorts and in particular those with gout. I've sent someone there to find him and bring him here to treat Mr. Peake."

"Will he, nill he?"

"I've offered him a handsome sum. He seems the type to respond to that."

"Not hopeful," she said.

"No. Best not to tell Peake yet. Grammaticus might have moved on, or he might flee at the sign of serious interest. We don't want to raise false hopes." He kissed her hand. "Be of lighter heart, Beth. Gloom won't bring Hermione's beloved back to life."

Hermione woke in a room lit only by firelight, with a muddleheaded feeling that told her she'd been dosed with laudanum. She didn't remember taking it. She didn't remember much after the coroner had convinced her that Thayne was dead.

He was dead.

Her heart didn't believe, but her head knew the truth. The silken rose. There could be no doubt. Thayne was dead and buried.

She was in her shift. She'd been undressed, but not to nakedness.

What time was it? It was dark outside.

She pushed up to sit against the pillows, trying to accept the truth. Thayne was dead and buried — as Edward Granger. That wasn't right. Had she told the coroner that Edward Granger was Mark Thayne? She didn't think so. She really should. Or was it a secret she should take to the grave? She remembered thinking that and bursting into tears, but she seemed to be drained of tears now and left only with the leaden ache.

The door opened and Beth looked in. When she saw Hermione was awake, she came over to the bed in a rustle of silk. She was in a dark red evening gown and the firelight shone on rubies around her neck. "How are you? Is there anything you need?" she asked.

Hermione took the question at the ordinary level. "No, thank you. You look lovely. The party."

"I hope you don't mind it going on."

"Of course not. What time is it?"

"Nearly seven. The dinner guests will be arriving soon." Beth took Hermione's hand. "I'm so very sorry that you've lost someone dear to you."

"Thank you. It doesn't seem quite so terrible now, but that's the opium."

"Yes."

"The pain will come back."

"Yes."

Hermione dragged out a sensible thought. "Will Mr. Delaney be here tonight?"

"Indeed, I expect him."

"Please thank him for me. He was very kind. Very understanding."

"Of course." Beth went to the mantelpiece and then brought something over. "The coroner sent these and Nicholas thought you should have them."

Puzzled, Hermione took a white handkerchief that had seen rough wear. When she unfolded it, something fell out. A tangle of stained silk.

"Oh." She started crying again, but in a softer way, with sadness, but with memories as well. "His handkerchief, too. Both from the river."

"Are you all right?" Beth asked again. "I wasn't sure you should have them."

"I'll treasure them. They help. But the

talisman didn't protect him in the end, did it?"

"Would you like anything else? There's water by your bed."

Hermione saw that was true and reached for the carafe. Beth poured the water for her. It tasted strange, but she knew why. "Opium affects the taste of things."

"Yes. It's a blessing," Beth agreed, "but it blunts our emotions and plays games with our minds. Try to rest. You'll feel better. . . ." She halted. "No, not better, but clearer, later. Nicholas has some good news. Dr. Grammaticus is said to be in Tunbridge Wells. Nicholas is arranging for him to come here to treat your great-uncle."

"That is good news." It was, but Hermione couldn't feel it yet through the cotton wool of her mind. "Has Edgar been told?"

"We decided to wait until we're sure he's more than a charlatan."

Hermione nodded.

Beth squeezed her hand. "I must go. It's a weak platitude, but time does heal."

Alone again, Hermione fingered the handkerchief and the rose, grateful to have something of Thayne's, even if they made her cry again. Perhaps crying washed away grief. She doubted that. She conquered tears and focused on the good news about

Dr. Grammaticus. That had once been so important, but now it fell flat.

She slid back down into the bed, holding the handkerchief and the rose, and eventually drifted back to sleep.

She woke again and had to get out of bed to use the chamber pot. Once up, she didn't want to return. Her head was clearing, bringing back the pain, but she preferred piercing truth to fuzzy blankness. She found the handkerchief and the rose in the bed and put them in her trinket box for safety.

Better to think about Grammaticus. He might be here tomorrow, and his cure might be true. Edgar could enjoy life again.

What of her? She supposed she'd return to Selby. Even with ten thousand pounds, where else did she have to go? She could stay with Edgar. Yes, that would be better. Perhaps he'd want to travel again. Foreign shores would distract her. Perhaps in time she'd forget.

She went to the window and found she could see the moon floating in and out of clouds. Below, the garden had been turned magical by colored lamps. She remembered earlier, watching Beth's son playing there and having been so sure she could make a future with Thayne and children of her own.

It had already been too late. Thayne had

died days ago. She hadn't known it, which seemed unbelievable, but he'd been dead for days. He must have been killed almost as soon as he arrived in London. Killed by his vile, revolutionary enemies. Perhaps she could help find them. The Frenchwoman and the brute's brother. The idea of a goal strengthened her. She drank the remaining water and then rang the bell.

When Nolly came in, all anxiety, Hermione said, "I'm much better. I'd like something to eat and drink."

"Oh, that's good, milady. You need your strength. What do you fancy? There's all sorts, what with the party going on."

"Choose a few items for me, please. And I'll have some port. It's supposed to be strengthening."

"Very well, milady. I won't be a tick!"

Hermione put on her brown woolen robe — the robe she'd lent Thayne in the King's Head. That memory brought tears, but she conquered them and lit more candles. In memory of that night, she put more coal on the fire so it burned brightly. No need to ration it here. She sat nearby recalling all their encounters.

The button. Where was it? She saw her pockets draped over a chairback and searched them. She looked at every surface and even in some drawers. What had she done with it? How could it be lost?

She sat back by the fire to weep. How could she have been so careless?

The door opened and she quickly wiped away her tears. Nolly came with a tray and set out delicacies on a table to Hermione's hand, along with a small carafe of port and a glass. "Anything else, milady?"

"No, thank you. Have you been able to see anything of the party?"

"I have, milady! One of the others showed me a spot where we're allowed to watch the guests arrive if we don't have duties then. As my duty's to you, milady, I watched for quite a bit. Such fine gowns. I'd love to have a fine gown one day. And jewels. One lady wore diamonds that were like stars around her neck."

Hermione was pleased Nolly was enjoying herself, but she worried about these new ambitions. In a fair universe there was no reason Nolly shouldn't wear silk and diamonds, but with the world as it was, the only way for her to get them would be through wicked ways.

"Such fine gentlemen, too," Nolly said. "Some of them right handsome, milady, like the marquess. But I shouldn't be going on so, milady, not with your loss."

"I welcome the distraction." Hermione took a bite of a savory tart. It was more like dust than delicacy, but she forced it down and drank some of the rich port.

"There's something fierce about his lordship," Nolly said. "Now, that Mr. Delaney, who brought you back today, he's a good-looking man, and kind."

"Yes, he is. And kindness is important." She probably should give a lecture on the folly of wickedness and the importance of kindness, but perhaps people should take their pleasures when they could. She'd avoided wickedness in Riverview and see what had come of it.

Nothingness.

She'd been frightened of conceiving a child, but now she'd welcome one, no matter how scandalous that would be. She'd have something of Thayne to remember.

"Oh, here, milady." Nolly was holding out the brass button. "Fell out of your clothes when we undressed you. Don't know where it came from."

Hermione grabbed it and held it in both hands. "I do. Thank you."

After a moment, Nolly said, "Right, then. Is there anything else you need, milady?"

"No. You go and enjoy the performance."

"It is like a play, isn't it, milady? There's a

place where we can watch the dancing."

Nolly left and Hermione held the button as she nibbled a salmon patty. She needed her strength, but could hardly swallow it. She put that aside and tried a jam tart. It was too sweet, so she simply drank more port. The pain was a part of her and she supposed it always would be, but she was more than the pain now. She had purpose.

A number of purposes.

His body shouldn't be interred under a false name. Even though his parents were dead and he seemed to have no close family, she was sure he'd had friends. There'd been Mitchell, for example. She'd never heard of him, but she knew there were parts of Thayne's life they'd not had time to share, just as she'd not had time to tell him of her pleasant time in Hampshire.

She paused in raising the glass to her lips. Mitchell had identified the body as Ned Granger. If he knew him only as Ned Granger, mustn't he be in league with the villains? He could even be the murderer!

She rose, wanting to run out and tell someone, but it was nighttime. It could wait, but she had an even stronger purpose now. Through Mitchell, she'd find Thayne's murderer. The one who did it and those who ordered it. All of them.

She drained the glass of port. She would avenge him. How violent that sounded! But she wanted whoever had killed him to be hanged, and yes, though she'd never attended an execution, she might go to watch that.

For a moment her furious purpose had burned through her grief, but it seeped back. No matter what, Thayne was still dead. She'd never see him again.

She poured the last of the port into her glass and took it to the window. There was no one out there amid the pretty lanterns and she saw why. Rain glimmered on leaves and paths. The heavens had wept, but some time ago, for now the moon was shining through scattering clouds.

She put aside her glass and opened the window, welcoming the dampness on the air. But then she heard merriment. There must be windows open in the house, letting fresh air into crowded rooms and letting out music and chatter. She was glad people were happy. It was proof that happiness existed despite the deadness inside that said it didn't.

She'd mourned her parents and Jermyn, though not deeply. She'd grieved more for Roger, but not like this. Nothing at all like this.

Roger had been too young to die, and too full of life, but the Company of Rogues had known him better than she. She and Roger hadn't shared childhood games or secrets. She'd been in her schoolroom world with Polly and Miss Chandler, and he'd been in his with his tutor until going away to school. Jermyn had been an even more distant figure, eight years older and off to school almost before she knew him, then in another sphere when at home. His death, two years ago, had stung only because it meant the title would go elsewhere, along with their home.

She'd encountered Thayne so few times, but each meeting had been intimate and left a deep impression on her mind and heart, like the mark pounded into silver or gold to prove it true.

The garden below was not a terrace, but it took her back to that first encounter. The moon was almost as bright tonight. How sad that no one was out there to talk and flirt, and perhaps to sow the seeds of love. She supposed that even the most amorous lady wouldn't risk silken dancing slippers for a kiss.

She could go out there. She could wear her leather half boots. Yes, out there, under the moon, remembering.

Where were her own clothes, the ones she could get into and out of easily?

CHAPTER 36

She found them in a bottom drawer, but realized that if she was seen in the house so simply dressed, someone might take her for an intruder. She wanted no fuss, which meant she must dress for the party.

She rang the bell again.

Nolly took a long time in coming. "I'm sorry, milady. I was watching the dancing. They were waltzing!"

Waltzing. She'd dreamed of waltzing with Thayne. . . . "I want to walk in the garden. I need an evening gown so I won't look out of place."

Nolly stared at her. "Are you sure, milady?"

"I'm not out of my wits, I promise." *Though I may be a little drunk, but it doesn't matter. I need to do this.* "I need fresh air," she said, trying to sound rational, "but if I leave this room in an ordinary dress, one of the guests might think me an intruder."

"Oh, I see," Nolly said, though clearly she didn't. "Right, then, which one? The pink? That's the prettiest, milady."

"No!" It came out too sharply. "Not pink tonight. The bronze stripe. It has a frill around the hem that can be unpicked for cleaning if soiled."

As Hermione endured the process of corseting, she knew she wasn't thinking quite as she should. She was tipsy with port, and perhaps still affected by opium, but the greatest disorder was grief. Even so, it would do no harm to escape into a deserted garden and she wanted it. Perhaps among the simplicity of plants she could mend her mind.

The gown slithered into place, and as Nolly fastened the back, Hermione looked in the mirror. The unfamiliar gown that exposed her shoulders made her seem almost a stranger. That was good. She didn't want to be Hermione Merryhew. Not tonight.

"The slippers, milady." Nolly was offering delicious confections of silk and lace.

"They'll be ruined in a wet garden. I'll wear my half boots."

"Brown leather, with that gown, milady?" Nolly was reacting as if Hermione had suggested showing her breasts.

"I hope no one will see me, but if they do, they won't notice my footwear in a moment."

Once she was shod, Hermione sat before the dressing table mirror to deal with her hair, impatient with the necessity. If she met anyone in the house, she couldn't look disheveled. She gathered her hair into a knot on top, skewering it with pins.

"My trinket box, Nolly."

She fixed two pinchbeck sprays of flowers in her hair. She needed something around her neck as well. She owned a few good pieces of jewelry, including a string of pearls — the ones she'd worn to her first ball — but she'd left such valuables at Selby. She chose a necklace of quartz beads. At a glance they might even look like pearls. Matching earrings and she should pass muster.

Nolly was offering long white gloves. Hermione almost rebelled, but she pulled them on. Then she surveyed herself in the mirror. "That will do. Thank you, Nolly. You may return to your diversions now."

"Wouldn't it be best if I come with you, milady?"

"Into the garden? I'll have no use for you there." She saw the maid was still concerned about her. *Am I mad? Perhaps the deranged*

475

don't know.

"At least take a shawl, milady," Nolly said, offering a rectangular shawl in a bronze paisley pattern and with a deep fringe. Another gift from Beth. "You don't want to catch your death."

Hermione didn't care if she did and the shawl would be in the way, but she couldn't bear any more fussing. She draped it around herself and sent the maid off, saying only, "Do not tell anyone where I am, Nolly. On your honor."

"If you say so, milady."

Once she was sure Nolly had gone, she opened the door and checked the corridor. The coast was clear. The ballroom, the drawing room, and the other more public apartments were on the opposite side of the central hall, but she'd have to go down by the grand central staircase. She knew no other way.

She went to the top of the stairs, but then stepped back. Late guests were still arriving. She remembered that some had been invited to dine before the event, but others would arrive throughout the evening for the dancing. She peered around a pillar and saw two groups of people, four in one and five in the other. A bevy of servants, footmen and maids, were taking cloaks and coats.

One group of two couples began to climb the stairs. One of the men had a patch over one eye, but the patch didn't conceal a scar on his cheek. Wounded in the war, and not neatly, but he was alive. The lady on his arm hadn't lost him to the grave. The two couples turned toward the other side of the house, leaving the coast clear, but the other guests lingered in the hall.

Where were the servants' staircases? There would be some all over this mansion, but she didn't know them, and in any case, with such an entertainment in progress they'd be busy with people going up and down. Perhaps she had gone mad, but now getting outside, into the garden, seemed the most important thing in the world, as if then everything would change. As if then everything would be right.

She headed down the main staircase, attempting a vaguely distracted air, as if on an urgent mission, but feeling like an exposed malefactor. She was braced for someone to call, "Stop, thief!" The party of five began to climb the stairs, still talking. They merely inclined their heads in passing.

Once in the hall Hermione turned quickly toward the back. Beth had said there were doors to the garden somewhere down here.

This part of the house was quiet, but when she arrived at a room with glass doors into the garden, she found it lit by lamps and with a fire in the grate. It was set up as a possible retiring room for anyone wanting a peaceful spot.

It was unoccupied now, however, and when she tried it, the door to the garden was unlocked. She was soon outside and could breathe at last. She inhaled cool, damp air full of greenery and the delicate perfume of night-scented flowers that glimmered pale in the lamplight.

Like flowers on a grave.

She wept then and had no handkerchief. She stemmed her tears with the shawl, crying even more over ruining it.

Stop this. Stop this. It does no good.

She inhaled again and became aware of the cold. She pulled the shawl close around herself, grateful for Nolly's common sense. Nolly was a treasure who should have everything she dreamed of. But not wickedly.

But as she'd thought before, why not? No one should go to the grave with dreams unfulfilled, with desires unfulfilled, and death could come in a moment. She remembered Edgar saying that the greatest danger came without warning. How wise he was, and she wasn't wearing the kris!

She wouldn't burst into tears again, but the music and lightheartedness spilling out of the house grated on her. Lamplight and moonlight showed the paths quite well, so she followed one toward the back of the garden, farther from merriment. The paving stones were merely damp, but rain lingered between them, and here and there on leaves and stones. She was glad of her leather boots, and held up her gown so it wouldn't be too much soiled. The path wove around, creating small, private areas walled with shrubs and bushes thick and high enough to create an illusion of being alone. Some held benches, inviting one to linger, but they were too damp to sit on in silk.

One area held a statue of a woman in classical robes sitting on a rock. Hermione wondered whether it was a memorial of some kind because the woman looked sad and she was surrounded by rosemary. She pinched off a little and drew in the aroma. Rosemary for remembrance. She tucked the sprig down the front of her gown. Perhaps rosemary was also for truth, for acceptance settled in her mind.

Thayne was dead. Dead and cold in his grave. She'd never see his lopsided smile again, never argue with him, never talk, talk,

talk throughout a stolen night. She'd never kiss him again, and she'd thrown away their one chance to do more. Truth sat leaden in her heart, but she was sane again. Sane enough to know she should go back inside before she caught a chill. She retraced her steps, and then a turn gave her a view of the lit windows of Belcraven House.

It looked like the fairy palace she'd once thought it. In the brilliance of an extravagance of candles, men in dark elegance and women in a rainbow of colors were talking, laughing, and dancing to the music she could faintly hear. Part of her still wanted to protest, but she pushed that aside. Let them take pleasure in the moment. Let everyone take pleasure in every precious moment, for who knew what might happen in the next?

Some of those cheerful men would have fought in the war. Many of the revelers would have suffered the death of a dear one as she had. She remembered the wounded man she'd seen mounting the stairs. Another of the men entering the house had had an empty sleeve. Their friends and relatives would have suffered over their maiming, but they'd count themselves blessed because their loved one was still alive.

Behind the windows, the smiling dancers

wove up and down a line to a tune she knew. It was one of the two dances she'd enjoyed with Thayne so many years ago. She wouldn't resent the dancers. She'd rejoice that there was still dancing in the world.

One day she would dance again.

Week by week, day by day, minute by minute. She began to find some balm in the dancers' pleasure, but then she frowned to focus. A man had faced her briefly, but then turned so his back was to her. Still, her heart had flashed with recognition.

Now she saw only broad shoulders in a dark evening suit and dark hair that was rather short for fashion. This was indeed madness. The hair was nothing like Thayne's, and Thayne would certainly not be here. Despite a pounding heart, she refused that mad path of grief — seeing him in every passing dark-haired gentleman in London. There must be a thousand.

Turn again, she willed at him.

Show me you're not Thayne.

Give me back my sanity.

He stayed in position for a maddening length of time, but then went to the middle to dance with a lady, turning this way and that, smiling at his partner.

A lopsided smile?

Stop it! You can't possibly see that detail at

this distance. It isn't him. It can't be him. He's dead and buried.

Her head was buzzing, however, and she had to clutch onto a nearby lamppost to stay upright. *Mad with grief.* Like his mother, she'd gone out of her mind because she couldn't accept the truth. But knowing she was mad didn't cure it. Her mind saw Thayne, moving on along the dance line, and madness conquered sense. Her heart screamed: *He's alive!*

She picked up her skirts and ran toward the house, then tripped on a stone and almost fell. Heaving for breaths, she made herself slow, and some sanity returned. It wasn't him. It couldn't be him. Still, she needed to find that man so she could prove that to herself. Otherwise, she'd never be sane again.

She hurried into the breakfast room and froze, fixed by the stares of two older ladies. Was one truly wearing the wide skirts of the past century, or did her insanity extend to everything? Both looked down at her shoes. The strangely dressed lady raised a quizzing glass. At her boots. And at muddy marks on the carpet.

"Are you quite all right?" asked one. The rather gaunt one who was dressed normally.

"Yes, completely!" Hermione said, and

fled. Once out of the room she heard low conversation behind her. She was muddying Beth's house. Resenting every moment it took, she untied the ribbons of her boots and took them off.

She dropped the shawl on top of them and abandoned them there to hurry toward the front of the house and the stairs up to the ballroom. Her rational mind knew that the man, whoever he was, wouldn't be leaving at this moment, but the rest screamed to hurry, hurry, or she'd never know.

Some servants were still in the hall. A footman said, "Milady?"

She ignored him and ran upstairs, aware of passing some people on the staircase, but no longer caring. She raced along the corridor in her stocking feet, weaving past startled couples and into the ballroom.

The dance had ended. People were standing, strolling. Where was he? Where was he?

Dark hair. No, that was the man who'd lost an arm.

That other one was too short.

"Hermione?"

She heard Beth's voice somewhere nearby, but she'd seen him now, across the room, laughing at something a blond lady had said to him. The one in diamonds. He was at ease here and so exquisitely well dressed, with such pristine white linen at neck and wrist and touches of gold and jewels. Even his hair was different. There was a red to it.

It wasn't Thayne.

But her heart wouldn't believe what her mind told her, and when he turned, perhaps alerted by a mood in the room, her heart ruled.

"Thayne!" she cried, and ran to him.

CHAPTER 37

Mark caught Hermione, bewildered by her being at this party, and alarmed by her demented, shoeless wildness. She was all too like his mother, though she was laughing and crying as well as babbling nonsense.

"Hermione. Has someone hurt you?"

In response, she fainted. He caught her up into his arms, stunned and with no idea of what to do.

"This way." That was his host, the Marquess of Arden. Telling him to take Hermione away from here. *Good idea.*

They escaped the ballroom, but faced a gauntlet of people in the corridor, all staring and speculating.

"This way."

Now it was the marchioness, the hostess, steering him past the stairs. "Arden will devise a story," she said quietly. "Let's get her to her room."

Her room? Here? He'd been searching

London for her and she'd been in Belcraven House? He followed down a corridor, around a corner, and into a room with a rumpled bed.

Lady Arden pulled back the covers. He put Hermione down, smoothing her silken skirts, touching her stockinged toes. She was dressed for the party except for slippers, but she hadn't been there. He'd have known.

She was beginning to come around, blinking and grimacing in confusion. But then she saw him and clutched at his arm.

"It is you!"

"It is me. But why that turns you mad I can't imagine."

"Because you're dead!"

"Because you're supposed to be dead," Lady Arden corrected.

He looked at her. "Dead?"

But Hermione had knelt up to turn his head so she could stare desperately into his eyes. "It is you? You look different."

Though still perplexed, he smiled for her. "It is me. I needed to change my appearance a little."

She was still frowning, doubting. "Tell me about Tranmere," she demanded. "The last night at Tranmere."

"Before a witness?"

486

Then she smiled. He'd never seen such brilliance light someone's face. She pulled his head down for a kiss, shocking him with raw passion, then broke apart to stare at him again, but smiling, smiling. "It *is* you."

"It is. But why think me dead?" He looked to the side to the more rational person here, but the marchioness had gone. She'd closed the door behind her. He should open it again and ring for a servant or demand a chaperone. . . .

Hermione pulled him back to face her again, touching his hair, sending shivers down his spine. "So short."

"The only unfashionable thing about me." He captured her wandering hands and tried to make sense of all of this. "Hermione, how are you here? I've been searching the inns of London for you and your relative."

"The Curious Creatures. They brought Nicholas Delaney to the Cross Keys, and he sent Beth Arden to bring us to the fairy palace, and now you're alive."

Dear God, she'd run mad. Like his mother.

"You were searching for me?" she asked, seeming pleased.

"Desperately."

"Come on the bed," she said, moving over.

Not wise. The chaise in Tranmere had

487

been perilous enough.

"I need you to hold me."

He couldn't resist the intensity in her voice. He took off his shoes, then joined her on the bed and took her into his arms to soothe her back into her wits. But she kissed him again. Soon he was entangled in her perfumed silks with her hair sliding beguilingly free.

He found the strength to stop the kisses, but stroked her lovely cheek.

"I'm alive, love. I'm not going to disappear." He took her hand and held it over his deeply beating heart.

"I know," she said, looking at him as if she thought he was insane. "I need to touch you, though."

She began to work off one of her long silk gloves. It was stained with mud or dirt. Where had she been?

He helped her, gently asking, "Curious Creatures? Fairy palace?"

Suddenly she laughed. "Did I sound demented? Poor love. I'm not like your mother, I promise you."

Only she would grasp that so instantly.

She tossed the gloves to the floor and touched his cheek with a bare hand. "The Curious Creatures are a philosophical society and I've come to think of Belcraven

House as a fairy palace. That's all."

He covered her hand with his own. "Nicholas Delaney?" He remembered meeting a Delaney at the party. A dangerously charming fellow.

"He's the leader of a group called the Company of Rogues. My brother Roger was a member, which means they think they can take charge of my life."

He chuckled. "Foolish men."

"They brought me here. Though I shouldn't complain about that."

"Except that it hid you. I've been searching inns. When we couldn't find you, I began to fear you'd come to harm."

She brought his hand to her lips and kissed it. "I thought you were *dead.* You are. Dead and buried." She frowned in thought. "If you're not, then who's in your grave?"

"No one, love."

"I mean Edward Granger's grave."

"Ned Granger has a grave?"

"I didn't believe it until the silk rose."

Suddenly he understood. The silk rose he'd forgotten until too late, until his old clothes had gone to a ragman. With so many urgent matters, he hadn't felt he could hunt down a shabby coat for a tattered scrap of silk, but he saw how this dreadful mistake might have been made.

He cradled her hands in his. "Love, love, the dead man must have bought my cast-off clothes with the bit of silk still in a pocket. I shouldn't have let it slip out of my mind for a moment."

"No matter about that. You're alive. You forgot more than the rose, though. He had your cards, too, though they could hardly be read."

Now he began to suspect the truth. Ned Granger had never carried calling cards. "Then how was the body identified?"

"Someone came forward to do so. It must have been one of your revolutionaries. But then, why claim it was Granger when it wasn't?"

"An excellent question. Name?"

"Mitchell."

He saw it all now, and he'd have someone's guts.

"I know no one called Mitchell. This is the Home Office people pursuing their course without thought for the pawns. If Ned Granger is dead, Solange Waite might lower her guard. A pity that she rarely reads English newspapers."

"So you do work for the government. I thought as much."

Of course she'd worked it out, his clever lady. The woman he'd held in his heart through the long years. He kissed her again, letting free all his passion and need, and felt it ignite in her. She kissed him back as she'd never kissed him before.

"When I thought you dead . . ."

"When I couldn't find you . . . ," he murmured, trailing kisses down her warm, silken neck, past cool beads and onward. "I thought I'd lost you." His lips found her plump breasts and the hollow between them, where he inhaled her delightful scent. "This is a wonderful gown."

"One of Beth's," she breathed. "I own nothing so fine."

"You will. Beth's?"

"Lady Arden."

"She's an old friend of yours?"

"No." She raised his head so she could kiss his lips. "It doesn't matter. Kiss me more. And more."

He remembered the kiss at the King's Head. The passion that had flared. And in Riverview House. She wasn't mad from grief anymore, but she was close to it from relief.

He fought free of her. "We can't do this, love. You'll regret it."

"I won't." Her lips were red and moist from kisses and her gown in wanton disarray. A slight nudge and her nipples would rise free. . . .

"Hermione, you're not in your right mind."

"I've never been righter." There was something steely amid the seductive lusciousness. "I've thought about this."

He groaned.

"I thought you were dead," she said. "I believed you were dead and I knew then it had been wrong to be sensible in Tranmere. The future is always uncertain and I want to know you. I want to know all this, with you. Show me. Teach me. If you love me, Thayne, pleasure me. Please."

She drew his head back down toward her breasts and he couldn't resist. Soon her nipples were free and he teased gently at them so that she stretched like an ecstatic cat. Then he turned rougher and she clutched his hair in a way that told him the measure of her excitement. She was made for passion, and she soon shattered into the gasps of pleasure she'd so boldly demanded.

The intensity of her response consumed him. Vaguely he knew he should be surprised by it, but he wasn't. From her bright eyes at that ball to the kiss in Ardwick, passion had crackled in her from the first, only waiting to be released. He gripped a handful of skirt and drew it up so he could stroke a silk-stockinged leg. He found the cotton frill of her drawers, maddened by the little noises she was making, by the way her body still moved with desire.

"Stop me now, Hermione," he said.

But she laughed. "Why? This is wonderful."

"Yes, but we can't. Not yet."

He tried to pull her skirts down, but she dragged them higher, up to her waist. "We can. We must. You could die. I could die."

"No one's going to die."

"Everyone dies."

"Eventually." He caught her grasping hands. "Have sense, woman!"

"You could die tomorrow." How anyone in such glorious disarray could be so purposeful, he didn't know. "You still have enemies."

"Yes, but . . ."

"And they'll kill you if they can."

"Yes, but —"

"So love me now. Here. Tonight. If you die, I want your baby."

"No."

She pushed him back down and crawled onto him. "Please." But then she hesitated. "Unless you don't want to."

Her sudden uncertainty broke him. He clutched her to him. "Oh, I want to. More than life. But only if you promise to marry me."

She shocked him by pulling back, frowning. "That's a very shoddy proposal."

He burst out laughing. "I'll never understand you." He rolled off the bed and went to one knee. "My dear Lady Hermione . . ."

But she grabbed for him, laughing. "I'm sorry. I'm sorry. Of course I'll marry you, Mark Thayne! I wish it could be now." She looked up at the bed hangings. "I remember a story about someone getting married with a curtain ring. . . . No clergyman. There's probably one at the party."

"You propose we go down there to demand an instant wedding?"

She was grinning. "I would if I could."

"Alas, no license."

She waved a hand. "Such fiddling legalities. At Gretna we'd only have to say we were man and wife."

"That's Scottish law, not English."

"Does God mark borders? I claim you, Mark Thayne. . . . You are truly Mark Thayne, aren't you?"

"Truly, though I have to confess that I'm also Viscount Faringay."

"You're suddenly a peer?"

"I've had the title for years." Her frown

worried him. "You mind?"

"You could have told me."

"Would you have believed me?"

"Perhaps not, but I've fretted so about how we were to live."

"You have?"

"Don't look so pleased."

"I can't help it."

"You're not a *poor* viscount, are you?"

"Will you not marry me if I am?"

"I'm too far gone for that, but as it happens, I have money now. My great-uncle's giving me a dowry of ten thousand pounds." She eyed him mischievously. "So perhaps, sir, you're a fortune hunter."

He laughed again. "You do like to win, don't you?"

"I do, and I've won you. I claim you, Mark Thayne, Viscount Faringay, as my prize."

He kissed her hand. "And I claim you, Lady Hermione Merryhew, as mine. We are man and wife. Strictly speaking, we need witnesses, but no, we are not going to the ballroom to recruit any."

"I could have a ring, though," she said, scrambling off the bed, opening a drawer, and taking out a trinket box. He noticed again how gracefully she moved, but not with languid grace — with strength and poise.

He delighted in how she showed no embarrassment at the way her bodice exposed her and her hair was tumbling loose. Its thickness pleased him. He would brush it for her at times. When they were married. Such a deeply satisfying thought.

She closed the lid and returned to him with a ring in her fingers. It was a slender golden band holding three small dark stones, probably garnets.

"It was my mother's, when she was young."

He'd give her rubies, but this would always be precious. He slid it onto her ring finger. "My wife."

She climbed back onto the bed. "And wife means wedding night."

He'd never wanted anything more, but he said, "Better to wait."

"I thought we'd dealt with that." She grabbed his coat and began to push it off his shoulders. "I need you now. In case you die, I must." Her hands stilled and she rested her head against his shoulder. "I never expected this, to feel like this. In my heart, yes, but in my body? I fear I might explode."

"Oh God, yes." He kissed her, but then fought free again. "Let us do this right, my love." He left the bed, shed his half-off coat, and then locked both doors — the one to the corridor and the one into a dressing room, knowing he should fling them open and even call for help. What the devil were they all doing, the Ardens, this Company of Rogues, the whole damn party, not stopping this?

There was only him to stop it, but when he turned back, his Hermione sat expectantly on an unruly bed in a nest of striped silk, nipples full and rosy, looking at him as if he were her moon and stars.

Explode. Definitely. But this was their wedding night. He couldn't just toss her down and plunge into her.

He shed his waistcoat and cravat. "Care to join me in disrobing, wife?" That came out more brusquely than he'd intended, but she obliged, blushing, eyes bright.

"You'll have to play maid, husband." She turned her back.

He hadn't noticed before how low the back of her gown was. Never had the hollow of a spine been so alluring. It demanded to be kissed, then licked, and so he did. She inhaled, stretching her neck back, rising up on tiptoe so that his fingers turned clumsy and almost lost their strength. Thank God there were only four hooks.

He slid the gown down her arms. She

wriggled to help it slither off onto the carpet, which did nothing for his control. He set to work on her corset laces. He'd heard of men cutting them and had thought it barbaric. Now he cursed the lack of a sharp-enough knife.

He was only half-done when she said, "It's loose enough," and worked it up and over her head. "There," she said, turning to him in only her shift. She'd pulled it up in taking off the corset, but nipples jutting beneath plain cotton were as potent as when exposed. Her breasts needed little help from whalebone to stand full and high. She saw where he was looking and blushed, but then laughed. "I'm glad this isn't our real wedding night."

"What mad thought's in your head now?" he asked, dragging off his waistcoat.

"I'd have been undressed by my maid. I wouldn't be watching you undress."

He laughed. Laughing came easily now. As with a maniac? But who the hell cared?

Waistcoat gone. Pantaloons unfastened and off. Drawers and stockings off. Only the shirt left. She was still watching, bright with pleasure.

He picked her up and put her in the bed in her shift, then lay beside her in his shirt and pulled the covers over them.

"I thought of this once," he said, pulling a remaining pin out of her hair.

"About us together in a bed?"

"That? Frequently." He fingered her hair around her, finding a few more pins. "In Riverview House, I went first to your bedroom. Your nightgown was over a rack by the fire. I wanted you naked in a bed with me, but I liked the idea of nightgown and nightshirt. It said marriage to me, and permanence, and even growing old together."

"I like that," she said, stroking his cheek. "I also like the look of you clean-shaven."

"Only managed by being shaved just before coming here."

"I must grow accustomed to whiskers?"

"If you object, I'll razor myself by the hour."

She chuckled. "I liked your hair longer."

"It'll grow."

He took off his shirt then and helped her with her shift, adoring her for the blush she couldn't help and for the smile she meant. He cradled her full, firm breasts. "So beautiful."

"Am I?"

"Everything about you is beautiful, Hermione. And you are mine." He kissed her then, doing his best to go slowly.

As before, the passion flared, even more fiercely now for being stirred, then banked, again and again. He fought but lost. No matter. She was as wild for it as he, and wetly ready for him. She flinched when he broke through, and he stilled for as long as he could to let her adjust.

"Perfect," she breathed, and he felt her inner muscles clench around him. That set him free.

CHAPTER 38

She'd unleashed a storm, but she'd always loved storms. Hermione could only match his rhythm, aware of gasping in time to his thrusts and of wanting more and more until thought burned away in sensation and sensation exploded everything for a blinding moment that rippled on and on and then gently down into wonderful heat and sweat.

"No wonder people in hot countries go naked," she murmured, flexing her fingers on luscious flesh.

"Does that make sense?" he mumbled.

"Skin to skin. Delicious."

He licked her shoulder. "Mmmmm."

The most convenient part of him was his ear, so she sucked the lobe. His leg stirred against her and she smiled. "If I were a cat, I'd purr."

"If you were a cat, I wouldn't be here."

"Idiot."

He chuckled.

"This is lovely, too," she said. "Being here like this, so relaxed, at ease. No wonder people get married."

"We're not married."

"Yes, we are. In all ways that matter."

"We should marry as soon as possible."

"In case there's a child, yes."

"You wouldn't marry me otherwise?"

She smiled at the tease, but said, "If we couldn't, it wouldn't bother me as long as we could be like this."

"Are you always so coolheaded?"

It was her turn to chuckle. "Most people wouldn't think this coolheaded."

"And earlier, not at all."

"Should I have been calm?"

He leaned up to kiss her. "Never. You were wonderful, in every way, and I am happier than I've ever been. To have you. To have found you. Again."

"And again, and again." She sniffed. "I'm going to cry."

He kissed her lashes. "Don't, please. I know women talk of tears of joy, but don't."

She sniffed again, deliciously touched by his distress. "I'll try. But they are tears of joy. I do want us married, child or not. How soon? A license is quick, isn't it? We could marry tomorrow."

"You wouldn't mind not having your family with you?"

"Not as much as I'd mind waiting, but you're right. We should marry at Selby."

He sat up against the pillows, taking her with him in his arms. "I want to marry you tomorrow, love, but I can't leave London yet."

She sighed. "The Frenchwoman and the rest. It's time you told me exactly what's going on." When he stayed silent, she added, "I'm your wife, Thayne. . . ." She looked up at him. "Should I still call you Thayne?"

"You can call me anything you want, including nodcock when justified."

She wouldn't be beguiled away from her questions. "You're working for the Home Office and it has something to do with the black, red, and green some people wear. One man I saw wearing those colors was trying to stir sympathy for rebellion, and I suspect a woman I saw in Ardwick was your vile Frenchwoman. Then there's your urgency about that letter. It was addressed to Sir George Hawkinville, who doesn't sound like the leader of a band of thieves."

"Too clever for your own good."

"Better that than stupid. I need to know. I have the right to know."

He sighed. "You do, and I've never found

it easy to keep secrets from you. Impossible now. So here's the truth. I've vowed to prevent bloody revolution coming to Britain, and I work to that end."

Her heart clenched with fear, but she did her best to hide it. "I suspected as much, but revolution? As in France?"

"I know it can seem unlikely, but unrest seethes everywhere and the London mob explodes at every spark. The situation here is too like the Paris mob a generation ago, ready instantly for mindless violence."

"Mindless? There's true hardship and injustice."

"The mob isn't agitating for reformed laws or a lower price of bread. They thirst for violence and destruction as if blood would wash away their pain."

"There is pain."

"But that will be eased by reform, not violence."

So work for reform in safe ways. In Parliament. He wouldn't say yes. She saw that. Not until the task was finished.

She settled back into his arms, carried into deeper waters than she'd expected. She'd known his enemies were ruthless and violent, but from what she knew of the French revolutionaries, they had been far worse. There was a reason the bloodiest time had been called the Terror.

The Terror that had slaughtered his mother's family, which was why this fight was his crusade.

"But hasn't the mob always been the same way?" she asked. "Wasn't it the Gordon Riots when Parliament was attacked, back in the last century? Nothing came of that in the end."

He pulled the covers farther up over them. "Touch and go. Carriages and houses were attacked as well, and prisons broken open, releasing the inmates to do their worst. The army had to be called in, but they killed hundreds of people, many of them innocent bystanders. No one should ever rouse a mob. Someone said that there are three ungovernable forces — torrential flood, wildfire, and a human mob. All three destroy, and indiscriminately."

"Yet people do rouse them," she said. "Like Orator Hunt and Arthur Thistlewood."

"And Julius Waite."

"Isn't he a moderate?"

He kissed her hair. Such a butterfly touch to create havoc inside. "Only more subtle in how he stokes the fire. He frames action in terms of Magna Carta and the Crusades."

"Ah. The man I mentioned, who was

wearing the black, red, and green — I encountered him at an inn where he was talking about righteous rebellion. He cited Magna Carta, the Glorious Revolution, and such, and made rising up against an unjust king seem a virtuous crusade."

"He'll have been a member of the Three-Banded Brotherhood."

"What's that?"

"Julius Waite's secret organization that works for revolution. A flag with three bands of color has become popular with those in favor of revolution, hence 'Three-Banded.' "

"Like the French tricolor," she said, "but black, red, and green." She touched his face. "You've had to live within them to oppose them. That must have been hard on your conscience when you planned to destroy them."

"My conscience wasn't comfortable about killing people in the war. It had to be done."

"We who stay at home don't think enough of what we ask soldiers to do."

He turned his head to kiss the palm of her comforting hand. "It's better so."

"Perhaps, but if we thought on it more, there might be fewer wars."

"Not as long as war serves some people's purposes, and if evil rises, it must be fought."

"Your spying days are over now."

"My adventure in Warrington exposed me. I had no choice."

She didn't like the tone of that. "You'd rather have carried on?"

He took her hand in his, then kissed her knuckles, then held it against his naked chest. "I was achieving something. I passed on information that helped prevent gatherings from developing into riots, and riots into worse. Once I gained membership of the ruling committee, the Crimson Band, I had access to secret information."

"If that information leaked, didn't they suspect you?"

"They suspected someone, but I was careful. I only let out the most important details. My main purpose was to find a way to bring them all to court and gallows. The letter that endangered you should have done that if Solange Waite hadn't slipped out of sight."

She'd thought it was over, but he was still involved. Not as Ned Granger, but still involved, still in danger. It was hard to stay clearheaded when so afraid, but if he was locked to his task, it must be completed quickly.

"The middle-aged Frenchwoman. She's disappeared?"

"Yes, and we don't know what she's up

to. There's always a chance that she'll make contact with her husband or one of the others, and so they remain free and watched."

"Could she not have grown disgusted with her husband's plans and left him?"

"She probably has, but not in the sense you mean. Waite is too slow and cautious for her. She pretends to be a sober matron, but she's a fanatical revolutionary. As a young woman she was an ardent Jacobin. God knows what atrocities she was involved in during the Terror, but I've seen evidence enough of her heartless resolve. I gained my place in the Crimson Band because she had another man tortured and killed. She thought him a traitor on very skimpy evidence, though she was right."

"And you still took his place?"

"Danger has never deterred me, Hermione. You should know that."

But do you like it too much to stop?

She'd envisioned an ordinary life, and when he'd told her about the title, she'd been sure of it. They'd be Lord and Lady Faringay, with an estate in the country and a house in Town, plagued only by the regular challenges of life. But when had he ever known such a life? He'd had a difficult childhood with an unbalanced mother, then gone into the army. From there he'd gone to his dangerous secret work.

If he noticed her silence and read it correctly, he didn't mention it.

"Solange has sent the Boothroyd brothers to threaten men's families if they showed signs of wavering in allegiance. She's clever enough not to apply pressure to the target, but to those he cares for. All sensible villains do the same. Or heroes. I've seen the army use the same measures."

She pressed her head to his shoulder. "I wish no one was duty-bound to see and do such things."

"So do I."

"I still can't believe there's real danger. Not here in Britain. It could never work."

"The French Revolution didn't work, but think of the destruction and suffering it caused as it careened toward its end. Many of the early leaders had noble aims, but the wildfire consumed them. Most of the royalty and aristocracy who died were no more vile than others, and many were too young to have done anything to deserve death. Perhaps the greatest suffering landed on the weak and powerless, who were trampled, pillaged, and left in the dust, unnamed and unremembered, and all because of careless trouble-mongering."

Hermione held him close, tears stinging

at his passion for his cause. She felt that foreign suffering and dreaded it coming here, but she shuddered at how Thayne's resolve had entangled him in dark and dangerous ways.

"I was wrong to tell you," he said. "I've upset you. I never wanted to do that."

He tried to pull away, but she wouldn't allow it. "I see that you can't abandon the cause, but you must believe that nothing like the French Revolution could happen here. That man talking of Magna Carta and such didn't get much support, and that only mild, and then a trenchant widow poured water all over his ideas. She tangled him up in details of warming pans and the place of the common people in great events so that he ended up befuddled and obliged to toast to the health of Princess Charlotte."

She won the chuckle she'd hoped for. "I wish I'd been there."

"So do I. You'd have seen that most people have too much sense."

"I can't trust to that."

She recognized defeat. "So what are you doing now?"

"Trying to find Solange Waite before she blows up some part of London, quite possibly Drury Lane while the Regent is attending a play."

That startled her into sitting up. "Can you be serious?"

"Completely. I know her plans involve gas, and the theater has recently been renovated to use it in all areas. To blow it up and take royalty and any number of other important people with it is exactly the sort of grand gesture she'd aim for."

She'd never expected such a precise and perilous plot. Of course he'd risk anything to prevent it. She should feel the same way, but she'd rather see the Regent blown up than him.

As if he could read her mind, he laid his head against hers. "Don't try to weaken me, love. You might succeed."

"I've suffered your death once. I can't bear to do it again."

"I can only be careful. I can't draw back."

Why couldn't she have fallen in love with a comfortable, hearth cat of a man? She loved Thayne, however, and she knew what she must do. "Then tell me everything. Perhaps I can help."

"Jupiter, I'd forgotten. Perhaps you can. Can you draw?"

She was bemused to be plunged into the mundane. "Anyone can draw."

"I can't. I was never taught, but perhaps it wouldn't have helped. Some people can make a sketch of a person recognizable. My attempts look like nothing human. Can you better that?"

"I suppose so, but I'm no gifted artist. What do you need me to do?"

"You're one of the few people we can trust who've seen Nathan Boothroyd. Can you attempt his likeness?"

She couldn't help but shiver. "I remember him all too clearly, but whether I can capture that from memory . . . It's not like attempting a portrait of a sitter."

"Will you try? We're trying to draw out Seth Boothroyd by posting requests for help in identifying his brother's body, which is in Chester. They're alike, remember. We've had no luck so far, but if we could display a picture, Seth Boothroyd might come forward. If not, somebody might report seeing such a man in London. Either way, we'll have found Seth and can follow him to Solange and Isaac."

"That's ingenious."

"We had the idea because the Three-Banded Brotherhood have a sketch of me. Or rather, of Granger."

"They're *hunting* you? Dear heaven. That's why you had your hair cut short. It's not much of a disguise."

He kissed her forehead. "The 'disguise' is

mostly my being fashionable Lord Faringay. Who would assume that transformation?"

"All the same, you're in danger at every moment. I can't bear it."

"You have to."

His tone caught her up. She was definitely not made to be a warrior's wife, but she'd do her best to be strong. "I'll attempt a sketch now," she said. "Where can I find pencil and paper?"

He held her back. "A few hours won't make any difference. I'm sorry, love. I was too blunt."

"But right. Now that I know you're hunted, I want that madwoman found as much as you or more. I don't care about the Regent or the whole government, but *you* will be safe. I intend to be a respectable married woman into a happy old age."

"And I very much want to be a respectable married man." His kiss was tender, but no less passionate for that, and she was willingly sliding into more delights when he put her apart. "Desist, you wanton woman. We have to decide how to face the world."

"What world? Who cares?" She tickled and teased up his side.

He captured her hand. "The world cannot be denied, love."

She became aware again of music. It was

faint as fairy harps, but it told her the dance party continued. The world was there and everyone there must wonder at her frantic appearance and subsequent disappearance. And Thayne's.

Scandal! All very well to brush aside thoughts of scandalous intimacy, but this was real and close.

"What do you think people assume?" she whispered.

He grinned and whispered back, "The worst." Then he spoke normally. "We can hope not. Arden was supposed to devise a story. I assume no one but he and Lady Arden know I brought you to your bedroom and stayed. People might wonder, but if I never reappear at the party, I can plausibly have left the house at that point. Time for me to dress."

She held on to him. "Doesn't that depend on the story Lord Arden devised? If we were long-parted lovers, reunited in dramatic circumstances . . ."

". . . which seems the only likely explanation . . ."

". . . would you leave?"

"I am noble and restrained, but was so overcome by joy that I chose not to face others."

"Then how are you going to summon a

carriage now without the servants knowing?"

"I love a sharp-witted woman. I'll walk."

"When there are people intent on *killing* you?"

He grinned. "Cosseting."

She remembered their conversation in Tranmere. "I'd tie you to the hearth if I could."

"I might like it, but not now." He pulled free and she had to let him go. As he began to dress, he said, "There could be cozy hearths in our future, love. Will you mind a country life? I've an estate to learn about and look after."

"Not at all, and I know something of the business."

"It's been somewhat neglected, by my father and then by me."

"We'll care for it together."

"There are ghosts. Not real ones — if that makes sense, but . . . My mother killed herself there."

She left the bed, snatching her shift to pull on before taking his hands. "We'll deal with that together. We'll make it a happy home. Trust me to do that for you."

He raised their hands to his lips. "You're astonishing."

The look in his eyes made her blush with

pride. "Note, sir, that this requires that I be your wife. You must stay safe." *It will take at least a week to marry in Selby. In a week the Frenchwoman could be captured and the danger over.*

But he said, "A special license. That permits marriage in any church at any time. Anywhere, in fact, but I think you'd like a church."

"I suppose we could obtain one quickly." She must be a better actress than she'd ever imagined. He didn't seem to hear her hollow dismay.

"I think so. Someone will know." He kissed her hand again. "You could be my wife tomorrow."

"I don't think so." She'd found a sliver of hope. "Tomorrow's Sunday. I'm sure no one can obtain a marriage license on a Sunday."

She wished he didn't look disappointed, but when he said, "I must wait, my dearest dear?" and seemed to mean it, she melted.

"Perhaps only until Monday."

"Or Tuesday at the most." He drew her in for another deep kiss.

It was hard to part, but they managed it and he set to finish buttoning his waistcoat. She found the strength to keep up the carefree act and perched on the edge of the bed. "It's almost as delightful to watch you dress as undress."

"And it's entrancing to see you in your shift. Do you want to dress again?"

"Only in my nightgown."

He smiled at it, spread over the frame near the fire. "Nightgown and nightshirt next time."

"Husband and wife."

"Wife and husband."

They chuckled at their own nonsense.

He completed his dressing and then went to the mirror to put on the neckcloth, grimacing. "Braydon's man tied it for me. I'm no hand at fancy knots. You?"

"I'm sorry, no."

He achieved something and stuck a gold pin in it, but it wasn't very elegant. She found that endearing. Despite his present appearance, she suspected he'd been more comfortable in Ned Granger's clothes. She didn't mind that. "Who's Braydon?" she asked.

"An old acquaintance who's been helping me. He was with me on the road from Warrington, driving the curricle."

"I hardly remember anything except that man, fear, and you."

He came to her to touch her cheek. "I deeply regret putting you in danger."

She covered his hand with hers. "Without

that, would we be here? But who exactly is Sir George Hawkinville?"

He sat with her on the edge of the bed, holding her hand. "I served under him for a time on the Peninsula. He's left the army, but holds a special commission from the Regent to seek out the revolutionaries. When I took on that crusade, we came together again. He's here in Belcraven House tonight as a guest."

"So he's a friend."

"A colleague, say. In large part a superior officer. You're thinking me friendless."

"How did you know?"

"The concern in your eyes. I had any number of friends in my youth and in the army, but my recent work has cut me off from them. Those friendships can be revived, and Braydon has become one. Since resuming my true identity, I've met a few other good fellows. You don't need to mother me."

"Mothering wasn't quite what I had in mind," she teased. "But I do hope we have children. Is it bold of me to say so?"

"Very practical, I'd say, given the way we explode." He kissed her slowly, and again. "Odd that it's so hard to part. We've had practice."

"But we must. Promise you'll return

tomorrow."

"On my honor. I'll help you work on the sketch."

He rose, and she had to loose his hand. He put more coal on the fire, which had almost gone out. When it was burning well, he turned back to her. "Tomorrow, my wife."

He went toward the door, but she said, "Oh, wait!" She went to her trinket box. "It's in a sorry state, but perhaps it will still work."

She offered him the scrap of stained silk. He looked at it, then kissed it. "With this, I'm invincible." He unlocked the door and left.

Hermione hugged herself, amazed that she could be infused with delight but riven through with dread. She must do everything possible to put an end to his enemies. She'd execute the drawing and help him find the brute's brother. That would lead to the Frenchwoman. All the danger could be over before they said their vows.

Solange had received a report from Chester. Sarah Lawrey must have played the grieving sister well, for after she'd identified the body she'd obtained not only the name of one of the men who'd found it but his

London address so she could write her thanks. Solange hadn't yet told Seth, for he was a man of rash action. But that wasn't her biggest concern. Rather, she had to wonder whether this Braydon had found the corpse or created it. Apparently he'd found the body by the roadside but then persuaded a carter to take it to Chester. Perhaps he was an innocent passerby, but she'd like to know more about the man described by the coroner as a member of one of the finest families in the north.

She sent Betty to Parsifal Street to learn what she could. Betty was clever at gossiping with servants and shopkeepers.

"Fancy house with rooms for six idle, worthless types," Betty reported hours later, "each set of rooms enough for a household. Braydon goes by the name Beau Braydon, so he's the sort to waste a fortune on fine clothes and drink. He'll be first to embrace Lady Guillotine." Betty was one of the fiercest for the revolution, but she secretly bought lottery tickets, so she was fueled by envy, not principle. Still, she was useful for now.

"You found out nothing about Braydon himself?"

"Course I did. Went to the mews where they keep their horses and found a groom there willing to chat. He has horses for drawing his curricle and another for riding around the parks. If he goes traveling, he's too fancy-dancy to take a common coach. He drives himself in his curricle!"

"Shocking," Solange said, holding on to her patience. "What of Granger?"

"No sign of him. Braydon's just another damned aristo." Betty emphasized that by spitting on the floor.

"Yet he discovered Nathan Boothroyd's body."

"Likely he just came across it, Solange, like he said. If he had anything to do with the death, he'd not get involved, would he?"

That made sense, but Solange had a feeling about Braydon. Granger had disappeared. He'd visited Waite, then disappeared. Through Betty she was in touch with the Brotherhood groups in London, so she knew no one had reported seeing a man resembling Tregoven's portrait.

Could Granger be Braydon?

"Did you find out how long Braydon has lived there?"

"A few years," Betty said, "but he's often away. Traveling in his sodding curricle."

Could Granger have juggled the two identities? She wouldn't have thought so, but he hadn't always been in her presence.

"His appearance?"

"Dandy, like I said."

"Dark or blond?"

"How the hell would I find out that?"

By asking, Solange thought. Why were all her tools so inadequate? She dismissed Betty and rolled everything in her mind. It was very unlikely that this Beau Braydon was Granger's alter ego, but the great moment was too close to be careless.

She went to the kitchen, where Seth sat moodily staring at the fire. "I have sad news. Nathan is dead."

She was braced for instant rage and surprised when his lips wobbled and his eyes glistened with tears. He rubbed them like a child. "No. No, he can't be."

She sat and took his hand. "It's a shock to us both. He was killed, Seth. Struck from behind and killed."

The lie about the cowardly attack summoned the anger she wanted. "Who? Bloody Granger?" He rose to his feet, fists clenched. "Where is he? Where is he?"

"I'm sure Granger was involved, but the only name I have is Braydon. A piece of nothing called Beau Braydon. He lives at number 23, Parsifal Street."

"Where's that?"

"A hackney will take you there, but we

522

must think about this. About how to pay him for what he's done. You won't be able to gain access to his lodging."

"I'll wait outside. Kill him when he comes out."

"It's dark. You won't know him. We must think."

Boothroyds didn't think. He glowered, his hands working in frustration, which was a bad sign. He'd once put his fist through a door when in this mood.

"Go and watch," she said quickly. "Watch who goes in and out, but don't do anything unless you're sure it's Braydon. Come back and report to me, especially if you see whether his hair is blond or dark. You might even see Granger there. If you do, kill him."

"I'll bring him back," he said. "Need to do him slow."

She wanted Granger dead and all others who might stand in her way, but there was no reasoning with Seth at the moment. "If you can. But don't let him slip away."

When he'd left, she sighed with relief. Boothroyds were useful, but unpredictably dangerous, especially Seth without Nathan to keep him in hand. *Like an explosive, in fact.* She smiled as she watched Isaac across the room, so thoroughly enjoying his work.

CHAPTER 39

Mark considered the layout of the mansion. It was divided by the central hall and grand staircase. The public rooms on this floor — the ballroom and anterooms — were on the other side, so he'd stay over here. Where? He hesitated to enter a bedchamber.

He hadn't mentioned it to Hermione, but his danger might not come only from the Three-Banded Brotherhood. He suspected one or more gentlemen were keen to have words with him. True, Lady Arden had left him alone with Hermione, but that wouldn't have carried approval of what had happened. Arden could consider himself an outraged host, and these Rogues seemed to see themselves as honorary brothers. He couldn't run from them.

A manservant emerged from a concealed door and turned into the corridor bearing a short pile of white linen. He paused, eyeing Mark uncertainly.

Mark reminded himself that he wasn't an interloper, but a guest and a peer of the realm. "I'm seeking the library," he said. "Is it on this floor?"

"Yes, sir. Toward the back. May I take you there?"

"Thank you."

Mark followed him and found himself in a small, elegant, and apparently well-stocked room of glass-fronted shelves. The only light came from a lamp, but the servant used that to light two others hanging from pedestals.

"Would you wish me to light the fire, sir?"

"Thank you, no. When you have time, please tell Lord Arden that I'm here. I'm Viscount Faringay."

"Yes, milord."

The servant's expression had shifted to more respect, but revealed nothing more. Either the earlier drama hadn't spread, which seemed unlikely, or the servant was well trained. Mark couldn't imagine any way that servants or guests could know everything. He hoped not, for Hermione's sake. He'd not have her embroiled in a scandal.

Should have thought of that earlier, shouldn't you?

He wandered the room, glancing at shelves and seeing the occasional book he'd like to dip into, but his mind preferred to dwell on delights, when not braced for trouble. At the time, in that room with Hermione, it had seemed the most natural thing in the world, and their fantasy wedding a true blessing. Any man responsible for her would see it otherwise and he judged Arden to be a man of action. He hoped a degree of respect for books and fine furniture would restrain him.

The door opened and he turned.

It wasn't Arden, but the man he'd met earlier as Delaney. He seemed calm enough.

"I'm pleased to find Hermione's beloved alive and hearty," he said.

Mark inclined his head, unable to read him. "I gather you're the leader of a group called the Company of Rogues, and something else called the Curious Creatures?"

Delaney smiled. "You must think me very odd. I was the leader of the Rogues at school. As for the Curious Creatures, I helped found it to explore the more obscure crannies of knowledge, but I rarely attend the meetings these days, as I prefer country life."

Both smile and tone were unthreatening, but Mark remained tense, waiting for the first blow. "I gather you've taken Hermione under your wing," he said, "because of her brother."

"After a fashion. I helped her find Dr. Grammaticus. That's where the Curious Creatures come in."

"Damn the Curious Creatures! We're to marry."

The smile seemed genuine. "I'm pleased. I'm sure everyone will be."

"Everyone?"

The smiling lips twitched. "Your summons to meet here reached Arden when I was nearby and I persuaded him to let me come instead. He has a hasty temper. I don't."

"But you're angry?"

"Not at all. He might be, depending."

Mark tired of dancing around the subject. "He would have cause."

"Ah, you conventional thinkers. It's clear Hermione loves you, and likely that you love her. Assuming you are to marry, no one will make difficulties. Of course, if you are ever less than kind and loving toward her, your life will become very difficult indeed."

"That's blunt."

"That is simple truth," Delaney said, in the same equable voice. "Are you likely to be less than kind and loving?"

"Yes. Isn't everyone? Are you perfect? Is

Arden?"

After a moment, Delaney winced. "That's a far sharper blow than you can imagine. I apologize for indulging in drama and even hyperbole. You understand the message, however. I've only known Hermione for a few days, and until she believed you dead, she gave the impression of enjoying a good enough life, but it can't have been that way. Both parents dead, and from things Roger said, neither was ideal. Both brothers dead, which led to the loss of her home."

Mark hadn't thought of all that. "Her only remaining family is a sister with whom she's not entirely at harmony. If your message is that she deserves loving kindness, I intend to do my best."

"I can't know what she deserves, but it's what I'd wish for her, for her brother Roger's sake."

Mark chose to cut through this. "Do you know how to get a special license?"

"Archbishop of Canterbury, money, and oaths that all's aboveboard."

"Omniscient, are you?"

Delaney smiled. "Annoying, I know, but it's more of a magpie mind."

"I don't have time to go to Canterbury."

"There's an office in London. Knightrider Street."

"Thank you. Does the magpie know about my secret work?"

The smile turned wry. "Hawkinville is a Rogue by association and I've been somewhat involved in his current work myself. That's why I'm in London. I gather you met Beaumont."

"Yes."

"Rogue."

"Arden, of course," Mark said. "How many of you are there?"

"Rogues? Like maggots in meat. No, in strict fact we are ten, and, as long as you're on the side of the angels, all well-disposed to a brother-in-law."

Mark wasn't used to feeling out of his depth and didn't like it. "All I want is to marry Hermione as soon as possible, find Solange Waite and put an end to her and her plans, and then . . ."

"Settle on your estate?" Delaney said.

"More magpie finds?"

"My family home is Grattingly in Berkshire. Faringay is close enough for talk to reach there."

Mark deeply disliked talking about his intimate affairs, but it came with the situation. "It's been neglected, yes, but I'll take it in hand."

"I'm sure you will. I was wondering

whether you can settle at all. You've never had the opportunity to try."

"For Hermione, I will."

"And your work?" But then Delaney shook his head. "We'll talk of it tomorrow. I gather Hermione is to draw a likeness of one of the conspirators."

"She claims not to have great skill."

"We'll hope she's modest," Delaney said.

Mark's mind was stuck on, *And your work?* He knew Hermione worried about that, too, and he didn't know the answer. Could he abandon the fight when the danger remained? Solange and Waite were only one head of the hydra. But Hermione shouldn't live in fear.

In face of that predicament, Mark was in danger of threatening the fine furniture himself, as he'd feared Arden would.

"You wish to leave, I assume," Delaney said. "I'll arrange for one of Arden's carriages to take you back to Braydon's, but Braydon should accompany you. Foolish to lose you at this point, when you know the enemy best." He left without another word.

Mark ran a hand through his hair. His annoyingly short hair. He remembered Hermione's irritation at being taken over by the Rogues and understood exactly how she felt, but he drew on his usual steadiness. If the Company of Rogues could help win her happiness, he'd do his best to be gracious.

Delaney's unanswered question was now a worm in his mind, however. He'd spoken to Hermione of a rural life, but could he settle to it? As Delaney had said, he'd never tried, so he couldn't know. He'd said he'd do it for Hermione's sake and he'd meant it, but that didn't mean he'd be able to do it well. He had no good memories of his family home.

Hermione would have drifted in dreams, but practical concerns forced their way in. The world hadn't disappeared and neither had the consequences of her actions.

She changed her shift for her nightgown. She picked up her scattered clothing and arranged it all neatly on two chairs, as if she'd undressed in an orderly manner. That didn't deal with the blood spot on her sheet. It was small, but it was there, along with some dampness. Laundresses would speculate. Servants would gossip. . . .

She rang the bell, hoping Nolly hadn't gone to bed.

The maid was there in minutes. "Are you feeling better now, milady? I heard you fainted."

And more, Hermione could see. "What

are people saying?"

"That you recognized a gentleman, milady — a Lord Faringay — and fainted. He carried you away with her ladyship going along with you. That you'd been close to Lord Faringay and thought him dead. And that you were in your stockinged feet, milady."

Hermione put a hand to her head. "I left my boots by a door."

"Should I go and get them, milady?"

"No, no, they're not important."

"What happened, milady? Did that man *do* something to you?"

"No, but . . . Yes." There was nothing for it. "The sheet."

Nolly went over. "I'd say he did something, all right."

"Nothing terrible. We're going to be married."

"Happen they all say that, milady."

Hermione giggled. "Yes, but it's true. Lady Arden knows."

Nolly's eyes went wide.

Hermione had meant marriage, not marriage bed, but she'd let the lie live. "Even so, I don't want the laundresses to see that sheet."

"I see that, milady, but I don't know where to get a clean sheet here. I reckon we'd best wash this one. I mean me, milady."

" 'We' is fine, but then it will be wet."

Nolly looked around. "I have it. You have some of that red wine left. We'll pour it over."

"I was drinking port in bed?"

"You were doing something in bed, milady," Nolly said, deep with disapproval no matter what Lady Arden was supposed to know. "It's the best I can think of."

"And it's very clever. We'll use food as well. I was eating in bed and spilled everything." She poured the bit of port over the stain, then upended the remains of pastry, cake, and fruit on top and smeared the mess around. "Thank heavens for raspberry jam."

"Lawks, milady, that's a terrible mess."

There was a knock at the door. Hermione wanted to ignore it, but everyone would know she was in here. She nodded to Nolly, who went to open it. Then opened it wide.

Beth Arden came in.

Hermione instinctively stepped in front of the messy bed, but then moved aside. "Beth, I'm so sorry. I'm afraid I've made a horrible mess eating in the bed. I know I shouldn't have."

Beth's lips twitched. "It is often tricky, isn't it?" she said. She addressed Nolly. "Ask

Mrs. Tailstock for fresh sheets, and bring back another maid to help you remake the bed." When Nolly had left, Beth dropped the lightness. "Are you all right?"

Hermione knew she should probably feel confused or even guilty, but she couldn't help a beaming smile. "Wonderfully. We're to marry as soon as we can. We did marry in our own way, but properly. I mean we'll do it properly! I'm sorry. I'm giddy. To find him alive!"

Beth came to hug her. "I'm so glad. I felt some qualms at leaving you alone together, but your grief had been so powerful, and the way he reacted to your distress and collapse . . ."

"The way he reacted?"

"With all the distress and ardor you could want. He would have fought off armies for you at that moment."

Hermione exhaled with delight, but then she remembered the real enemies. "He's in danger, Beth. I can't say how."

"I know. Hawkinville explained some of it."

"That's a relief. I wish there was something I could do. I want to protect him."

"Regard him as a soldier, Hermione. We can't go with them into battle."

"We can wish we could."

"We'd be a hindrance to them."

"Not if we were trained to fight."

"Indeed, but this is not the time to debate such a change in the natural order."

"Boadicea? Amazons? Oh, what am I saying? I don't have the nature for violence."

"I understand you have a more normal skill that might be of use."

"The likeness. I've never been a skilled artist. I can attempt a tolerable watercolor landscape, but faces?"

"We can only ever do our best. Did Faringay explain how it seemed he was dead? I've heard no explanation of that."

Hermione told the story, but then the maids came in to remake the bed. Hermione wanted to babble excuses, but she attempted a haughty expression of indifference. She knew Beth had stayed to lend propriety. If the marchioness saw nothing suspicious in the stained sheet, then how could a servant suggest it?

When the bed was pristine and the servants had gone, Beth said, "I'll leave you to rest now. The party is coming to an end, but I still have guests."

"Thank you. You're very kind."

"I hope we can be friends."

"I hope we already are. Will you be a witness?" Hermione asked. "At the wedding?"

Beth smiled. "It would be an honor."

When she was alone, Hermione stood dreaming of her wedding. It could be the simplest affair in a plain room and she wouldn't care. She would be married to Thayne.

He'd always be Thayne to her, but once married, she'd be Lady Faringay.

Hermione, Lady Faringay.

She was tempted to write it down, over and over, as lovers so often did. Years ago she remembered attempting "Mrs. Thayne," but without a first name it had lacked magic. She laughed when she remembered trying "Mrs. Lieutenant Thayne," but that certainly hadn't worked. Laughter faded when she remembered attempting a portrait of him. She'd thrown it away because it could have been any man, and an ugly one at that.

She looked out again at the garden. It was still deserted, for now a light rain fell through dying lamplight.

She remembered the grief she'd felt out there. It had been overwhelmed by joy, but she never wanted to feel the same pain. He must live and her drawing could help. She must find the ability to create a recognizable likeness of the brutish Boothroyd.

■ ■ ■ ■

Seth Boothroyd kept watch outside the Parsifal Street building, untroubled by mizzling rain, or by not knowing what Beau Braydon looked like. He would find a way to avenge Nathan, struck from behind, with no chance to fight.

Men began to return from their evenings in hackneys and carriages, hurrying into the building beneath umbrellas. He caught scraps of conversation, but none of interest until a fancy carriage halted and two dandies climbed down, shielded from the rain by a large umbrella held by a liveried footman.

"There," one said. "Safe and sound."

"You're not inside yet," the other said.

"A rifle from a distance, Braydon? In this light?"

The men went inside. The footman closed his umbrella and took his perch on the back of the carriage, and it went off down the street.

So that had been Braydon. Fine dark clothing and natty hat, worn at a good angle. Not sure about hair color.

Nathan would have liked that hat. Nathan knew how to dress. He bought my clothes, made sure I wore them right. Nothing's the same without him. Nothing will ever be the same without him.

Slowly, a new thought came to him.

Bloody Ned Granger had killed Nathan. Nathan had gone after him, and Nathan was dead. That other man had sounded a lot like Ned Granger. Hadn't looked like him, but sounded like him.

He set off back to Great Peter Street. Mrs. Waite would know what to do.

Chapter 40

The next morning Hermione breakfasted in her room, then went to see Edgar, hoping no sign of her adventures showed.

He was sitting up in his chair, watching the square. She thought he might be watching for Grammaticus, but then remembered they'd decided not to tell him in case the man was clearly a fraud. Was that fair, though? She hated being treated like a foolish female, but she was treating Edgar like a foolish old man.

She sat beside him. "We've found Dr. Grammaticus."

He turned sharply, eyes bright. "He's coming here?"

"I hope so. He's living in Tunbridge Wells. He may have no true cure to offer, Edgar."

"I know that. I've always known that. But it'll be good to try. Good to be doing something."

"I hope his cure works quickly, then, so

you can dance at my wedding."

"Wedding? To whom?" But then he said, "*Quickly?* Why the hurry? Wait a moment. Yesterday you were in a state because the man you loved was dead!"

"Then I found he wasn't. He's Lord Faringay and we're to marry."

His brows met in anxiety. "You've never mentioned anyone called Faringay. Someone asked about a Granger. What have you been up to, girl? Are you being duped?"

"Don't get in a state. Faringay and I met five years ago, then again recently, and found we love each other."

"So who was the dead man? And who's Granger? You're spinning me a tarradiddle, girl."

"I'm not a girl!" She reined in her temper. "Very well. Here's the story in brief. I met Faringay at a ball five years ago. He was a lieutenant in the army then, and soon left for the war. We lost touch, but met again in Lancashire on my journey to you." She skipped the bit about his stealing into her room. "By then he was using the name Ned Granger and engaged in secret work for the Home Office, though I didn't know it." Perhaps she'd leave out the letter and abduction, too. "For that reason, we didn't have many opportunities to meet, but I hoped to encounter him in London, which I have."

"So what's this business about him being dead?"

"Ned Granger had taken a position in a group of dangerous revolutionaries, but he was discovered, so the Home Office staged his death and Faringay took up his real identity. He'd assumed a scruffy appearance as Granger, but he's now very neat and stylish."

"He played this trick without telling you?"

"He didn't know," Hermione said quickly, but really, she was exasperated by Edgar's trying to rule her life.

"I knew you were caught up in something dangerous," he said, scowling. "The less you have to do with Faringay, the better."

"I love him, Edgar, and I have for years."

"Love. More dangerous than poison, that is. I've known people die for love, and not in a swooning sort of way. But there's no cure for that ailment, is there?"

"I fear not."

"You're marrying quickly. Why?" Hermione felt herself go red. "Never mind. I know how young blood runs hot and sense flies up the chimney, but he'd better do right by you."

"He will."

"Is he worthy of you, Hermione?" he asked, in a gentler way. "You're a grand lass and marriage is for life."

This sort of protectiveness she could welcome. She took his hand. "He's a grand lad, and I want him for life. Edgar, will you give me away?"

Perhaps red showed in his grayish cheeks. "Your brother-in-law would be more suitable."

"He's not my family and I don't want to delay, not even for days. I can't explain, but I can't."

"All these things you can't explain," he muttered. "And you haven't thought. I can't walk you down an aisle."

"Very well. We'll marry here. In your room. A special license permits that."

"Are you sure? No church? No people gathered outside to see the bride?"

"I'm sure."

"Then I will, and gladly. Annie'll be pleased. You'll need your dowry."

"There's no hurry. He has adequate money."

"All the same. I had my banker over here yesterday and I've set it in hand. You'll need some extra for bride clothes and all such stuff. I have some cash to hand."

"There's no time for that and I have

Beth's finery. But thank you." She kissed his cheek. It wasn't as gray as it had been when she'd first seen him, but she'd have kissed him anyway. "Your gift of money will mean a great deal to Polly."

He shrugged that away and said, "Settlements. You'll have good settlements to secure your future. I'll have my solicitor back here immediately. Some of my money'll be put in trust for you. And your Faringay will provide generous pin money."

"You're acting like a father, Edgar."

He pouted. "If I'm to give you to him, I'll see it's done right."

"You are very dear to me, Edgar. Truly."

He wiped his eyes. "And you to me. Be happy. And be safe! You've still the kris on you?"

She took it out of her pocket to show him. "But I'm in no danger here."

"Keep it on you. Like I told you, the worst danger sends no heralds. I wish I weren't so damned feeble!"

She squeezed his hand. "Try not to worry. I'll be careful at all times. Now, we're to go to church, and afterward I'm supposed to attempt a drawing."

"A drawing? Of whom?"

"A man I saw in Warrington. The one who was pursuing Thayne."

"Thayne, Granger, Faringay. What honest man has so many names?"

She chuckled. "Most peers have both title and surname."

"And how many of them are honest?"

She laughed again and went to dress for church.

She walked to a nearby church with the Ardens and some of their household. When she returned, she heard Thayne waited in the library. Never had anyone shed outdoor clothing so quickly, but still by the time she joined him, Arden was there, and also an elegant, fine-boned man who was introduced as Braydon. Another lean, but tougher, man was Sir George Hawkinville at last.

"Of Peel Street," she said when they were introduced.

He inclined his head. "I regret your involvement, Lady Hermione, but your effort today could be crucial. Shame most men aren't taught drawing skills."

"My lessons can only take me so far, Sir George, but I'll do my best."

Braydon said, "My gift is memory, Lady Hermione. I hope to be able to help that way."

She smiled, but then became aware of a tension in the air. "What's happened?"

"No matter," Hawkinville said, but Thayne answered her.

"Last evening a gentleman in the government received an oilcloth package at home, which he opened himself, in private because it was perfumed with violet. He thought that indicated that it was from a lady of his acquaintance. Inside he found a letter, also perfumed, to such an extent that it was damp. He hid it in a locked box in his bedroom until he could attempt to read it. This morning, he was woken by an explosion. It was fierce enough to break the lock and fling the lid back so that it broke. The box burst into flames, but they were extinguished, so there was no disaster. But that is the second attempt."

Thayne hadn't told her there'd been one earlier. "Surely now everyone will know about the damp letters," she said.

"Given the involvement of servants in this case, it can't be kept quiet, but what if they send a package out of town, or to a military barracks? There's more. There was an explosion at the Customs House last night, apparently caused by gas. There's no evidence of outside interference, but we have to wonder. We have to stop Solange now."

"Yes, of course."

A small easel had been set up on the

library table, with paper ready, and pencils. Hermione sat before it and picked up a pencil. This was important and, above all, key to Thayne's safety, so she must create a good likeness, but when everyone gathered behind her, it didn't help her nerves. She tried to summon an image of the man who'd snatched her, but saw only implacable eyes and terror. Instead, she turned her memory back to that encounter at the Lamb and found she could remember him quite well.

"Square," she said, glancing behind at Thayne. "I remember thinking that. That he had a square head on square shoulders."

"Yes, that's right."

She lightly drew that, then began to sketch eyes into the square head. It wasn't right, and she remembered the shrill voice of Miss Chandler, their long-suffering governess. "The eyes are in the *middle* of the face, Lady Hermione, not toward the top!" Miss Chandler had drawn a line across the middle of the oval of a head. "Draw the eyes *there*."

Hermione lightly drew a line across the middle of the square. It looked far too low, but Miss Chandler's way had worked, so she drew two ovals along the line.

"Not so excessively close together,"

Thayne said, leaning forward over her right shoulder. His closeness didn't help her concentration, but otherwise it was magical. And his comment was helpful. She'd made the same mistake in that long-ago drawing. "Put the nose in first," Miss Chandler had commanded.

"His nose?" she asked Thayne. "I think it was quite broad."

"That's right." Thayne's voice, close by her ear. His breath against her cheek. His warmth and smell surrounding her. She pulled herself together and sketched in a broad nose, remembering rather flaring nostrils. Then she corrected the ovals at a better distance.

"Low forehead," Braydon said.

"He was wearing a hat," she remembered. "Quite a smart one."

She sketched in a tall beaver hat with a curly brim. Things were easy. It was faces she found hard. "Is that beginning to resemble him?"

Thayne said, "Yes. But it's not distinctive enough."

"His mouth," she said. "There was something odd about it. Something frightening."

"Pointed canine teeth," Braydon said. "Filed that way, I assume."

"That's right!" She drew an open mouth so the teeth showed.

It looked ridiculous.

She tossed her pencil down. "That doesn't even look human!"

"It's certainly not right," Thayne admitted, "but Nathan wouldn't have been walking around showing his teeth, and the main thing is that Seth sees the poster and thinks it might be his brother. Draw him with mouth closed. We can put the filed teeth in the description. It should have been in the earlier one."

"Mea culpa," Braydon said.

There was a piece of rubber to use to correct errors, but it left a smudge. She drew a closed mouth over it, unhappy with the result. She did an easier part and added a high collar and a wide neckcloth.

Braydon said, "He was wearing a gold pin in it. A simple circle."

She added that. Dark jacket. She sat back to consider it. "It's still not right."

Braydon said, "His head wasn't completely square. It curved down to the chin."

Hermione corrected that, then said, "Thick neck! I remember how thick it was. And broad, heavy shoulders. Like a bull." She roughly widened neck and shoulders to what seemed an extreme amount, but it did convey the man.

"Might that be good enough?"

"It might," Thayne said, "but there's something else."

"About the ears?"

"Long whiskers," Braydon said. "Side wings. Dark and dense down to the corner of the jaw."

"Yes!" Hermione said, and drew them in. "That really might be recognizable." She looked up to Thayne for confirmation.

Smiling, he kissed her. "It is."

She was blushing again, but she'd happily settle to more kisses if not for her audience. And if Thayne weren't already studying the drawing again.

"If there weren't so many barbers in London, that might be a line of enquiry. I'm sure both Boothroyds had to shave frequently to keep up their natty appearance, but I never knew their intimate details, thank God."

"Hair in the nostrils, too," Braydon said.

Hermione added them. "It's him. It would never be accepted for the Royal Academy, but I do believe it's recognizable."

Thayne swept her up and spun her around.

Hawkinville took the drawing. "I'll have

this prepared for printing along with the details of his appearance. You'd best come with me, Braydon."

Braydon grimaced humorously at them before following orders.

Hermione looked up at Thayne. "When the Boothroyd man is found, will you go in pursuit?" She knew the answer. He'd feel honor-bound to.

But he said, "Not unless I'm essential. I want to be in at the end, but I need to marry you before taking unnecessary risks."

"That could tempt me to delay the wedding. No, I won't. I wouldn't try to tie you that way."

He wiggled his eyebrows. "But in other ways?"

"Don't," she murmured, aware of the Ardens still in the room.

"But I love to make you blush."

"And I prefer to be decent. In public, at least."

He grinned. "Such promise for privacy."

They might have flirted on if a servant hadn't entered with a card to present to Arden. Arden brought it to Hermione. "A gentleman to see you. The Marquess of Carsheld."

"Porteous!"

"You don't have to see him if you don't

want to," Thayne said.

"I'm not alarmed, only surprised. He must have learned I'm in Town. Beth, will you come with me?"

Beth raised her brows, but came as chaperone. Porteous had been taken to the drawing room and was standing, hands clasped behind him, looking out of a window. He turned at their entry with a weighty expression.

"Cousin Hermione. I came as soon as I heard."

"Heard what?" Hermione asked, but then realized that talk of her precipitous entry to the ballroom last night must be whirling around Town. "Oh. It was a misunderstanding, Cousin. All is well now."

Beth suggested they all sit and offered tea, which was declined. Hermione saw that Porteous had not improved over the past months. He wasn't enjoying his wealth at the table, for he was even thinner and his hair had retreated even more.

"As head of the family," he said, "I felt I must enquire as to your welfare."

"That's very kind of you, Cousin, but as you see, I am quite well."

"I have come to offer you the protection of my house."

"I assure you, Cousin, I'm well situated

551

here with my friends."

"All the same, it would be more suitable if you were to remove to my house."

She remembered past conversations. Politeness never worked. "No, thank you."

He turned to Beth. "Lady Arden, you must see the propriety of it."

"Must I?" Beth asked amiably. "Please, Carsheld, don't attempt to deprive me of my dear friend's company."

"My mother is most anxious to have Cousin Hermione's company."

"I'm so sorry to disappoint her," Hermione said, trying for Beth's tone. "But for now I must stay here."

"You will remove to my house soon, then? Or should I say, *our* house." His expression was probably intended to suggest a loverlike innuendo, but it made her think of a particularly nasty cat outside a mousehole.

"I'm afraid that won't be possible," she said, doing her best to hide her glee. "I'm pleased that you will be one of the first to know that I am betrothed, Cousin. I have accepted an offer from Viscount Faringay."

His thin cheeks flared red. "Faringay? Who is he?"

"A very suitable gentleman," Beth said. "He was in the army, and subsequently involved in delicate diplomatic work, but now he intends to settle on his estates."

"And he takes you without a dowry, Hermione? The man's a fool."

"Then you're a fool," Hermione retorted, "for you tried to do the same."

He rose. "I come to do my duty to you as family and receive scorn in return. You and your sister will get no more kindness from me. Not one penny."

Hermione rose, too. "We have no need of it, Carsheld. A relative on my mother's side has provided for us most generously. Good day to you, and do give my warmest regards to your mother."

He picked up his hat and gloves and stalked out of the room.

"My, my," Beth said. "I see why you wanted a companion."

Hermione blew out a breath. "Mostly to stop me from murdering him."

"He wanted to marry you?"

"He's been trying to force me to it by offering assistance to my sister and her family. If not for Edgar, I might have had to give in."

"I would have stopped you if I could. I assume he's not invited to the wedding?"

Hermione slapped a hand over a giggle. "I'm tempted to invite him in hopes that he would choke. Probably I should, but he's

the sort to attend and play the specter at
the feast, bringing his mother with him,
dressed in mourning."

"It's almost worth it."

"No. Do you know, when he inherited, he
never offered us any extra items from the
various houses? We'd taken what we were
entitled to, but there were other things that
held meaning to us and could have no
significance to him. I hinted to him once
about two miniatures. He replied that they
would be wedding gifts."

"We can only hope that he marries suit-
ably," said Beth.

It took a moment for Hermione to catch
the meaning. "Oh, yes indeed!"

"Come to my boudoir so we can discuss
your very suitable wedding. Who you want
to invite and all other details."

"There's too much going on to think of
that now."

"There is nothing going on here and now.
Your part is done."

"Thayne —"

"Quite likely he's left."

"No. He'll want to know I'm all right. I
must speak to him, but then I'll discuss
wedding plans, if you wish."

"You're a very unusual bride."

"Were you all in a tizzy over your bridals?"

Beth's smile was wry. "After a fashion, but perhaps your way is best."

Hermione hurried in search of Thayne, and found him alone in the library. "I knew you'd want to know."

He took her hands. "Was there any difficulty? I watched him leave. A sour skeleton."

She chuckled. "Very sour. I refused to move into his house and refused his implication that I would soon be his bride, informing him that I was to marry you. I crowned the moment by telling him Polly and I were well funded and free of his screws. It was, all in all, very satisfactory."

He drew her to sit on a velvet-covered bench. "I wanted to act as your protector, but I see there was no need."

"Do you mind? Remember, I have no physical courage, so I'll accept protection there willingly."

"I pray you're never in danger again."

"And I you." They couldn't help but kiss, again and again. "But my prayers won't work."

"Pray for my safety, love. I do intend to be as careful as I can."

"Only until we're married."

He didn't deny it. "That will take a day or two. By then this might all be over. We're clearly near the end."

She pushed for more. "The other revolutionaries? Hunt and Thistlewood. You'll leave that fight to others?"

She thought he'd deny that, but in the end he said, "I'll help, but from the sides. I've become aware of my other responsibilities to Faringay. But that makes me regret that I trapped you with me last night."

"Trapped? I was willing in every way."

"But you have no escape."

"Nor want one!"

"You haven't experienced life as my wife yet."

She put her fingers over his lips. "We'll find a way, love. We have to, for you will always do your duty, and I must always be at your side."

"I'd have it no other way." He rose. "I must go. There's much to be done." She thought he might have forgotten the license, but he added, "Arden's offered to go with me tomorrow to the archbishop of Canterbury's office. With his glittering power we might be able to marry late tomorrow."

She'd take the blessings of that and push aside the fear. As she went with him to the door, she said, "I wish I could do more to help find Mrs. Waite. As it is, Beth wants to talk about guests and a wedding breakfast."

"It'll be our only wedding. A shame to have a scrambling affair."

She was surprised. "Do you want something grand? I've asked Edgar to give me away, so I thought we'd marry in his room."

He smiled. "You, me, a clergyman, and witnesses. That's all we need for perfection."

"Yes." She could see he shared her reluctance to part, so she steered him out into the corridor, and went down with him to the hall. She managed not to say anything more about him keeping safe. She knew he would. Until they were married, at least.

CHAPTER 41

Hermione was crossing toward the stairs when she heard someone knock at the door. She turned back and heard a man say, "Dr. Grammaticus for a Mr. Peake."

The porter opened the door somewhat grudgingly and directed the man to a reception room.

Hermione hurried over. "Dr. Grammaticus. Welcome!"

As she saw him more clearly, however, her excitement deflated. His sober black was appropriate for a doctor, and his old-fashioned gray bob wig could be excused, but shouldn't a good doctor present a picture of health? He had spindle legs, but was round as a ball in the belly and had the swollen nose and red face of a drunkard.

He smirked and bowed with too much of a flourish and the creak of a corset. "At your most devoted service, my dear lady! Do I have the honor to speak to the Marchioness of Arden?"

"No. I'm Lady Hermione Merryhew, your patient's great-niece." She felt inclined to take him into the reception room, but it wouldn't do. She wasn't going to take him to Edgar yet, however. She took him up to the library. It wasn't quite as welcoming as the drawing room, but no insult. Once there, she invited him to sit and went right to the point. "We understand you have a cure for kala-azar, Doctor."

"I do, your ladyship."

"Then how is it not widely known and available?"

His eyes narrowed at her tone, and she felt they were decidedly shifty. "I have not been able to prove its effectiveness, your ladyship. I cured people in Egypt and then in Algeria, and brought home signed testimonies, but the government dismisses them. They will not pay me without proof, and I do not trust them to pay me once they have the details of my treatment. I need a patient with the disease so I can demonstrate, but there are none in Britain. Until now, I gather."

"Why not travel to India, Doctor, where I understand the disease is common? You could demonstrate your cure there, under the eye of military doctors."

He spread his hands. "So everyone asks, your ladyship, but I am a broken man. I was a ship's surgeon during action, and then I was plagued by the climate of North Africa. I dare not visit the tropics again, so I need your relative as much as he needs me."

He could be a clever mountebank, but she sensed true desperation in his words. "I gather your cure depends on a particular fungus, Doctor. You have a supply?"

"I have the preparation ready, your ladyship, but in a secret location."

"You are very intent on secrecy. People are rewarded for inventions and cures, even when the details are known."

"I have enemies. I have been tricked in the past. I need my one case here in Britain, and then I will reveal all."

He was half-mad, but that didn't mean he was a fraud. Hermione realized she was again trying to protect Edgar in a way that would infuriate her if anyone tried to do it to her. She rose. "Come and see my great-uncle."

He rose eagerly. "He is the patient?" But then he added, "He will pay?"

"I'm sure he'll be generous to one who cures him, Doctor. Come with me, please."

When she introduced the doctor to Edgar, she saw the same assessment in his eyes, but he listened to the story without comment.

"So you want paying to cure me," he said in the end. "That's fair enough, but I need to know what you're dosing me with."

"Antimony and fungus mirabilis."

"Aye, but you admitted that you made up that name, and no amount of searching has found it."

"Of course not. That's my secret. My key to a fortune."

"You expect me to swallow whatever you give me without question?"

The doctor's lip curled. "I'm sure you've taken many medicines without question, sir. You have no other hope. I know this disease, and death marks you already."

"My great-uncle has improved since coming to London," Hermione protested.

"But the effects are inexorable. He will soon die."

"How much?" Edgar asked.

"A thousand guineas."

"That's outrageous!" Hermione protested.

"For a life?" the doctor replied.

Hermione suddenly remembered what Nolly had said about doctors being paid for treatment, not cure. "How do we know it will be a life? I propose that you be paid when Mr. Peake is cured."

"What? What?" Grammaticus spluttered. "What sort of business is that?"

"A sound one," Edgar said with a chuckle. "We'll make a trader of you yet, my dear. I'll pay you a hundred now for your expenses, Grammaticus, but the rest when I'm restored to health."

"Absurd!" Grammaticus protested. "I'm not offering you an elixir of youth, sir."

"Pity. I'd pay a great deal more for that. I expect to be able to get around in a normal way for a man of my age and have my innards behave as they should. That's a low enough standard, isn't it?" When the doctor remained in scowling silence, Edgar asked, "What's the problem? Debts? Duns at the door?"

"A few temporary embarrassments. I need at least two hundred now."

"Very well."

"And at least two doctors to see you before treatment so that no one will be able to doubt the cure."

"More poking and prodding," Edgar grumbled. "But I agree. There's a Dr. Onslow in the Wirral who can say how I've been, and a ship's doctor, Aaron Johnson, as well. But make the others quick, or you'll have no one to try your potions on."

Edgar wrote a draft on his bank and gave

it to Grammaticus, whose hand shook as he took it. A good thing he wasn't a surgeon. Hermione escorted Grammaticus out of the room, but at the door she looked back. Edgar had sagged down. He, too, thought Grammaticus a fraud.

Once the doctor had left, she went to her own room, wishing Thayne were here to discuss the matter. What was the best thing to do? She tried to concentrate on that, but her mind flitted elsewhere.

She and Thayne had been apart so often, but now it felt intolerable not to have him here or at least know exactly where he was. She needed to know he was safe.

Beth knocked and entered. "We do need to talk about the wedding. . . ." But then she said, "What's the matter?"

Hermione told her about Grammaticus.

"I can't say whether the man's a charlatan or not, but our doctor is an excellent man. I can summon him tomorrow to be one of the witnesses."

"Thank you. I want Edgar to be able to at least try the cure, though I must confess my mind is full of Thayne."

Beth smiled. "A bride is supposed to dream as her wedding approaches."

"I'm not dreaming. I'm worrying. Or rather, I'm fretting because there's nothing

I can do." She couldn't stay still and rose to pace the room. "The poster could take days to prepare and print, but that mad French-woman is planning to blow up London, perhaps this very day!"

"I thought the plan was for Drury Lane."

"I don't think they're sure of that. I'm not sure they're sure of anything!"

"And you want to solve all the problems."

"I certainly would if I could. Wouldn't you?"

"Of course. But there probably isn't the urgency you see. You have no more reason for thinking something will happen today than the men have for thinking it will happen later. Come to the nursery. Children are an excellent distraction."

That proved true, and after lunch with Edgar, Hermione agreed to sit with Beth and discuss the basic necessities of a wedding. The matter of which gown and what accessories did capture her interest, and then what clothes she would take on her honeymoon. Beth had offered the Ardens' country home, Hartwell.

"It's what's called a cottage *orné*. Somewhat large for a cottage and very *orné*, but it's a place for simple living."

As time passed, the lamps were lit so Hermione could write lists. She had to admit that planning her honeymoon was delightful, because she'd be there with Thayne. A whole week or more with nothing to part them, day and night.

When Lord Arden joined them, she asked, "Is Thayne with you? Faringay, I mean."

She blushed at the others' amusement, but couldn't help her eagerness.

"I'm sorry, no," Arden said. "I left him at Braydon's room many hours ago."

"So you don't know what's planned?"

"No."

Beth said, "We could invite him to dine. And Braydon as well, of course."

"We could," Arden agreed.

Beth went to her desk to write the note.

"I could take it," Hermione said. She went even hotter, but sanity seemed to have escaped her. "I'm so restless. Perhaps he might need persuading. And we could discuss the wedding on the way back."

Beth looked at her husband. "Is it safe?"

He was looking somewhat exasperated, but he said, "I can make it so. A closed carriage, with armed attendants." He looked at Hermione. "My footman will have instructions to bring Faringay out to you. Don't leave the carriage."

That seemed excessive, but Hermione had won what she wanted, so she hurried to summon Nolly and put on spencer, bonnet, and gloves. They went down, but had to wait until the carriage came to the front door, by which time she was feeling all the eccentricity of her impulse. She couldn't back out now, however.

The carriage was quite plain, and as well as a coachman, it had a groom at his side and a liveried footman at the back. She climbed inside feeling well guarded indeed. It was no great distance and the gaslit streets made it especially safe. They soon drew up outside a fine brick building and the footman went to knock. Hermione twitched to go with him, but she'd promised.

Time passed and she began to worry, but then Thayne came out of the house in hat and gloves and the footman swung open the door.

Hermione leaned forward to smile, but then a shape hurled forward, slamming the footman aside and barreling on into Thayne, howling, *"Bloody murderer!"*

The brute's brother!

"Thayne!" she screamed, stumbling out of the carriage because she couldn't stay inside. Not when Thayne looked so slender in the massive arms. She clung to the doorframe of the rocking coach. "Help!

Someone!"

The footman was sprawled on the ground unconscious. She looked up to see the coachman struggling with his horses, but the groom had a pistol ready.

"I can't shoot, milady! I could hit either of 'em."

The brute seemed to be trying to break Thayne in two. She heard voices calling, but no one was going to be here in time.

Just then, Thayne twisted free and drove a fist at the Boothroyd's throat, but the brute lowered his chin to take it, then grappled again, getting an arm around Thayne's neck that looked likely to break it.

Kris!

Hermione dragged it out and ran toward the brute's rocklike back, despairing that the delicate blade could even make a dent. *Stick it in hard,* Edgar had said. *Go through leather, flesh, and even some bone.*

Neck. She wrapped both hands around the hilt and drove the blade with all her strength into a spot between collar and hair. It went in! *Like a knife through soft cheese.*

The brute made an odd gargling noise and then crumpled, taking Thayne with him. They fell together, just as she'd fallen with Nathan when he was shot. Darkness threatened and she staggered to some railings and clung to them, her trembling legs almost too weak to hold her. Nolly rushed over to put an arm around her.

She watched Thayne scramble to his feet. Thank God he was all right. He came quickly to take her into his arms. "Don't say anything."

Say anything? She was struggling to breathe, but at last people were all around, babbling and exclaiming.

"What happened?"

"Attack."

"Madman!"

"What's the matter with him?"

"Madman indeed," Thayne said. "He attacked me. Thank God I got a knife into him."

"That's the truth, sir!" There were other supporting voices, but none of them could have seen. Not with how fast everything had happened and the darkness between the pools of gaslight.

"I must take care of the lady," Thayne said. He picked her up and carried her into the house. She was glad of it, for she wasn't sure her legs could hold her unassisted. He took her into a luxurious room, where he placed her on a sofa, then knelt beside her. "Are you all right, my darling?"

She found her voice at last. "Yes, I think

so. But . . ."

"Not now. Say at little as possible. I must go back down."

"No!"

He freed himself from her clutching hands. "Just for a few minutes. Look after her."

"I will, milord!" Nolly said.

"Yes, sir," said another hovering servant. A male.

"Sweet tea with brandy," Thayne ordered, and then he was gone.

Hermione slumped back — and heard the straw of her bonnet crumple. "Not another one."

Nolly took the damaged bonnet off and stroked her hair. "There, there, milady. Such nasty goings-on. I don't know what happened, I'm sure I don't. That madman attacking your gentleman, and then you running at him screaming."

"I screamed?"

"Well, more yelled, I suppose, and you trying to hit him. Perhaps he collapsed from the shock. ."

Nolly hadn't seen the knife?

Hermione's wits were returning, in scattered bits but still coming together enough for her to understand. Thayne had claimed he'd had a knife in order to protect her. It probably wasn't a crime to attack someone who was attacking someone else, but a lady striking an attacker with a blade? Killing an attacker? That would be a nine-days wonder.

Nine days? The story would dog her all her life, and not to her credit. Many would think her mad. She grasped the offered cup and drank hot, sweet, brandied tea. It tasted marvelous and settled her nerves a bit, but as her mind cleared completely, she realized something terrible.

Her drawing had been for nothing.

She'd killed their means of finding Solange Waite.

CHAPTER 42

As soon as Thayne returned, she told him that.

"I'd realized. I'll send a note to Hawkinville. He might have become philosophical about it by tomorrow. There are other ramifications, however. Seth being here and attacking must mean that Solange knows I'm Ned Granger. When this event gets back to her, she'll know you're involved again."

"I could be any woman."

"In the Duke of Belcraven's town carriage? She'll easily find out more and if she digs deep enough, she'll learn that you're the woman in Warrington, the one she sent Nathan after. My hope is that she's too busy with her grand design to try to harm you, especially now she has no Boothroyd to employ, but we'll have to take special steps to guard you."

"And you."

"I'll be careful. But you could have been

killed, and again it would have been my fault."

Hermione still wasn't feeling very strong, but he needed her to be, so she sat up and then stood, and put herself in order. "Not entirely this time. I came here."

"And saved my life."

"Thank heavens for the kris."

"Is that what's it's called? A devilish weapon. I tucked it behind the umbrella stand because I couldn't conceal it anywhere without slashing my clothes to ribbons."

"Edgar gave it to me and insisted I carry it. Here." She tore the sheath free of her stitches. "Use this."

He took it. "You don't want it back?"

She couldn't prevent a shudder. "No. I hope to never be in such a situation again, but I don't think I could use it. The feel of it. The sound he made . . ."

He took her into his arms. "I'll take you back to Belcraven House."

They went downstairs, where he did retrieve the kris and slid it safely into its sheath. When they went outside, she looked away from Seth Boothroyd's sprawled body, which was being attended to. She was pleased to see the footman on his feet, though leaning against the carriage. He couldn't be asked to travel on the perch at the back, so she told him to travel inside and he didn't make much protest.

When they arrived at Belcraven House and told the tale, Arden said, "That's the last time I give in to love's idiotic whims."

Hermione didn't argue and when Beth suggested a quiet supper in her room, she happily agreed. She wanted to spend more time with Thayne, but she was still badly shaken. She'd killed a man. No matter how vile he'd been, it would take time for her to put it out of mind.

Thank heavens, her practical nature won out and the next morning, when she was told Thayne wished to speak to her, she could be calm and sensible. Until, that was, she entered the drawing room and saw him, and had to take his hands, smiling.

"I'm just come from Hawkinville," he said. "We're forgiven."

"Without so much as a scold?"

"Perhaps a frown, but he's soothed by having found the trail of Isaac Inkman. It contains some indelicate aspects."

"If you don't tell me for that reason, I'll become extremely indelicate!"

"Very well. Isaac enjoys a whore now and then."

She was annoyed to blush, but said, "And . . . ?"

"He doesn't visit brothels, but when the mood takes him, Solange gets a woman in for him. Hawkinville had Isaac's description sent to such places with the offer of a reward. He's a very distinctive type. It seems he was in the mood yesterday."

"You have the address?" Hermione said. "Mrs. Waite's address?"

She didn't know whether she was thrilled or terrified. It could soon be over, but please without putting Thayne in danger.

"Number 10, Great Peter Street, in Westminster. It's being acted on now, mostly by the military."

Without him. Thank heavens.

But then she saw his expression. He wanted to be in at the end.

She wanted desperately to keep him here, but he'd dedicated years of his life to this fight and it wasn't as if he'd be on the front line. She managed a smile. "You must want to be there." She had to add, "Without throwing yourself carelessly into danger?"

He kissed her hand. "I never have, love. My word on it."

Even so, her courage failed her a little. "I always knew I could never be a soldier's wife."

"I'm done with army life."

"You're going into battle now."

"Not really. The plan is to surround her, at which point she'll have to surrender."

"Truly?"

He grimaced. "I see you have a sense of Solange. That's why I should be there. I might be able to guess what she'll do and advise."

"And if she decides to set off whatever explosion she has planned?"

"Then I hope we'll have moved the nearby residents."

I hope you'll have moved. But how could he skulk at a distance and do the job? He'd do his best to keep his promise to her, but he'd also do what was necessary to protect others.

"You'd better be on your way," she said, "before it's all over. But after it's over, remember the marriage license. All the plans are made."

That got her the smiling kiss she wanted and she maintained her own smile until he had left. She wept then, but only a little. Tears were for grief, and he would return to her. He wasn't fighting alone anymore.

Beth came in. "Are you all right?"

"After a fashion," Hermione said, rather

helplessly. "He's going off into danger again."

"I share all your feelings," Beth said grimly. "When Faringay arrived, he told Arden what was happening. Of course Arden couldn't resist, especially as he considers the attack on you and Faringay a personal insult, you being under his protection." At Hermione's expression, she said, "Truly. But it was also an excuse. He sent a message to Nicholas, which means that probably all the Rogues in Town are now dashing to help bring down the mad Frenchwoman. I could murder them all!"

Hermione shivered. "We can only hope Solange Waite doesn't do it for us."

Mark left the house thinking he was probably safer on the streets than he had been since returning to London. Seth Boothroyd was dead and Solange was encircled. He found a hackney and instructed the driver to go close to Great Peter Street, Westminster.

"Close to, sir?"

"Precisely."

"Not very precise, if you ask me," the old man grumbled, "but you're the one as is paying the fare."

Mark didn't know where Great Peter

Street was, but the hackney went down Whitehall, past the military headquarters and other government offices, and then between the Abbey and the Palace of Westminster. He hoped they still had a long way to go, but the carriage soon drew up. It was a residential street of the simpler sort, but very close to the seat of power. What exactly was Solange planning to do from here?

When Mark got down, the driver said, "This is Smith Street, sir. Great Peter Street's just ahead. You can see the gasometer over the rooftops."

Mark turned to look down the street to the one ahead. There indeed was the brick-clad cylindrical tower that was filled with gas by whatever chemical process the gas company used. From there it could be pumped through miles of pipe to light up Westminster, the heart of the British government.

Oh, Solange, you do have a warped kind of brilliance.

He'd read the notes he'd stolen in Ardwick, but they'd not made much sense to him. There'd been details of how gas was produced and delivered, including many technical terms. Chemists had gone over those notes and had been unable to work out what plan was involved. He thought they'd dismissed fire, but perhaps they'd not considered such a grandiose design. Could she set off a fire here that would race along the pipes into the Palace of Westminster?

He paid the driver and walked forward, looking for Hawkinville or anyone he knew. Hawkinville's people wouldn't be conspicuous. He came upon a group of people arguing with two soldiers.

"No one's to go through just now," one was saying. "Orders."

"Whose orders?" a woman asked, shopping basket on hip. "Bet it's that gas tower. We never asked for it to be put here. Dratted thing blew up four years ago. I suppose it's going to do the same again."

There was a general muttering, but no one tried to get by the soldiers. Mark looked at the tower again. Was Solange going to blow the whole thing up? He assumed the previous explosion had been an accident and clearly it hadn't flattened the area, but it might have given her the idea.

How big an explosion was possible? Could debris reach as far as Westminster, killing hundreds and perhaps more? The death and destruction would be blamed on the gas company and the government. Could that ignite the mob and start an uprising when the government and all its offices were in disarray? If so, Solange would want to survive to take advantage of it.

He walked forward and one of the soldiers said, "No further, sir, if you please."

"I'm with Hawkinville," Mark said.

"Name, sir?"

"Faringay."

Hawkinville must have prepared the way, for the soldier said, "Very good, sir. Go straight ahead and turn to the right. There's a passage through to Laundry Yard."

How mundane it all sounded. This would have been a quiet area before the gas station had been built and there must have been a large laundry to need a drying yard.

He turned into the gloomy passage and emerged into an area of rough green dotted with soldiers patiently waiting for orders and a few clusters of men in urgent debate. Hawkinville was conferring with three military officers.

He spotted Arden and Delaney and went over. "How did you get in?"

Delaney smiled. "Ever try to keep Arden out of anything? Hal Beaumont's around, too."

Mark remembered Delaney saying Beaumont was one of the Company of Rogues.

"Maggots?" he said drily.

"Maggots are very useful creatures," Delaney said.

Mark also remembered that Hawkinville was a Rogue-by-marriage. Another man was standing by. Lord Darien, whom he'd known somewhat in the army before he'd had the title and met a few days ago at a club.

"You a Rogue, too?" Mark asked him.

"I damned well am not," Darien said, but with a touch of humor. "Hawk pulled in a number of military people a while ago. Quite a few of them are Rogues, but there are some normal humans."

"Not favorites of yours?"

"We've made our peace. I married the sister of one. I have to admit they can be damnably effective, especially in matters where the normal processes are best avoided."

"As now? There are soldiers everywhere."

"For contingencies. The military are keeping people out of the area and have cleared people out of some of the houses, but they haven't evacuated the closest ones yet to avoid alarming Mrs. Waite."

"She's in her house?"

"That's the general opinion, but it's stitch it as we go."

Mark smiled at the common complaint of army officers — that the plans weren't thorough enough. Mark went to Hawkinville, who nodded a greeting. "Know what's going on?"

"Only to an extent. You have to admire her imagination."

"I don't have to admire anything about her. We assume she plans a massive explosion from her property, hoping to explode the gasometer."

"Is that possible?"

Hawkinville nodded to the huddled group. "The chemical men are debating it, along with some of the army engineers. Those notes you stole were all about creating havoc by using the pipelines."

"They seemed to be, but gas production was mentioned. What do the experts say?"

"Nothing but questions. How big an explosion might she begin with? Exactly what explosives? From what level of the house? How the devil are we supposed to know? One suggested she might fire a projectile of some sort, which set them off about penetration and ingress of air. Apparently air must mix with the gas for it to explode. Otherwise it would merely go up in flames."

"Merely," Mark said drily.

"A mighty fire would be unfortunate, but an explosion could hurl projectiles for a considerable distance. My question for you is, when threatened, will she set off the explosion?"

"She won't want to blow herself up."

"Sure of that?"

"Yes. Her aim is living triumph, not martyrdom. However, I suspect she'd rather die than live to go on trial and be executed."

"In extremis she'd choose death. You should have killed her when you had the chance."

"I know that now."

"We have men positioned to shoot her if she appears at a window."

"They should have orders to shoot Isaac Inkman if they can. He's the one who'll set it off."

"Even if it kills him?"

"He'd enjoy the bang. Truly. He's half-mad. Damnation —"

A woman shrieked. For a moment Mark hoped it was Solange, but he knew it was too shrill. He ran with Hawkinville and others out into Great Peter Street.

A young woman had broken through the cordon of soldiers. She was running toward the row of houses shrieking, *We're betrayed, Solange. Betrayed!"*

A shot rang out, shattering a window in a house. Solange must have shown herself, but there was no shout or scream to indicate she'd been hit.

Soldiers recaptured the young woman and dragged her away. One had his hand over her mouth, but she kicked and writhed like one demented. Why did people fight so hard to destroy?

Mark moved forward cautiously to get a view of the front of the house with the shattered window. That window was on the ground floor, but Isaac appeared at an unbroken one on the upper floor, his owlish face staring. No one fired. Mark cursed himself for not having a pistol, though it'd be a devil of a shot at this distance.

Isaac was dragged away and Mark moved back again to Hawkinville's side. "The cordon's secure?"

"As secure as can be in this warren of streets with hoi polloi desperate for a glimpse of the excitement. So she's there."

"And knows all's lost."

"Will she fire out at anyone who approaches?"

"Unlikely. My guess is she's trying to escape. Can you have your men at the back show themselves? Deter her from trying to slip out that way."

"If she slips out, we'll have her," Hawkinville objected.

"But not Isaac. She'll leave him behind to set off the explosion. If she can't get out, she won't order him to."

"Right." Hawkinville nodded and left. Mark questioned what he'd just said. Might Solange decide that martyrdom was worth it?

Then he wondered about Isaac. Would he truly blow himself up? He was fervent about explosions, but was he willing to die for it? Did he believe there was chemistry in heaven?

"You have a plan?" Delaney asked.

He'd come up from behind, quiet as a cat. Mark saw Arden, Beaumont, and Darien on hand. "You men are mad," he said. "This isn't your war. You've never even been in the army, Delaney. Nor you, Arden."

"All the more reason to act now," Arden said, as if discussing a game of cards.

"We'll only act if there's anything useful to do," Delaney said, sounding like a reasonable man. "I have strong objections to wasted lives."

"No wonder you didn't join the army, then. Yes, I have a plan, but it's one only I can carry out. I need to discuss it with Hawkinville."

He went over and indicated he needed to speak to Hawkinville alone.

"Yes?"

"I'm willing to gamble that Isaac Inkman can be persuaded out of the house."

"Gamble how?"

"By going in there to persuade him."

It was typical that Hawkinville only said, "What are the chances?"

"I truly don't know, but I wouldn't attempt it if I didn't think it could work. You allowed Delaney and his people into this?"

"They've been in it all along to one extent or another. Arden less so. But they're all useful fellows and not encumbered by official protocol."

"I see."

"If you're going to do something, sooner will be better than later, for a range of reasons. But one is that I'm expecting someone from the Home Office to turn up soon to take charge."

Mark gave a humorous grimace. "With all possible speed," he said, and returned to the willing Rogues. "The plan is approved. I'm going in to talk out a deranged chemist."

None of them showed alarm.

"What can we do in support?" Beaumont asked.

His empty sleeve made it impossible to be scathing, and in fact, some possibilities came to mind. "It would help if Solange can be kept busy with distractions from the front. Any and all."

"Right."

"And I need a pistol." Beaumont supplied one. Mark checked the loading and priming. No one would object to that when the shot could be life-or-death.

"Right, then," he said.

Delaney put a hand on his arm. "Hermione's suffered your death once already."

"For her sake I'd let someone else do this if I could, but I'm the only one who might get Isaac's trust, and that could be key to all."

Delaney nodded and no one else made an objection. "We're under your orders, then."

CHAPTER 43

Mark said, "I need the soldiers to shoot occasionally at the front of the house, but without killing people. Any other distraction that comes to mind."

Arden nodded and went off.

"Hal and Darien," Delaney said. "Any good at arson? Could you manage a lot of smoke from a house across the street?"

The two men hurried away.

Delaney turned to Mark. "Anything else?"

"Not that I can think of."

"I'll be your backup." Before Mark could voice his protest, he said, "Only that, I promise. You know what you're doing."

Mark hoped to God that was true, trying not to think of Hermione and promises made. He remembered the scrap of silk in his pocket and fingered it, then ran down the street close to the wall where Solange couldn't see him if she looked out. He'd seen a narrow passageway between two houses and he slipped into it. As he'd hoped, it brought him to the space behind her house and the backs of another row.

It wasn't divided into individual yards, but instead was a shared open area with a well and a few small gardens. It was crossed by washing lines. Mark hoped the houses on the far side had been evacuated.

"Good that there aren't individual walls to climb," he said to Delaney, "but if she's looking out, nowhere to hide. Even the washing lines are empty."

Movement drew his eye to the opposite row of houses. A soldier was showing himself at the window of one, with a bright flash of scarlet. Another opened a back door to look out, rifle at the ready. That part of the plan was working. Solange would be mad to try to run out this way.

Despite thrumming urgency, Mark waited for the other distractions.

A rattle of shots from the street. A small explosion somewhere to the right. That should have her peering out at Peter Street, trying to understand. Trying to find a way to escape. Or had she given up? Was she preparing to depart in glory and take as many with her as she could?

He ran for the back of the house, counting doors to find the right one, hearing

Delaney behind him. This one. He listened, but beyond that, there was no precaution to take. He opened the door and went in.

He found himself in a kitchen. Deserted, but with kettle steaming away on the hob. He heard footsteps above. Brisk. Solange's? Where was Isaac? Would a bomb do most damage from the ground floor or the upper one?

The house was small. He moved forward into a dingy parlor that had a door that opened directly onto the street. Solange wouldn't have enjoyed living in such poor surroundings. The ground floor was deserted and he saw nothing that might be a bomb.

He glanced back at Delaney, who shook his head in agreement.

Narrow stairs rose up from one side of the room. Mark took off his boots, cursing silently at having to struggle with Braydon's Hessians. Delaney helped. His own came off easily.

Mark went silently upstairs, listening all the time for clues. He wanted Isaac, not Solange. He'd shoot Solange if he saw her — he was resolved on that — but then Isaac might set off the explosion in panic. Once he had Isaac under control, the main danger was over. He came to the top and saw two closed doors, one to his right, one to his left. Two rooms, one back and one front. The back one would look out on the gasometer, so if that was the target, the bomb should be in there. He hoped Isaac was with it and Solange in the front room, distracted by the mayhem.

He stepped toward the back room and opened the door.

Isaac was there, looking out of the window, his hand resting on a long, fat cylinder that was held at the back in a sort of sling. At first Mark could make nothing of it, but then he realized what it was. A beam ran across the room beneath the window. The sling — in fact some kind of woven rope — stretched back from it at great tension. When released, the cylinder would hurtle toward the gasometer like the bolt from a crossbow.

Dear Lord in heaven. And Isaac could release the mechanism at any moment.

"Very clever, Isaac," Mark said as calmly as he could, closing the door behind him to lessen the chance of Solange hearing voices. Delaney would have to fend for himself.

Isaac turned sharply, but then grinned. "Told you it was a good plan, didn't I? But what are you doing here? I thought you were a traitor."

Typical of Isaac to be so absorbed in his explosive toy that he wasn't aware of the drama all around, but that didn't make him less dangerous.

"Not at all," Mark said. "I've come to help. We just release the cord, and bang?"

"Bit of a delay, but that's about right."

"Are you sure it'll work?" Mark asked, going closer. A pistol shot might possibly set off the explosive. If he couldn't persuade Isaac to leave with him, it would have to be hand-to-hand. "Could be dangerous from here," he pointed out.

"But glorious."

Isaac had looked away as he spoke, however, and his tone had flattened. Was he lying? About what?

"Better not to die," Mark said. "Come with me. I'll get you out of here and you can try again another day."

Isaac looked at him in that blank way that could make him seem simple. "You're on Solange's side?"

Now, there was a double-edged sword. Mark went with instinct. "No. She's too cruel."

Isaac sat down on a nearby stool and blinked at him. "That's what I think. She talks me into doing terrible things."

"Like this?"

"The exploding letters."

"You seemed happy about those," Mark said, his hearing alert for warnings. He could hear the occasional shot and some shouting, but nothing from within the house. How long would Solange leave Isaac unattended? What would Delaney do if she emerged, armed?

He forced his mind back to the main purpose. He'd thought Isaac better dead, but now he wasn't sure. What was more, he doubted that Isaac was needed to deploy the weapon. If it was, in effect, a crossbow, Solange could release it alone.

"I was happy about the *idea,*" Isaac said. "It was a new one. Fun to try out an exploding letter and see that it worked. But she said it should have done more damage. She made me make a bigger one. When she heard it hadn't hurt anyone, she got that look in her eye. You know the one?"

"I do."

"It wasn't *my* fault someone put it in a box. I didn't let her know I was glad."

It was hard to see Isaac as a victim, especially when he was sitting by the weapon he'd designed and made, but his story made some sort of sense. Solange had persuaded and intimidated far stronger men than he. When it came to it, until the first exploding letter, Isaac's actions had all been experiments.

"What about this?" Mark asked, nodding at the long tube. "I assume if I cut the sling, it'll fire at the gasometer?"

Isaac nodded, wearing a particularly idiotic grin.

Mark managed to speak calmly. "That will do a lot of damage. Can it be made harmless? We don't want to leave it for Mrs. Waite to set off, do we?"

"I don't mind," Isaac said. "Could be fun."

Idiot. Perhaps he was better dead.

Mark heard movement outside the house. He stepped closer to the window and saw some soldiers dodging around. They were distracting as ordered, but wasting their time. There was only this one window at the back. He could only pray no one tried a random shot at it and exploded the device.

"This isn't my idea of fun, Isaac. How do we disarm it?"

"Don't need to. Won't do much good."

"Disarming?"

"Firing." Isaac patted the tube again. "I suppose I should have said it won't do much harm. Disarm. Dis-harm. Interesting, that." He suddenly scowled. "You've got that look."

"What look?" Mark asked, trying to adjust

his face to patient friendliness.

"As if I'm annoying. But perhaps I am. I'm only really interested in chemistry. And aspects of engineering. Most people aren't."

"Which is why they can't understand you. Try to explain this to me, Isaac. Why won't the exploding projectile do much damage?"

"It won't explode. It'll just smash into the gas tower. According to my calculations, it'll break some bricks, but not even dent the gasometer inside." He turned wistful. "It would have been interesting to see what would happen if an explosive missile broke into fourteen thousand cubic feet of gas, but I don't think there'd be enough air."

Mark managed not to roll his eyes, but what should be done with this man-child genius?

"Are you sure, Isaac? About little damage?"

"Oh, yes. But she won't like it."

"No. But I'll deal with her for you."

The door opened and Mark turned, pistol at the ready. It was Delaney. "It's getting quiet in the street."

"Who's this?" Isaac had stood, his eyes wide. What had Solange told him might happen if he was arrested?

"He's a friend," Mark said. "He'll help me get you to safety."

Mark would like to have Delaney take Isaac away and stay to arrest Solange, but he remembered his promise to Hermione. He'd broken it, but with reason. He had no excuse to do more. Others could take care of her.

Delaney's brows were raised and he nodded toward the device.

"It won't do much damage. That's right, isn't it, Isaac?"

"I told you so! Do you think me a dunce?" A bang from the front of the house made him jump. "She's coming. You said I'd be safe!"

Instinct. Mark grabbed Isaac's arm and pulled him out of the room. Isaac broke free and ran downstairs, Mark and Delaney following. Then in the kitchen Isaac paused to take the steaming kettle off the hob.

"Outside," Mark said, steering him toward the back door, but at sight of the soldiers, Isaac shrank back. "Come on. It's safe."

Delaney gave Mark the boots he'd picked up and took Isaac's hand. "Come along. We'll take care of you."

Isaac looked at him and then let Delaney lead him out. Mark couldn't help thinking, *Like a lamb to the slaughter.* Delaney couldn't keep that promise. Isaac had been hand in glove with violent revolutionaries and responsible for two acts of violence.

They paused to one side of the door to put on their boots, taking turns to watch the door, pistol ready. The bangs and explosions had ceased at the front and the house might as well be uninhabited. What was Solange doing?

It didn't matter as long as she didn't escape. Delaney shepherded Isaac to safety. Mark followed as rear guard.

When they arrived in Laundry Lane, Hawkinville said, "You got him, then. Good work." He gestured to some soldiers to arrest Isaac.

"I promised him safety," Mark said.

"That promise wasn't in your power to give."

"He's a pawn. He's only been responsible for one thing that could have done serious damage — the second exploding letter. He says Solange forced him into that and I believe him."

"What of all this? There is no bomb?"

"He says it's a dud."

"And you believe him?"

"Yes. You don't have any wish to hurt people, do you, Isaac?"

Isaac's eyes were shifting around the angry faces and armed soldiers and he had a death grip on Delaney's hand. It was to him he spoke. "None. Truly. I particularly didn't want to damage the gasometer. I've been reading all about gas." In a moment he transformed, glowing with excitement. "We can light up the world with gas. No more night. Heat it, too. No more cold. Gas engines. Like steam engines, but better. Gas fireworks. Gas ships. Big, big balloons powered by gas."

Hawkinville looked as if he wanted to shoot Isaac on the spot, and Mark had qualms about setting the man loose in the world, but Delaney was smiling. "You have some very interesting ideas, Isaac. They should certainly be explored." To Hawkinville, he said, "If we can sweep aside the one unfortunate letter, there's really nothing to hold against him. May I pledge the Rogues to take charge of him?"

"How? If he takes it into his head to burn up the world with his precious gas, he will."

"I won't!" Isaac protested. "I don't like hurting people."

"We can say he assisted us here today," Mark said. "It's true."

Hawkinville shook his head. "We'll review this later, but he's in your charge now, Nicholas. Our priority is to seize Solange Waite before she proves to the world that your idiot lied."

Nicholas winked at Mark and steered Isaac away. They were already talking about heating a house with gas-powered pipes.

"What will the woman do when she realizes that Isaac has escaped?" Hawkinville asked.

"Fire the projectile. Let's go and watch."

"Watch?"

"I trust Isaac on this. It seems he truly doesn't want to harm the gasometer."

Hawkinville muttered about lunatics and madmen, but he went with Mark to one of the houses opposite Solange's row. They took a position by an open window.

Mark said, "Have a soldier fire a shot toward that window there. One who can be trusted not to hit it."

The musket ball smashed into brickwork beside the window and some of the soldiers gave a muted cheer.

Mark heard Solange call, "Isaac?" Did he hear the string of French curses, or only imagine them? He saw movement in that back room but had no clear sight of her. "Any moment now," he murmured, praying he'd been right.

There was a great *twang!* He instinctively ducked, but the metal cylinder hurtled over the rooftops. Then they heard an appalling crunch, followed by a cacophony of falling bricks.

"Not damage the gasometer, you said!" Hawkinville ran for a front room to see what had happened, but Solange was in the window opposite now, her expression telling Mark all he needed to know. She screamed her frustration, the red-faced personification of fury.

Mark pulled out Beaumont's pistol, praying it shot true. He steadied himself against the window frame, calming his breath. Then he aimed and fired. He'd aimed for her heart, but the gun fired high. The ball went into her screaming mouth.

She fell out of sight as Mark slowly lowered the smoking pistol with a shaking hand. Right or wrong, he'd killed a woman, if not in cold blood, then with cool, clear calculation. And he'd do it again in the same situation.

Hawkinville returned. "The gas engineers will have the final say, but it looks like superficial damage. You fired a shot?"

"Solange Waite is dead."

"Good work, but let's make sure."

Mark went with him across the communal yard and back into the house. An officer was already coming downstairs. "One dead woman, sir. No one else."

"He's dealt with," Hawkinville said. "Satisfactory," he said to Mark, "especially if she was the linchpin as you say. Now to find something to link Waite to this."

"You won't. He dislikes violence and destruction."

"Then he steers a damned odd course."

"He longs for glory and deludes himself about how it can be achieved. By all means arrest him. Hold him and frighten him with the possible consequences. The lack of habeas corpus allows that. That, along with having to face what Solange planned, should break him. He'll help you destroy the Brotherhood and be grateful to be allowed a quiet, scholarly life. Without Durrant his writings will lack all fire."

"I wish we could hang him, but you're probably right about him going free. When people like him are found not guilty, it makes matters worse. What of Durrant and the others? Pity we can't tie them to this. We don't have much else that would hang them."

"Tregoven will disappear. He has no true conviction. He'll find some other slimy way to try to glitter. Durrant will probably attach himself to another prominent speaker, so you might get him one day. There's Ezra Croke, but he's nothing more than a bookkeeper. You could squeeze him if you want to know any secret contributors to the cause, though as best I know, Waite funded most of it himself. Now, I go to prove to my bride-to-be that I've survived."

"I assume I can't call on you again?"

Mark was tempted, but he said, "Only for the theoretical end of things."

Mark traveled back to Belcraven House with Arden, who complained of his tame part of it. "Though Beth would have no patience with pointless heroics."

"I hope Hermione agrees mine weren't pointless."

Their ladies berated them, but with shining relief. Mark took Hermione to the drawing room and confessed what he'd done. "It was necessary, love, but I promise, only advisory roles in the future."

"Truly?" she asked.

"Truly. I don't regret killing Solange, but it was different to killing people in the war. I don't want to be in that situation again short of the most dire need."

She drew him down onto a sofa. "I'm glad. I don't want you in danger, but more than that, I don't want you scarred inside."

He kissed her tenderly, at length. "How delightful to be betrothed," he said, "and this permitted."

"Being married will be even better. The license?" She was eager for it now.

"Somehow it slipped my mind. I'd better drag myself away and get it."

"Then we could be married tomorrow." But then she added, "I do worry that you'll grow bored."

He laughed. "With a too-prosperous estate, a poorly cared-for house, and Rogues watching my every move as husband?"

"They have no right."

"I'm glad of them. You have no other men to protect you."

"I have you, and I need no protection from you. When I think on it, you have no protection from me."

He chuckled. "I could probably summon some army friends if you turn overwhelmingly violent."

"That smug look could tempt me, sir. There will doubtless be times when I want to hit you with a poker."

"Which is where we began our adventures." He kissed her soundly. "I'm off to get that license, you bold piece, so you'll soon be mine in all senses of the word."

They married the next day, in a simple way Hermione found perfect, in Edgar's room, with the Ardens in attendance, along with

602

Thayne's friend Beau Braydon, and Nolly and Peter standing by.

She'd discussed the Rogues with Thayne the evening before.

"They might like to attend. I feel perhaps I should invite the ones in Town for Roger's sake."

He'd picked up on her reluctance. "But they do tend to take over. Arden will do, love."

"I'd forgotten he's one. Perfect. Edgar's room's too small for more in any case."

They were alone after having signed the rapidly drawn-up settlements. Thayne had made no objection to restrictions or demands and the Ardens had witnessed them. As the evening was mild, they'd strolled out in the garden, which was delightful even without the lamps. They'd remembered the past and shared more of their lives during the five years they'd been apart.

There, Thayne had given her an unusual gift. "About the new Marquess of Carsheld," he'd said.

"Porteous?"

"You felt he was cleverer than you to find coal on the estate, but I had someone look into it. Pure luck, love."

"Luck?"

"More new developments. Apparently there was an obstacle to deep mining called the ninety-fathom dyke, but it's been recently overcome. Carsheld didn't do anything for his new wealth. Other landowners and their engineers approached him."

She'd stared at him. "I don't know whether to be pleased not to have been foolish or outraged at the injustice of it. If Father had lived another year . . . !"

He kissed her. "Don't we have good fortune enough, love? In all meanings of the word?" Which was completely, perfectly true.

For the wedding she'd chosen the pink evening gown. It wasn't suitable for day wear, even though she'd added a white silk shawl, pinned together at the front, for decency, but it was perfect. She'd fashioned a pin with white silk rosebuds and fixed the shawl in place with it at the front of the bodice. When she entered Edgar's room, she saw Thayne's eyes light.

She beamed back at him. His dark blue coat sported bright brass buttons.

She went to Edgar, who was sitting in a chair with a rug over his knees. He took her hand. "I've had a talk with him," the old man said. "He'll do."

"Of course he will."

"If I'm giving you away, I'll know and approve. I'll be a father to you if you'll let me, Hermione."

She kissed his cheek. "Of course I will, with thanks."

"Then you'll take a father's gift." He brought out a long red box from under the rug and gave it to her.

"I hope it's not sharp," she teased as she took it. The cover was fine leather.

"Served you well enough, so don't complain. Open it."

She did, expecting jewelry, but inside was a slender, pale carving.

"Jade," he said. "It's supposed to give long life and happiness to the owner."

"A precious gift," she said, showing it to Thayne.

He said, "Amen," then looked at Edgar. "I may have her, then?"

"And if I said no?"

"Despite your age and infirmity, I'd insist."

"Good man. Get on with it."

They joined hands and faced the clergyman and simply made their vows.

An hour later they set off for Hartwell, the Ardens' country retreat in Surrey, where they'd begin their honeymoon. Hermione had feared it would be too grand, but though luxurious, it was a small house set in rustic gardens and completely delightful.

She had to laugh, however, when she saw a nightgown and a nightshirt spread neatly before the fire to be warm. They hadn't brought attendants. He didn't yet have a valet, Nolly wasn't really a lady's maid, and they wanted to be alone, so she asked, "How?"

"Simple planning. But that doesn't mean we have to wear them."

"We certainly do. I expect . . . Yes," she said, opening an adjoining door. "Here's my dressing room, and you must have a matching one." She grabbed the nightgown. "Off you go, husband, till we meet again."

She needed help to undress, so she rang for a maid, but once gown and corset were off, she dismissed the woman. She washed and put on the pristine nightgown, then sat to brush out her hair. She took her time, enjoying the delay. Enjoying the tingling anticipation building inside her.

Eventually she put down the brush. It was time. As she went to the door, however, she felt oddly nervous. The last time, the first time, it had been in white-hot passion fueled by her grief and relief. This. This was different.

She looked at her golden wedding ring,

smiled, and went in. He was standing by the bed in his nightshirt. He'd extinguished the candles, so the room was lit only by firelight.

"Wife," he said.

"Husband," she replied. "How perfect this is."

"From first to last and ever more." He turned back the covers. "Will you, Lady Faringay?"

She climbed onto the bed, still decently covered. "With pleasure, Lord Faringay." She grinned at him. "I wonder how other couples do this."

"In all ways known and then some," he said, joining her and pulling the covers over them. "But this is perfect for us." He gathered her in against him, cloth thick and rumpled between them. "This is home and hearth and tranquil days. That's what I want for you, my love, and what I'll strive to give you."

"Thank you," she said, turning to kiss him. "But perhaps I should mention that I'm not completely averse to adventures in bed, sir."

He laughed. "For some reason, you don't surprise me one bit."

Epilogue

Faringay Hall, October

The blast of a horn from the gatehouse warned Hermione that guests were arriving. She went to her room for her warm cloak and then ran downstairs, pausing to send some servants off to the kitchen. They'd been scrubbing the join between the stair treads and risers, which hadn't been touched for an age. She'd found the whole house like that — superficially in order but with no deep cleaning ever done. Many of the hangings had been too moth-eaten for use.

The house was full of servants as she tried to correct years of neglect, and she was glad to be providing employment for so many, but she'd wanted to present a more normal appearance for their first guests.

Thayne was coming from the back of the house, where he'd doubtless been fighting the records and ledgers. He'd thrown out the old estate steward just as she'd dismissed the upper servants in the house, but that meant that their weeks here had been tumultuous and busy.

After a week at Hartwell they'd traveled north to visit Polly and her family. William had looked curious about the rapid marriage, and had perhaps seen a resemblance to the groom who'd returned her on the road to Tranmere, but he'd not asked questions. Polly had been so excited by the visit, the marriage, and Edgar's gift of ten thousand pounds that she'd not probed. It would have come to that in time, but Hermione had used the excuse of a house needing much attention to keep the visit to just three days.

William and Thayne had rubbed along together well enough, especially as Thayne had asked William's advice on estate management. He had the knack of getting along with people.

She smiled simply to see him and he smiled back. All was in order there. Their love only deepened and their private times were perfect. She knew, however, that the ghosts lingered for him. Though it would draw on her capital, she intended to have the whole house repainted and some of the furniture changed. She would erase the memories.

What to do about the French Wing, she didn't know. She was tempted to tear it down, but she didn't think Thayne was ready for such a decision, especially when his mother had killed herself by throwing herself off the roof walk.

It had happened the winter before last when a great storm had split an elm near the house and men had set to clearing the dangerous branches. No one had thought about how Thayne's mother might react. She'd heard men and violent sounds and run up to the roof to see the danger. Presumably the roughly dressed men wielding axes and mattocks had triggered her deepest fears, for the wall around the walk was too high for an accidental fall.

Thayne hardly spoke of it, but she knew he felt guilt. The tree would have had to be dealt with, but if he'd been here instead of infiltrating the Three-Banded Brotherhood, he might have arranged the event better. Hermione couldn't argue that was untrue, so only time would heal it, but obliteration of the French Wing would help.

They went out together to greet the chaise and the curricle bowling down the well-tended drive. That had been her most recent achievement, and completed only in time.

Braydon was driving his showy curricle and Edgar and Peter were in the chaise. She watched with pleasure as Edgar climbed out with very little assistance and walked toward her with only his cane.

She went to meet him, noting the normal color of his skin. "I assume you've paid Grammaticus, then."

"I have, but the man's a foolish wretch."

She left Braydon to Thayne and walked with Edgar toward the house. "He's thrown it all away on cards or dice?"

"Not that. He's still refusing to tell anyone the details of his magical mushroom."

"Why, now he's proved it works?" She gave him her arm to go up the six steps.

"As to that, the doctors are being doctors. Only one case. Can't be entirely certain. But I had a word with some East India Company men and they're interested in paying him well for the formula. Grammaticus gets greedier at every turn, however. He's now insisting on setting up a workshop to produce the cure and sell it as doses. Might work if he was willing to travel to India, but not as he is. And he's not a well man. He often seems on the edge of an apoplexy. When I think of the people who'll die for lack of his secret, I wish we could put him on a rack."

They were in the hall by then. "Please be calm, Edgar, or I'll lose you to an apoplexy."

He shook his head and looked around. "A tolerable house, I suppose."

"The decades of neglect linger, don't they? But it improves every day and our latest treasure is an excellent cook. Are you able to manage the stairs without help?"

"Aye, though it'll be slow. I won't get stronger by letting people mollycoddle me."

She accompanied him on his slow progress up the stairs, half listening to the conversation below. She didn't know Braydon well, so she was only trusting that he'd help brush away the dark. She knew he'd be bound to bring news from London, but she couldn't cosset Thayne from wider events, much though she'd like to.

She settled Edgar in his bedroom and went to be sure Braydon's was in order. His valet was there, looking rather sour. "Is something amiss?"

"No, my lady. We have everything we need."

She remembered then that Thayne said Braydon's valet disliked rural living as much as his master. A few days would kill neither of them. She went down the back stairs to check on matters below. With so many new servants she kept a firm hand on everything.

She was tempted to warn them about Braydon's valet, as she feared he'd be a discordant element, especially as she had no lady's maid of similar status. She'd tried to persuade Nolly to train into the position, but the maid had wanted to return home.

"It's been grand, milady, but home's home, isn't it? I have ambitions now, though." Hermione had worried about that until Nolly added, "Reckon I could be a housekeeper one day if I put me mind to it. In a big house, even."

Hermione thought she could indeed. The housekeeper who'd just started work here was a very down-to-earth woman.

She tracked the men's voices to the drawing room and found Thayne had provided them both with ale. She was suddenly glad the room was rather shabby, for they both looked at ease in their sagging chairs, legs stretched out, smiling at something.

They both rose, but she waved them back to their seats. "At ease, gentlemen." Grasping the nettle, she asked, "How are matters in Town?"

"All calm," Braydon said. "Perhaps in part because they keep delaying Parliament. It's put off now until mid-December."

"Thus shortly after assembling," Thayne said, "everyone will disperse for Christmas.

613

No chance for the reformers to make their case."

They hadn't yet spoken of Christmas. She was determined to celebrate it here, but not quite sure how when any local traditions had been broken for so long.

"I can't regret your not having to leave to take your seat yet," she said.

"And I'm blessedly free of all such obligations," Braydon said. "In addition, it seems the world holds its breath as it awaits the birth of Princess Charlotte's baby, all hoping it will be a son."

"A daughter will do," Hermione pointed out. "Charlotte herself will be queen in time, and before either of you say anything, remember the Elizabethan age was glorious."

Thayne smiled and Braydon toasted her. She could feel improvement already.

In a while she took Edgar around part of the estate in her gig, talking of improvements in hand and those to come. "Much of this work is done with your money," she said. "Soon the estate will be earning more, but for now we're plowing money back to redress the wrongs and neglect."

"He should have taken more care."

"He knows that now. He was driven by his purpose, and it was for the good.

Without him that woman might have achieved a great disaster and might even have stirred the mob into revolutionary violence."

"True enough. Now her lot are finished and insurrection is largely in the hands of that Arthur Thistlewood, who's a dangerous man but not nearly as cunning, so I doubt he'll achieve his end. There's Orator Hunt and his sort, who should stop stirring up the mob, but they don't intend revolution. Are you happy, my dear?"

It was no time for provisos. "Yes. And you? What will you do with the decades to come?"

"Enjoy London. I've joined the Curious Creatures for a start, and I'm looking into leasing a house. Reckon I might hold the meetings there. Be a bit of a center for adventurers and curious minds."

"I'm sure Nicholas Delaney will be delighted."

"Interesting man. I've agreed to house that chemist, too."

"Isaac Inkman?" she asked, startled. "He'll blow you up."

"He promises not to. Odd young man, but I've known some like him. Never be normal, but can be very clever. Delaney's of the opinion that he only does what he intends to do, so I'll keep his intentions on the right things. I like the idea of exploring greater use of gas. And steam. Steam engines for transportation. It's a grand world, Hermione, and I hope to live to see even more wonders."

They turned back toward the house and he peered ahead. "What's that conical turret on the house?"

"That's the French Wing, built for Thayne's mother."

"The place she threw herself off? Demolish it."

"Just like that?"

"Just like that. I've little patience with this clinging to old stuff, but especially poisonous old stuff. Would you cling to a thicket of deadly nightshade because it was old?"

She gave a little laugh. "I like your way of looking at it."

That night as she joined Thayne in bed, she shared the conversation.

To her surprise he agreed. "I hadn't quite reached that brutal point, but he's right. Better it goes before there are children." He put a hand on her belly. "There's still hope?"

"And more with every day. A summer baby, perhaps. We'll have Faringay ready for him or her."

He gathered her into his arms. "We will.

You were right. Having guests here is clearing so many cobwebs."

"Right?"

"Are you claiming not to have that plan?"

She chuckled. "You know me so well. The next step is a dinner for the local gentry." It seemed the moment. "And then we must plan for Christmas. I've been told that when your father was young, it was held in grand style."

He kissed her nose. "Which might be a local tale, hoping for largesse."

"It might be, but I want it anyway."

"Then you shall have it, and anything else you desire."

"Which at the moment," she said, shifting, "is only you."

Later, on the edge of sleep, she murmured, "Is it folly to think that for this little while the world is perfect?"

"Probably," he said, "but I share your belief. May it be so for everyone."

But next morning the postbag brought a letter for Braydon. He apologized, saying, "I didn't direct that any post be sent on." He opened it and read it. "From a lawyer insisting it's urgent. What impudence." But as he read on, his expression changed and he muttered something that might not be suitable for a lady's ears.

"Sad news?" Hermione asked.

He looked up. "The worst. I've inherited a title. And an estate to go with it. Probably a decrepit estate. The wretched man's suggesting I make haste to take up my duties. It's taken months to find the heir. There are implications of chaos and," he added direly, "dependents."

Thayne's humor escaped in a laugh. "There are worse fates."

"I'll be damned if there are. Johns will desert me."

"Once settled in rural contentment, what need you of perfectly polished boots?"

Braydon raised a fist and Hermione, laughing, rose to stand between them. "Gentlemen!"

Thayne stood to put an arm around her and hold her close. "What you need, Braydon, is a wife. I assure you, she will much improve your life, no matter what challenges await."

AUTHOR'S NOTE

I've been saying to friends that I've been writing a Regency antiterrorism undercover cop, and that's pretty close to the truth, isn't it? It's a passionate love story as well, of course.

Antiterrorism is part of the Regency, because the postwar period was one of economic depression, which led to great unrest and fear, some of it fed by the French Revolution only a generation earlier. Many people were connected to victims. For example, one of Jane Austen's relatives was the widow of a French aristocrat who died on the guillotine. It's not surprising that the government was willing to take drastic measures to oppose the threat.

Much of the unrest and demand for reform was justified, but it was also exploited by those intent on a violent overturning of law and order. Waite and the Crimson Band are my own invention, but I took my inspiration from Arthur Thistle-wood, a true character. In 1820 he and his co-conspirators were hanged for the Cato Street conspiracy to murder the prime minister and the cabinet as trigger for a violent insurrection. The event in Ardwick was my own invention, but it was modeled on the earlier one mentioned in the book, the Blanketeers' March. Unfortunately, that didn't fit with my Rogues timeline.

The Company of Rogues books have a clear timeline, and it's not a very long one. Though there are now fifteen books, the first one, *An Arranged Marriage,* opens in April 1814, and this one in September 1817. The men are in their mid-twenties, a prime time for marrying and "starting a nursery" as they said, especially those with titles and fortunes to pass on.

On to explosions. I had fun researching this! Gas-lighting was rapidly spreading throughout London's streets, and was being introduced for indoor lighting as well. As mentioned in the book, the smell of coal gas was a problem. You might remember that in *The Rogue's Return,* Simon and Jancy made a rapid retreat from their town house because gas had been installed. Shops using gas-lighting kept their doors open.

The gas was produced by private

companies that stored it in huge gasometers and pumped it through the pipes. It's true that making coal gas explode isn't simple. It will flame, but for explosion there needs to be the right blend of gas and air in a confined space. Just like the chemists in the book, I couldn't come up with a way to make that happen, so I devised the plan to attack a gasometer with a missile. Very likely it wouldn't have worked, even if Isaac had really tried, because of needing that mix of gas and air. Which Isaac knew.

I've put up pictures connected to the book on Pinterest, including a map of the area around Great Peter Street, showing the Chartered Gasworks. You can find the photographs by going to Pinterest.com and searching for my boards. There's one for *Too Dangerous for a Lady*.

As for the exploding letters, I found a mention in a period record that the insurrectionists were experimenting with them. I couldn't resist. I'm not a chemist, but I found a few chemicals known at the time that might do the job. I deliberately didn't give any details just in case they would work!

Now, medicine. Edgar suffers from kalaazar, which is a real disease and still exists in the tropics. It's now called visceral leishmaniasis. It was thought to be caused by bad air, but in fact it's caused by protozoan parasites and spread by insects, like malaria. Antimony was the standard treatment and could work, but treatment improved when it was discovered that vanadium enhanced its effectiveness. I discovered that some fungi draw up vanadium and store it and ran with that. This isn't a scientific novel, after all, and I only needed to feel some plausibility for my own satisfaction. As the vanadium connection wasn't discovered until recently, I fear poor Dr. Grammaticus is going to have the threatened stroke before he can reveal his secret.

And the Curious Creatures? Did you recognize the name? I tossed them into a book years ago as yet another odd thing Nicholas Delaney was involved in. When I needed a philosophical society for this book, I knew there'd been something and it would be a perfect fit. Thank heavens for my readers, because some of them remembered the details for me.

The employees of Thorndike Press hope you have enjoyed this Large Print book. All our Thorndike, Wheeler, and Kennebec Large Print titles are designed for easy reading, and all our books are made to last. Other Thorndike Press Large Print books are available at your library, through selected bookstores, or directly from us.

For information about titles, please call:
  (800) 223-1244

or visit our Web site at:
  http://gale.cengage.com/thorndike

To share your comments, please write:
  Publisher
  Thorndike Press
  10 Water St., Suite 310
  Waterville, ME 04901